C000205820

First published in 2013 by Harper Collins Publishers.

This edition published in 2019 by Sharpe Books.

The Secret Life of James Cook

GRAEME LAY

CONTENTS

INTRODUCTION

The year is 1745. Sixteen-year-old James Cook leaves his parents and siblings in their inland Yorkshire village and walks to a coastal town to begin an apprenticeship as a grocer's assistant. There, for the first time he sees the sea, and falls in love, events which dramatically alter the course of his life.

And the course of world history.

The year is 1771. Forty-three-year-old Captain James Cook RN, recently returned from a circumnavigation of the world, is presented to King George III at St James's Palace, London. A celebrity now, the onetime village farm boy has proved himself the greatest seaman the world has known.

How did this remarkable transformation occur? What qualities did James Cook possess, to enable him to overcome his humble beginnings and rise to the summit of his profession? And what of his young wife, Elizabeth, who bore his children and had to cope with his prolonged absences from hearth and home?

A Man of Endeavour is a fictionalised account of Cook's youth, early naval career and first world voyage. With the unique insights which fiction provides, it tells a grippingly intimate story, of James Cook not only as naval commander, but as husband, father and family man.

London, 15 July, 1771

The coach made its way through crowded Whitechapel, then passed into Mile End Road. When he saw the street sign James leaned out the window and called up to the coachman: 'Assembly Row. Number 7. Another one hundred yards, on the right.'

'Very good, Lieutenant Cook.'

He, Banks and Solander had come ashore from *Endeavour* yesterday, at Deal. A week short of three years, it had been since they had left. Almost three years, and scores of thousands of nautical miles. It seemed like half a lifetime. But he had kept his promise to Elizabeth, he had returned safely to her and the children. His official journals had already been delivered to the Admiralty, in Whitehall, and he was wearing the crisp new uniform the Navy had issued him. On top of the coach, his cabin trunks were crammed with mementoes of the world voyage: native dolls for little Elizabeth, for the boys miniature weapons and what the New Holland natives called 'boomerangs', Tahitian bark cloth and Maori jade pendants for Beth, several of Parkinson's landscapes and botanical illustrations to hang on the walls of their house. And, at the bottom of the trunk, the other journal. For Elizabeth's eyes only.

The inside of the coach was stifling in London's mid-summer heat, and James took the handkerchief from inside the jacket sleeve of his uniform and passed it over his face. It was not merely the heat that was causing the outbreak of dampness. So much had happened to him during the three years, but what had happened to her, and the children? Would things be the same between them? *Could* things be the same, after such a time apart?

As the coach drew up outside the terraced brick house, he saw a shadowy movement behind the curtains of an upstairs window. *Elizabeth.* He had instructed the Admiralty people to send word to her that he would be arriving late this morning, in order that she and the rest of the family would be prepared for his arrival.

He placed his tricorn hat firmly on his head, then stepped down from the coach. Assembly Row was dusty and rutted with scores of coach wheel tracks. Almost-forgotten smells - horse dung in the street, gin from the nearby distillery - filled the air. As he went to help the coachman take down the trunks he felt himself swaying, as if he was still at sea. The sailor's sway. It would last for weeks, he knew.

The front door of number 7 opened, and she was there, running to him.

'James! Oh James!'

He held her close, murmuring her name, feeling the yielding shape of her body against his, drinking in the lavender scent of her fair hair, touching the softness of her cheeks and neck. She said nothing, but he could feel her sobbing, hear the sporadic intakes of her breath, as if she had just ceased running. Still holding her, blinking away the moisture from his own eyes, he looked over her shoulder. The two boys were standing on the step, gowned in the miniature Royal Naval uniforms she had sewn for them. James, now eight, Nathaniel, now seven. They were silent, staring at him with grave, apprehensive eyes, as they might be eyeing a complete stranger. Releasing Elizabeth, he went to them, bent down, said softly, 'Lads, my lads, how you've grown, both of you.'

Then, looking around for the other children, he turned back to his wife. Perplexed, he said, 'But where is little Elizabeth? And our newest child?'

One

The lad stepped outside the cottage, looked up. The sky was overcast, but beyond the peak of Roseberry Topping there was a slash of blue. It was mid-summer, 1745, and fair conditions for the longest journey of his life. There was no wind, but he knew that in an hour or two there would probably be a north-easterly breeze, blowing up from the Tees. His boots were beside the door of the cottage. As he bent down and pulled them on, his mother appeared in the doorway. She was holding a gunny sack. When he finished lacing up his boots she passed it to him. 'There's a clean shirt and vest, the scarf and the two pairs of socks I've knitted, and jam butties and the fruit cake I baked yesterday. Two apples, an' all.'

'Thank you Ma.'

Her expression was anxious. 'You'll need water along the way...'

'Aye, Ma.' He smiled down at her. 'But the road follows the river, so I won't stay thirsty long.'

The lofty figure of his father appeared behind her, in vest, woollen trousers and socks. Older brother John and younger sisters Margaret and Christiana pushed their way past their father and stood beside James. Although their eyes were shining, their smiles were crimped. He smiled at them, tightly. This day had been a long time coming, and now that it had come, he needed to be gone quickly. No sense in drawing out the leaving business. From inside the cottage he could hear the gurgling from his cradle of baby William, whom he had already kissed goodbye. He hoisted the sack over his left shoulder, pulled his cap down hard on his head. His mother came forward, he embraced her and felt the bulk of her body against his.

'Bye Ma. I'll write. And Christiana will read my letters to you.'

Christiana nodded. His father held out his big, calloused paw and clutched James's right hand.

'Good luck, laddy. And take care. Look after yerrself.'

'I will, Pa.' He tried to smile. 'And I'll work as hard as you do.'

Then he held his mother again. There were tears working their way down the creases in her cheeks. Holding her at arm's length, he smiled down at her, but he was thinking, *she is looking so old,*

3

so careworn. She managed a smile. 'Bye Jamie. God bless, God bless.'

'Bless you too, Ma. Bye.'

The others came up one by one, embraced him, then stood back. Christiana's blue eyes glistened, John tugged at his thumbs, awkwardly, mumbled, 'Bye brother.' His father hesitated, then came forward with a rush and took him in his arms. They held each other for a moment. Then his father backed away and said, 'Bye Jamie. We're proud of you, laddy.' Then he looked at the ground, shaking his head, as if bewildered by his own feelings.

Later, after he left Ayton and was on the path across the moors, passing the alum works on the far side of Roseberry Topping, James realised - and the thought came suddenly, and jolted him - that it was the first time in the sixteen years of his life that he and his father had held each other in such a way.

By mid-morning the sun had broken through the clouds. He came down from the moorland and rested under a willow tree, beside the river that wound its way through the lowland. After drinking gratefully from its icy waters he ate several of the chunks of bread and plum jam his mother had packed for him, and one of the apples. Where the track joined the road, a milestone declared, Staithes 7m. He saw that the sun was high. Near midday, he reckoned. Mr Skottowe had told him when he farewelled him yesterday, that it would take him half a day to reach the coast. So another three hours should see him there.

He removed his boots and socks and sloshed across the ford, the water chilling his feet and ankles. On the other side he dried his feet with tufts of grass, pulled his socks and boots back on, then resumed his journey. He thought back to the conversation he had had with Mr Skottowe, four months ago, when the landowner had ridden up and spoken to James and his father as they were digging out a weed-infested drain beside Aireyholme Lane.

'Well young James, what are your plans?'

'Plans, Sir?'

'Yes. For the future.'

Mr Skottowe dismounted from his roan. Taking this as a sign that a discussion was coming, James and his father stepped up from the drain. Their landlord removed his cocked hat and wiped his brow. Adgowning James's father, he said:

4

'The lad did well at his schooling, Cook, in arithmetic in particular. Even better than I expected when I had him enrolled.'

'Aye, Sir. Thanks to you, my family now has someone who can read and write, beside Christiana.'

James felt himself reddening.

Mr Skottowe nodded. Then, looking at young James, he said, 'And it's time that he put his schooling to good use.' He grunted. 'He needs to get right out of the ditch. Don't you agree, lad?'

'Aye, Sir.'

James sensed that this conversation was going somewhere unusual. But where?

The owner of Ayton Manor took a pipe and a wad of tobacco from the pouch slung across his chest and began to pack the pipe bowl. As he did so he said,

'Last week I was in Guisborough, for a sitting of the North Riding Quarter Session, along with other Justices of the Peace. Afterwards, over dinner, I was speaking with William Sanderson, a Staithes businessman. Sanderson told me that he was looking for an apprentice.'

Frowning, James's father asked, 'What is Mr Sanderson's line of business, Sir?'

'He is the proprietor of a grocery store, and a haberdashery.'

'A sound business, is it Sir?'

'It is. Sanderson is a well-known merchant, with an estimable reputation in the district. When mention was made of the apprenticeship, I immediately thought of your second so. The one who can read and write.' He looked solemnly at James. 'What say you to the idea, lad?'

James's mind tumbled. An apprenticeship. In Staithes. He had never been further than Ayton, but he knew that Staithes was a seaside town. A chance to get away from the farm, and from Ayton. A chance to make his own way, to live his own life. Frowning at the landowner, he said:

'What is the term of the apprenticeship, Sir?'

'Three years. Sanderson will teach you the skills of the retail trade. It would be a chance to put your arithmetic skills to practical use. Giving change, tallying up the day's takings.' He paused. 'Board and lodging will be provided at the store, along with a small allowance.'

James Cook looked hard at his son. 'What d'you say to the master's suggestion, lad?'

'I think I will accept it, Papa.' He nodded at Mr Skottowe. 'Thank you, Sir. Thank you very much.'

It was mid-afternoon, and the land was rising to the east, when he first caught the strange smell. He stopped and sniffed the wind. A salty tang filled his nostrils. He walked on, upwards. Then, just before he reached the brow of the hill, he heard a sound like none he had ever heard before. He stopped, inclined his right ear towards the sound. It was like steam escaping from a kettle spout, but a thousand times stronger. The noise rose and fell, rose and fell, but even when it fell it did not cease altogether. Instead it seemed to fill the air and race up towards him. Although he had felt weary before, he now increased his pace, striding forward on the track which zig-zagged up the slope, his heart pumping with anticipation.

The track turned once more, then opened out to a grassy clearing. There was a railing at the edge of the clearing, before the land fell away, and a bonneted woman and a young boy were standing at the railing. A dog was racing back and forth behind them, its tail wagging furiously.

James went to the railing, a little way along from where the woman and the boy were. He stared down. Oatmeal cliffs, a foot bridge, and houses, huddled around the mouth of a river. He looked out at what lay beyond the cliffs, beyond the town, beyond the estuary, to the source of the salty aroma and the roaring. Waves, driven by the north-east wind, racing in towards the land, waves, breaking as they came closer to the land, and white water like the streaming manes of galloping horses. Further out the sea was an expanse of grey, flecked with white, and he could see the triangular sails of several small vessels. Beyond the sails, the great expanse reached to a cloudy horizon. *The German Ocean.* He stood for some time, entranced by the sight. Then, with a spring in his step, he began to make his way down the track that led to the town.

He quickly came to know Staithes. Its face was turned to the sea and the townsfolk lived off its bounty. It was relatively prosperous, James came to realise, compared to Great Ayton. Its income was based on its fishing fleet, augmented - he was informed after a time - by the nocturnal smuggling of brandy, wine, perfumes and other high-excise contraband from the Continent. Rough and functional, Staithes' houses were nevertheless more substantial than those of the village he had come from. Its streets were cobbled and there were alehouses as well as shops. Littering the seafront were oars and boat-hooks, lobster pots, netted glass floats and fish nets stretched out on poles to dry. The raucous cries and bickering of sea birds were like a constant chorus to the town's waterfront activities.

William Sanderson's shop was located on the waterfront. There was a drapery on one side of the building and a grocery on the other. The shop sold standard commodities from its two sides: bolts of cloth, made-up clothing, ribbons and reels of cotton from its haberdashery side; biscuits, ham, bacon and poultry from the other. Of the two sides of the shop he preferred the grocery, with its aromas of bacon, cheddar, kippers and the mushrooms that were collected from the fields above the town and sold to Mr Sanderson by Zachariah Gillon, Staithes' dimwit.

The Sanderson family – the two parents and a young boy and girl - lived above the shop, while James slept downstairs. Although the shop was a modest enterprise, William Sanderson was a prosperous businessman who owned several other properties in and around Staithes. He showed an early trust in James, and appreciated the fact that after instructing him in the presentation, cost and dispatch of the goods, allowed his young assistant to serve the shop's customers without close supervision.

At the end of the week he added up the takings from Monday to Saturday, passed the list to Mr Sanderson and on a separate sheet wrote down the goods which needed ordering. And on the Saturday Mr Sanderson paid him his allowance of two shillings. Of the two shillings, James saved one. That was not difficult - the Sandersons provided him with all his meals, which he ate from the grocery counter. And he slept under the same counter, on a palliasse, with a straw-filled pillow and covered with a pair of blankets. It was comfortable enough. And he liked the independence he had in Staithes, compared to the Ayton cottage and the constant demands of his brothers and sister. His closest companion in the shop was Isabella, its tabby cat, who slept at the foot of the palliasse and from time to time brought in a dead rat which she would place triumphantly at James's feet.

Before long he knew all Mr Sanderson's customers.

'Morning Mrs Acklam. It's a cool wind we have today.'

'Aye, it is, but we mustn't grumble. How is Mr Sanderson?'

'Well. He is in Guisborough until Friday.'

'Ah. Business, I presume.'

'I presume so, ma'am.'

The woman's husband, Samuel Acklam, was also a businessman in the town. A hawk-faced man in his mid-thirties, Samuel bought fish from the men who operated the cobles and smacks. He had the fish split and wood-smoke dried in a warehouse at the far end of the town, then sold them on to fishmongers in the region's larger towns: Newcastle, Durham and Stockton. It was also rumoured, a boatman had told James, that Samuel Acklam dealt in goods which were fishy in another sense of the word - mainly cognac and perfumes from France. How else to explain the Acklam's grand house at the top of Church Street, and the fact that the household could afford to employ two servants?

'How is Mrs Sanderson?' Ackland's wife asked James.

'Well, although the children keep her very busy, ma'am.'

'Yes, yes.' Drawing her dark blue shawl up over her shoulders, she said, 'I need some ribbon, James, to edge the hem of my daughter's gown.'

'Certainly, Mrs Acklam. What colour ?'

'I think ...' Placing her wooden-handled bag on the counter, she stared at the row of reels behind him. 'The red, I think. The dark red.'

'And the width?'

'The one inch, please.' Nodding, she added, making a mental calculation, 'Yes, a yard and a half of the one inch.'

He uncoiled a length of the ribbon and measured it against the brass yardstick set into the counter. Then he took the scissors, snipped the ribbon to the ordered length, folded it and passed it the customer. As he did so he noticed the three large rings on the middle fingers of Mrs Acklam's left hand, two encrusted with diamonds and the third with scarlet stones. Rubies, were they? She placed the ribbon in her bag, drew out a small leather purse and bulged her eyes. An expression that James had learned meant, and the price?

'That will be six pence please, Mrs Acklam.'

She passed over a one shilling piece which James set down on the counter. He opened the drawer, took out a sixpenny piece and gave the change to her. She nodded dismissively, said goodbye and left the shop.

He picked up Mrs Acklam's silver coin and was about to place it in the shilling bowl when he paused and looked at it more closely. It was worn, and quite unlike any coin he had seen before. The date - 1723 - explained its worn surface, as it was over 20 years old, but what were the strange coats of arms on one side? He brought the coin closer to his face and peered at the three letters in the spaces between the coats of arms. SSC. What did they stand for? Intrigued, he placed the shilling in the bowl with the others and slid the drawer shut. The shilling was ... what was the expression Mr Sanderson used? *Legal tender*. 'As long as it's legal tender, lad, into the drawer it goes.' But all the same, he thought he would take the strange shilling to the Customs House to see if anyone there could explain its origins.

He entered the office, which was located in the High Street. The Customs Officer, Edward Goddard, was behind his large desk, making entries into a ledger book.

'Sir?'

'Yes?'

Edward Goddard was stout, with pouched cheeks and pronounced dewlaps. It was said in the town that he couldn't tell a smuggler from a pirate's parrot, and didn't care, so long as his salary was paid by the government. James took out the shilling.

'I was wondering, Sir, if you are familiar with a coin such as this. A customer used it to pay for some goods at the shop. ' He handed it to the Customs Officer, who placed a pair of pince-nez on his nose and peered at it, first on one side, then the other.' Then, removing the glasses, he said:

'It was minted by the South Sea Company, during the reign of George I.'

'What is ... the South Sea Company?'

'One that trades with Spain's South American colonies. Argentina, Chile, Peru.' He chuckled. 'Lots of people invested their savings with that company, and their shares rose in spectacular fashion. Then they collapsed, in 1720 I think it was, and fortunes were lost. People called it the "South Sea Bubble"'.

'But the shilling is still ...legal tender.'

'Oh yes. The company's still trading, Lord only knows how, so their shilling's legal.' He handed the coin back to James.

'Thank you, Sir.'

James walked back to the shop, one hand in his breeches pocket, holding the shiny shilling. To himself he said the words over and over: South Sea Company, South Sea Shilling. There was something exciting about those words, *The South Sea, the South Sea*. He knew that no-one knew what really lay deep in the South Sea, the Mar Pacifica, as it was marked on maps. People wondered, but no-one knew. But one day, surely, men would discover what lay in the rest of the ocean. As for the shilling, he would see that it was put back in the shop till tonight.

Staithes' fishing fleet - small boats the locals called cobles, and larger smacks - were clustered inside a wooden sea wall which broke the force of the ocean waves. From his very first days in the town, James felt himself drawn to the seafront and its activities, sights and sounds a world away from those of the farm and village. Fishermen sailed their cobles out at first light and brought them back in by mid-afternoon, six days a week, except when the wind was impossibly strong. Back in port, the men hauled wicker baskets of cod, herring and plaice up onto the quay, accompanied by shouting, cursing and laughter. There was a constant wash of waves against the sea wall and a pervasive stench of fish, seaweed, pitch and salt spray.

James drank in these sights and smells, and was spellbound. As he watched the cobles' sails hoisted, then catch the wind and buck their way out into the grey, cold sea, he envied the fishermen their lot. Their lives raised questions in his mind, too. What was out there, beyond sight of the land? What lay beyond that gravestone-grey sea and its gauzy horizon? What skills were needed, to confront and combat it? And as the months passed, a question grew, nagging within him. Would he, James Cook, have the courage to make a life on the sea?

Turning up the collar of his jacket, he walked back along the waterfront. Hearing laughter and shouting coming from one of the town's public houses, the Cod and Lobster, he put his face to a pane of one of its mullioned windows. Sailors were sitting on upturned beer kegs, tankards of ale in front of them, talking and laughing. A log fire burned in the grate next to the alehouse's servery. Even from the outside, James could feel the camaraderie radiating within, and appreciate it. These were men who worked hard, he had come to realise, and who risked their lives every time they set their sails. He admired them for it. Reluctantly he moved away from the Cod and Lobster's window. For another two and a half years he was bound to Mr Sanderson, and a life of ribbons, cotton reels, flour and sugar. He crossed the cobbled street to the shop. Tonight he would write another letter to his parents, letting them know of his recent doings, knowing that Christiana would enjoy reading it to them.

Through the shop window James could see a coble approaching the harbour entrance, its sail close-reefed, a fish net draped along its port gunwale. A gang of gulls was following the high-bowed vessel, squabbling as to who would get the first pickings. The gulls were the highwaymen of the sea, James thought. He saw that the coble was Isaac Thompson's *Patricia* and kept watching as she rounded the end of the breakwater, admiring the dextrous manner in which her sail was lowered and furled by Samuel's fishing partner, Alexander Holloway. *Lowered, furled.* James was learning this new language, picking it up from the fishermen he spoke to on the seafront. *Close-reefed, gunwale, bollard, boom, mizzen, windward, leeward, going about.* It was a special language which people who lived on the land had no knowledge of. He had bought a small notebook and in it was carefully listing these strange new words, and their meanings. 'Mizzen', he wrote, then, as Isaac had defined the word for him, 'the mast that is next aft of the mainmast'. In this way he observed, listened to and learned, this special vocabulary.

Isaac threw out a mooring line as the coble came along side the mole and John Coulson the wharfinger caught the line and made it fast to a bollard with a few deft figure-of-eight turns. James averted his eyes from the scene. The sea was so close, but for him it was also far away, shackled as he was to the shop, six days a week. The one day of the week the fishermen never ventured out was Sunday, the same day that James was free of his shop duties. He yearned to be able to ask one of the coble owners if he could go out his boat, if just for a day, but this was not possible.

Yet always, peering through the windows of the shop by day, or standing on the harbour wall of an evening, watching the waves and observing the rise and fall of the tides, James felt the tidal pull of that grey sea. His eyes would stray to the river mouth and the harbour, watching the comings and goings of the cobles and smacks. The harbour entrance was an opening into another world.

William Sanderson had a glass-fronted bookcase in his parlour upstairs, in which he kept a collection of history books. Medieval history was a particular interest to him, he explained to James, taking out a leather-bound volume and showing it to him. *The Cathedrals of England*, by Charles Knightly. But James's eyes had alighted on the spine of one of the other books. *Sir Francis Drake's Famous Voyage Round the World, 1580*, by Francis Pretty.

'Might I be permitted to read this one, Sir?' he asked, placing his finger on its spine.

'Certainly.' Sanderson took it down. 'Francis Pretty was a Gentleman-at-arms on *Golden Hind*.' Handing it to James, he added, 'It's a rattlingly good account.'

And reading it for hours on end, by candlelight under the shop counter, James had to agree. Drake's voyage – including as it did so much high seas misadventure and death – was enthralling. He began to borrow and read more of his employer's books, eschewing the medieval histories for accounts of the great voyagers: Magellan, Da Gama, Columbus. And when at last he snuffed out the candle by which he had been reading, and fell asleep, his dreams were invariably of the sea.

He was peering through the window again, watching Alexander Holloway and Isaac Thompson unloading baskets of fish from their vessel and onto the mole, when the shop's doorbell rang.

Mistress Jackson, a basket over her arm.

'Good morning James.'

'Good morning, Mrs Jackson. It's a cool wind today.'

'Aye, but we mustn't grumble.' She placed her basket on the counter. 'One reel of white cotton, please.'

'Certainly, Mrs Jackson.'

But as he reached for the item, he sighed with the tedium of it.

Sometimes on his evening walks to the mole, James would come across Nicholas Bartholemew, a recently retired mariner who lived alone in a cottage above the town. 'Old Nick' as he was known, had spent eighteen years as a Royal Navy able seaman. The old man had long lank hair which he covered with a woollen cap, and his left eye was entirely white, like a milky marble. One of the bollards on the mole Old Nick considered his exclusive territory. Sitting there, staring out to sea, he found a ready audience in young James.

'Have you heard of George Anson, lad?'

'Was he the commander who sailed around the world?' He remembered Mr Skottowe speaking of Anson.

'Aye, that's the one.' The old man cocked his head. 'I were with his fleet. On the *Gloucester*. Eight hundred and fifty-three tons, a fifty-gunner.'

James crouched down beside him. 'So you sailed in her .... right around the world?'

'No. *Gloucester* were lost along the way. I came back on *Centurion*.' He scratched the white stubble on his cheek. 'Almost four years, it took. From 1740 until 1744.' Old Nick laughed, harshly. 'We were meant to raid Spanish settlements in South America, but the campaign were a disaster.'

'In what way?'

'In every way.' The old man looked down at his boots. 'We started out with eight ships, we ended up with one. We started out with nearly two thousand men, we came back with 188. Including mesself.' Two of the ships never even made it around the Horn.'

'Were the men lost in sea battles with the Spaniards?'

'Some.' His one good eye brightened. 'We did capture one of their galleons, off the coast of China. But we lost over a hundred men in the taking of that prize.' He put a hand over his left eye. 'That's how I lost this. From a short sword.' Grimacing, Nick adjusted his buttocks on the bollard. 'But most of the men what were lost died of the scurvy.'

He recited the grim facts, appalling James with the details. After several weeks at sea, most of the men fell ill. Their gums became swollen and bled and their teeth were so weakened they could hardly chew their salt beef and ship's biscuit. Dark blue blotches appeared on their skin and they fell into a lethargy from which they could not be aroused. 'Men died like flies,' Old Nick concluded. 'Hundreds of 'em.' Nick and the remainder of a skeleton crew were left to work the ship.

He closed his one eye for a moment. 'Yes, it were the scurvy that were worse than the battles, it were the scurvy that were our curse.'

'How did you survive?'

'By eating the weevils from ship's biscuit. I were a quartermaster, so I could get to the biscuits first.' He chuckled. 'Yerr didn't need teeth t'eat the weevils.' He sat up straight. 'And d'you know lad, I saw sights on that voyage that you wouldn't believe.'

'In South America?'

'Aye. Natives, entirely naked, who painted their selves with coloured clay. Great eagles which soared above the plains. Strange furry pack animals, like a cross between a sheep and a small horse. An island where there were huge stone statues, mountains that exploded.' He shook his head in awe at the memories. 'Yes, there were many, many deaths ...' his one eye shone again. '... but lad, I tell you, if I were fit and able, I'd sign on again termorra.'

Walking back to the shop, James was lost in thought. What sights the old man had seen, what wonders there were in the world beyond. Anson's fleet and Old Nick had merely skirted the west coast of South America, before crossing the north Pacific. The rest lay undiscovered. What adventures there were yet to be had. By others. For him there were only ribbons and kippers, and sleeping not in a galleon hammock but a palliasse under a grocery store counter.

It wasn't enough, he thought. Not nearly enough.

Two

The door-bell tinkled, the shop door opened.

A young woman, small, dark-eyed, someone he had not seen before.

'Good morning, Miss.'

'Good morning.'

The small figure stared about the shop, her eyes flicking across the shelves. Only just over five feet, he estimated, she wore a gown of pale brown tweed, cinched tightly at the waist by a wide black belt, and a bonnet tied under her neatly pointed chin. Her nose was narrow, her lips prominent and shapely. There was a round wicker basket over her arm. Her attention returned to James.

'I need to buy some bacon.' There was something strange about the way she spoke. *Bay-con.*

'Yes, Miss. How much?'

'Six pieces, please.' *Seex.*

He took the roll of bacon from under its gauze cover, placed it on the cutting board and carefully sliced off the rashers, conscious of her eyes following his movements closely. As he wrapped the bacon in brown paper, he said,

'Are you new to Staithes, Miss?'

'Yes.' Her eyes were large and dark, contrasting starkly with her very pale cheeks, her lashes long and curling. Strands of dark hair curled from the sides of her bonnet. 'I am just employed as a servant by Mr and Mrs Acklam.' *Serr-vent.*

'Aah ...' Handing the parcel over, he said, 'There you are. And is there anything else your household needs, Miss?'

'No, thank you.'

'Well then, that'll be tuppence, please.'

She took a small purse from the basket, took out the two coins and handed them to him. Her hands were small, ringless and rather chaffed. Nodding, she said, 'Thank you, and good-day.'

'Good-day to you, Miss.'

Through the window he watched the small, neat figure walk across the cobbled street, then in the direction of Church Street. Where had she come from, he wondered, and why did she speak in that strange way? And he thought it must be true what they were saying in the town, that the Acklams were growing rich from Samuel's business dealings. They already had a groom and a caretaker, now it seemed they could afford another servant. And one who was unusually beautiful. He had never seen anyone quite like her.

His gaze returned to the waterfront, where Joseph Coster was readying his smack, *Duchess*, for its departure to the fishing grounds. Turning away, he wondered what it would take to break the bonds that were shackling him to this shop. He still had another two years and eight months of his apprenticeship to serve.

He walked out onto the breakwater. It was October, the days were drawing in and it was already nearly dark. The sky was black and threatening, the cuticle moon low in the sky. A strong cold wind was blowing onto the coast from the north, causing waves to slop up against the stones of the sea wall on its ocean side, flinging up spray. A line of gulls stood like sullen sentries along the edge of the mole, their backs to the wind, and on the harbour side the cobles and smacks of the fishing fleet jostled against one another in the chop.

Peering into the dusk, James was surprised to see that he was not alone on the sea wall. A diminutive figure was standing at the far end, close to the harbour entrance. The hood of a cape was drawn up over its wearer's head. As he stared up ahead through the gloom, a large wave reared, then dashed itself against the sea wall, sending up a shower of spray which reached the caped figure. Hearing a cry, seeing the person spin away, James ran forward.

She peered up at him from within the hood, blinking away the seawater from her eyes and brushing away the spray from the front of her cape. 'Come back Miss,' he said, 'you're too close.' Instinctively he held out his hand. She took it, and he led her back along the breakwater. At the end, above the area where the cobles and smacks were tethered, they stopped. Their hands parted. James frowned down at her. 'That were dangerous, Miss, to go so far along the wall at nightfall.'

Then he realised who it was. The Acklams' servant girl. Staring up at him, she pouted. 'And who might you be, to tell me what I should and shouldn't do?'

Feeling a flash of anger at her reaction, he said, 'I were concerned for your safety, that were all. The tide's rising. You could have been washed into the sea.'

Meeting his reproachful look, she said defiantly, 'I didn't know that the tide were rising.' Then her hand went up to her mouth. 'Oh, you're the boy from the shop.'

The boy. He nodded, brusquely, then said, 'Come on, it's time we were both off the wall.'

She walked beside him in silence, her head barely reaching his shoulder. At the end of the wall, where a set of stone steps led to the quay, they both stopped. The wind was bitter, and he saw her shudder with the cold. She was so small, and seemed so vulnerable in the face of the wild sea. Noticing the dampness of her cape, concerned for her, he said, 'You need to get dry.' He looked along The Beck, to where a buttery light glowed in the window of The Cod and Lobster. 'Come over to the alehouse and get warm by the fire.'

She stared up at him doubtfully, then glanced over towards the inn. She nodded, conceding, 'I need to get warm.' That strange way of speaking. *Ay need t'get war-rum.* Was she from the Borders?

He led her to the inglenook, bought a handle of warm milk for her and a half pint of ale for himself. The only other people in the inn were three old men sitting around a table in the corner, enveloped in pipe smoke. One of them was Old Nick. He raised his chin and his pewter mug in greeting when he saw James and the girl walk in. The trio stared at them curiously, muttered comments to one another, then returned to their ale and conversation.

Before sitting down she removed her cape, then her bonnet, shaking her head to free herself of the remaining drops of seawater that clung to the sides of her face. Her long hair was raven black, matching her eyes. Her green velvet gown was mostly dry, except at the cuffs and neck, where the frills were stained with seawater. The stylishness of her clothing made him feel conscious of his own rough woollen topcoat, calico trousers and worn boots. What startled him most about her was the size and darkness of her eyes, and the contrasting whiteness of her cheeks. Her skin was as white and delicate as the bone china plates that he had seen in Mistress Sanderson's parlour.

She sipped the warm milk, making little gasps between sips. As she did so, he said, 'My name is James.' He took a mouthful of ale. 'And you are?'

'Michela.' *Mee-kay-la.*

He put his face a little closer to hers. 'And you do not hale from Staithes.' It was part-statement, part-question.

'No. I was born in Genoa.' *JEN-o-uh.*

His mind raced. Genoa. Where on earth was that? Oh yes, the city where Christopher Columbus came from. Columbus, the man who had conquered the Atlantic. The navigator was one of his heroes, along with Francis Drake and William Dampier.

She explained. Her parents and their two daughters had left the port town of Genoa six years ago, her father seeking work after the wool industry in their home city collapsed. He was a weaver. Following other Genoese migrants, the family had made the long overland journey to Calais, and thence by sea to Scotland, where they knew there was a woollen industry. Once there they had had to learn to speak English, and that had been very hard, especially for her mother. Her father had found weaving work and cottage accommodation for his family in Cumbernauld, but five months later he was trampled in the street and knocked unconscious by a runaway horse. He died a short time later.

By now almost destitute, Michela, her mother and younger sister, Ione, had been forced to move on again, this time south across the Scots border, seeking domestic work in north-east England. Her mother and Ione were now in Durham, working as servants in separate households, but Michela had had to move here to Staithes, where she had found work and accommodation in the Acklam's household. She was nineteen years old, she told him. That surprised him. She looked younger, whereas she was actually two years older than he was. And the tragedy of her story also explained the melancholy air she had about her.

She had related her story calmly, even matter-of-factly, leaving him to imagine the upheavals and sadnesses she and her family had witnessed. And her voice captivated him. Her 'i' sounds were pronounced 'ee', but she also rolled her r's, in the Scottish manner, the way his father did.

He told her something of his own life. Growing up in a village, learning to read and write, moving to Staithes to learn the grocery trade. He told her how much he enjoyed to read sea stories at night, but couldn't bring himself to tell her that he slept under the counter on a palliasse. It all seemed so dull compared with her sad but eventful background.

Finishing her handle of milk, she placed it on the hearth. 'I will be going back now,' she announced. 'I must be up at daybreak to prepare breakfast for the Acklams.'

James stood up. 'I will walk with you to their house.'

'I can see myself there.'

He nodded. 'As you wish.'

Once again she had given him that direct, almost defiant look. The one that seemed to see right through him, with those strange black eyes. There was a quiet determination about her, a steely core wrapped in that small, apparently vulnerable body. He was reminded of a saying of his father's. *Strong spirits come in small bottles.*

Outside the alehouse she put on the bonnet and drew the cape around herself. Head tilted back, fixing him once again with her unflinching gaze, she said, 'Thank you for the milk. It has warmed me considerably.'

'It was no trouble.' There was a pause. 'Perhaps we will meet again on the quay.'

'Perhaps,' she replied, non-commitally, before turning away.

He watched the small huddled figure walk to the end of the quay, then turn into the street that led to the far end of the town. What a strange creature she was. Troubled, but beautiful. And different to any girl he had met before. Not that he had met many, but...

That night, as he lay under the counter, sleep did not come easily. And when at last it did, her face was present in all his dreams. And that face and figure continued to haunt him over the following days. He had to see her again, had to talk with her again. By day and night he thought of her, and every evening after shutting the shop, he returned to the seawall and the quay, in the hope that she might be there, but she was not.

One evening he went to the Acklams' large house and watched it for a time from across the street, but could see no evidence of her. And when he saw the hulking figure of Samuel Acklam emerge from the front door of the house, brass-handled cane in his hand, James melted away into the night. He began to think that he might have imagined the whole episode on the sea wall and at the inn, while at the same time knowing for certain that he had not. Confirming this, she again came to the shop, three times over the next fortnight, shopping for her mistress. Each time she was courteous but distant, speaking with that strangely exotic accent and according him only the faintest of smiles when she departed. But each time that shadowy smile lingered in the air, and in his consciousness, long after she left.

A much duller figure entered the shop.

'Good-day James.'

'Oh, Mrs Acklam, good-day. It's a chilly one again.'

'Indeed it is. A dozen eggs, if you please.'

'Certainly, Mrs Acklam.' Carefully removing the eggs from their pottery bowl, he said, with feigned indifference, 'Do you still employ the same servant girl?'

'Michela?'

'That is the one.'

'Aye, we do.' Mrs Acklam gave him a somewhat suspicious look. 'Why do you ask?'

'Oh, it's just that ... I have not seen her in the town for some days.'

'She is supervising the children, as she is paid to do. The work keeps her well occupied.' Then she made a disapproving face. 'Somehow, though, she finds the energy to walk in the evenings.'

'Really? Where?'

'Above the town. She takes the Cleveland Way path, she tells me. She enjoys the view from there, she says.'

'It is a fine view, certainly.' He placed the eggs in a bag, put it into her basket and took the payment of threepence, noting again the large gem-stoned rings Mrs Acklam wore. There were four, now, on her left hand.

'Thank you.' Glancing out the window at the grey sky, she said, 'It's my hope that the rain holds off. I'm wanting to go to Danby for the week, to see my parents.'

'Very good Mrs Acklam.'

He thought he would wait for two or three days, then found he could not wait that long. So it was the very next day that he walked to the end of the town, then climbed the steep path that was Cleveland Way. He had put on his newer jacket, and his cleanest shirt and waistcoat, the one with brass buttons. He just wished he could afford a decent pair of boots. The wind had dropped, the sky was leaden and the clouds were obscuring a rising gibbous moon.

The track levelled out at the top of the cliff. At once he saw her, sitting on the seat at the place where the path turned inland, staring seaward.

'Michela. Good evening.'

'Oh, hello.' That voice. *Hay-low*.

'How are you?'

'Well, thank you.'

She was wearing the same dark brown cape, but with a matching bonnet which framed her pale, oval face and its delicate features. Frowning up at him, she said, 'I've not seen you walking here before.'

'No. I prefer the sea wall.'

'And I prefer the view of the sea.'

'And here you are well out of reach of its waves.'

She gave a little laugh, then said, moving along the seat. 'Would you like to sit?'

'Thank you.'

For a time there was silence as they both sat and stared out to sea. Far below, the town's houses, shops and inns comprised a dark, huddled mass along the estuary of The Beck, and the seawalls enclosed the boat harbour like giant jaws. It was Michela who broke the silence.

'I like it up here. It's peaceful.'

'Aye, it is.' A pause, then, 'Do you like Staithes?'

She thought for moment. 'It is ... *satisfactory*. Is that the right English word?'

'I suppose ... if the place gives you satisfaction, then it is.'

She laughed, but not in a happy way. 'Well, Staithes is far better than Genoa, and Cumbernauld. And my employer is kind to me.'

'Mrs Acklam.'

She flashed him that sharp look that he well remembered from before. 'Mr Acklam is my employer. It was he who engaged me.'

'Oh. And Mrs Acklam?'

'She supervises my work in the house.' Her tone was resentful.

James said, 'Her husband is a successful businessman, they say.'

She nodded. 'He is planning to buy another property in the town, so he must be.'

Again, James felt his inadequacies. But determined too to press on, he said, 'I wondered if we might walk together of an evening, here, or ... elsewhere ...?'

Turning, she looked directly into his eyes. Hers were so large and dark that they seemed to be her only feature, and they seemed too to be assessing him, absorbing him, drawing him in towards her. He yearned to reach out and touch her, to hold her close to him, to protect her. But she looked away.

'I cannot,' she said, flatly.

The words were like a slap. After a pause he said quietly, 'May I ask why not? My intentions are entirely honourable, I assure you.'

Swivelling around towards him, she again fixed him with that penetrating gaze. 'I will tell you, then.' There was a pause, and he could see her chest rising and falling as she took breath to compose herself. And when she spoke, she did so slowly, choosing her words with obvious care.

'You are, I am sure, an honest person. You are kind, and strong, and hard-working.' James felt his pulses quicken. How astute she was, how quickly she had summed him up. Then came the blows, like a hammer on an anvil. 'But you are a shop-worker. And you have no ... *prospects,* I think that is the word.' She paused, before adding, 'So you can offer me nothing.' Her eyes still fixed on his, she spoke quietly but with obvious feeling. 'I have been poor, and I am poor still. But I have a determination not to be poor for the rest of my life. I have my own plans for the future.' She tilted her head slightly. 'And I do not wish to be poor. Can you understand that?'

He made no reply. He still felt like holding her, but now he felt like crushing her. Because of the penetrating impressions of him that she had so quickly formed, because of the cruel truth of her words, because he had no answer to what she had stated. Standing up, she drew her cape around herself. 'Now I must go back. Good-bye.'

And she was away, walking down the track in small, quick steps, without a backward glance.

He spent some time sitting on the seat, staring down at the town but seeing nothing but her face, listening for night sounds that might distract him, but hearing nothing except her accusations, seeking excuses but feeling nothing but the lash of her words. Then at last he got up and began to walk back down the path to the town.

For the following two days he did nothing but go about his usual business: working by day in the shop, eating the meals Mrs Sanderson prepared for him, reading by candlelight and falling asleep in the small hours on the palliasse. But during that time the accusatory sting of her words did not lessen, and neither did the vivid image he had of her. By the third night he knew he had to see her once more. He would tell her that he *did* have a plan for the future, that when he had finished his grocery apprenticeship he would make an offer of his savings to William Sanderson, so that he could become a part-owner of the shop. That would demonstrate that his prospects were *not* unfavourable, and that he meant business.

The Acklam house was near the top of Church Street, a sturdy, two-storeyed brick and tile building whose front entrance opened directly onto the street. There were large leadlight windows with white-painted frames on either side of the front door. A narrow lane ran beside the house, running into the neighbouring street, Seaton Garth, and James approached the house via the lane. The rear area of the Acklam property was enclosed by a high wooden fence, into which was set a gate with an iron latch, and the small windows at the side of the house, on both the ground floor and upper storey, were curtained and blank. He paused and stared up. Which room was Michela's? There would be servants' quarters surely, probably at the rear. And Mrs Acklams had said that the family was going away to Danby, so Michela would be in there, alone he hoped.

He emerged from the lane and walked out onto Church Street. A faint light showed through the curtains which covered the window to the left of the front door. He approached the house and went to the window on the left-hand side of the entrance. Although the curtain was heavy, there was a slight opening in the centre of the window where its two halves had not quite come together. James thought that he would raise the knocker in the centre of the front door. Then he hesitated, and instead put one eye to the not-quite-joined curtains.

Peering into the drawing room, he saw that the light came from a circular candelabrum fixed to a bracket beside a small fireplace, assisted a little by the glow from the dying embers of the fire itself. These two sources were insufficient to shed light on the entire room, yet strong enough to show the two figures on the large rug in front of the fire, one large, the other much smaller.

Samuel Acklam lay on his back, spread-eagled, his bare arms and legs flung wide, mouth agape; Michela was sitting above him, legs apart, hands flat against his chest. Her head was tipped back and she was rocking back and forth, her naked back and buttocks luminescent in the flickering half-light. Around the pair, garments and undergarments were strewn across the floor: a gown, a vest, hose, a wig, waistcoat, a pair of breeches.

Simultaneously transfixed and repelled and by the sight, James's eyes were for some moments riveted to the tableau. The full realisation of what he was witnessing struck him like a lightning bolt. *I have my own plans for the future.* Then he turned away and put his forearm across his eyes. Scheming, treacherous little vixen. He dropped to his knees and remained briefly in that position. Then he stood up and ran, past the house, down the lane to Seaton Garth and from there along the High Street to the quay. Beside the boat harbour he stopped, his breath burning in his throat. There was a strong, cold wind blowing from the north-east, bearing the scent of the sea, and he crouched on the harbour edge for some time, drawing in the salty smell, using the coldness of the sea wind to dispel the loathsome image from his consciousness. *I have my own plans for the future.* Yes, as a rich man's doxy. Well, good luck to you Michela, he thought, bitterly. But in a way, he also knew that what she had done had helped him come to a decision. Even before he reached the shop, he knew what he would do.

'Mr Sanderson?'

'James. Hello.'

'Can I speak with you, Sir?'

'Of course. Please, be seated.'

There were two padded chairs under the bay window in the parlour. James took one, Mr Sanderson the other. The shop-owner steepled his hands as he looked quizzically at his apprentice.

'Well? You wish to borrow another book?'

James shook his head. 'It is another matter I wish to discuss, Sir.' He paused, to draw a very deep breath, then continued. 'I am not convinced that the grocery trade is one I am best suited to.'

Mr Sanderson sat up. 'Really? Why so?'

'I feel ... that a life spent working indoors is not what I wish to do, Sir. I have developed other ambitions, and they do not include selling cheddar to housewives and ribbons to old ladies.' He looked directly into the shop-owner's eyes. 'So ... I wish to be released from my apprenticeship.'

The furrows on William Sanderson's brow deepened. Leaning forward, he said,

'Are you certain about this?'

'I am, Sir. My mind is made up.'

Clearly displeased now, Sanderson asked, scathing, 'Well, what is your alternative, lad? Returning to Great Ayton?' He flicked up his eyebrows. 'Working in an alum mine?'

James continued to look him levelly.

'No, Sir. I have no wish to be a farm labourer either. Or a miner.' He hesitated for just a moment, then declared: 'I intend to go to sea.'

Three

Again he said his farewells, to his parents and John, Christiana, Margaret and little William. It was the end of October, 1746. This time there was more of a sadness about the family, he sensed, as he bid each of them good-bye. It was as if they thought he was volunteering for war. This displeased him. He knew they did not really approve of his giving up the grocery trade and moving to Whitby. Taking up a seaman's apprenticeship? The decision baffled them. No one, on either side of their family, had ever gone to sea. His mother had said, her face crumpled with worry, 'But the sea's such a dangerous place to go, Jimmy. The German Ocean especially.'

But his mind was made up. Knowing that William Sanderson had ship-owning friends in Whitby, he had asked his former employer to recommend him to them as a prospective apprentice merchant seaman. At first Sanderson had suggested that, if he wished to make his living from the sea, he stay in Staithes and obtain work as a fisherman. But James had dismissed this idea, arguing that a coble was a boat, not a ship. Real ships he had seen from the clifftop above Staithes, colliers under full sail, making their voyages north to the river Tyne or south to the port of London. And he had learned that these ships were based in Whitby. Sanderson had then relented, informing James that he would send a letter of recommendation to his friends there, ship-owning brothers, John and Henry Walker. During their discussion, James made no mention of his other reason for wishing to be quit of Staithes. That humiliating fact was a secret he would share with no other person.

Now there was to be another beginning, another opportunity, and he was determined to seize it.

It was a fifteen mile walk from Marton to Whitby and at first the path took him across the bleak, wind-swept North York moors. The sky was leaden grey, seeming to reach right to the ground, and as he circled Beacon Hill light snow began to fall, forcing him to turn up the collar of his jacket and wrap around his face the woollen scarf Christiana had knitted for him. But this did not worry him, for he knew that every step he took on his way south took him further away from Staithes and its horrible associations.

The wind eased and the snow stopped falling when he descended from the moors to the village of Danby. There, beside the river he knew must be the Esk, he removed his boots and ate the bread, mutton and plums his mother had packed for him. Half an hour later he set off again, the path following the river which tumbled its way down the valley.

As the valley broadened the water began to flow more languidly and at mid-afternoon, around a meander of the river, he came to Whitby. He paused on the outskirts of the town, staring down the river towards its estuary. The tide was low, exposing the mud-flats along the river's course.

If Staithes had been large after Ayton, then after Staithes, Whitby was huge. The town's buildings occupied both banks of the river. Where James stood, on the west bank of the upper harbour, slipways led up to sheds where vessels were in various stages of construction, some with just their keels laid, others with their stems and sterns added, a few with their rib-cages completed. Men swarmed about the shipyards, sawing, hammering and chiselling into shape the bones of the boats. On the opposite bank were moored dozens of vessels, fishing smacks, sloops, barges, cobles.

He followed the pathway down the river. Warehouses, chandleries and sail-makers' lofts gave way to two-up and two-down brick and tile houses, and shops and taverns, buildings which stood cheek-by-jowl along both banks of the river, their high piles exposed by the ebbed tide. A high wooden bridge, built on piers of stone, connected the west and east banks of the town. He saw that its central span could be raised by a series of ropes and pulleys, allowing ships to pass underneath the bridge to the upper harbour. He watched, fascinated, as a single-masted sloop passed slowly under the raised drawbridge, its sail catching the slight afternoon breeze.

A few minutes later he came to the quayside, which was crowded with people, wagons, horses and carriages. Ladies in bonnets and crinoline gownes held the hands of children, wigged men in frock-coats and high boots stood about chatting and seamen sat outside the taverns, yarning and smoking their pipes. Goods were being unloaded from barges by men in leather jerkins, carried up gang-planks to the waiting wagons on the quay. In the distance James could see the river broaden as its mouth, turning slightly south as it flowed past a breakwater and into the ocean. In the roadstead in the distance, two three-masted ships were at anchor, waiting for the high tide, he presumed, before they could enter Whitby's tidal basin.

The crowded quay, the movements of people and vessels and the generally purposeful air of Whitby, excited him. This was a place where he could forget his foolish infatuation with Michela and make a new beginning. Here he would immerse himself in reading and study, in preparation for a life at sea.

He now needed to find Mr Walker. He stared about the quay, then approached a group of what appeared to be sailors, as they wore seaman's jerseys and canvas trousers, sitting outside an alehouse whose sign declared it was the Cat and Fiddle. Adgowning a man with a grizzled beard and woollen cap, James said:

'Sir, I wonder if you could direct me to the residence of Mr Walker.'

'John Walker or Henry Walker?' came the gruff reply.

'John Walker.'

The man nodded. 'Grape Lane, lad. That's where you'll find 'im. Or at least 'is 'ouse.'

'And where might ... Grape Lane be, Sir?'

Leaping to his feet, the seaman pointed upriver. 'That slipway there, see? The third one up from the bridge?'

'Yes.'

'The house at the top of the slipway is John Walker's. Take the bridge across the river.'

The house was tall, three storeyed, with a steeply pitched slate roof into which a dormer window was set. As James approached he noticed, high above the house, a great grey stone building on the cliff-top above the town. Whitby's abbey, he assumed. He knocked on the front door of the house and it was opened by a thin, elderly woman in a pale brown gown and matching crocheted shawl. She looked him up and down intently, and James doffed his cap.

'Good-day, madam. I am here to see Mr Walker. Mr John Walker.'

'I will tell him you're here, young man. He's in his study. What name shall I say?'

'James Cook. I am to take my able seaman's rating with him.'

John Walker came out from behind his desk. The study was lined with filled bookshelves, and pinned to the walls were several ornate charts of coastal waters. A brass barometer hung beside the study's single window, and on the large desk was a model of a ship, a yard long and fully rigged. James thought it was a collier, but couldn't be sure. John Walker was stout, with a round, sagging face and wide sideburns. Although his cheeks seemed to have collapsed, his clear green eyes were those of a much younger man. Taking James's hand, tipping his head back and half closing his eyes, he looked him up and down before saying, 'So, you're the young man Sanderson wrote to me about.'

'I am, Sir.'

'The one who tired of the grocery trade.'

James hesitated. The comment made him sound feckless. By way of reply he said, 'Better, I thought Sir, to withdraw from a calling to which I was ill-suited, than to remain in the shop and so satisfy neither my employer nor myself.'

'Hmph.' John Walker continued to scrutinise him. 'You're unusually old to be starting an able seaman's rating. Eighteen, are you?'

'I am, Sir.'

Walker looked at him challengingly. 'And what makes you think you're fitted to a life at sea?'

'I think ... it may well suit my abilities, Sir.'

'Which are?'

'A knowledge of mathematics, the capability to read and write, a desire to experience the world, physical stamina ...' His voice died away. What more could he say, without sounding like a braggart?

Eyes still fixed on him, the shipowner said, sternly, 'Well, you're a strong lad, that I can see, and Sanderson's vouched for your skills in arithmetic. But have you the courage to go aloft in gale and furl a mainsail, or swing a lead-line on a lee shore - and there's many of them on this coast - or hold the helm on a stormy, moonless night with only a compass to steer by ....'

Having made his point, he did not need to go on. James inhaled deeply, then said calmly, looking the shipowner straight in the eye, 'I cannot say whether or not I have those very abilities, Sir, but I can say that I will do my very best to learn them.' He paused, then added, forcefully, 'I have a mind to do so, so I believe I will.'

Walker laughed, softly. 'Good. The will to do so is all, when training for the sea.' He placed one hand on the model ship. 'This is my flagship, *Freelove*, a Whitby cat. She carries coal from the Tyne to London. If you study hard and prove your worth, you could be sailing on her.' He folded his arms. 'The coal trade's the best nursery there is, for seamen, but it's a nursery with no tenderness. It's harsh, but here you'll learn the ropes, first on shore, then at sea. And Whitby sailors make the best top men, that's well known.' Unfolding his arms, he stared up at James. 'Do you understand what I'm saying?'

'I do, Sir.' He lifted his chin. 'When do we start?'

As the only apprentice not from the local parish, he was accommodated in the attic room of the Walkers' house. The room was small, its walls sloping to the apex of the building. Accessed by a steep staircase from the second floor, it had a floor of worn bare boards. There was narrow leadlight window in one wall, beneath which was a chair and writing desk on which, beside the candle-holder and ink well, James placed his note book and sheets of writing paper. The bed was under one wall slope, and although for the first few days he banged his head when he sat up in it, it was a considerable improvement on sleeping under the shop counter. Under the other wall opposite the bed was a wash-stand, chamber pot, basin and water jug.

Mr Walker's lessons were given in the ground floor front room. The other apprentices were five or six years younger than James. One, a freckle-faced boy called Thomas, was only twelve. To James they seemed like children, often giggling behind Walker's back, and he found them tiresomely immature. He sometimes felt like clipping them round their ears. It was always a relief when, after the evening meal, which he took in the kitchen, he mounted the stairs to the little attic room, imagining as he did so that the stairs were a companionway and the little room was the cabin of a ship. Once in his room he would read by candlelight the books Mr Walker had loaned him, references such as Charles Leadbetter's *Compleat System of Astronomy* and for pleasure, more accounts of epic sea voyages, such as the English sea captain Woodes Rogers'

A Cruising Voyage Round the World. And invariably, before he got into bed, there would be a call from the top of the stairs.

'Master James?'

'Oh, Mistress Prowd. Good evening.'

'Evening to you, Master James.'

Her head appeared, her face heavily lined, her grey hair tied back tightly in a bun. She had a wooden tray in her hands, on which was the usual handle of hot milk and a plate of cake slices. Taking the tray from her, he said,

'Carrot cake, my favourite. Thank you, Mistress Prowd.'

'It is no trouble at all, Master James.' She frowned. 'Just don't you be staying up till all hours doing that reading of yours, will you. You need your sleep.'

He smiled. 'I won't, I promise.'

'Good. And when you've finished with your supper, just leave the tray at the bottom of the stairs.'

'I will. Good-night Mistress Prowd.'

The more he learnt, the more he realised he didn't know.

Astronomy and the constellations, the compass and its variations, fixing latitude, reading and drawing charts, setting a course, sails and how to maintain them, types of rigging, soundings and how to take and report them - all these arts and many others were taught to James and the other apprentices in the front room of the house in Grape Lane.

He also learned of Whitby's importance to England's east coast counties. Cut off from the rest of Yorkshire by high moorland, the town was a hive of marine activity, looking to the sea instead of its hinterland. In all but the months of December and January, its merchant vessel fleet sailed out through the estuary of the Esk, around Whitby Rock and thence north to Tyneside or Shields, south to the Thames and upriver to London, and east to the ports of Scandinavia and the Baltic. The main cargos carried were coal from the Tyne and Durham, timber from Norway, and from the Baltic other shipping industry necessities such as hemp, sail-cloth and pitch.

James's respect for the Walker family grew. Everyone in Whitby knew that the brothers' word was their bond. As for the family's strict moral code, some of the other apprentices resented the Walkers' rules about their conduct during those times when they were released from their tuition. James and his fellow apprentices were forbidden to play dice, cards or bowls, or to frequent the taverns or playhouses on the other side of the river. But although some of the other apprentices chomped at this bit, the regulations did not bother him. He was well aware that he had a great deal of study to complete if he was to succeed, and there seemed scarcely time to complete his studies, let alone gamble, drink or seek the company of loose women on the waterfront. And although the bruise on his heart over Michela had not completely faded, his time in Staithes was otherwise almost completely forgotten.

The War of Austrian Succession had been waging for six years when James came to Whitby. It was a conflict which began under the pretext that Maria Theresa of Austria was ineligible to succeed to the Hapsburg thrones of her father, Charles VI, because she was female. In reality though, shrewd observers agreed, this was merely an excuse put forward by Prussia and France in order to challenge the power of the Hapsburgs. So, in 1740, another European war had begun.

With Britain and the Dutch allied to Austria against Prussia and France, the conflict the Americans scathingly called 'King George's War' touched the port of Whitby and made James keenly aware of the role the Royal Navy was playing in the defence of Britain's realm. Whitby had become an important cog in the wheel of the war, with troop transports, store-ships and occasionally armed vessels of Britain's naval fleet calling at the port. And after nearly seven years of war, the tide had lately turned in favour of the British, on both land and sea.

James and John Walker stood on the quayside, watching a British man o' war, HMS *San Nicolas*, being worked into the harbour. It was August, 1747. James noted the cannon ports along the ship's gunwales, instinctively counting them. A three-decker, sixty guns. Returning from battle against the Prussian fleet in the North Sea, she was a handsome vessel, but was showing the wounds of war. Midships on her port side, just above the middle deck, there were two jagged tears in her strakes, and the port railing on the after deck had been partly blown away.

Oblivious of this damage, crewmen scrambled aloft, as agitated as feeding ants amid the shrouds, lowering and furling first the main topgallant staysail and the main topgallant, then the foretopsail and the maintopsail. The remaining sails slackened as the ship was belayed slowly but methodically to her mooring by a team of men on the quay. There too, local stevedores and ships' provisioners waited to begin their work. As he watched the vessel being manoeuvred to her mooring, saw the men scuttling aloft and heard the commanding shouts of the *San Nicolas*'s mate, he felt a surge of pride. Was there a sight better intended to stir the heart of an Englishman?

The great ship was brought closer to the quay. John Walker, hands clasped behind his back, was also watching the docking proceedings closely. But his expression was not one of admiration. James said,

'She's a fine sight, Mr Walker.'

'Aye. If you approve of warships.'

James looked away. This was a subject they had discussed before. And disagreed on.

'Do you not agree, Sir,' he said carefully, 'that the Navy has served our King and country well?'

Walker drew a very deep breath, exhaled slowly, then said:

'It has.' He pouted. 'But war solves no problems. To my mind, it only creates the conditions for further conflict. So, we will be fighting the French again before long, in my estimation.'

'In England's interest, nevertheless.'

Walker's frown became a glare, with which he fixed James. 'Is it in our nation's interest to lose so many young men, to death and grievous injury? The loss of so many sons and brothers? Where, pray, is the good in that?'

Returning the older man's baleful look, James said, 'But Sir, your own ships at times transport troops and horses to the war, do they not?'

Walker looked away, then said, flatly, 'Only because if my ships do not, others will, and that will be my loss.' He grunted. 'I see no contradiction in making money from war, when the opportunity arises.'

The logic of this escaped James. If the man was to have principles, they should at least be consistent. He said, 'And what of the guns your ships carry? I admit to being surprised when I first saw that they carried an armoury.'

'For *defensive* purposes, purely. It would be the height of foolishness to carry commercial cargoes and not have the means of defending their value.' He thrust his face forward. 'Don't you see that?'

James nodded, but remained unconvinced. Mr Walker was a Quaker, like the rest of his family. As such, they believed that progress lay not in military alliances and war, but through concord and commerce. Yet the sight of the naval ship they were watching, the flags that she flew and the sailors racing so purposefully amid her decks, stays and masts, continued to stir James. He tried another tack.

'But if we bow to pressure from our foes, Sir, the French and the Prussians, and do not support the Austrian cause, surely we risk a loss of our authority in the world?'

His employer looked at him in disbelief. 'Austria? What is Austria to us? A landlocked nation with not even a mercantile fleet to call its own? And allied with *Bavaria*, a mere province, also with no coastline.' He shook his head, adamantly. 'No, James. This war, like all wars, is folly. And I will have no part of it.'

James fell silent. He had great respect for John and his brother Henry, for their probity, their industriousness and their faith. He had learned a great deal from them, and not just about seamanship. The personal example they set all their apprentices was beyond reproach. There was no doubt that in some respects, the Walkers and the other Quakers were right, in that if all men believed in peace, then war would be rendered unnecessary. Yet while there were foreign politicians, admirals and generals who would threaten England's sovereignty, there must, James was convinced, be a need to combat such foes. That was why he could not himself become a Quaker. That would be a change too far. So, he and Mr Walker would have to agree to disagree. He would let the matter stand without further dispute, and continue to think his own thoughts. Mr Walker turned his back on the ship. Tapping his left foot irritably on the cobblestones, he said, 'I shall return home now. Are you coming?'

'Not yet, Sir. I'll tarry awhile here. Please tell Mistress Prowd not to keep supper for me.'

'Very well then. I shall see you in the morning.'

'Yes. Good evening, Sir.'

As the sun slipped down the sky the dockside became crowded with naval sailors and officers from the man o' war, along with local people who had come to watch, and horses drawing carts loaded with provisions for the ship. There was no doubt, James thought as he watched barrels being rolled down from the quay and into *San Nicolas*'s hold, that Whitby had done well from the war. Scarcely a week went by when a Royal Navy troopship did not call in to the port for provisioning. And as with the *San Nicolas*, sometimes a man o' war to discharge wounded sailors. This latter thought was prompted by the sight of injured seamen being brought up from below decks. Most of them were heavily bandaged, their gownings stained with blood. Several had their arms in slings. Watching the distressed, staggering figures, James thought that Mr Walker was well right in one respect. The personal cost of war was high.

San Nicolas was now moored firmly to the quay, all her sails furled. The sailors not yet on leave still scampered about her rigging, and the cries of the boatswain who was the cause of their agitation reached James. He continued to watch for some time, absorbed by the scene. What must it be like to serve on such a ship in time of war? What courage and discipline there must be, to ensure that she was not destroyed by cannon fire or taken by the enemy as a prize. He turned away, intending to take supper at the Mermaid Inn. There in a little while he knew there would be sailors on shore leave from the *San Nicolas*. They would be recounting the experiences of the sea battles they had lately survived. And the old Whitby sea dogs would counter these stories with their own. Men like old Charlie Wilkinson, who had sailed with Woodes Rogers on the great circumnavigation of 1708-11, and who had helped rescue the castaway Scotsman Alexander Selkirk from the Juan Fernandez Islands, off the coast of Chile. And James would eavesdrop on their conversations, hearing the seamen's rodomontade, knowing full well that there was nothing in his experiences on Whitby's quayside that could remotely compare with theirs.

The port of Whitby became busier by the month, in spite of the fact that the War of Austrian Succession was at last over. Although this meant that there were far fewer naval vessels calling, there were still constant shipping movements, mainly the Walkers' colliers bound for the Tyne and London.

And at last, in September 1747, he went to sea.

His first voyage was aboard the appealingly-named collier *Freelove*. She was a cat of 341 tons, built at Yarmouth, and James sailed on her with nine other apprentices and seven crew. Like the rest of her class, *Freelove* was broad in the beam and had a shallow draft, which made her well suited to sailing the coastal and estuary waters of England's east coast.

With James aboard, the sturdy vessel sailed north, from Whitby to Tyneside. There she tied up for a week beside the river, first unloading her ballast stone, then taking aboard her cargo of coal, 170 chaldrons in all. All the apprentices helped with the loading. It was grimy work and James and the others were greatly relieved when the ship was cleaned, the taxes on the coal and ballast paid and they cast off the lines, cleared the heads and were at sea again.

They then sailed south, with a predominantly following wind, to the Thames and Wapping dock, in London.

The city and its river captivated him at first sight. So many ships, so much energy and activities! But there was no for him to explore dockside. After their dark cargo was discharged, they back-loaded timber for the Walkers' Whitby boat yards and returned to *Freelove*'s home port in time for Christmas. There the collier was laid up and wintered over in the shipyard until February.

During his eleven-week maiden voyage, James was forcibly struck by the difference between studying navigation in the comfort and warmth of the study in Grape Lane, and being at sea. Employing a quadrant while safe on a hill above Whitby could not be compared to standing on the foredeck of the collier and using the instrument while the vessel and crew were being lashed by winds of thirty knots, as happened between Whitby and the Tyne. On the voyage he also spent hours in the chains in these conditions, swinging the lead. In coastal waters this was a duty of utmost importance, and he was pleased that he proved equal to the challenge. Several times he was given a turn at the helm, overseen closely by *Freelove*'s Master, John Jefferson, and feeling the ship respond to his turning of the wheel to follow the compass needle thrilled him. By the return sailing he was used to employing a handspike to heave on the windlass, eating while standing upright as the ship pitched sharply, and setting the barometer. In this way he was learning everything of what Mr Walker called 'The three L's' - lead, latitude and lookout. He couldn't wait to be sent aloft, but Jefferson did not allow that promotion until the apprentices were on their second voyage.

Sailing, James realised after that first voyage, consisted of combating a combination of the elements: wind, water and tide. But wind, water and tide could also, by deploying certain time-honoured skills, be exploited. And that was what skilled seamen did. The sea itself was utterly indifferent to the fate of those who sailed upon it, and as such it was to be at all times respected. But it could also be taken advantage of, and, occasionally, defeated.

The sea excited him in so many ways. The exhilaration of a strong following wind, the setting of a course, the hoisting or reefing of sails, the timing needed to tack effectively into the wind, the skills involved in measuring depths or manoeuvring the ship towards a harbour light, the satisfaction of making it safely alongside the wharf at Tyneside and in the Pool of London - it all amounted to a life which he knew would fulfil his ambitions and capabilities. Even the discomforts - the long hours on watch, the cramped spaces below decks, the rain and wind - did not in any way dismay him, for the satisfactions of sailing compensated for these. The onboard food was plain and unvaried - salt beef or pork and ship's biscuit mainly - but he had never been one to complain about what he must eat. He had once roasted on an open fire, then eaten, a weasel that he had killed with his slingshot on Roseberry Topping.

The life of an apprentice merchant mariner was arduous, but aware of how much he was learning, James now wished for no other. John Jefferson was a man who had been at sea for most of his life. He and the mate, Robert Watson, were not only greatly experienced seamen, they were also fine instructors in all the arts of seamanship. He obtained more knowledge from them during the eleven weeks that he was at sea on *Freelove* than he had during his previous fourteen months of land-bound study.

But a short time later, from Great Ayton, there came painful news.

May 11, 1748
My Dear Parents,

Yesterday I received a letter from Christiana, informing me of the death of little William. This news greatly distressed me, and I can imagine the grief the child's passing has caused you all. That our dearest William should have been taken by the ague at the age of just three years is a lamentable event, and I feel doubly anguished that I am not with you to offer my consolations in person. He was such a lively little fellow, full of fun and mischief. Christiana also informed me that my little brother has been interred in All Saints' graveyard, in the sad company of Jane and our two Marys - all taken from us far too soon. I cannot help but wonder: what kind of God is it that does not permit so many children to flourish and attain adulthood? It is enough to make me question God's very existence, although I am well aware that these thoughts will not be yours. Your faith, I know, will be unwavering.

It was of some consolation to also learn from Christiana that she is betrothed. I must confess to some surprise at this news, as she seems to me to be so young, but on reflection, at 17, she is of a natural age to marry. I wish the couple every happiness following their nuptials, which Christiana informed me would be held at All Saints. No doubt you, John and Margaret will be in attendance. Christiana provided few details of her fiancé, Mr Jonathan Cocker, apart from the fact that he is a carrier. But from memory the Cockers are an old north-east family, so he should be of sound stock. I will look forward greatly to receiving news of the couple's nuptials and events subsequent to them.

Life here in Whitby continues busy, both by day and in the evenings. There are my studies - mainly navigation, astronomy and chart making - which Mr Walker oversees, and which I find I have some aptitude for. It is good too that I have an attic room at the Walkers', and a desk for my drawing and note-taking. The Walkers' housekeeper, an elderly childless lady, Mistress Mary Prowd, seems to have adopted me, as she brings me mugs of hot milk and cake when I am studying into the late hours. She is very kind.

Of my studies, astronomy in particular fascinates me. Mr Walker has kindly given me his copy of Compleat System of Astronomy *and it has absorbed my spare hours for the last weeks. After sunset on clear nights I cannot forbear to walk to the top of the cliff above the town, lie on my back on open land and observe through a glass the phases of the moon, the placement of the planets and the sky's constellations. The planet Venus has been particularly bright these past few weeks, and captivates me on a clear evening.*

The contents of this missive will be read to you by Christiana, and by the time it reaches you I will be at sea again, on one of the Walkers' colliers. But wherever I may be, my thoughts are always of you both, and of John, Margaret and Christiana. Once again, my condolences on the loss of poor little William. Although I cannot be with you to share your grief, my thoughts are much with you at this time of our great loss. Now, in my twentieth year, I look back on my own childhood with the deepest affection. I will be forever grateful for the kindness, wisdom and sober habits you imparted to me, and it is my sincerest hope that I can also lead such a life.

Your loving son, James

After another two years of study and crewing on *Freelove,* James's prospects as a professional seaman appeared favourable. In April 1750 he completed his seaman's apprenticeship. Now there was a rumour that a longer voyage was in the wind, on a new collier, *Three Brothers*, and that her destination would be a Baltic or Scandinavian port. Anticipating this voyage caused James's pulses to quicken. And as the new vessel had first to be fitted and rigged at one of the Whitby yards, and he was assigned to assist in the work, this excited him too, as he knew he would learn even more about the rigging of a cat. As indeed he did.

It was in the spring of 1751 that he sailed to his first foreign port.

'Take the helm, Cook. Steady as she goes.'

The master, Robert Watson, moved away from the wheel and James took his place. He glanced down at the compass, then up at the billowing mainsail. Watson stood a little way away, watching him closely. James knew he was under surveillance, but held his nerve. Peering up ahead, he moved the wheel a few points to starboard, to catch more wind, and *Three Brothers* responded. Her hold was filled with Tyneside coal, and she moved sluggishly, slowed further by the out-flowing tide. James looked around him. Minutes ago they had entered the great sound, Sognefiord, whose rock walls rose up sheer from the water. Dark clouds covered the tops of the fiord walls, sheets of rain streaking from them. Half an hour later the breeze dropped to a zephyr, and James called for more sail. Two hands scurried aloft and loosed a second foresail, and *Three Brothers* surged forward. James, feet planted wide apart, was exhilarated. There had been storms in the North Sea, and the collier had taken a beating, but in this enclosed, silent world she was moving eastward steadily towards the headwater. James turned and called to William Steed, on the afterdeck. 'Break out the Norwegian flag.'

The flag was unfurled by Steed, and hung limp alongside the Jack. Watson chuckled. 'You remembered, then.'

James nodded. Another test passed. But as it was his first time in Norwegian waters, he was unlikely to neglect the protocols. Glancing to port, he saw that the water was almost black, since little sunlight penetrated the sound. No need for soundings here, he knew from studying the charts last night. The water in the fiord was hundreds of fathoms deep. Scope to his eye, Watson said, 'The mill's on the eastern shore. Two points to starboard.' James obeyed, squinting into the distance. He saw a wharf, a bare-poled ship tied up there, and stacks of logs on the shore. *Three Brother*'s back-load. There would be casks of turpentine, too, for stowing.

Watson nudged James's side. 'I'll bring her in.'

James gripped the wheel. 'No, I'll do it.'

'Are you sure?'

Another test. James held the spokes tight. 'Yes.'

'Do it, then. And when we're just off the wharf, bring her round into the wind. We'll warp her into the dock.' There was a pause, then, 'You did well, Cook,' Watson said, gruffly.

As *Three Brothers* inched closer to the shore, James called for the top sails to be lowered and six of the crew scurried up the shrouds. The ship moved forward under its own momentum for a few minutes, then he spun the wheel and she came around into the light air. A cutter rowed by six sailors put out from the shore and began moving towards them, two uniformed Norwegian customs officials standing in the stern. An hour later, his vessel securely moored, James stood on foreign soil for the first time.

Several more years passed. Promoted to the rank of able seaman, and then to Mate by the Walkers, during fourteen voyages on four different ships - *Freelove, Three Brothers, Mary* and *Friendship* - he had brought all his cats safely to ports as distant as Oslo and Kiel, then back to Whitby. And with each voyage the sea entered deeper into his bloodstream, until it seemed to be as one with it. Even after just a few days ashore, he found himself longing to be back at sea. On land, all days seemed the same; at sea, every day was different.

But as he gained more experience, the more his discontent with the collier trade grew. Passing into his twenty-seventh year, the restlessness within him intensified. The very sight of a three-decker naval vessel being sailed majestically from the Chatham dockyard to the pool of London, or an elegant East Indiaman moving downriver, setting forth on a voyage to Cape Town and ports beyond, was the source of both admiration and envy for him. How could working on Whitby cats possibly compare with the challenge of serving his King on a ship of the line, or on a trading voyage half-way across the world?

One evening in May, 1755, there was a knock on the open attic room door, then a call.

'Cook?'

He stood up. 'Mr Walker. Come in.'

His employer entered. Looking at the open book in James's hand, he said, 'What's that you're reading?'

James held it up. '*A Voyage to New Holland,* by William Dampier. It was loaned to me by Charlie Wilkinson.'

'Wilkinson? He cannot read, surely.'

'He has learnt to, since retiring from the sea.' He paused. 'Do you know this book? '

The shipowner scowled. 'I know of Dampier. He was a rogue. A pirate.'

'Perhaps so. But he was also a great voyager. Three times, he sailed around the world. No other man has gone so far. Not even Sir Francis Drake.'

'That is true, but his conduct while he did so was unbecoming. He was not an honourable man.'

'A brave one nevertheless, Sir.'

Walker laughed. 'You're a stubborn man to come up against in an argument, Cook.' Placing his hands behind his back, he flexed his shoulders, the way he did when he wished to discuss matters of business.

'I need to talk with you. And not about Dampier.'

'Certainly. Here or in your study?'

'Here will do.'

James set the book aside and the shipowner took the chair beside his writing desk. Stroking his chin thoughtfully, Walker said, 'How long is it since you first came to Whitby?'

'It will be nine years next October.'

'It does not seem that long, to me.'

'Nor me, Sir. The time has gone by swiftly.'

Walker nodded. 'And you've done well. Uncommonly well. Not just completing your apprenticeship in three years, not just passing the examinations to become a Mate, but the way you've sailed *Three Brothers* and *Friendship*. On this coast, and in Scandinavia. You're a born seaman, Cook.'

James laughed, lightly. 'My parents would be surprised to hear that, Sir, being people of the land. And remember, I was born in a farm biggin.'

Walker gave a grunt. 'Well, you've certainly put that life behind you. I've seldom seen a more natural sailor. Your practical nature, your diligence in your studies, they produce a rare ability. *Friendship* has been sailed profitably, and safely, with you as her Mate.'

James did not reply. Instead he wondered what this was leading to. John Walker rarely dispensed praise in this manner. Instead he repaid diligence with other encouragements - incidental promotions, financial disbursements, invitations to express one's opinions frankly. Verbal commendations were far less forthcoming.

Walker leaned back in his chair. Again he placed his hands behind his back, signalling that something significant was coming. James noticed the hammocks of flesh beneath his hazel eyes, the crepey flesh of his jowls. He looked weary. But when he spoke again, his voice was as it always was, authoritative and decisive.

'Cook, it greatly pleases me to say that I'm offering you a command. Of *Friendship*. Starting with her next run. To Kiel.'

James was jolted. A command? Of the very ship he had sailed on for more than two years. The one he had navigated to Tyneside, to Wapping, through the Skagerrak, and to Rostock and Stockholm. She was a sturdy ship, and one that he had come to greatly respect. And now she could be his, not just to navigate, but to command.

Walker was looking at him expectantly, eyes half closed, his mouth set. Aware that his offer to the seaman opposite him was irresistible, he was relishing the fact. Meeting the older man's expectant stare, James paused for some time before replying, and when he did so his voice was firm.

'Thank you Sir, for the offer. But it is one which I will not accept.'

Walker looked as if he had walked into the edge of a door. His head twitched, then twitched again. At last he found his voice, saying carefully, 'Am I to deduce from that statement that you intend to leave the sea?'

'No, Sir. The sea has come to be my life, and I hope that it always will be.'

'Pray then, why ...'

'I intend to join the Royal Navy, Mr Walker.'

'The Navy?'

'Yes, Sir.'

'Cook, are you mad?'

'I sincerely hope not, Sir.'

'Then why ...' An expression of exasperation replaced the one of disbelief. 'Here are some reasons why that is unthinkable.' Holding up his left hand, he began to count with his right forefinger in an admonitory way. 'One, there are the hazards of battle ...Two, the pay is meagre ... Three, the food is abominable ... Four, the discipline is brutal ... Five, there are the diseases of long voyaging - scurvy, typhus ... '

James cut in. 'I am aware of all that, Sir. But I have long harboured an ambition to join Britain's navy. And to see places more exotic than the Tyne and Wapping. '

Walker tossed his hands in the air. 'Then why not join the East India Company? They would recognise the qualifications you have gained here. You could sail with them to India and the Indies. Exotic destinations, certainly. '

'I wish from now on to serve in the ships of our King, Mr Walker, not in trading vessels.' He went on, earnestly. 'I believe there is no greater calling. And I would rather serve as a volunteer, instead of being pressed into service. It's fortunate for me that I have so far escaped the gangs, when so many others have been pressed.'

'Yes, but ...' Walker now waved his hand in circles, like a wayward orchestra conductor. '... you would have to begin all over again, from the very bottom of the ranks. As a mere able seaman. No rank, no authority. And, war with the French is coming again, if the rumours are to be believed. If that is so, the deck of a man o' war is a perilous place to be.'

James nodded. He retained the greatest respect for this man, his tutor, his mentor, and he always would. But his horizons were limited, and he, James, had outgrown their limits. Quietly but forcefully he said, 'I fully understand the implications of my decision, Mr Walker, including the perils of naval life. And I am prepared to start again.'

The other man shook his head. 'I cannot believe that you do understand. If you did, you would not entertain this notion.'

James bridled. 'It is not a *notion*, Sir, it is an ambition. And one I have long held.'

Silence filled the small room. Then, heaving a sigh, John Walker said, 'So I cannot persuade you to alter this course?'

'No, Sir. My mind is made up.'

He nodded. His mouth was a straight tight line. He stood up, and held out his hand. 'Very well. But I'll not deny that you will be sorely missed on our ships. And in this house.' He gave a mirthless little laugh. 'Mrs Prowd will be bereft. You are like a son to her, I believe.'

'And I will miss her, Sir. As I will miss you all. You and Henry and all your children. I will never forget your many kindnesses. I was but a boy when I first came to Whitby. I have become a man here, with a man's responsibilities.'

Walker nodded, briskly. 'Yes, yes. So, when do you plan to leave?'

'Next month. I will take the coach to London, and report to the naval recruitment centre.'

'Where is it?'

'In Wapping.'

'Then there will be no need to take the coach. *Three Brothers* sails for Wapping the week after next. If you wish, you can sail with her. As a supernumerary.'

'Thank you Sir, that is a generous offer. I will first return to Cleveland, though, to farewell my family.' He hesitated, then continued. 'May I carry a letter of recommendation from you, to the naval authorities, testifying to the qualities of my seamanship?'

Walker nodded, but his face remained mournful. He put his hand on James's shoulder. 'As I said, you'll be much missed in Whitby. But I wish you the very best of luck.'

Four

James walked from Mrs Rigby's boarding house in Shadwell, and followed the street she had told him led to the Thames. He had been awarded five guineas long-service pay by John Walker, the most money he had ever had in his life. The jacket he had bought yesterday from a tailor in Mile End Row had brown velvet lapels and matching cuffs. It was the most stylish garment he'd ever worn, and it made him feel grand, even though he knew that soon he would be exchanging it for naval garb.

He walked on, briskly. Today he would lunch in The Bell, in Wapping, then visit a bookshop and buy a copy of Anson's *A Voyage Round the World*, to take with him to Portsmouth. His new life was under way, at last.

Wapping High Street was crowded. It was market day, and the stallholders were busy, calling out to the potential customers who milled about – women mainly – shopping baskets on their arms. Outside the town hall, three beggars in ragged clothes squatted on the cobbles, heads bowed. The upturned hats on the ground before them contained a few farthings. Thin, mangy dogs roamed about, dodging kicks from passers-by and cocking their legs to piss on the wheels of the stallholders' carts.

As James made his way through the busy square, he passed a butcher's cart draped with blood-stained hares, plucked ducks and sides of yellowing mutton. Shooing away the flies which hovered about the meat, the stall-holder called to him. 'Now there's a prosperous looking young man. Fancy a nice joint or a poultry, guv'nor? Everything fresh, all ready for the pot. Take a lovely duck home to your missus!'

Suppressing a smile, James walked on. *Guv'nor*. Did he really look the part?

He came to the lane which led down to the river and the Bell. Standing on the corner of the High Street and River Lane was a small, thin, middle-aged woman. She was wearing a grubby bonnet and there was a shawl drawn around her hunched shoulders. Her green velvet gown looked several sizes too big for her. As James approached, the woman raised one hand to him, beseechingly.

'Sir? Good sir?'

James stopped, peered into the pallid face and the huge, dark eyes. The cheekbones of her emaciated face were prominently delineated. But she must have been beautiful once, he thought.

'Sir ...'

Her hand shot out and gripped his arm. She tried to smile. 'Come with me, sir, to my room. I weel geev you a good time there, sir. A very good time. For only sixpence.'

James froze. That accent, that face.

'Michela?' he said, haltingly.

Now she went rigid. Releasing his arm, she said, in a whisper. 'You know my name? How?'

'I'm James. From Staithes.'

Her hand went up to her mouth, the shock of recognition widened her eyes.

'The boy from the shop ...'

'Yes. The boy from the shop.' He allowed a silence, then said, 'Nine years ago.'

She stared, as if seeing an apparition. 'And now you are ... grown.'

They faced each other in silence for a few moments, both unwilling to speak, neither knowing how to bridge the yawning gulf between them. Until at last James said, 'What happened? With you and ...'

'Meester Acklam.'

'Yes.'

The vile memory came rushing back.

She clutched the shawl, drawing it tight across her breasts. 'He gave me a room, in Staithes, in a big house. He bought me clothes, and jewellery. He said he loved me.' She stopped for a moment. 'I had his child, a girl. I called her Laetitia.' Her eyes filled with tears. 'She was born very weak, and became ill, but he refused to get a doctor. She died two days after she was born. After that, he told me to leave.' Closing her eyes, she looked away. 'He had found another young woman. Another mistress.'

'Where did you go?'

'Back to Durham. But my mother had died of consumption, and my sister had disappeared, no-one knew where.' She put one hand to her brow. 'So I sold the jewellery and came by coach to London, seeking work here as a servant. But the only work I could get here was ...' She turned away with the shame of it. '*Thees.*' Then her eyes returned to his, and now they were gleaming through the tears. She moved close to him, and slipped her hand inside his jacket. 'Come with me, James, *come with me,*' she implored.

He recoiled, smitten with horror and guilt at her story. Why had he not warned her? Why had he not challenged Acklam? He could have warned her, could have tried to help her, could have pointed out the folly of her way. And now, it was much too late. Backing further away, he reached inside his jacket, withdrew his wallet and from it took a one guinea note.

'Have this,' he said, handing it to her.

Her small hand reached out, took the large note, stared at it wonderingly. And as she stood staring, James turned from the pitiful sight, quite unable to bear it. Then he broke into a run, racing down the lane towards the river, not looking back.

The greatest difference, he noticed from the very beginning, was the sound of the guns. In Portsmouth and Plymouth, his new home ports, it seemed that the waterfront cannons were forever being fired. Salutes for the King's birthday, salutes for the Queen's birthday, salutes for admirals, for homecoming vessels, for the bringing in of prizes. The hills and waters around both ports echoed with the boom of the twenty-pounders, the smell of cordite drifted across the harbours and the very air seem to tremble and reverberate with their thunder and smoke.

It thrilled him, this cannon fire, for it immediately and dramatically denoted the difference between the merchant service and the Royal Navy.

For what he later thought of as his able seaman years, the first ship he was assigned to, and the first armed vessel he had sailed on, was HMS *Eagle*. A fourth rater of 1,240 tons, she carried 48 cannons. His first commander was Captain James Hamar, his first voyage part of a patrol line between the south of Ireland and the Scilly Islands. *Eagle*'s role there was to intercept any French ships she encountered.

James had quickly learned that Portsmouth was a political as well as a naval town. He was aware that although a state of war between the two nations had not yet been officially declared, France was considered a threat to Britain's growing imperial ambitions. Accordingly, the Royal Navy considered it its duty to do all it could to disrupt trade between France and what she called 'New France' and what Britain called 'Canada'. James had read that the French had been involved with the fur trade there since the early seventeenth century, and when studying maps of the north-eastern seaboard of North America, he saw that the principal means of egress to that region was the Gulf of St Lawrence and the river of the same name, a funnel-shaped channel leading to a French fortress at a place called Quebec.

Now, in the second half of 1755, one of the Royal Navy's functions was to intercept French vessels carrying vital supplies of food, clothing and armaments from mainland France to its colonial outposts across the Atlantic, such as Quebec and Louisbourg. James's first naval voyage was not auspicious, however. After *Eagle* encountered gale-force winds and mountainous seas in the Irish Sea, Captain Hamar declared that the ship's mainmast had been split. He informed the crew that he was taking the ship back to Plymouth harbour. On the way back to port, James examined the mainmast for himself. Although the driver boom was obviously broken, and one of the topsails had blown out, he could see no evidence that the mainmast itself was split. The boom could be replaced at sea, as could the topsail, so why, James wondered, was the captain taking the ship back to port? As a mere able seaman, he had to keep this thought to himself, but he experienced silent satisfaction when after arriving safely in Plymouth, naval carpenters confirmed that the mast was indeed seaworthy. A week later the Admiralty relieved Captain Hamar of his command of HMS *Eagle* and replaced him with Captain Hugh Palliser.

This taught him a lesson which he never forgot: that the Admiralty was a force which always had to be reckoned with. At sea a commander's authority was absolute, but on land the Admiralty ruled. However high the commander considered himself on shore, the Admiralty was always higher.

From the beginning, James liked Captain Palliser, and not just because he was also a Yorkshireman. After all, Palliser came from the gentry, so his background could not have been further removed from his. Five years older than James, he had been at sea since he was twelve, and had already served in the West Indies and India when he assumed command of *Eagle*. After they had been just a few days at sea together, Captain Palliser commended James in a phrase which he never forgot. After he had demonstrated to two fumbling able seamen how to go aloft and furl the topgallant properly, Palliser scowled at the hapless pair and remarked to James, 'Seamen they may be, able they are not. Amid this rabble, Cook, you're like a honed cutlass in a drawer full of blunt cutlery.'

It was under Palliser's command, and as *Eagle*'s master's mate, that James first experienced naval action. The conflict which would become known as the Seven Years War began in 1756, and on 30 May 1757, in the Bay of Biscay, *Eagle* engaged and sank the French ship *Duc d'Aquitaine*. Under fire for the first time, and although he saw ten of his shipmates killed by French cannon fire, James was surprised to find that he felt no fear. He was too concerned, he later realised, assisting with the ship's placement, to be fearful. And having once overcome fear by ignoring it altogether, he never subsequently felt frightened in battle. There was just far too much to get on with.

In June 1757 Captain Palliser received a letter, forwarded to him in Portsmouth by the Admiralty in Whitehall. It was from the Honourable Charles Derby, Member of Parliament for Scarborough. Curious as to the contents, Palliser read the letter.

To Captain Hugh Palliser RN

Some months ago the vessel under your esteemed command, HMS Eagle, *sank an enemy ship,* Duc d'Aquitaine, *in the Bay of Biscay, a feat which all Englishmen rejoiced in. None so much as the members of my constituency, when we learned that the Master's Mate on His Majesty's ship was James Cook, late of Great Ayton, where his parents still live. His father's employer, Thomas Skottowe JP, a landowner in the said village, has asked that I write to you conveying the strong recommendation that James Cook be promoted to the rank of officer in His Majesty's Navy as a consequence of his reported courage under fire and his part in ensuring the sinking of the French vessel and the safe return to port of HMS* Eagle.

Accordingly, Captain Palliser, I would humbly request that you make representations to this effect, to the Lords of the Admiralty.

I am, Yours Sincerely,

The Right Honourable Charles Derby,

Member of Parliament for Scarborough.

Palliser went below to James's cabin, where he was preparing for a forthcoming examination which would decide if he would be promoted to full Master.

'Cook?'

'Sir?'

He handed James the letter. 'I received this today.'

James read it. Then, shaking his head, he said, 'This embarrasses me, Sir. Does he not realise that I have only served only two years in the Navy, and that promotion is based on seniority? What he suggests is impossible.'

'Quite so. Obviously Misters Skottowe and Derby are not familiar with naval regulations.'

'That does not surprise me, Sir.' He smiled. 'But as you know, all Yorkshiremen close ranks, when the occasion suits it.'

Palliser laughed. 'Yes, yes.'

James said, 'Will you reply to Mr Derby?'

'Yes. I will explain. And I will also include the information that you are shortly to sit your Master's examination.' Then, folding the letter, Palliser said thoughtfully, '*Do* you have an ambition to be an officer, Cook?'

'Yes, Sir.'

'I thought so. Good.'

Two days later James took the coach from Portsmouth to London. On 29 June 1757 he sat and passed the examination at Trinity House, Deptford - the institution responsible for training harbour pilots - and was subsequently promoted to full Master. As the role of a ship's Master was to sail the ship, this new qualification gave him deep satisfaction. He was even more satisfied when on 27 October 1757, his twenty-ninth birthday, he was appointed Master of HMS *Pembroke*.

Seven months later, in the spring of 1758, *Pembroke* sailed for Canada.

Five

18 May, 1758
Dear Mr Walker,
I hope things are well with you, Mr Henry and both your families, in Whitby.

I write from the port of Halifax, on the peninsula of Nova Scotia, where the English fleet is gathered preparatory to attacking the French fleet at Louisbourg and thence, it is hoped, to wrest control of the St Lawrence River and Quebec from the French forces.

So, I have 'crossed the pond', as the old seafarers put it, and what a mighty pond the Atlantic is! I am currently serving as Master of the man o' war, HMS Pembroke, *under the command of Captain John Simcoe. She is a new ship, Plymouth built, launched only four months ago. Fully rigged, she carries sixty guns and so is a 4th rate ship of the line. These figures I know will not impress you, Sir, given your feelings about war, I convey them to you only so that you will be aware of the vessel on which your former apprentice is serving.* Pembroke *is considerably larger than a Whitby cat, but regrettably does not appear to have been constructed to the highest standards. Her mizzen mast cracked during a mid-Atlantic storm, and two of the bilge pumps malfunctioned.*

You will recall, Sir, how much I desired to sail on the world's great oceans, and how this desire played a large part in my leaving the merchant service and joining the Royal Navy. Well, I have now at least crossed one such ocean, but it was a voyage scarcely intended to encourage further expeditions. We sailed from Plymouth for Canada last February, calling at the island of Tenerife – an exotic port of call off the African coast, administered by the Spanish. There we provisioned the vessel and spent five days ashore before setting sail again on a south-west course. Thus far all was well. But four days out of Tenerife the weather turned against us, and we suffered adverse winds for the ensuing three weeks, necessitating long reaches which slowed our progress considerably. You will recall my telling you of the voyage on Freelove *in the autumn of 1754, when John Jefferson and I were making for Oslo, and how contrary the winds were throughout.*

Well Sir, the voyage to Halifax was ten times worse. The worst part of it was not the sailing - I was confident of my handling of the ship throughout the voyage, in spite of her construction deficiencies - but an outbreak of illness on the lower decks, which severely curtailed Pembroke's manpower. I intend to write to the Admiralty, reporting on this epidemic.

As paper is scarce and costly here, this letter will necessarily be brief. Two sheets only. In concluding it, Sir, I trust that you will convey the news of my recent activities to Mr Henry Walker, Mistress Prowd, and the Chapman and Sinclair families. Please tell Mistress Prowd that I greatly miss her supplies of hot milk and fresh baking! I hope too that your most recent intake of apprentices is proving equal to the challenges your seamanship instructions present. Should I return safely to England following this tour of duty, Sir, I will most assuredly visit you all in Whitby, on my way further north to Cleveland see my family.

My fondest wishes to you all,
James Cook

Report to the Admiralty by James Cook RN, Master of HMS *Pembroke*, 25 May, 1758

The Lords of the Admiralty, Whitehall, London

I am aware, my Lords, that my commander Captain Simcoe is reporting to you on matters pertaining to the unsatisfactory physical condition of HMS *Pembroke* during her recent voyage to Halifax. It is my intention here, as Master of the vessel, to report candidly on the dire physical condition many members of the ship's crew developed in the course of the voyage.

Towards the end of the third week out of Tenerife, many of the men fell ill. One after another they became so weak that they could not leave their hammocks, then eventually descended into a comatose state. To give but one example, Able Seaman Francis Partridge, with whom I served on HMS *Eagle* in the Bay of Biscay last year, fell victim to this illness. While at the helm one morning I received a message from *Pembroke*'s surgeon to say that Partridge had requested my presence. Going below decks, I found him languishing naked in his hammock. Others of the crew were also lying in their hammocks, groaning piteously, so weakened that they could not even leave them to reach and use the head, and so had soiled themselves. I had seldom witnessed such a distressing and horrible scene. Partridge, recently a strapping West Country lad, was almost unrecognizable to me. His eyes had receded into his skull, much of his hair had fallen out, and blood was oozing from the side of his mouth. When he recognised me he gave a little cry, held out his hand and attempted to grip my arm. 'Cook,' he said, 'I am so poorly. My strength has gone, all gone.'

There was nothing I could do for the poor fellow except reassure him that I would convey his story in writing to his wife in Plymouth. This I did earlier this day, prior to writing to you. Partridge died the following day, along with two other able seamen. The three victims were buried at sea, the services conducted by Captain Simcoe, while I held *Pembroke* on her course in gale force winds, which continued unabated, adding to the frustration and sorrow the entire ship felt.

No fewer than twenty-four of *Pembroke*'s crew died before we reached Halifax - twice as many who died in the battle against the French, in May 1757, when I was serving aboard HMS *Eagle*. And most of the remainder of the men on *Pembroke* were so weakened for the remainder of the crossing that the poor wretches were unable to work the ship. As soon as we reached Halifax, thirty-four crew members were admitted to the naval hospital there, where they eventually recovered, but only slowly.

As you will doubtless have concluded, my Lords, *Pembroke*'s afflicted crewmen had fallen victim to scurvy. It is my earnest hope that physicians, both naval and civilian, will apply themselves to discovering the cause and treatment of this affliction, whose extent and effects I had not before directly witnessed. With respect, my Lords, I suggest to you that this scourge is a matter which requires the authorities' utmost attention, particularly in the case of prolonged sea voyages, when the disease worsens the longer a ship is away from shore. I trust that your Lords will adgown this matter with the greatest urgency.

I am your humble servant, James Cook

He stood in the stern of *Pembroke*'s launch, glancing in the direction of the cove but keeping constant watch on the swells which were building up in the bay. It was August, 1758. The boat's four sailors were watching him, trailing their oars, waiting for a signal. All five men were aware that yesterday when a dozen other longboats from the English fleet had attempted to land in Kennington Cove, all had been overturned by breaking waves. Several sailors were injured, one seriously after a blow to the head from a capsizing boat. Now the wind had abated somewhat, but it was still blowing on-shore, making any landing difficult. But as Kennington Cove was the only landing beach in the Louisbourg area of Royale Island, they had no option but to put ashore here. In the distance James could see a broad arc of yellow sand, and above it a sand dune foreshore covered in tussock grasses, and beyond, stands of dark green conifers. He brought the boat's tiller around, so that the bow pointed seaward, the better for him to judge the swells.

Three large swells in succession passed under the boat, causing it to pitch steeply. When they had moved on towards the shore, he pushed the tiller away, bringing the boat's bow around and towards land. As the oarsmen waited for his command, their faces were set and tense. They had all heard about what had happened yesterday, and none of them could swim, including James.

'Sir?'

The leading oarsman, Matthew Gibson, hands gripping the haft of his oars, was looking at James expectantly.

Legs braced, James stared out to sea. 'Await my command,' he told Gibson.

Feet wide apart, he held the tiller and stared seaward. Another swell moved under the boat, then raced towards the beach. Then there was a lull. Left fist bunched, James brought his hand down, hard.

'Now! Pull!'

The men dipped their oars, deep, and the longboat began to move beachward, James calling the timing.

'One, two, one two ...'

Still staring seaward, he saw a swell began to build. He called, calmly but more insistent now, 'Harder. One, two, one two ...'

The oarsmen, shoulders straining, eyes cast downwards, dug the blades of their oars deeper.

'One, two, one, two ...'

The swell rose and began to race towards them, building into a wave. The beach was only twenty yards away now and the longboat hurtled towards it like a harpoon. Holding the tiller firmly, James glanced seaward once more. The swell was rising, the offshore wind tearing at its crest.

'Ship oars!' he yelled, and the men obeyed, hauling their oars aboard. Knees bent, James gripped the tiller, ensuring that the rudder remained straight. The longboat skimmed into the shallows, then stopped suddenly as its keel touched sand. 'Disembark,' he shouted, 'and bring her in!'

They leapt from the boat and into the white water, two on the port side, two to larboard. They clutched the gunwales, then began to haul the boat further in. James held the tiller until the four oarsmen were clear of the water, then jumped into the shallows. Pushing at the stern while the others tugged at the gunwales, the boat reached the beach. Seconds later the swell, which had become a five foot wave, collapsed and swept into the cove, its white water surging into the launch's stern. The five men lugged the vessel clear of the water and up onto the beach.

Gibson grinned at James. 'Fine timing Sir,' he gasped.

He nodded, curtly. 'Well rowed lads.' He looked along the tideline.' Tide's dropping, but keep the anchor out to be sure she's safe. And one of you must stand watch over her at all times. I should be back within the hour.'

'Aye Sir.'

All four sank down on the sand, chests heaving but obviously grateful for the break. Walking up the beach, James was startled to see a solitary, uniformed figure standing on the foreshore in front of some sort of instrument. He was making notes in a small book. Curious, James strode up the sand towards him.

The man appeared to be about his own age, thirty. He was fair haired and of slim build, and instead of wearing naval garb he was gowned in the uniform of a lieutenant in the British army. As James approached, he looked up.

'Good-day, Sir.'

'And good-day to you, Sir.'

'Cook, James Cook. Master of the *Pembroke*.'

'Holland, Samuel Holland.' The men shook hands.

James said, 'You are not from the English fleet?'

'No, I am in the employ of Brigadier Wolfe.'

'I was curious, when I saw what activity you were engaged upon here. What is the instrument you're using?'

'A plane table. I'm carrying out a survey of this cove, for Brigadier Wolfe.'

The two men chatted. The man was Dutch, but spoke good English, albeit with a strong accent. His family name was Van Hollandt, he told James, and he had left his homeland to further his career as an engineer in the British army. Sent to North America to work as an assistant engineer, he had carried out surveys in the New York area before being transferred to Louisbourg to give engineering advice to Brigadier Wolfe, in preparation for the campaign against the French garrison. Now that the French had surrendered after a five-week siege, it was Holland's duty to survey this part of Royale Island for the records of the British army authorities.

James nodded, then said, 'And the "plane table". That is a telescope on it, is it not? And a compass.'

'Yes.' Holland tapped the scope and it moved. 'It rotates, so I can take a fix on a distinctive feature, like the headland there ...' He put his eye to the glass and swivelled it so that it pointed to the headland at the north end of the cove. 'Then I draw a draft of the principal aspects of the topographical features in my notebook, from a base line. I include its magnetic bearing, using the compass.' He looked up. 'So, by taking angles off certain fixed points - such as the headland there - I can later reproduce the features of a landscape precisely on paper.'

'Ah. So simple. But practical.'

'Ja. It was devised by a military engineer, Captain Woolcott, during the campaign against the French in India.' Brushing sand from his sleeve, he said, 'You are interested in surveying?'

'Very. I have studied mathematics, including trigonometry. And as a naval man, I have a particular fondness for hydrography. It is among my duties as *Pembroke*'s Master to produce charts of the areas we find ourselves in.'

'Have you produced such charts already?'

'Some. But I have much still to learn.' James paused. 'I wonder ... since the Louisbourg campaign is over, whether I would be able to accompany you during your survey. I would be greatly obliged if I could take some tuition from you.'

The Dutchman considered this for a moment, then said, 'Is your vessel here for long?'

'We will not be leaving until at least the autumn.'

'Then I cannot see why not.' Holland smiled. 'So long as a man of the Senior Service has no objection to receiving tuition from a mere foot soldier.'

James laughed. He liked this man. And clearly he could teach him a great deal about coastal surveying. So he would request that Holland meet Captain Simcoe, and that he, James, be given leave to stay ashore and accompany the Dutchman during his survey of Royale Island.

They worked well together, the pair of them, during that summer, surveying Gabarus Bay. With *Pembroke* at anchor off Louisbourg, they worked ashore for days on end, then brought their draft sketches back to the ship. Holland was a patient instructor, and James learned a great deal from him, in particular how to establish a reliable baseline and to use triangulation to establish accurate co-ordinates. In this way he learned to marry the techniques of land and sea cartography, linking his nautical mapping with Holland's sophisticated land surveying techniques.

On *Pembroke* they worked in the great cabin, over a drawing table, under the supervision of Captain Simcoe. He helped them to render the vast amount of trigonometrical data and calculations made ashore into charts sufficiently accurate for ships' masters to employ while navigating the region's coastal waters. Captain Simcoe had loaned James his copy of Leadbetter's *Uranoscopia, or the Contemplation of the Heavens*, along with *The Young Mathematician's Companion*, references which he made great use of during that summer. And it was aboard *Pembroke* too that James and Holland compiled the materials for, as the Dutchman entitled it, 'A Chart of the Gulf and the River of St Lawrence.'

As for his letter to the Admiralty on the subject of the outbreak of scurvy on *Pembroke*, he received neither acknowledgement nor reply. He brooded on this lack of response, first affronted by it. He then affirmed, to himself: *I will act upon the scurvy, if given the chance.*

5 February, 1761

Dear Mr Walker,

I write from Halifax, Nova Scotia, in my cabin on HMS Northumberland, *the flagship of the English squadron here. I was transferred to her last year and I am her Master. You will no doubt be interested in her figures. At 1,414 tons, and 164 feet by 45 feet, she is the largest naval vessel on which I have so far served. She was built at Plymouth eleven years ago and is under the command of Captain Nathaniel Bateman. Lord Alexander Colvill is in overall charge of the English squadron here. He is ten years my senior, and a greatly experienced seaman who has served in the West Indies as well as North America. We were both present during the siege of Quebec, when he availed himself of the charts of the St Lawrence which Samuel Holland and myself had produced. Although I have no proof of it, I suspect that it was Lord Colvill who arranged for my transfer from HMS* Pembroke *to* Northumberland. *If it was indeed his work, then I am deeply grateful to him for having faith in my navigational and hydrographical abilities.*

But Sir, those days of the Quebec siege now seem distant. You will doubtless have read in the broadsheets of the details of the battle for Quebec and General Wolfe's momentous victory. It may surprise you Sir to learn that I too am relieved that the conflict with the French appears to be over. I have over these last five years seen far too many good men killed and maimed - from lowly seamen to commanders - to believe that war is an entirely noble cause. Thus, my beliefs and yours are now much more convergent than they once were. When I joined the Navy I was a callow fellow - now I have a far greater awareness of war's cruelties and privations.

The deaths of our leaders are just as affecting. John Simcoe, my commander on HMS Pembroke, *and a loyal supporter of my surveying programme, died on the ship from natural causes prior to the siege of Quebec. I felt this bereavement keenly, as he had become a close friend. The death of General Wolfe at Quebec moved us all greatly too, just as Montcalm's demise must have affected the French forces. They were both fine leaders of men.*

This is an unusual shift in my sensibilities, you may think Sir, and perhaps a paradoxical attitude for a man who still wears the King's uniform with pride and dedication. It is still my conviction that Britain is the greatest nation on Earth, and thus I will willingly give my own life in its defence, but with my knowledge now that if conflicts can be resolved without warfare - on either sea or on land - then that course must be pursued to the utmost. The French may still cause trouble in this region. There are rumours that they still covet the port of St John's, north of here, in which case it will be our duty to defend the fort to the best of our ability, but we hold out hope that the present peace will prevail. This region is now almost entirely under the Union Jack, and should remain so.

And now, Sir, since I have used up my ration of notepaper, I must conclude. Please convey my best wishes to all my friends in Whitby.

I remain Sir, yours faithfully, James Cook

He learned again that winter in Halifax was the bleakest of seasons. Although the port itself was ice-free because of the warm current known as the Gulf Stream, which passed Nova Scotia from the south, outside Halifax harbour great chunks of floating ice lurked, brought down from the high northern latitudes by another, much colder current. It was the same coldness which had caused his party such discomfort during their survey of the St Lawrence. James realised too that it was the mixture of the cold and warm air above the two differing currents which caused the dense fogs which afflicted so much of the coasts of the region and presented a persistent hazard to navigation. The results of this mixture of warm and cold air could be compared, he thought, to the clouds of steam which emerge from a boiling kettle, then condense in the surrounding colder air.

During the months when he and his crew were kept entirely within the harbour's confines by the ice mountains outside, he spent the time productively, increasing his knowledge of astronomy and mathematics. He read avidly the work of an ancient Greek Mathematician, Euclid, of Alexandria, in particular his 'Elements', which had been loaned to him by Lord Colvill. He found it a brilliant work of geometry. Learning that Euclid was born in 300BC, he appreciated that the mathematical knowledge of the Ancients was remarkable, and that his theories were highly applicable to the art of navigation. While *Northumberland* lay at anchor in Halifax, awaiting the arrival of the spring thaw, Euclid's 'Elements' and its diagrams and theorems absorbed him by day and night.

As well as studying, he spent many days surveying the harbour, an activity which the inclement weather did not entirely preclude. And when the fog and ice did prohibit outdoor activities, he retired to his cabin to work on his charts of the harbour, work which fully absorbed him. He had come to regard a finely drawn and precise chart as a work of art, as well as being the most practical assistant a ship's master could possess, and he now took the greatest pride in the researching and compiling of coastal charts of waters hitherto unsurveyed.

But while the fleet awaited the spring thaw the rest of *Northumberland*'s crew, lacking constructive activity and with the imperatives of war gone, became lax. In the town there was the usual agglomeration of taverns and houses of ill-repute, and while on shore leave the men took every advantage of these dens of inequity. Drunkenness became widespread, and the fleet's marine corps and bos'uns were kept busy apprehending, arraigning and punishing the numerous miscreants. James was concerned by the number of repeat offenders among the crew of *Northumberland*. The most notable example was the inaptly named Edward Lovely. Last August this seaman had been lashed for theft. He was lashed again for drunkenness, in two instalments, on December 1 and 2, for various crimes and misdemeanours. Then, the very next month, he was sentenced to receive 600 lashes for absenting himself unlawfully from his ship. This last flogging was carried out 'around the fleet', as the saying had it, with 180 lashes being administered alongside each British ship.

James watched from *Pembroke*'s poop deck as Lovely, tied to a grating in *Northumberland*'s launch, received his second round of lashes from her bosun. Already the seaman's back was bleeding meat, and his initial cries, which had carried across the harbour, were subsiding to agonised whimpers. This led James to wonder if the prolonged and repeated punishment he was witnessing would cure the man of his reoffending. He knew that the cat o' nine tails was an essential part of naval life, but it also seemed to him that 600 lashes was manifestly excessive. He had given much thought over the last few years to the role of a ship's commander, and while fully aware that a captain must at all times insist that discipline be maintained, and that violations of the code of naval conduct be punished with the lash, it seemed to him equally important that the commander was seen to lead a team of men who worked a ship in as harmonious a way possible.

Having served much time on the orlop deck, he was well aware that disharmony occasioned by unjust or disproportionate punishment led only to festering resentment among the crew, with a consequent lack of willingness to carry out essential duties. As a consequence, a ship became not only unhappy, but inefficiently crewed. Long ocean voyages and sea battles demanded discipline of the most rigorous nature, but the need for teamwork at sea remained paramount. If he ever had the privilege of a command, he would never resile from prescribing the cat – to be lenient with the lash was viewed as a weakness by the lower deck. But teamwork was just as necessary, as without cooperation a ship could not be worked efficiently. A commander's crucial challenge was to achieve a balance between crew discipline and solidarity.

As fresh fruit was unobtainable in Halifax during the frozen season, and the men still refused to eat the pickled cabbage which was made available to them, they continued to suffer the effects of scurvy. Witnessing this scourge again, it now seemed to James to be a matter of the utmost importance to insist that a dietary regime at sea which included scurvy-combating ingredients, called by the physicians 'anti-scorbutics', be made mandatory. He was aware that it was now thought likely that a regular intake of pickled cabbage – which the Europeans called 'sauerkraut' – could prevent the onset of scurvy. Yet the Navy had done nothing to make such an intake compulsory on its ships. Until it did so, James felt certain, scurvy would continue to afflict its crews.

With March came the thaw, and the seemingly endless winter was over. Eagerly he resumed his surveying programme, beyond the confines of Halifax harbour.

Six

It was a mid-morning in November, 1762, when he left Mrs Rigby's boarding house in Shadwell, on the north bank of the Thames. He walked briskly along Candle Street, passing rows of brick and tiled houses whose front doors opened directly onto the street. Groups of children were at play in the street and some called 'Mornin' Sir' to him as he passed. Smiling, he nodded a greeting in reply. His day was planned: he would walk into the City, then visit James Sheppard, John Walker's London agent, who in a recent letter John had recommended he meet. An open carriage approached, carrying two ladies, and James stepped aside to let it pass, raising his hat to them as it did so.

The autumn air was chilly, the sun low, and he was glad of the stout navy-issue cape he had put on before he left. He was glad too of the five days' leave he now had, having at last completed and delivered the charts of the St Lawrence to the Admiralty in Whitehall. He was pleased with the charts, which had been completed in his room at the Shadwell boarding house. They were the culmination of two years of surveying and note-taking along the river, and he was confident that should hostilities against the French be resumed, they would be valuable to the Navy and the Admiralty.

Last month he had turned thirty-four. He was proud of what he had achieved in the seven years he had been in the Royal Navy. Although he detested boasting, to himself he could admit that signing on with the Navy had been a successful move. But now, in his thirty-fifth year, he felt that there was something vital missing from his life. A hollowness deep within himself, he thought of it as, a kind of scurvy of the spirit. This was not the result of a lack of friends, for he had forged strong comradeships in the Navy, with men such as Samuel Holland, and he had gained influential patrons who knew of his abilities and respected his work. Men like Sir Hugh Palliser and Lord Colvill.

He crossed Dellow Street, stepping over the deepest of the muddy coach tracks, then walked on towards the City.

However the melancholia that he had been experiencing lately was becoming more and more difficult to dislodge. In a year or two he would have spent half his life at sea. Nearly sixteen years, spent entirely in the company of men. That was how it had to be, for the sea was no place for a woman. But now that he was back on land, on English soil once again, he found himself longing for the touch and the warmth of a woman. Not merely a carnal relationship, but someone he could know as a friend and companion. He was struck again by a guilty memory, of the harlot he had used in a waterfront whorehouse in Halifax, during his last bitter winter in Nova Scotia. That woman, part-Indian, part-French, had been used purely for the relief of his base urges, and afterwards James had felt nothing except pity for the poor creature and a lingering shame for himself. The act had been the recourse of a sad and lonely man.

He paused to look up at the grey, brooding sky. It matched his mood. Perhaps it was the memory of the death of his brother John, at the age of 23, that was prompting these considerations of mortality. His three sisters and his other brother, William, had died too, but in infancy. This was a sad but inescapable part of life. But for brother John, his parents' first-born, to reach maturity and then die before them, had been a bitter blow for his surviving family. At sea James had seen a good deal of death, men dead from disease or battle wounds. As he watched their canvas-shrouded bodies committed to the deep, the words of the naval chaplain had come increasingly to just wash over him. His thoughts instead were always with the victims' bereaved families on land, the ones who would not learn of the fate of their lost men until many months after the event.

He walked on. If he too were to die, after he returned to sea, who would there be to remember him, beside his parents, and Christiana and Margaret?

He passed the Tower of London. Every other day he took this walk, west from Wapping, along the river and into the City. He relished the exercise, while the sights and sounds of London's streets usually cheered him: the cries of the kerbside hawkers and broadsheet sellers, the elegant sedan chairs and their curtained occupants, the fine carriages and their horse teams, the delicious smells from the coffee houses and food stores.

Near Garraway's coffee house in Clement's Lane, he came to one of his favourite haunts, Lambert's Book Emporium. It was narrow, with diamond-patterned windows, rough-hewn ceiling beams and bare, sagging floorboards. It was so dark inside the shop that its lamps barely illuminated the crammed shelves. But by searching them carefully, James usually discovered something of interest: a book of maps of North America, accounts of East Indiamen's voyages, histories of European wars, astronomical tables.

He stooped as he entered the shop, to avoid banging his head on the low lintel, then squinted into the dim light. The proprietor, Charles Lambert, sat at the desk just inside the door, absorbed in a copy of *The Spectator*. By now James was well known to him. A fellow with a furrowed forehead, dimpled chin and heavily powdered wig, Lambert looked up with obvious reluctance from his reading.

'Ah ... good day Sir. Are you keeping well?'

'Quite well, thank you,' said James.

'And are you looking for anything in particular today?'

'Just browsing, as usual, thank you.'

His eyes returning to his *Spectator*, Lambert waved his hand airily towards the shelves. 'Well, browse away.'

James moved down the narrow space between the shelves, which gave off a smell of leather, ink, candle smoke and camphor, a not unpleasant combination. Heading towards the 'Explorers' Chronicles' section, he noticed a shelf entitled, 'Dietary Advice and Digestive Treatments'. One word on the dark blue spine of a shelved book caught his attention. *Scurvy*. He reached up and took the book down. Its full title was *A treatise of the scurvy*, and the author's name was James Lind. Opening it, James saw that it had been published nine years earlier, in 1753. The author was not familiar to him, but as the subject was of close interest, he paid Lambert three pence for the little book ('The only copy I've yet sold') and placed it in his haversack. Leaving the shop, he walked down Lombard Street and past Wren's Monument to the riverbank. There, on a bench beside London Bridge, ignoring the cool east wind blowing along the river, he began to read Lind's treatise, and something of the author's life.

A Scotsman, Lind had been a naval surgeon and was now chief physician at the Royal Naval Hospital at Gosport. As part of a study of naval hygiene, he had conducted at sea an experiment on the causes and possible cures for scurvy. James read on, fascinated.

Postulating that the disease had multiple causes and therefore required multiple treatments, mainly of a dietary nature, Lind considered that scurvy could be combated not merely with pickled cabbage, but also by an intake of acids in the body. While in the Bay of Biscay he had treated scurvy-afflicted sailors with various fluids, including cider, barley water and vinegar, along with citrus fruits. The latter, he concluded, were particularly effective. Reading on, James saw that Lind also advocated a strict regimen of personal cleanliness in naval vessels: better ventilation below decks, regular washing of bodies, bedding and clothing and fumigation of a ship with sulphur and arsenic.

James put the little book back in his haversack and began to walk back along the river, contemplating Lind's theories. He passed the fishing smacks alongside the Billingsgate fish market, smelling the stinking fish stalls beside the quay, hearing but not really listening to the calls and curses of its porters. What Lind had postulated made sense to him. On that first voyage to Halifax on *Pembroke*, when scurvy had taken such a terrible toll, he was aware that the outbreak only happened after their supplies of fresh cabbages, lemons, limes and oranges – taken on at Tenerife – had been exhausted. The men on the upper deck, encouraged by Captain Simcoe, had continued to consume regular intakes of lime juice and pickled cabbage, and had remained in sound health, but the men below deck steadfastly refused to consume these items, stubbornly continuing to eat only salted beef, pork and ship's biscuit. Considering again what Lind had written, James was aware that citrus fruit was acidic, and therefore anti-scorbutic. Thus, Lind's medical experiment may well have made a vital connection. So why, he also wondered, had the Navy not acted upon the doctor's findings?

Deciding to take lunch at an alehouse he knew, The Bell, which was a short walk from his boarding house, he made his way back, over Tower Hill and down Wapping Lane towards the river. The streets became crowded with carts, wagons, carriages and men on horseback, jostling for the right of way. Minutes later he could smell the industries of the Thames: boiling pitch, fresh-sawn timber, the reek of roperies, tanneries and breweries. He loved the mixture of odours that pervaded Shadwell, the smells of maritime industries. Quickening his step, he soon heard the familiar sounds coming from the riverside: the cries of lightermen, wharfingers and the ferrymen who plied the Thames. Rounding another corner, he came to The Bell, a half-timbered building on the corner of Brewhouse Lane and Wapping High Street, its eponymous sign swinging in the cool breeze. He wiped his boots on the iron scraper beside the entrance, then went inside.

The ceiling was low and cream-coloured, the beams blackened, the bare floorboards undulating. A coal fire was burning in the capacious fireplace, which was lined with rows of horse brasses. A portrait of George III hung above the mantelpiece. A few men sat about at tables in the room, mugs of ale in front of them, playing cards. At one end of the room was a servery, and James went directly to it. It was attended by a young woman. James removed his hat. Then, inclining his head towards her, said, 'Good morning, Miss. I will have ....' he stared at the row of barrels behind her '... a pint of Steele's ale, if you please.'

'Certainly, Sir.'

She turned and fetched down a pewter tankard from a shelf, placed it under a spigot and began to fill it. James studied her as she did so. She was of medium height, shapely and fair-haired. Her lilac gown was pulled in tightly at the waist, accentuating her full hips. She wore no bonnet, and her hair was drawn up high on her head and pinned in place with a tortoiseshell comb. The tankard filled, she passed it to him. He noted her cornflower blue eyes, and the scattering of pale freckles on her rounded cheeks. They reminded him of a quail's egg. He thought too that he had seen the young woman somewhere before. But where?

'Thank you,' he said, sliding a penny piece across the servery counter. Then, frowning, he said, 'Have you worked here long, Miss?'

'Since I were eighteen, Sir. And I'm 20 now.' She smiled. 'I don't usually work on Mondays, but Constance, the publican's daughter, slipped in the yard and turned her ankle.'

He nodded, then said, 'Do you know Mistress Mary Batts, who used to own The Bell when I first came to London?'

The young woman gave a delighted laugh. 'I should think I do know her, Sir, as she is my mother.' Her smile faded. 'But since my father passed away, she has remarried. She is now Mary Blackburn, and living in Shadwell.'

'I see. And do you live there too?'

She picked up a cloth and wiped the top of the servery. 'No. I live with the Sheppard family, in Barking.'

'Is that James Sheppard?'

'It is. Do you know him?'

'I do. Through my onetime employer, John Walker of Whitby.'

'I have heard of Mr Walker.' She began to squeeze the cloth out into a bowl.

As James sipped his ale, he cast his mind back. Then, watching her spread the cloth out on the counter, he said thoughtfully, 'You must be the little girl who once dined here with your parents and me, when I was serving on a Whitby collier. I used to stay in a room upstairs.'

She tilted her head on one side. 'And when would that have been, Sir?'

'Before I joined the Navy. It would have been ... 1748 or 49.'

'That would have made me ... six or seven then.' She smiled, apologetically. 'So I'm sorry, Sir, but I have no memory of the occasion.'

He did. He well remembered the vivacious child who had joined the adults at table one evening. *Elizabeth.* When he had told her that he sailed on a cat, she had looked puzzled and asked: 'A cat? How can anyone sail on a cat? Where does the mast go?' The questions had caused great mirth at the table. And now, here was the same Elizabeth. No, not the same, now a grown woman. And a comely one.

'I was a mere lad then,' James said. 'But I remember the occasion, as it was one of my first voyages to Wapping. And I well remember your father, Samuel. And your mother. Is she well?'

'She is, Sir.' She began wiping the counter again, and as she did so he noticed that she wore no wedding ring. 'She will be visiting here after midday, and so too will my stepfather, John Blackburn.'

'Perhaps I shall see them then.'

The young woman moved away to serve another customer, an elderly man whose wig was decidedly lopsided. James watched her as she poured the man a tankard of ale. How lovely she is, he thought, so fresh and ... wholesome. A fine example of young English womanhood.

He finished his ale, and it formed a warm, satisfying pool within him. When the young woman returned to where he stood, he said, 'I would like a pork pie, please, Elizabeth.'

Her blue eyes widened with surprise. 'You have remembered my name, Sir, after all these years.'

'I have. And please, Elizabeth, my name is James. James Cook.'

His visits to The Bell became more frequent. Remembering that she did not usually work on Mondays, he ensured that his lunch was taken in the alehouse on the other days of the week. And each time, she greeted him warmly. Their conversations became longer. She asked him about his work in Nova Scotia, he asked her about her wider family and their interests. Then, several lunches after they had first talked, and anxious to converse with her beyond from the confines of The Bell, James plucked up the courage to ask her to walk out with him on a Sunday. She blushed at his invitation, but smiled too, nodding her agreement.

They crossed the meadow behind Shadwell. It was only a month since that first conversation in The Bell, but James felt himself being drawn more and more deeply into Elizabeth Batts's orbit. Her gentle company and utter naturalness delighted him and was bringing a new dimension to his life. After so much male company over the years, much of it brutish, he found her feminine presence enchanting. That he had found a woman he already knew he loved, and whom he dared to hope returned his love, seemed a kind of miracle to him.

The ground was still frosty and the sun, low in the eastern sky, gave off a lemony light. He wore a heavy topcoat, she a red and brown checked woollen gown, a matching shawl and woollen gloves. The grass crackled underfoot as they made their way up a low rise in the meadow. There was an oak tree at the top of the rise, its leafless branches appearing to implore the grey sky for warmth. James led Elizabeth to a carved seat under the tree. She read from a brass plate on the back of the seat. *In memory of Joseph Finlay 1694- 1752. Rest and be Thankful.* Spreading her gown first, she sat down carefully. 'Well, thank you for your help, Joseph Finlay, whoever you might have been.' Laughing, James sat down beside her.

They sat in silence for a time, staring in the direction of the Thames, across the roofs of Shadwell and the chimney tops that stuck up from them like the stumps of a felled forest. A sinuous mist hung over the river, marking its meandering course westward towards the estuary. Since they had first walked out together they had learned a great deal more about each other. He had told her about his family in Cleveland, his apprenticeship in Whitby, his adventures in North America; she had told him about her life in Barking, her mother's remarriage and the way she and her second husband had built up their business interests.

James had been invited to stay with James Sheppard in his commodious house in Barking. There they spent the evenings beside the fire, reminiscing about their connections with the Whitby-based coal trade, sometimes joined by Sheppard's business partner, Erasmus Cockfield. The two men, Quakers like the Walkers, were timber merchants and sail-makers, as well as master mariners in their own right.

And during that time, James's interest in the vivacious, intelligent young woman who was part of the household, intensified.

Now, breaking the silence, he said to Elizabeth, 'Two weeks more and it will be the winter solstice.'

She smiled. 'Do you always think of the year in such terms, James? I only think December means that Christmas is on its way.'

'I suppose it is because of my concern with astronomy. At sea I live with the moon and stars as much as the sun.'

'It is a life that suits you, then?'

'I cannot imagine one without it.'

She looked thoughtful for a time, then asked, 'And when will you return to sea?'

'When I am ordered to. In the spring, I presume. The decision is not mine to make.'

She frowned, but nodded too. 'Yes, I know other naval people. That is how it must be.'

Turning towards her, he placed his hands over hers. 'But in the meantime, I am quite happy to be on land.' He looked earnestly into her eyes. 'Elizabeth, forgive me, I am unused to speaking in this way ...' he hesitated, then pressed on '...but I must tell you that these past few weeks, walking out with you, speaking with you, getting to know you, have been the happiest of my life.' She met his gaze, felt his big hands tighten around her much smaller one, smiled. 'And through you, I have discovered something about myself that I did not know existed.' He looked down at their joined hands, and Elizabeth waited for him to continue. 'That discovery was that I am capable of loving a woman.' Hastily, awkwardly, he corrected himself. 'Not just "a woman", but you, Elizabeth. There was another, longer pause. She could see that he was struggling to find the words he needed, and as she watched him do so her feelings for this big, strong but awkward man flooded through her. He looked up again and said, decisively now, 'Elizabeth, I love you, and I wish to marry you. Will you do me the honour of becoming my wife?'

She stared into his craggy face, into the deep-set grey eyes that seemed to be at one with hers. She too felt the strength flowing from his resolution, felt his hands on hers, felt a stirring within herself that seemed to flow up and towards him. Leaning forward, she placed her lips against the side of his neck. Then she drew back, took her hands from his, put her arms around him and said. 'I will, James, I will.'

On 21 December 1762 they walked across the meadow outside Barking to the parish church of St Margaret's. No banns had been issued, neither of them thought it necessary to do so. Eschewing any ceremony or fuss, the couple were married in a plain ceremony at St Margaret's before three witnesses who the minister, the Reverend George Downing, had arranged, and who neither James nor Elizabeth had met before. This was of no concern to them. The most important thing for both of them was, they were now man and wife. After their unadorned nuptials they moved into Elizabeth's parents' old house in Upper Street, Shadwell.

And there they made further discoveries about each other, ones which brought both of them great happiness.

They had been married just four months, during which James had been putting the finishing touches to his St Lawrence charts, when a messenger on horseback delivered a letter to Upper Street. The envelope carried the seal of The Admiralty Office, Whitehall. Surprised and curious, James opened it in front of the fire, Elizabeth watching him intently as he did so. For a few moments he said nothing. Instead he stared at the page, his brow set.

'What is it, James?'

'I am ordered to sea again. On HMS *Antelope*. Under the command of ... Thomas Graves.'

'As Master?'

'No.' He peered at the notepaper. 'As a supernumerary. I am to be ...' He began to recite:

"...employed in making surveys of the coasts and harbours of Newfoundland, and in making drafts and charts thereof". Looking up, he could not withhold a note of pride from his voice. 'I am to be The King's Surveyor. On the schooner *Grenville*. And I am to be paid ten shillings a day for carrying out these duties.' He inhaled sharply. ' Ten shillings a day ...'

She went to him, put her arms around him, set her face against his chest. 'Oh, James, that is wonderful news. Congratulations.' Then she drew back and stared up at him. 'I have news too. I meant to tell you later, but after hearing this, I must tell you now.'

He looked down at her. 'What is it?'

'I had a consultation with Doctor Bartlett last Thursday.' She reached up and touched his lips, gently. 'I am with child.'

Seven

15 July, 1763, St John's, Newfoundland
Dear Mr Walker
Firstly, my thanks to you for your letter of congratulations upon the occasion of my marriage, which I received shortly prior to departing for Canada. I was very touched by your message of goodwill and ensured that Elizabeth, my wife, shared your letter with me and the good wishes it contained.

My thoughts have of late been with you all in Whitby, busily engaged in your mercantile activities. With the population of London growing so rapidly, as I have read, no doubt the demand for Tyne coal continues unabated. Please remember me to your family, and Mistress Prowd. Your daughters and sons must now be almost grown up. Do the boys intend to train for a career at sea?

I write from St John's, on the island of Newfoundland, the base for my surveying activities. The Governor, Thomas Graves, has placed a schooner, HM Grenville, *at my disposal while the coastal survey of the island is carried out. As I am her Master,* Grenville *represents my first command in the Navy. The surveying project will be a lengthy one, as the island has a long and complex coastline (its total length, I estimate, is more than 10,000 miles) with a great many bays, promontories, estuaries and smaller islands, all of which must be thoroughly charted. It will be a task requiring several years of work, that is certain.*

You will doubtless want to learn of Grenville*'s characteristics. She was built in Massachusetts, in New England, was named after George Grenville, our First Lord of the Admiralty. A compact vessel, she is 55 feet in length, has a 17 foot beam and at only 69 tons is quite suited to working in the inshore waters which are the object of my expedition's survey. But she is also well capable, I believe, of making the eastward Atlantic crossing, which I shall be undertaking in her after the onset of autumn.*

To carry out the survey of this island, I spend most of my time ashore. There I first set up a baseline and with my compass accurately determine the direction of north. I then choose the most prominent geographical features - usually a headland, hillock or islet - and once selected, use them as triangulation points.

Bearings are then taken on these features, employing a plane table and sextant.

The charts drawn up as a result comprise a merged image of the coastal features, to which are added the depth soundings taken from the water by William Parker, Grenville's *master's mate. I also add, where fitting, recommendations for potential anchorages, advice for pilotage, fisheries and future settlements, as given the likelihood of future English migration to this large and strategically situated island, such information will be essential.*

As the summer here is brief - even briefer than in the north of England - it is imperative that the surveying continues unabated while the weather permits us to do so. Those who have lived here for some time quip that, 'There are three seasons only in Newfoundland, July, August and winter', and I am bound to agree that it is a saying which contains much truth. But it is also true that I have become hardened to the cold and wet, so that it seldom interferes with my work. This is no doubt due in part to my Yorkshire upbringing, which thus has much to recommend it.

So, Sir, that is my news for now, from the far side of the Atlantic. I trust you will receive this letter - dispatched from St Johns by the Governor's secretary - within the next two months. It is my intention to spend most of December and January in London with Elizabeth and her family, but if time, work and weather permit, I will also journey north to Yorkshire to visit my parents. When I do, be assured that I will also call at Whitby to visit you and your family.

I am,
Yours most sincerely,
James Cook

After HMS *Grenville* was safely at anchor in the harbour at St John's, James was taken ashore and to the residence of Thomas Graves, lately commander of HMS *Antelope* and now Governor of Newfoundland. It was October, 1763. James's first question to the Governor was, 'Is there a letter from home for me? From my wife?'

There was no letter from Elizabeth, but there was one from the Admiralty. It contained an order that he put to sea for England in *Grenville* no later than the end of October. This was a command which he had been expecting, so it did not disconcert him. But the timing was poor. Their child had been due in early October, Elizabeth had informed him in her last letter, meaning that it would probably already have been born by now. A letter took at least a month to cross the Atlantic, as Elizabeth well knew, just as she was aware of the approximate date of his departure from Newfoundland. That unfortunate combination of circumstances meant that there was no way that she could inform him of the birth until his return to London.

He walked out onto the St John's waterfront. Beyond the fleet of local fishing boats, *Grenville* was at anchor in the harbour, her poles bare. Over the next few days he would supervise the provisioning of the schooner in preparation for their departure. The voyage would take over a month, even with favourable winds. Childbirth was a dangerous business, he well knew. In Great Ayton village, several women the Cook family knew had died giving birth. Sometimes the child had died too. If it survived, the grieving father had been left to raise the child alone. In James's mother's case, she had been exceptional, bearing eight children who had survived, even though five of them subsequently died. Yet childbirth and death were never far apart, it seemed. So, he wondered constantly, what was the fate of Elizabeth and their child? When he returned home, would it be as a father or a widower?

This was a worry which he took aboard *Grenville* with him and which was stowed firmly in his mind for the next five weeks. At nights he lay in his cabin, sleeping fitfully, feeling the heave of the sea, listening to the little ship's straining timbers and the howl of the wind in the shrouds, knowing that each day's hard sailing brought him closer to home and news of Elizabeth.

At last, on 29 November 1763, he brought *Grenville* into the Solent, sighted Portsdown Hill, sailed her past the ancient Round Tower and docked her beside Portsea Island. After making sure the ship was secure he went directly to Navy headquarters. There, a letter awaited him. It was dated 16 October, 1763 and was adgowned to 'James Cook, the King's Surveyor, HMS *Grenville*, Portsmouth'. As he had hoped, it was in Elizabeth's small, well formed hand-writing.

My Dearest James,

By now, I hope with all my heart that you will be safely back in England, having completed your surveying duties for another year. If so, you will receive this news before you prepare to return home here.

Three days ago I was safely delivered of a son. My labour began in the early hours. My mother sent immediately for the midwife, Miss Ella Thompson, she arrived here just after daybreak and was of great assistance and comfort to me.

The child was delivered two hours later. He is a bonny baby and as hungry as a horse. When he wishes to feed, his lusty cries fill the house. He wakes from his crib about every three hours, demanding more milk, which I am delighted to provide him with. People ask who he resembles and I have to say his father, as he has the nose of a typical Yorkshireman. He is a Cook, indisputably, and so perhaps a sailor in the making! Mama adores him already and is like a second mother to the little chap, fussing about him so. I have not yet had the chance to take him outside, but will do so when the weather becomes favourable.

You will remember that we discussed what we would call our child, before you left in April. We agreed that if it was a son he should be a James, after your father and yourself, and that is still my wish.

I will be writing to Christiana to inform her of the birth, and will also request that she notifies your parents, and Margaret, of the glad news. I have arranged for the little one to be baptized in St Pauls in Shadwell by the Reverend Arlridge, on Sunday, the first of November. The ceremony will be followed by tea and cakes here at the house. It is a great pity that you will not be able to attend the baptism, but the Lord willing you will see our child, not long afterwards.

Oh James, I cannot tell you what joy it is to be the mother of such a healthy child. Now there are two James in my life, and I have the greatest love for them both. My only regret is that you are not here to share my happiness. But in your last letter you said that you would be home by Christmas, and that the Admiralty would inform me as to the approximate time when that would be.

So, husband, my next wish is for safe passage for you to Portsmouth, and thence to London. Perhaps over the winter weeks,

*if you have time to spare from your chart-making, we can search
for a house of our own. That is another dream that I have for us.*

*Take every care, James. I cannot wait to be safe in your arms
again, my darling, and for you to see our beautiful son.*

Your loving wife, Elizabeth

Thus was established his seasonal itinerary for the next four
years: sailing for Newfoundland in the spring, then spending
summer engaged in hydrographical work on the coast of
Newfoundland and its adjacent islands. When there happened to be
time to spare, he wrote letters to friends and family, to Elizabeth,
to his parents and Margaret via Christiana, and to John Walker.
The surveying work would occupy him until late autumn, when he
would make the eastward crossing of the Atlantic to London, the
precious drawings, notes and soundings locked in his sea trunk.
Once at home again in London he would spend the winter drawing
the final drafts of his charts. And in the spring he would once more
sail westward, to his summer home, the island of Newfoundland.

In this way three more years passed, industriously and peaceably.
Until 4 August, 1764, at Quirpon, Newfoundland.

They followed their well-established routine. While William
Parker, the very capable master's mate, sailed *Grenville* slowly
along the coast and the calls of the men casting lead and line were
recorded on board, James, assisted by boatswain Jimmy Griffiths,
worked ashore with a plane table, sextant, theodolite and flags,
taking fixes on the most prominent landmarks and sketching them.
Grenville shadowed the little shore party, standing a few hundred
yards off wherever they went. Although she was but a minnow
compared to the great ships-of-the-line he had served on during the
war years, he had already developed an affection for the schooner.
She was a suitable vessel for the work, being able to be worked in
close to the shore, although her lack of a back-sail sometimes gave
him cause for concern, as this made it difficult to avoid unexpected
hazards such as reefs and shoals.

When he returned to the ship and sat at the chart table in his
cabin, drawing and recording, he revelled in the work. There was
such beauty, as well as such utility, he thought, in a finely drawn
chart. A headland, a cove, a reef, a contoured hill, a cliff slope -
being able to capture and depict such features on paper, along with
precise soundings of the inshore depths - this was work that

absorbed him totally. He felt as a portrait painter must when rendering his subject faithfully on a canvas, making meticulous observations in order to reproduce the essence of his subject, not just for current reference but for generations to come. But whereas the portraitist worked with the human face and frame, he worked with the face of the land and its many diverse features. His first published map, the draft of the harbour and bay of Gaspe, which had appeared six years ago, he was inordinately proud of. But he was aware that that survey had been a relatively straightforward exercise. Gaspe was regular in shape, its profile reasonably predictable, unlike the coast of Newfoundland, which was infinitely irregular. Thus, every section of the island's coastline presented a challenge.

Griffiths unslung his musket and leaned it against the trunk of a tall spruce. They had made an encampment at the foot of the tree.

'When shall we be returning to the ship, Sir?'

'In an hour or two.' James glanced over to the west, where the sun was already low. 'It's mid-afternoon now, by my estimation.'

'Shall I boil tea for us, then?'

'Yes. I'm going to climb the headland again, to check the sightings. And I'll be as thirsty as a hunting hound when I get back.'

The two men had been working together on the survey for a year and a half now, and each knew the other's habits well. Ginger-bearded Griffiths carried James's equipment and their food and other supplies in his pack, while James worked on the survey and Griffiths erected the canvas shelters they slept under, and heated food and brewed tea for them both. From Swansea in South Wales, the boatswain was also a skilled fisherman, and most days cast a line from the rocks and brought in a cod or a halibut, which he would then cook for them over a fire.

A man of few words, Griffiths always had a lit pipe in his mouth, on which he puffed away like an Indian chief. James sometimes wondered, does any man love tobacco as much as he does? It's a wonder he doesn't smoke his pipe in his sleep. Also, as the Admiralty had instructed, Griffiths always carried a musket, a full powder horn slung over his shoulder and a bag of musket balls at his waist, although in truth they had seen neither Indians, nor even a French fisherman, for over a week now. Still, the musket did have a practical application. When conditions were misty, as they often were in the early mornings, Griffiths would fire it to alert Parker and the others working on the cutter as to their precise location.

This was James and Griffiths' third day ashore, and James knew they must return to the ship before nightfall. It would take him at least two days to make decent drawings of this, the eastern side of Quirpon Bay. Now, with the sky already dimming, he took a swallow of tea from his tin cup, then declared, 'That'll do for today, time to get back to the ship. Call the cutter in.'

He had decided that after the evening meal on the ship he would retire to his cabin and work late by lantern on the charts. He felt increasingly concerned about the project. There was perhaps another six weeks' surveying possible, before winter and the ice chunks returned, and only half the northern coast had been surveyed. Could he complete the remainder of the survey in the time they had left? He thought not. That would mean returning to Newfoundland next summer, a prospect that did not dismay him. But the decision was the Admiralty's to make, and whether they agreed to send him again depended upon how they regarded the work he had accomplished so far. His report to the Admiralty would be important, he knew, but would it be enough? He had done his very best, he was certain of that.

The plane table, compass, sextant and sheets of drawing paper had been packed into his canvas carry-bag and Griffiths had already carried the equipment down to the rocky shore. Crouching beside the dying fire, James reached out and tossed the dregs of his tea onto the embers. Griffiths, lit pipe still clamped between his teeth, bent over the embers and began to cover them with earth, using a spruce branch for a brush. As he did so his powder horn slid around his hip, it tilted, and its contents spilt into the remains of the fire.

Sparks flew up, then seconds later the world erupted in a ball of orange fire. Through the fireball, James glimpsed Griffiths being flung back and hurled against the trunk of the tree. Staggering backwards, James stared at the gory mess that was his right hand and wrist. His left hand's grip tightened on the wrist as he instinctively applied a natural tourniquet to it. He brought the hand up, to slow the flow of blood, and saw that the explosion had opened a gash in his hand, from the webbing between his thumb and forefinger and across his palm to the wrist. The right hand felt as if it was clutching red hot coals.

Appalled at the sight, and at the implications of the injury, he looked away. His right hand, his drawing hand, his writing hand. How could he work with such an injury? *Grenville* carried no surgeon, so how would he be treated? He looked across at the crumpled figure of Griffiths, lying against the tree trunk. His face was a bloody mask.

Still gripping his right wrist, James staggered down to the shore. He heard shouts from the cutter and was dimly aware that it was being rowed towards him. The men must have heard the explosion. At the water's edge, he fell to his knees, closed his eyes and waited.

He opened his eyes. He was in his bunk. Parker was clumsily wrapping a bandage around his hand and trying to tie it to the book shelf above. The blood flow had been staunched, James saw, but the pain was unrelenting. 'How is Griffiths?' he asked Parker, from between gritted teeth. William shook his head. 'Not good. The blast took him in the face.' Dimly, James was aware of the windlass grinding.

'Why are we weighing anchor?' he asked Parker.

'I'm taking the ship round to Noddy Harbour.'

'Why?'

'So we can get there before nightfall. The French fishing ship we came alongside four days ago, *Sablon*, she's probably still anchored there. And she carries a surgeon.'

He closed his eyes. *Grenville* began to move. The rolling and creaking of the ship was comforting, but the burning and the throbbing in his hand was worsening. More painful though were the thoughts that tumbled over and over in his mind. Will I lose the hand? What are the prospects for a man with one hand? How will I support Elizabeth and the child?

Hours later. He was semi-conscious, but aware that darkness had fallen and that there was another man with Parker. Both men carried lanterns. Parker came forward.

'Cook?'

'Yes.'

'This is M'sieur Jacques Aubert. He is the surgeon from *Sablon*. He has come to treat your wound.' Parker paused. 'He speaks little

English, but I know French.' He stood back, respectfully. 'M'sieur Aubert. C'est James Cook. Le Capitaine.'

The Frenchman wore a pale blue frock coat. In his late twenties, he had a thin, sallow face but brown, kindly eyes. Placing his medical bag on the floor of the cabin, he knelt beside the bunk and said, 'Votre main, s'il vous plait, M'sieur.' Parker translated. 'He wishes to examine the hand.'

When he presented it to him, still wrapped in its blood-sodden bandages, the surgeon carefully removed the crude gowning, turned the hand outwards and studied the wound. The blood was crusted and streaked with black. He asked a question in French, and Parker said, 'He wants to know if you can move your fingers.'

He opened and closed his hand, very slowly. The surgeon grunted, then spoke again, this time directly to William, who again adgowned James. 'He thinks there are no bones broken. Now he needs warm, salted water and brandy to clean the wound. I'll get some.' After Parker vanished the surgeon again peered intently at the injured hand, his brow puckered. He opened his bag and took out what looked to James like a pair of shiny pliers, a square of muslin, a roll of bandage and a large cotton reel through which a needle had been skewered. The surgeon laid out his equipment out at the foot of the bunk, and as he did so Parker returned with an enamel bowl filled with water and a bottle of brandy.

Frowning with concentration, the surgeon worked very slowly, dipping the muslin cloth into the water bowl, to which he had added a half the contents of the brandy bottle, then dabbing the wound. James closed his eyes against the pain. It was as though his hand was being held over a flame. At one stage the Frenchman made a clicking noise with his tongue and muttered something to Parker. 'What does he say?' asked James, keeping his eyes closed.

'Gun-powder. He is trying to remove all the gun-powder from the wound. Before he inserts the stitches.'

James drew a deep, painful breath. 'Yes, yes.' Then he was struck by a thought. 'How is Griffiths now?' he asked Parker.

'He will live.' The mate's voice was just above a whisper. 'But he has lost his eyesight.'

17 August, 1764
Dearest Elizabeth,

I trust that you and our baby son are well. I have been thinking of you both, keeping each other company in Mile End Road and perhaps walking in the meadow if the weather conditions have made such activities possible. I already look forward greatly to seeing you again, and little James, and to walking out with him by the river. I hope that the odours from the distillery have not been as bad as they were during the previous winter. Gin is a vile spirit in both smell and taste, in my opinion, and the proximity of the distillery to our property, along with the density of the coach and wagon traffic along Mile End, leads me to think that we should give consideration to moving to a larger house upon my return. Mile End in other respects suits my professional purposes, as you know, being home to so many other naval men of my acquaintance, and so close to Trinity House, but the reek of gin cannot be good for you or the child. As far as the cost of buying a more commodious dwelling is concerned, I am confident that I will be in possession of sufficient accumulated capital to make this possible.

Your mother is doubtless proving of great assistance to you in your domestic duties. For that I am truly grateful, as I know how much of the administration of the household you would otherwise have to bear alone. You must know how much I am looking forward to seeing you and little James again. Sadly, I will miss the very day of his first birthday celebrations, but we will still be able to enjoy festivities to mark the occasion, albeit some weeks after the event. I have a birthday present for the little one, a ship in a bottle, a model of Grenville, *made by one of my crewmen, Daniel Parsons. It is a very fine creation, fashioned by Daniel over the winter months. When he is a little older, James will appreciate it, I am sure.*

Our new child grows too, no doubt, and I hope that your confinement is as comfortable as can be expected. It is possible, but by no means certain, that I will be home in time for the next birth. If I am not it is of little consequence, as a man can play no useful role when it comes to the arrival of a child, save perhaps in the choice of its name.

I have also been applying myself to the matter of a name for the new little one. I thought Elizabeth, after your good self, if it should be a girl, and Nathaniel if it should be another boy. Nathaniel after no particular person, but I very much like the musicality of that name.

You will surely have noted by now the disorderly nature of my hand-writing in this letter. An explanation of this follows.

Two weeks ago a calamity occurred which has greatly disrupted my surveying work. A powder horn exploded accidently, causing a grievous injury to a member of the ship's crew, Jimmy Griffiths, who was blinded, and a severe wound to my right hand. As Grenville carries no surgeon, the ship's Master was obliged to make contact with a nearby French vessel, whose surgeon treated my injury. It was poor Jimmy who bore the brunt of the explosion, and I am afraid that this will be his last voyage. The Navy will, I hope, award him a pension for his service. That will certainly be my recommendation, as his assistance with my surveying duties has been invaluable.

I have been confined to my cabin and the decks for two weeks now, unable to draw or write, which has caused me the greatest frustration. I am impatient for the programme to proceed, as the work yet to be completed is immense and the knowledge of what remains to be done only compounds my frustration. The injury to my drawing hand could hardly have come at a less opportune time.

It was my greatest fear after the explosion that I would lose my hand, and hence my naval career, and indeed this was a possibility. However when the surgeon, Monsieur Aubert, returned to Grenville to gown the wound again three days later, he was able to report that the healing process had begun, aided by regular rinses with alcohol. Two days after that he cut away the stitches with his scissors and was able to confirm that the gash had closed. There will be a scar, but no permanent impairment. My gratitude for the surgeon's skills was immense, although inexpressible, given my inability to speak his language.

And now at last I can manage to put quill to paper again, albeit clumsily.

However I now face other worries, dear wife. The days have already begun to draw in, and in another month or so conditions will not permit our coastal survey to continue. However I return to my on-shore duties the day after tomorrow. This also means, I believe, that Grenville will be ordered to sail for Spithead in November. This means that it will not be a great deal longer before

*I am with you and little James, and our second child, a prospect
that I anticipate with the utmost pleasure. The wifely warmth and
comforts which you provide me with have been the object of my
thoughts on many a long and lonely night, both on* Grenville *and
during my times ashore.*

*Once again Elizabeth, my apologies for the untidy nature of this
missive, but having been fully informed of the facts leading to its
construction, I am sure that you will well understand the reasons
for it. I managed to procure extra sheets of paper, surplus to my
surveying notes, to ensure that you have been given all details of
the regrettable events of 4 August. And I will arrange for this letter
to be dispatched from St John's in the next ship bound for home,
in the anticipation that you will receive it at the earliest possible
juncture.*

My deepest love to you and our little boy,
James

While he slowly recuperated from his injury, James's role and
that of William Parker were reversed. Parker continued the survey
of Cape Norman ashore while James remained aboard and took
sightings of the north-west Newfoundland coast from the poop
deck. This arrangement, although unavoidable, James soon found
unsatisfactory. Parker's drawings were cursory and crude and,
James suspected, lacked accuracy. Then, a fortnight after the
accident, his frustrations were compounded by the behaviour of
other members of his crew.

Able seaman Joseph Carstairs came up from below, lurched
across the main deck, then fell in a heap in front of the mast. Then
Peter Flower, an assistant surveyor, emerged from the
companionway. He staggered towards Carstairs, tried to pick him
up, but fell over himself. The two seamen lay in a heap, giggling
in a mindless manner.

James hurried down to the main deck.

'What is it?' he demanded of both men.

Flower looked up at him crookedly. 'Nothing, Sir.'

As James bent down, he caught a whiff of something strange.
Not grog, something else.

'Nothing, is it?'

'No Sir.' Flower's eyes were bloodshot. He looked away.

'What have you and Carstairs been drinking?'

'Nothing Sir.'

'Don't lie to me, man. What have you been drinking?'

Flower looked sullen. Then, realising the game was up, he said, 'A kind of spirits, Sir. Made from wood chips and sugar.' He looked at the other man. 'Carstairs brewed it. In a pot. In the galley.'

James felt a flash of fury. No wonder the crew had become so idle and derelict lately. Thinking to take advantage of his indisposition and not content with their grog ration, they had resorted to distilling extra spirits, a serious breach of naval regulations. *How dare they.* He turned and called up to Billy Corry, who was on the foredeck, greasing the windlass. Corry had assumed the boatswain's responsibilities since Griffiths' dreadful injury.

'Corry, report here!'

Corry, grease pot in hand, looked at Carstairs and Flower, who were now standing in front of James, hangdog expressions on their faces. He set his hands on his hips. 'These two men are to be punished with a gantlope, Corry. Immediately. Order all the rest of the crew on the main deck.'

They formed two parallel lines, on either side of the mast. Each man held a kittle – a length of knotted rope – and awaited the order. Carstairs and Flower stood at the head of the lines, heads down, naked from the waist up. Corry had thrown buckets of seawater over them, to sober them up for the punishment. Staring at the abject figures, James felt particularly angry at Flower's transgression. The young man had worked well on the survey until now, and regarded James as a kind of foster father. But now all sentiment was set aside. Foster son or nay, Flower must be punished.

Standing on the foredeck, James announced loudly to the crew: 'By distilling and consuming unauthorised spirits, for the theft from the ship's sugar supply, for being drunk and disorderly and neglecting their duties, these men have committed serious breaches of naval regulations. They will each run the gantlope, ten times.' He nodded at the bosun's mate. 'Carry on, Mr Corry ...'

Flower ran first, feet bare, head down. In the hands of his shipmates the knotted ropes rose and fell, rose and fell, striking him on his back and shoulders with short, dull thuds. When he reached the end of the gauntlet he staggered and turned, head thrown back with pain.

Then Carstairs began his run, squealing as the knots struck home.

The blows kept raining down, the cries kept coming, Corry keeping a watchful eye on the lines and the beating ropes. Withholding meted punishment was also an offence.

By the time Flower and Carstairs had done the run ten times, their backs were striped, livid and leaking blood. Panting, their faces crimson and streaming with sweat and tears, they crouched by the rail. As the two lines of men dissolved Corry picked up his bucket again and threw half its contents over Carstairs, the other half over Flower.

Surveying the scene from the foredeck, James felt a curious kind of satisfaction. *He had been given the authority to have men flogged, and now he had done so. This was authority. This was command.* He made a further announcement. Voice ice-cold, he declared: 'Conduct on this ship over the past two weeks has become lax. Duties have been neglected. Doubtless because some of its crew have been indulging in distilling and consuming illegal spirits. This indulgence must never occur again. If it does, the culprits will run the gauntlet *twice.*' He glared down at the silent, chastened crew. 'Is that understood?'

They nodded, and mumbled. 'Aye Sir ...' 'Aye Sir ...' 'Aye Sir ...'

The scar on his right hand was aching, and he clenched and unclenched his fist, slowly. 'Very well. Now resume your duties.'

Eight

'James?'

'Yes?'

Elizabeth appeared in the study doorway. She was holding the baby, Nathaniel, under her left arm, and in her right hand was an envelope.

'A letter has been delivered to you. I think it is in Christiana's hand.'

He got up from his desk and took the pale brown envelope from her. The letter was adgowned to, 'Mr James Cook RN, Assembly Row, Mile End, London', in Christiana's distinctively looped hand-writing. It was some months since they had heard from her. Now, no doubt, she was writing to wish him well for his next Atlantic crossing. Picking up his bone paper knife, he sliced the envelope open. Inside were two sheets of notepaper.

20 February, 1765

My dearest brother,

This letter will, I hope, reach you before you leave once again for North America.

It is with much distress that I must inform you that our dear mother died, on the eighteenth day of February. She had been visiting Ann Skottowe at Aireyholme Farm, in order to carry out some cleaning duties at the house, and upon returning home to Great Ayton in the late afternoon was caught in a bitterly cold rainstorm and drenched. That evening she developed a chill which quickly worsened. A fever developed the next day, and although Papa sent for Dr Rossiter, he was unable to arrest her decline. She passed away two days later. Although she had reached the fine age of 63, her health until then had been sound, and her passing shocked us all.

The funeral service was held at All Saint's, in Great Ayton, and was attended by a great many in the community, as mother was deeply respected for her devotion to the care of others, as well as her remaining family. Alas, our sister Margaret and her husband were unable to attend the service, as he was away on a fishing expedition, leaving her alone in Redcar to take care of the eight children.

Father is bereft, as you can imagine. It was always his assumption that he would pass away before Mother did, and the shock of his loss is still much with him. Margaret and I will do what we can to assist him recover from his grief. Although he is adamant that he does not wish to leave Ayton, it is the earnest wish of Margaret and myself that he comes to live with each of us in turn.

Mother was interred alongside our five brothers and sisters in the graveyard of All Saint's, in accordance with her wishes. Father has arranged for her name to be added to the family tombstone. A simple inscription, 'Grace Cook, born 1702, died 1765, a faithful wife and devoted Mother, much loved'.

Christiana's letter continued.

Shortly after the funeral, I was reading a collection of poems by the writer Thomas Gray. They were published some years ago, I think. One long poem in particular moved me greatly. It is called Elegy in a Country Churchyard, and is a kind of lament. I thought as I read it that it could well have been adgowned to our poor dead brothers and sisters, and that the Country Churchyard could well have been All Saints', our church in Great Ayton. Here are some lines from Mr Gray's poem.

Perhaps in this neglected spot is laid
Some heart once pregnant with celestial fire;
Hands that the rod of empire might have sway'd,
Or wak'd to extasy the living lyre.
But Knowledge to their eyes her ample page
Rich with the spoils of time did ne'er unroll;
Chill Penury repress'd their noble rage,
And froze the genial current of the soul.

Do you see what I mean, James, about these lines? I thought they were so beautifully written.

Perhaps Jane, Mary and Mary, and William and John, could have achieved what you have, had they but survived.

There is an Epitaph to Mr Gray's poem. It concludes:

Here rests his head upon the lap of Earth
A Youth to Fortune and Fame unknown.
Fair Science frown'd not on his humble birth,
And melancholy mark'd him for her own.

With these doleful but heartfelt lines I will end this letter, James. I hope it finds you, Elizabeth and your two boys well. No doubt little James and new baby Nathaniel are growing quickly. Please write if you are able to spare the time to do so. I always enjoy hearing news from you, as does Father. Even more so, now.

Your loving sister,

Christiana

He walked to the study's dormer window and stared out over the slate roofs, the leaden sky, the smoking chimney pots and the trees of the distant common, but seeing nothing except his mother's sunken cheeks and weary grey eyes. She had always seemed old to him, but such was her fortitude that he always thought that she would endure for many more years. Now, dead. He closed his eyes and put his hand to his face, picturing her in her small world. In the cottage, preparing meals. In the garden, tending her vegetables. In the church, following the service.

The death of his mother, the person who had borne him, cared for him those many years, tended his cuts and abrasions, scolded him when he needed it. He remembered the time when, while climbing Roseberry Topping, a thorn had pierced his foot and lodged there. Back at the cottage his mother had heated a poultice and applied it to the wound, holding it in place with a bandage. The poultice was so hot that he had cried out, several times, but she had determinedly held it in place, telling him that it was the heat that would draw the thorn and its poison from the wound. And she was right, the wound had healed. 'I had to be cruel to be kind, Jimmy,' she had said to him later, 'sometimes yerr have to be cruel to be kind.' As for his decision to go to sea, he knew that she had never understood it, could not comprehend how the sea had entered his being, was baffled by the way he had to be away from the land for weeks on end.

She had seen the sea only once, when both his parents had come to Whitby to visit him. The summer of 1753, it had been. He had taken them down to the harbour, thinking it would be a treat for them. But it was not. They had stared out to sea, then turned away, not able to comprehend the immensity and strangeness of it. Frightened of nothing or no-one on land, he could tell from the looks on their faces - part-fear, part-awe, part-confusion - that they found the sea unfathomable.

Neither were they able to comprehend why their second son was making this frightening environment his life.

But how could he have hoped to explain to them what he could not fully explain to himself? That with each voyage he took the sea seemed to run deeper into his being. He had never been able to explain this feeling to his mother. And now he never would be able to.

As he stared through the study window, his vision became blurred. I loved you, Grace Cook, there was no finer mother. And suddenly he was overcome with sorrow, that he had not been there to talk with her, to help care for her, to comfort her before she passed on. If he had known of her illness he could have taken the coach north, stayed with her for a few days at least. But how could he have known, until it was too late? The guilt he felt at this dereliction of filial duty lodged in his throat like a fish-bone. His mother had died without him, and his father would now be alone. Lifting his head, he closed his eyes, but the image of her stayed in his mind's eye. He was astonished to feel tears, streaming from his eyes, running uncontrollably down his cheeks. He tried to blink them away, but could not, so he let them run. Grace Cook, who had loved him, whom he had loved, now gone forever from his life.

Nine

Once the fog had cleared, the day was warm and still, the sky clear. *Grenville* was near the Burgeo Islands, off Newfoundland's southern coast. As James stood in the cockpit, his eyes kept returning to the sky. The date was 5 August, 1766. Would astronomer Leadbetter's prediction prove correct? Would it actually happen today? The ship was at anchor off the islands, and on her deck the crew was going about its routine tasks, two men scrubbing the foredeck, another two greasing the pulleys and mast with pork fat. Deliberately, James had not informed the crew about the predicted event, as he was curious to see how they would react, should it actually occur.

He waited, still staring upwards, telescopic quadrant at the ready.

Then, out of the blue, the sky began to darken. The crew looked up, their mouths agape. The sun began to disappear, the day darkened further.

Parker ran up from below and entered the cockpit, his expression bewildered. 'What is happening, Sir?'

'A cosmic event. A solar eclipse. The moon is passing across the face of the sun.' James held the smoked glass up in front of the man's eyes.

Parker gave him a wry look. 'Were you aware that this would occur, Sir?'

James kept staring at the shadowy orb. 'I was. Or at least I knew it was predicted.'

In awed silence they all watched as the shadow moved on and the day grew dimmer. He trained his refracting telescope on it, thrilled by the sight. Leadbetter had been right yet again, about the place and time of the event. What a prophet the man was! For some moments the sun's face was entirely covered, and the day briefly turned to night. The shadowy figures on the deck were silent and still. James could almost feel their fear. This event, which James knew was entirely natural, seemed to the sailors below to be quite the opposite. Then a glimmer appeared on the sun's eastern rim, its rays burst forth, and gradually the glowing ball was revealed again. The crew looked at each other with undisguised relief.

As an ardent astronomer himself, James had read of the eclipse's coming while at home last winter in Leadbetter's *Compleat System of Astronomy*. Unlike the rest of the ship's crew, however, he realised that what he was witnessing was something which had implications for ocean navigation. Eclipses and transits, Leadbetter had postulated, could be used to establish the precise distance between the Earth and its sun. An eclipse provided the opportunity, in Leadbetter's words, 'to determine the true Difference of the Meridians between London, and the meridian where the ship then is; which when reduc'd into Degrees and Minutes of the Equator is the true Longitude found at sea'. James had also read that another eminent astronomer, Edmond Halley, who had died four years earlier, concurred with this belief.

James was fully aware that the lack of a method to accurately determine longitude represented a great gap in navigational certitude. Determining latitude was a relatively simple matter, measuring the sun's varying angles to the Earth's surface, but without an accurate chronometer, to ascertain how far one had sailed west or east, was largely a matter of approximation. And because he always strived for complete accuracy, James disliked approximation. He was aware that the men of science were confident that the gap in astronomical knowledge would eventually be filled, but when? He had been told that instrument-makers had been working for some time to develop a precisely accurate marine chronometer which could be taken aboard ship and used to measure the progress of voyages westbound or eastbound from London. In particular James had heard the name John Harrison mentioned in connection with this work. Evidently, though, Harrison's chronometer was as yet insufficiently accurate. Successful navigation, James was well aware, demanded precision. Hence, any means which could be found to fill the longitude-measurement gap, he and others of the nautical profession would welcome.

When the crew had resumed their duties, he retired to his cabin and there began to write a detailed account of the eclipse, accompanied by sketches he had taken. Its significance may be of interest to the Admiralty, he thought. Or even the Royal Society, the academy of distinguished scientists who met in Crane Court, London, to discuss and debate such events.

As he made his notes, James gave further considerations to astronomical matters. He knew full well that it was not possible to harness the heavens, but he was aware that a study of cosmic phenomena - such as solar and lunar eclipses, and transits of the planets of Earth's solar system - allowed navigators, scholars and scientists to better comprehend the universe which all men of the world shared. And the desire for such a comprehension was one he felt too, with increasing keenness.

Nine months later a paper written by James Cook RN, the King's Surveyor, was read to the Royal Society by Dr John Bevis, and published in the Society's journal, *Philosophical Transactions*. It described an eclipse Cook had witnessed in August 1766, off the southern coast of Newfoundland. Bevis extolled the paper. It had made it possible, he said, to estimate the longitude of Newfoundland's Burgeo Islands. The Royal Society was impressed by the detailed account of the eclipse. Thus the name James Cook, nautical surveyor, became known to the Royal Society, a body of men whose influence in scientific affairs was growing.

He worked HMS *Grenville* in as close to the St John's waterfront as he safely could. It was 27 October, 1766. Eighteen months ago, at his urging to the Admiralty and under his supervision at the naval dockyard at Deptford, she had been converted from a schooner to a brigantine. The resulting additional sail pleased him, as her staying was now much more dependable when they came upon unexpected hazards. His affection for *Grenville* had grown over the years. She was a fine little vessel who had served him and the surveying programme faithfully.

This afternoon the St John's harbour was crowded, mainly with fishing boats flying a variety of flags: Spain, France, Portugal. There were also several larger vessels in port flying the Jack. Raising his telescope, James noted their details. A Royal Navy frigate. HMS *Niger*. Instinctively, he counted the cannons. Thirty-three, a fifth rater. Alongside her were two other Royal Navy warships, HMS *Favourite* and HMS *Zephyr*, along with Governor Palliser's ship, *Guernsey*. Noting that the tide was ebbing, James made a quick calculation. It was now mid-afternoon, so tomorrow they would weigh anchor just after midday, to take advantage of the outgoing tide. *Grenville* had been fully provisioned earlier in the day, from the warehouses at the other end of town, for her latest Atlantic crossing. Fourteen casks of pickled cabbage were stowed in the hold, along with the usual victuals. James knew the crew would make the usual grumbles about having the cabbage served with all their meals, but since he had made it a flogging offence not to eat it, their protests were soon followed by clean plates.

He returned to the business of docking *Grenville*. The harbour was sheltered and the wind was slight. Fifty yards from the seawall he turned the wheel hard to port, bringing the brig around and into the breeze. Her sails drooped and she stalled. 'Lower anchor,' he called to Parker, on the foredeck. The windlass spun, the chain rattled and seconds later *Grenville* was swinging at anchor. James ordered the launch hoisted.

The ship's boat drew up alongside the long sea wall, the bosun made a line fast to a bollard and he stepped from the boat onto the stone steps. He called down to the bosun. 'The Governor will doubtless want to discuss the survey, Parker, so I may be some time.' He smiled. 'You and the men will find a friendly tavern in which to pass the time, I dare say. But one of you must stay here with the boat at all times.' Parker nodded. 'Aye, Sir.'

He walked across the cobbled waterfront and made his way to the governor's imposing, grey stone residence. Above the entrance, the Jack hung limp from its projecting pole. After he rapped the knocker on the panelled front door it was opened by a short, bald, bow-legged man of about thirty-five. James introduced himself to the doorman, who led him into the drawing room, then withdrew to inform the Governor of James's presence. Minutes later Hugh Palliser appeared, his hand outstretched.

'Cook! Good-day! I watched you come in. How good to see you again.'

'Governor. It's good to see you, too.'

Hugh Palliser had been appointed Governor of Newfoundland two years earlier. As they shook hands warmly, James noted the extent to which his face had filled out since he had been appointed to his post. The sweep of his nose was now slightly capillaried, his complexion rubicund. He had always been fond of food and drink, and James supposed that his present position permitted him the maximum of opportunity to indulge in both. But his sardonic smile and decorous manner were the same. James had always liked this man, and not just because he too was from Yorkshire. More helpfully, he had been an unstinting supporter of the drawn-out Newfoundland surveying project. The Governor said:

'You'll dine with us this evening Cook, I hope?'

'If that is convenient, Sir.'

'Certainly, certainly. And you'll take a glass of sherry now? We broached a cask of best Sherez only last evening.'

'A small glass, thank you.'

The drawing room was capacious and carpeted. Although it was only mid-afternoon, the light was dim, there was a log fire burning and already the chandelier candles had been lit. A portrait of an elegantly robed Charlotte of Mecklenburg-Strelitz, the king's consort, hung above the fireplace. On both sides of the fireplace were glass-fronted bookcases crammed with large volumes. Several cut crystal decanters of liquor were arrayed on a sideboard beside the door that led through an entrance to the adjoining dining room. Ornately framed oil paintings, mainly of autumnal English landscapes, and a huge one of a stag at bay, adorned the other walls. A large globe stood on a circular table in the centre of the room. Canada and India were now both coloured red, James noted with satisfaction.

As he took in the room's decor and contents, he thought again how outlandish this residence was, grafted on to the very eastern rim of North America. It could have been a house or club somewhere in the wealthiest parts of the City of London, yet he was aware that Newfoundland - claimed by the Genoese voyager John Cabot for Henry VII of England in 1497 - was Britain's oldest colony, and St John's its oldest settlement. This consolidation of British authority abroad James found reassuring. The knowledge that this too was now the domain of the King of England justified the loss of all those lives, at Quebec and elsewhere.

The Governor gestured at the seats in front of the fire and both men sank down with their sherries.

As they sat and chatted, the pinkness of Governor Palliser's face became more pronounced. He seemed a little unsettled, too, James thought. From time to time he peered through the mullioned window opposite, frowning as he did so. Noticing James's curious expression, by way of explanation the Governor said,

'I am expecting other visitors from home, shortly.'

'Oh? More naval people, Sir?'

'Partly. They are from the frigate you no doubt saw in port.'

'Which one?'

'*Niger*.' He patted his wig. 'And as you are sailing for London tomorrow, in another day you would have missed her. And her shore party, which is coming here to discuss arrangements for the Governor's Ball.'

At that moment there was a rapping on the door and the doorman passed along the passageway beside the drawing room to answer it. As Palliser moved swiftly across to the doorway, James took in more of the large room's details: the known outlines of the continents on the ornate globe, the slobbering hounds in the stag painting, the crimson drapes with their golden tassels. What a comfortable life a Governor led. But how little James envied his position. This place was the very opposite of the freedom that the command of a ship offered. Hugh Palliser had authority, certainly, but his life must be as constrained and boring as that of a tethered gelding.

The Governor led the latest arrivals into the drawing room.

'Mr Cook. Meet the commander of *Niger*, Sir Thomas Adams, and Lieutenant Constantine Phipps, both of the Royal Navy, and Mr Joseph Banks.'

The men removed their hats and shook hands with James. Captain Adams looked familiar, leading James to think that perhaps he had met him some years before. In Quebec, was it? However since *Niger*'s commander gave no indication that he remembered him from an earlier meeting, James felt disinclined to prompt him. Adams was stout, with a broad forehead, a fleshy face and a double chin. He wore a naval captain's full gown coat, waistcoat and white cuffs.

Banks was in his early twenties, a tall, slim young man with thick brown hair which curled down both sides of his head, a pointed chin, narrow face and a well-shaped nose. He wore civilian clothes, including a maroon velvet jacket. Lieutenant Phipps was of a similar age, but short and stocky, with wavy blond hair, olive skin and blue eyes. He wore a lieutenant's dark blue gown coat, gold braid-edged waistcoat and white cuffs, attached to the jacket with brass buttons.

The Governor poured the other men glasses of sherry. They clinked glasses, toasted His Majesty, then the man called Banks turned to James and said, in a tone of pronounced uninterest:

'So, Cook, what brings you to St John's?'

'I have been surveying the coast of this island. Lately, Cape Anguille in the southwest, and the west coast, in the direction of Pointe Ferolle.'

The other young man sipped his sherry, then said, 'The islands of St Pierre and Miquelon are still in the hands of the Frenchies, is that correct?'

'Yes. Following the Treaty of Paris, they are the only part of Newfoundland not now under British sovereignty.'

The three men from *Niger* grunted with satisfaction at this statement. Then, half closing his eyes as he stared at James, Banks said, 'Your voice defines you as a Yorkshireman, if I'm not mistaken.'

'You are not mistaken. I was born in Marton and raised near Cleveland.'

The younger man pursed his lips. 'Not an area it has been my good fortune to visit. Although I once went to Whitby, to stay with Phipps.'

James turned to the naval officer. 'I undertook my seaman's apprenticeship in Whitby. Did you live in the town, Lieutenant?'

Phipps smiled, condescendingly. 'My family lives outside the town.' He paused, then said pointedly, 'In Mulgrave Castle.'

James began to feel uncomfortable.

'And I have workers on my estate who are from Yorkshire,' Banks put in. 'That is why your dialect is not unfamiliar to me.'

The man's mocking tone was unmistakable, and James felt himself colouring. He was insulting his accent, something he abhorred. Staring hard at the young man, he said:

'And where might you be from, Banks?'

'My estate is in Revesby, in Lincolnshire, but I live in London. I am an Oxford graduate, in the botanical sciences.' He turned to his friend. 'Phipps and I were at Eton together.' He paused. 'The great public school, near Windsor.'

James felt an urge to reach out and cuff this privileged puppy over the ear. He may be a gentleman and a landowner, but he had no right to patronise anyone in this manner. Having no wish or reason to continue this conversation, James was about to excuse himself and prepare to return to the ship when to his surprise the Governor stepped forward. Having sensed the awkwardness which had arisen between the two men, Palliser said hurriedly,

'Cook is the King's Surveyor. He works from the brigantine *Grenville*, which entered port today.'

The expressions of Captain Adams and the two younger men sharpened. Adams said, carefully, 'You are the James Cook who surveyed the St Lawrence before the battle of Quebec?'

'I am.'

The other man's face was transformed, the tone of his voice was now respectful. 'Cook, my deepest apologies, I did not realise ... I first saw a copy of your chart of Gaspe Bay not long after it was published. It is magnificent.'

Banks put in, 'And Captain Adams employed your chart when we entered the St Lawrence Gulf. That, and the one of the river.'

Adams nodded. 'Indeed, it was indispensable.'

James remained unsmiling as he said, 'I am pleased that it proved useful.' He still felt slighted that Adams did not recall meeting him, even if it had been some years before.

Addressing the sole civilian in the group, James said, 'So Banks, you and I have come to Canada for very different reasons.' He paused. 'You collect plants, I collect coastlines.'

The Governor clapped his hands, and smiled with relief. 'Good, good. Now we know who we are and what we do.' His expression was still a trifle anxious, however, before he said, 'And you will all dine with me, yes?'

James exchanged glances with the others. Adams nodded emphatically, Banks gave a wry smile, Phipps looked away. James nodded, gratified that his credentials had now been recognised. He would stay, after all. Parker and the other men deserved a decent time ashore, they had a long voyage ahead of them. He said to Palliser, 'Thank you Governor, I will accept your invitation.'

They dined at a long table in the adjoining room. The cook, a tall, angular woman from Portsmouth, wheeled in the dishes on a trolley and her husband, the bald doorman, served the food. Palliser uncorked a jeroboam of red wine and filled the men's goblets, explaining, 'The French send the wine to their community in St

Pierre, and we get it shipped in from there. It's from Bordeaux.'
He smacked his lips. 'It's rather good, don't you think?'

The others drank. Banks nodded, appreciatively. 'Very good.
The French have many weaknesses, as we Englishmen well know,
but wine is not one of them.'

When the main course arrived, the botanist showed an equal
appreciation of the food. Holding a chunk of fish up on his fork, he
said, 'This Sir, unless I am mistaken, is Atlantic cod. The genus
Gadus morhua.'

'It is, Banks. Poached cod. We almost live on it here.'

'It's a fine fish,' James put in. 'And plentiful, in these waters.'

'So plentiful ...' added Captain Adams, '...that when you put
down a line baited with six hooks, you can bring up twelve fish.'

Banks smiled. 'So this is a suitable area for me to frequent, then.'

When the others looked puzzled, he added, grinning at his own
joke, 'Well, the cod fishing grounds are known as 'The Grand
Banks', are they not?'

The visitors exchanged stories. Adams, Banks and Phipps had
been to Labrador, where Banks collected botanical specimens to
take back to London. He had gathered hundreds of plants never
before catalogued, he said with undisguised glee, and was a
supporter of the move to establish a special exotic botanical garden
in London. He and Phipps had also shot many small animals in
Canada, he added, which Banks had preserved and was taking back
to England.

James listened, impressed and resentful in equal measure.
Impressed by Banks's practical bent, but resentful of his aura of
class-derived superiority. Back in the drawing room, over crystal
glasses of tawny port, they continued their reminiscences of
Canada. Banks asked James, 'Have you visited any of the interior
yourself?'

'I have seen Quebec, naturally, following our victory in 1759.'
He set down his glass. 'Apart from that, my travels have been
confined to the coasts.' To remind the others of the importance of
his work, he added, 'In the course of my surveying and charting.'

Phipps nodded. 'We ventured inland, in Labrador. And had a
meeting with some Indians, while Banks was collecting his
specimens.'

'Were you threatened at all by the natives?' asked the Governor, with concern.

Banks shook his head. 'No. And there was a contingent of marines accompanying us, so we were not afeared.' He grinned. 'But we need not have been anyway. The natives were uncommonly hospitable.' He grinned. 'Their chieftain gave us two young squaws for the night, in exchange for a handkerchief each.'

The Governor leaned forward. 'What were they like?'

Banks laughed. 'Delectable.'

Phipps made a face. 'Once you got past the *smell*.' But he was smiling too, at the memory.

Banks chuckled. 'Constantine and I exchanged our squaws, at first light,' he said. 'It was a very agreeable business.' He turned to James. 'You have partaken of the local women, I assume, Cook?'

James again felt himself colouring, and not just from the port. He sat up. 'I am a married man, Mr Banks,' he said, reprovingly. 'And the father of young children.' He adjusted himself in his chair. 'I also believe that as Englishmen and the bearers of a civilised way of life, that we should set a moral example to savage peoples. In this way we can bring our enlightened ways to them.'

Banks did not hesitate. 'And I also believe we should set an example to them. Of shared pleasure.' His grin widened. 'To show the natives that we are truly human in our urges, and thus so not very different from them.'

When James did not reply, Banks continued.

'The natives also traded us four dried scalps. For a small mirror.'

'Human scalps?' said James.

'Yes.' Banks's expression was again gleeful. 'They trepan the scalps of their defeated enemies, then keep them as trophies.'

'I have seen them,' Captain Adams added. 'They have the appearance of dried fungus, but with hair attached. Black hair, naturally.'

'We shall present them to the London Museum, upon our return,' Banks added. He smiled at the Governor. 'The port is very agreeable, Palliser. I'm sure that Cook would like another glass.' He paused. 'I certainly would.'

They parted on the waterfront. There were a few lights from the taverns along the quay, but everything else was in total darkness.

Although James shook the Captain's hand warmly, then those of the two young men, in truth he was still resentful of their superior demeanour. Thank God that by the time the Governor's Ball took place - an event that the two upstarts had discussed for far too long during the evening - he would be at the helm of *Grenville*, being borne along by westerly winds and the Gulf Stream, Portsmouth bound. The Governor's Ball - what a frivolity!

'Goodbye,' James said, stiffly.

Lieutenant Phipps said, 'May the rest of your chart-making go well.'

Banks added, 'And take care, Cook.'

'I always do.'

'Good luck, Cook,' said Captain Adams.

'Thank you, Sir,' said James to the officer. He nodded curtly at the other two.

Phipps untied *Niger*'s painter and the three men climbed down the stone steps and into the boat, where two oarsmen were waiting, one holding a lantern. James stood and watched the trio being rowed away into the blackness. As he did so he thought, Captain Adams is of sound character, as one would expect of a commander in His Majesty's navy. But Banks and Phipps - what smug, impudent pups. He wouldn't care a jot if he didn't see either of them again.

Ten

The carriage stopped in front of the house in Mile End Road and James stepped out. It was mid-morning on 10 November, 1767, and the air was heavy with frost. *Grenville* had docked at Wapping at first light, two hours earlier. The driver took his bags from the roof and set them down beside the front step. As the carriage moved off, the front door opened.

'James!'

She wrapped her arms around him. For some moments he held her, burying his face in her hair, revelling in the smell of it and the softness of her body against his.

When she looked up, her eyes were brimming with tears. 'What happened to you?'

'What do you mean?'

'There was a message from the Admiralty. To say that *Grenville* had been sighted in the Downs, making for the Thames estuary. That was Wednesday. So I expected you three days ago. Where have you been?'

Looking over her head, he saw two small figures appear in the doorway. They were wearing the uniforms of Royal Navy officers, complete with blue jackets, navy blue tricorn hats and white hose. Officers in miniature. Releasing Elizabeth, he went to them.

'James, Nathaniel. How are you both?'

The little boys smiled shyly as their father shook their hands. James was markedly taller than Nathaniel, but both were sturdy and ruddy-faced.

'Why are you so late, Papa?' asked James.

Frowning, Nathaniel said, 'We been worried, Papa.'

Their father smiled. 'I'll explain, when I'm inside.' Picking up his bags, he smiled at Elizabeth. 'I would love a cup of English tea.'

He settled in the parlour, in front of the coal fire, the boys at his feet, Elizabeth alongside him on the divan. She had made tea and toasted bread on the kitchen fire. He sipped the hot tea gratefully. The room was so warm, his family so close now. Hearth and home, after seven months away, it was so good to be back. Unbuttoning his waistcoat, he told them what had happened.

'The ocean crossing was uneventful, with *Grenville* averaging four to five knots throughout. And with a following wind we made good progress moving up the Channel. By dawn on Wednesday we were in the Downs. But by late afternoon the wind grew stronger, and by the time we were approaching the Nore, it had increased to gale force.'

Little James looked puzzled.

'What is ... the Nore, Papa?'

'A large sandbank, at the mouth of the Thames. It is marked by a lightship, so I knew to keep *Grenville* well clear. But the sandbank steepened the sea, so that the waves were very large. I was obliged to lower all sails and put out anchors, to hold the ship until the gale blew itself out.' He took another sip of tea. 'But the sea was too shallow, the waves too big, and the anchors wouldn't hold. An anchor line broke, we tailed into shoal water and *Grenville* struck the sandbank. Hard.'

Elizabeth's hand went up to her mouth. 'Oh, no. What did you do?'

'We jettisoned everything we could, the ballast, guns and remaining provisions. But because she was laying on her larboard bilge, stuck fast on an outgoing tide, we had to take to the boats. The seas were driving hard, but we were able to row shoreward, and with difficulty eventually made Sheerness, on the north coast of the Isle of Sheppey.'

Little James, who had been following this conversation intently and with widened eyes, said: 'But what happened to your ship, Papa?'

'She was fast on the shoal, so we had to wait for the seas to go down before we could return to her. When they did, the next day, we rowed out on the high tide, boarded her, pumped out the bilges and when she was upright, floated her off.' Setting down his tea cup, he said matter-of-factly, 'That was why I was late.'

'But what of your charts? Your surveys?' asked Elizabeth.

'All my drawings and drafts were taken off the ship with me, when we took to the boats. They were wrapped in canvas, and are undamaged, thank the Lord.'

'So you will be working on them again over the winter.'

'I will.'

'And will you go back to Newfie, Papa?' asked little James.

GRAEME LAY

'Unless the Admiralty orders otherwise. My survey of the island is not complete. And the charts must be copied.'

Little James frowned. 'What is a chart, Papa?'

James considered the question carefully. How to explain it all to a four-year-old? He said, 'Do you know what a map is?'

The little boy nodded. 'It's a picture. A drawing.'

'Right. Of a place, though, not a person. And a chart is a kind of map, but of the sea. Of the place where the land meets the sea. And it shows what's under the sea, as well as on the land.' He glanced up at Elizabeth, who was smiling lovingly at them both. Nathaniel's thumb was in his mouth and he was beginning to doze. His father continued. 'A chart shows things like rocks and headlands and beaches. It shows how deep the sea is, beside the land.' He paused. 'Later, when I'm working on my charts, I'll show you how it's done.' The little boy nodded, keenly.

Elizabeth stood up. 'You must be hungry.'

'In truth, I am. There was no time for me to breakfast, after we made Wapping. And that was four hours ago.'

'Come into the kitchen. There are scones in the oven. And I'll cook beef sausages. Your favourite.'

The boys' bedroom was upstairs, in one corner of the house. They kissed their mother good-night in the parlour, then James led them upstairs, both in their night-shirts. He tucked first Nathaniel, then James into their beds, which were close together, with a chair between them. Clutching the piece of cloth which he carried with him whenever he was tired, little James said, 'Tell us a story, Papa.'

His father nodded. 'Which story would you like?'

'Indian story,' said Nathaniel, promptly.

'Yes, how you fought against the Indians,' said his brother.

They never seemed to tire of hearing this one, which had happened before the battle of Quebec, in July 1759, when he was sounding the St Lawrence River.

'I was in a small boat on the river with some other sailors, taking soundings and putting buoys in the water.'

Nathaniel said sleepily, 'Why were you putting boys in the river, Papa?'

'Not boys like us,' little James put in. 'The other buoys. The things that float.'

'Oh.'

104

Their father carried on. 'All of a sudden, four canoes came out from the shore, full of French soldiers and wild Indians. The Frenchmen carried muskets, the Indians carried axes they call tomahawks, and bows and arrows. Their faces were painted in bright colours. They began to attack us.' He paused. 'We knew it was no good fighting back, because there were too many of them, so we began to row our boat towards a big island in the river, called Ile d'Orleans, where there was a hospital for our soldiers. Musket shot and arrows were flying through the air towards us, and the canoes were catching up.'

The boys lay completely still, their eyes very wide. Little James clutched his piece of cloth, Nathaniel sucked hard on his thumb.

'We reached the island, with the Indians right behind us, and jumped out onto the shore. Two Indians leapt into the stern of the boat, yelling and waving their tomahawks, just as we were jumping out of the bow. I thought we were doomed, but as we ran up towards a forest on the island, a group of English soldiers appeared through the trees, carrying muskets. They had been guarding the hospital, had heard the cries of the Indians and came running. As we ran towards them, they fired at the Indians and the Frenchmen, who stopped, then turned away. They scrambled into their canoes and paddled away. We were safe.'

The boys sank deeper into their beds. Nathaniel's eyes closed. 'Night, Papa.'

He kissed each of them on the forehead. How precious they were to him. 'Good night, good night.'

They walked on the common, following the winding path that led to the top of the hill. It was nearly three months since James's return, and the boys were at the house, in the care of 23-year-old Frances Wardale, James's mother's great-niece and his second cousin. A plump, apple-faced young woman, she had come down from Middlesborough, at James's sister Margaret's suggestion, to help Elizabeth in the house. Although she worked hard at the cleaning and washing, Elizabeth found her complaints about life in London tiresome. Dirty crowded streets, the smell from the river, street urchins, the cost of food: there seemed nothing that she didn't find wanting about life in the city. When Elizabeth reported this to James, he listened, then urged her to be patient. 'It's all so different for her,' he said. 'She will become used to life here,' he averred. 'As I had to, after I left the North Riding for Whitby and London.'

They reached the top of the hill, then stood to admire the view. It was early February, and bitingly cold. Patches of snow like tufts of white hair were scattered across the common and their breath was visible in the air. Below, in the Pool of London, a winter forest of ships' masts could be seen, and a pall of smoke from a thousand coal fires hung over Wapping, Stepney and Shadwell. At the foot of the hill, horse-drawn carts filled with bricks, sand and timber were being unloaded in front of rows of half-completed terrace houses.

There was a large oak tree at the top of the hill. Its branches were bare and acorns littered the ground beneath it. James leaned against the trunk of the oak and Elizabeth leaned against him. Looking down at the building site, James said, 'London grows. Faster and faster, and further and further outwards.'

'It is already the world's largest city, they say.'

He nodded. 'Yes. England prospers, Elizabeth. Something that gives me great pride.'

He put his arms around her. For some moments there was silence, before he said, 'That letter that came yesterday was from Captain Palliser.'

'Oh? He writes to you often, doesn't he?'

'Necessarily so. Since he oversees the Newfoundland survey.'

'And what is the purpose of his latest letter?'

'He is pleased with my charts. So much so that he has recommended to the Lords of the Admiralty that they be published.'

'James, that is wonderful.'

'It is satisfactory.'

'More than satisfactory, surely.'

He looked troubled. 'But the survey is not complete.'

'And you will complete it over the coming summer?'

'That is my assumption.' He released her, then squatted at the base of the oak tree. 'Palliser wishes to meet with me again, presumably to discuss the survey programme.' He picked up a stick and in a patch of dirt, made a rough sketch of Newfoundland. Then he marked two sections of the northern coast with crosses. 'These parts remain to be surveyed.'

Elizabeth nodded. He had shown her the charts that he had completed. Adjusting her shawl over her shoulders, she said,

'When will you meet Captain Palliser?'

'The day after tomorrow.'

Elizabeth's brow crimped. 'James ... has he mentioned again the matter of a commission for you?'

He gave her a cross look. This was a subject that had come between them, ever since he had reported to her that Palliser had said that he would recommend James be promoted to lieutenant. That was six years ago. Looking away, he said, 'Palliser has not raised the matter again with me.'

Elizabeth frowned, deeply. 'But no one is more deserving of a commission than yourself, surely. Your war service, your surveying, your charts. What more do you have to do for the Navy before they make you an officer?'

He was silent for a time before he said, irritably, 'I am content to be the Master of *Grenville*. It is a role that suits me.' But even as he said it, he knew it to be a lie. He had long harboured an ambition to be commissioned, and he knew that Palliser had suggested to his friends in the Admiralty that he be offered one. To no avail. He could only assume that to the Lords he remained someone who had been born into the labouring class of Yorkshire, and such men did not become officers in the King's Navy. So he well understood Elizabeth's resentment, because it was a feeling he shared. Yet he was too proud to allow his wife to know this. Hoping to silence her protests, and aware that she knew the value of money, he said with feigned indifference, 'And I am paid ten shillings a day as Master. Were I a lieutenant, I would not be paid at that rate for a week.'

Elizabeth sighed, then said philosophically, 'Well, I suppose that is something we cannot disregard, with a growing family to feed and clothe.' She slipped her arm through his. 'And before long there will be another. Our new child is due in the autumn.'

'Captain Palliser, good-day Sir.'

'Cook, good-day to you. Are you well?'

'Apart from a slight chill, yes.' He took a handkerchief from inside his cuff and wiped his runny nose. 'This London air is not as healthy as an Atlantic breeze. Or even a Labrador fog.'

'Indeed it is not. I cannot wait to be at sea again, myself. I'm having a pint of ale, will you join me?'

'Certainly.'

They sat in the window seat of the Devil's Tavern, so-named because it was once frequented by pirates. Below them, on the river, vessels of all kinds, including barges and colliers, were moving up on the ebbing tide; smaller boats were rowing people from the north to the south bank of the Thames. The river's mucky brown sides were exposed by the low tide and a pair of ragged mudlarks were collecting bits of coal from the water's edge and putting them into a sack which they held between them.

As James reported on his progress with the charts, Palliser listened, nodding approvingly from time to time. His eyes were small and beady, like a gull's, his forehead broad below the wig-line, and a faint smile seemed always to play about his mouth. He told James that he would be returning to Newfoundland for the summer, for what he thought would be his last tour of duty there. The discussion then turned to the transits of Mercury and Venus. James had been reading a paper by the late Edmond Halley. In it he described how transits of the planets Mercury and Venus across the face of the sun, when scientifically observed in a parallax from selected, widely-separated points on Earth, could be used to measure the precise distance from the Earth to the Sun, a crucial step forward in the scientific surveying of the cosmos. James was aware from his astronomical studies that Transits of Venus recurred at intervals of 8, 121.5, 8 and 105.5 years. As the last transit had occurred in 1761, there would be another next year, in 1769.

Both men were also aware that Edmond Halley had drawn up a plan for the observation of the 1761 Transit of Venus. The Royal Society had enthusiastically sent several astronomers to observe the passing of the planet across the Sun's face. Other nations, including the French, Russians and Italians, had done the same, their astronomical instruments spread widely over the known world, from Siberia to China to the Cape of Good Hope. But the results had been disappointing. Cloudy skies had rendered most of the observations imprecise and the observations were poorly co-ordinated.

Palliser set his pewter mug down on the table. 'You are aware of the exact timing of the next Transit of Venus, Cook?'

'The third of June next year.'

'Precisely. And the next transit after that will not be until 1874.' Hugh smiled, ruefully. 'When we will both be long dead.'

'Yes. Just one more transit this century.' And James wondered, why all this transit talk?

Palliser's gimlet eyes bored into his. 'Last week I was speaking with the Astronomer Royal, Nevil Maskelyne, at Trinity House. He reported to me that the Royal Society is going to do its utmost to ensure that the 1769 Transit of Venus is scientifically observed and accurately recorded. There will also be a Transit of Mercury, in November 1769.' He paused. 'It is Maskelyne's considered calculation that both transits will be most favourably observed from points in the southern Pacific Ocean.'

James nodded. 'I've read that too. They say also that the weather in such a location is likely to be more favourable for an observation.' He gave a little laugh. 'There is just one problem. No-one knows what lies in the centre of the south Pacific Ocean.'

Palliser stroked his chin, thoughtfully. 'Samuel Wallis may be able to tell us, when he returns on the *Dolphin*. His instructions were to traverse the southern Pacific from east to west.'

'Wallis has not been heard of since he left last year. Nor Captain Carteret on the *Swallow*, which accompanied *Dolphin*.'

'True, but if Wallis does return safely, it will be with knowledge of the region in question. And thus perhaps with a suggestion for a suitable location for the observation.' Palliser closed one eye, conspiratorially. 'It is a tasty proposition, Cook, and one which could considerably enhance Britain's standing in the scientific world. Momentum for a transit observation is gathering. The King has agreed to support the expedition, and a suitable ship is being sought.'

James considered all this in silence. The implications of what Palliser was reporting were profound. And not just for scientists. An exploratory voyage to the South Seas, to observe an astronomical occurrence which would not occur again for more than 100 years, and in all probability to claim new lands for the King. What a prospect. He ran the middle finger of his left hand along the scar on his right palm and wrist. Palliser picked up his mug and drained the last of his ale. As he did so James asked, with undisguised curiosity,

'And should this expedition to the far side of the globe take place, who is proposed by the Royal Society to lead it?'

'Alexander Dalrymple.'

'*Dalrymple*, Elizabeth. They are proposing that he lead an expedition to the Southern Hemisphere to observe the Transit of Venus.'

Although she looked up from her knitting, the steel needles kept shuttling. She now spent any spare time she had in knitting for their new child, working so dextrously that it seemed to James that booties dropped from the end of her needles as effortlessly as wax from a candle. She said, calmly, 'Dalrymple? I don't know that name.'

'I do.'

'And ...?'

James leaned closer towards her. 'He's a high-born Scotsman and a hydrographer. He's worked for the East India Company, in Borneo and China. And he's a member of the Royal Society.'

Elizabeth's needles clicked on. 'He would seem then, to be well qualified for such a voyage.'

James shook his head. 'Not so. I have read what he postulates about the far side of the globe. He claims that a great continent lies in the south Pacific Ocean.'

Elizabeth frowned. 'Why does he hold such a belief?'

'Mainly because the Spaniard, Quiros, observed a large cloud bank in the South Pacific, when he was there in 1606. Dalrymple wishes to explore the ocean, merely on that basis. The man is a fantasist.'

Elizabeth paused in her knitting. 'But might there not be such a continent, in the Southern Ocean?'

'It is possible,' James conceded. 'To balance our planet's northern continents and so ensure its stability. And there is the land Abel Tasman touched upon, in 1642, New Zealand. John Byron too claims he found a southern continent, when he passed across the tropical latitudes of the Southern Ocean last year.' He undid two more buttons of his waistcoat. 'But I believe this was a figment of his inflamed imagination. He actually found only a few low islands.' James heaved a sigh. 'Elizabeth, it is the task of a skilled navigator to first determine whether or not there exists such a land mass, and if there is, to chart it faithfully. Precise surveying and practical recording is called for, skills which Dalrymple does not possess.' His voice becoming a mutter, he added bitterly, 'He is not a trained astronomer and he is not a naval officer. What he is, in my opinion, is principally a geographical speculator.'

'But if he is a member of the Royal Society, its members will favour him, surely?'

James made no reply. He recalled the last occasion when a non-naval man had been given the command of a naval vessel. The case had become legendary in Admiralty annals. The year was 1698, the vessel was HMS *Paramour* and the man was Edmond Halley. The voyage of scientific investigation - of the laws governing the variations of the compass - to the south Atlantic, had been characterised by insubordination from the naval officers aboard, who resented being commanded by a civilian. But Elizabeth was undoubtedly correct, James thought. Dalrymple had friends in high places, and his experience in the Orient was undeniable. So be it. He, James, had other matters to attend to. He stood up.

'I'm going up to my study, Elizabeth. I have more work to do on the charts.'

Still knitting rapidly, she nodded. Then she looked up. 'If the child is a girl, I think we should call it either Grace or Elizabeth. Which name do you prefer?'

At the same time that James was completing a final copy of his chart of the south-western coast of Newfoundland, preparatory to sending it to the engraver, Captain Hugh Palliser was taking a coach to the office of the Admiralty, a neo-classical building at the north end of Whitehall. It deposited him outside the colonnaded screen which ran in front of the building, and Palliser passed through the arched gate in the screen and walked up the steps to the door.

He rapped on the door, then waited. As he did so he thought back to the meeting he had attended two days earlier, in Crane Court, just off Fleet Street, in a two-storeyed, half-timbered building. The building housed an institution whose influence was increasing at a pace which matched the growing advancement of scientific enquiry - the Royal Society. The great Isaac Newton himself had acquired this home for the Society, of which he had been made President, in 1703.

Palliser had taken with him to the society's headquarters a leather case into which he had carefully packed several documents. Wearing his full naval regalia, he had been met at the door and shown into the study of the Royal Society's current President, James, the 14th Earl of Morton. After ushering him into his study, Morton indicated that he take a seat on the chair facing his desk, on which was one of Sir Isaac Newton's reflecting telescopes, along with a litter of papers. Glass-fronted cabinets filled with reference books covered one wall of the study, and above the fireplace was a large portrait of a glowering Isaac Newton, painted by Godfrey Kneller.

A Scotsman and a noted astronomer, Morton was a tall, stooped man of 65, with sunken cheeks, a stern countenance and eyebrows like overgrown hedgerows. His jacket was crumpled and the front of his waistcoat were marked with what looked like dried egg stains, causing Palliser to think, *a peer of the realm should not have egg stains on his waistcoat.* Still, he was a scientist, Palliser reminded himself, and they were known to be a different breed of men. He had not met Morton before, and he sensed a guardedness about the man as they faced each other across the desk. The tension between the Admiralty and the Royal Society which had arisen after the Halley-HMS *Paramour* fiasco had never quite been forgotten, and Palliser thought that this might explain the President's wariness. But he was aware too that the Society's Southern Ocean expedition could not proceed without the support of the Navy.

Peering at Palliser from beneath his untidy eyebrows, Morton said, 'Your letter said you wished to meet me in connection with the proposed expedition to observe the next Transit of Venus.' His voice was wheezy. Was he consumptive? Palliser wondered.

'That is correct, my Lord.'

'A highly significant astronomical event, which the Society is determined to obtain funding for. And suitable leadership.'

'Rightly so, my Lord. And it is the second aspect which you mention that brings me here today.'

'The leadership?' Morton blinked. 'What of it?'

'It is my understanding that Alexander Dalrymple is favoured by your Society to lead the expedition.'

Morton wheezed, then said, 'Your understanding is correct, Captain. The council of the Society intends to offer him the post of senior observer on the expedition.'

'I see. Then who will command the ship?'

The Earl hesitated, then said, 'Alexander Dalrymple has also stated that he wishes to manage the ship which will transport the expedition.'

Perturbed, Palliser said, 'But it must be an armed naval ship, my Lord. It must carry cannon, and marines.'

'Indeed. But that does not disqualify Dalrymple from such a role. He is a man of proven courage. And his experience in the East Indies will be invaluable.'

'With respect, my Lord, I would point out that it is proposed that the Transit of Venus will best be observed from a point in the central area of the Southern Ocean, not the East Indies.'

The Earl's expression darkened. 'I am an astronomer, Captain Palliser, I am well aware that that is the case.' He waved his hand airily. 'I merely meant that Dalrymple is experienced at navigating in exotic seas.' He waved his hand again. 'But continue.'

'I would like to suggest, my Lord, that there is a far better contender for the leadership of the expedition to the South Seas than Alexander Dalrymple.'

The Earl's eyebrows knitted. 'Oh? Who?'

'One James Cook, of the Royal Navy.'

'Cook ...' The Earl harrumphed. 'Is that the one who observed and wrote of the 1766 solar eclipse, off Newfoundland?'

'It is, my Lord. And it was that same paper which Dr John Bevis presented to your society, just a few weeks ago.' Palliser allowed a pause. 'And I was reliably informed that Cook's description of the eclipse was well received.'

The Earl nodded. 'Indeed it was. And from the description Dr Bevis was able to calculate the longitude of the Burgeos Islands, where Cook carried out his observation.'

Palliser saw his chance. Reaching for his leather document case, he said, 'And I have more strong evidence with me here, my Lord, of James Cook's abilities as a surveyor.' Opening the case, he drew out the completed chart of Newfoundland's Cape Anguille.

Palliser was greeted at the Admiralty door by Philip Stephens, Secretary to the Admiralty. Aware that Stephens was almost as influential within the Admiralty as the Lords themselves, Palliser had earlier written to the Secretary requesting a meeting with their Lordships with regard to James Cook, and this had been duly arranged by Stephens. Palliser was aware that Stephens had met and corresponded with Cook, and that the Secretary held his work and reputation in high regard.

The two men entered the meeting hall. It had a high, ornately decorated ceiling and a floral-patterned carpet in shades of pink and blue. At one end of the room were twin cabinets filled with naval histories, separated by a large globe of the known world. A chart of the Thames estuary and paintings of significant sea battles, including Admiral Vernon's capture of Portobello in 1739, hung from the wall at the opposite end of the hall. There was a long, polished oak table surrounded by upholstered chairs in the centre of the room and large windows in the wall that faced the street. A coal fire burned in the fireplace in the opposite wall. Numerous charts of different parts of the world were rolled up and attached to the wall above the fireplace. While Philip Stephens went to summon the Lords, Palliser stared around the hall. He immediately felt at home here, surrounded as he was by naval depictions and tradition. Far more so than in the untidy confines of the Royal Society's headquarters.

The First Lord of the Admiralty, Sir Edward Hawke, entered the hall, accompanied by the Secretary and three other Lords, Brett, Townshend and Carlisle. They all shook Palliser's hand. A big-boned man with a prominent nose and prominent jaw, Hawke was best-known for leading the British fleet when it defeated the French at the Battle of Quiberon Bay, off the coast of north-west France, in 1759. Palliser knew and respected Hawke as the man who had probably saved Britain from invasion by the French.

The five men took seats around the table, Stephens with notepaper, quill and ink pot in front of him.

Palliser described his meeting with the Earl of Morton, and the Royal Society's proposal that Alexander Dalrymple lead the expedition to the South Seas. He concluded, 'So it is my belief, my Lords, that the Society proposes to not only invite Dalrymple to lead the observation team for the transit, but also to command the naval vessel which carries the expedition members.'

Around the table, there were looks of astonishment. Lord Carlisle leaned forward. 'Do you mean, Captain Palliser, that a *merchant mariner* is demanding that he command one of the King's naval vessels?'

'I believe so, my Lord.'

Philip Stephens held his quill. 'But you also said that you showed the Earl of Morton some of James Cook's completed charts. In support of Cook's abilities.'

'I did, Sir.'

'And he was impressed.'

'He was. But he and his Council still favour Dalrymple.'

The imposing visage of Sir Edward Hawke looked fiercely at Palliser. 'Why?'

'Because ... he is a member of the Society. And because James Cook is merely a warrant officer.'

'Dalrymple may be a member of the Royal Society, but he is not an officer in the King's navy.' Sir Edward's voice dripped with contempt.

'To allow him to command one of His Majesty's vessels would be utterly contradictory to the Navy's regulations,' put in Lord Brett, witheringly.

'And he lacks Cook's battle experience,' said another, Lord Brett.

Stephens said, adgowning Sir Edward: 'It is my belief that James Cook is a far better candidate for the task, my Lord. His ability is proven beyond doubt. You endorse that view, do you not Captain Palliser?'

'I do. I have worked alongside Cook many times, and hold him in the highest regard. It is true he is non-commissioned, but that is a matter which the Admiralty can rectify, surely.'

There was a thoughtful silence, then Lord Townshend said, gruffly,

'Dalrymple's presumption that he would command the ship is offensive, in my opinion.'

Sir Edward, his face flushed, leaned forward: 'I would rather cut off my right hand than permit anyone but a King's Officer to command one of the ships of our Navy.' He brought the flat of his hand down on the table, hard. 'Cook is one of ours, Dalrymple is not.'

The others nodded. Stephens said: 'Then do I have your Lords' permission to convey that view to Lord Morton and the Council of the Royal Society?'

'Are you in agreement with that, gentlemen?' Sir Edward asked. All raised their right hands. Stephens picked up his quill and made a note. Sir Edward rose, and shook Palliser's hand again. 'Cook will get his commission, and his ship,' he declared. 'The Admiralty will order it, and the Royal Society must agree.'

After he and the other Lords had said their farewells and left the hall, Stephens smiled at Palliser and said, 'Will you be the first to inform Cook, or shall I?'

Palliser responded promptly. 'I'll tell him,' he said.

'And I'll tell Dalrymple.' Stephens chuckled. 'And suffer his ire,' he added, with obvious relish.

Eleven

On May 20 James received a note from Captain Palliser, requesting a meeting with him at Garraway's coffee-house, at mid-morning the following Wednesday. Assuming that he wished to discuss his next voyage to Newfoundland, James took with him a map showing the as-yet unsurveyed section of the island.

Garraway's coffee-house was located in Exchange Alley, between Cornhill and Lombard Street. It was a fine spring morning, the sash windows were fully open and daffodils bloomed brightly in its window boxes. Palliser ordered coffees for them, and while they waited for it to come, he filled, tamped and lit his pipe bowl. In the next booth seat James noticed a large, elderly man with hammocks of flesh under his eyes, a prominent chin and a wig which drooped at both sides. Gowned in a brown leather jacket and matching waistcoat, he was busy writing in a notebook. Leaning across the table, Palliser murmured, 'Dr Johnson.'

'I have heard the name. What does he do?'

'He's a writer.'

'Ah yes ...' James stole a glance at the earnest figure. 'He compiled a dictionary of the language, did he not?'

'Yes. This is his favourite coffee-house, he works here every day. He's a grumpy old codger, hates to be disturbed when he's writing.' Palliser puffed hard on his pipe. 'Never mind him, Cook, I have huge news for you.'

James replied brightly. 'The survey is to be concluded? I have been impatient for my orders. They're overdue.'

Palliser met his eyes, firmly. 'Yes, the survey is to be concluded.' He paused. 'But not by you.'

'*What*?'

'Matthew Lane is to complete the Newfoundland survey.'

James looked at Palliser in disbelief. He was being replaced by his assistant?

'Sir, I cannot believe this. The survey has been my life for nearly five years. Why I am being denied the opportunity to finish the work?'

Palliser set his pipe down on the table. 'Because your talents are required elsewhere.'

As Palliser summarised the recent decisions taken by the Royal Society and the Admiralty, James listened intently, scarcely able to believe what he was hearing. Command an expedition. To the South Seas. To observe the Transit of Venus. Commissioned. Lieutenant Cook. The prospect, and its implications, stunned him. *The South Sea*. The words had captivated him since he was a boy, since he had handled the shilling in Sanderson's shop, since he had read of the great voyages made by others. And now ...

'The first thing I must say, Cook, is congratulations. No appointment was more deserved, and I know that you will be equal to every challenge the expedition presents.'

Struck by another thought, James gave Palliser a demanding look. 'Was this appointment your doing, Sir?'

'No Cook, it was yours. Your naval record spoke for itself. Dalrymple could not match it.'

He reached into his leather satchel, drew out a sheet of notepaper and handed it to James. 'Your preliminary instructions, from the Admiralty.'

He held the sheet, unable to prevent his hand from trembling.

Dear James Cook

Whereas we have appointed you First Lieutenant of His Majesty's Bark, the Endeavour, now at Deptford, and intend that you shall command her during her present intended voyage; and, whereas, we have ordered the said bark to be fitted out and stored at that place for foreign service, manned with seventy men and victualled to twelve months of all species of provisions (for the said number of men at whole allowance) except beer, of which she is to have only a proportion for one month and to be supplied with brandy in lieu of the remainder; you are hereby required and directed to use the utmost despatch on getting her ready for sail accordingly, and then falling down to Gallions Reach, take in her guns and gunners' stores at that place and proceed to the Nore for further orders.

Ed Hawke, C.Townshend, PT Brett, T.Carlisle

James looked up. 'A bark?'

Palliser nodded. '*Endeavour*. A converted collier. Bought by the Naval Board. Built at Whitby, launched three and a half years ago as *Earl of Pembroke*. Three hundred and sixty-eight tons.' He waved in the direction of the proprietor. 'Let's add a brandy to our coffees, to celebrate.'

He leaned forward across the table and in a lowered voice, said: 'There is further news, Cook, unofficial as yet, but which will be of consequence to your expedition.' Glancing around to ensure that no one else could hear, he said, 'Samuel Wallis is safely back from his world circumnavigation in *Dolphin*. And there is a rumour going about the city taverns that he discovered a beautiful, mountainous island in the Southern Ocean, and has claimed it for our King.'

Taking a cab in Lombard Street, James was driven back to Mile End Road, the Admiralty letter in his case along with the chart. His mind still seethed. With the Transit of Venus occurring on 3 June next year, that was only a little over a year away. Therefore departure could be no later than August. The timing would be all. Then he had another thought. The Admiralty would doubtless instruct that he return, as well as enter, the Pacific via the Horn, for reasons of economy. But to do so would not constitute a proper circumnavigation. Wallis, Palliser had told him, had returned by the Cape of Good Hope, not the Horn. His *had* been a circumnavigation. James made a promise to himself. He would settle for nothing less than leading a round-the-world expedition. But in the meantime this additional ambition he would keep entirely to himself.

In the front room, Frances Wardale was holding little Elizabeth and spooning porridge into her mouth, the baby's face half-covered with cereal. James peered at the baby's comically messy face, then said to his cousin, 'Where are Elizabeth and the boys?' 'Upstairs,' she replied, dully. Ignoring her usual sulky mood, he went up the stairs, two at a time.

Elizabeth was sitting on the divan by the open window, embroidering a bodice. Pregnant again, she was taking advantage of the light cast by the early afternoon sunshine. Both boys were sitting on the floor, drawing with the pencils Nathaniel had been given for his fourth birthday.

Elizabeth smiled, wanly. 'How was Captain Palliser? Did he give you news of the survey?'

Sitting down at the other end of the divan, he told her the news. For some moments she did not reply. She just sat as if frozen, needle in her hand, thread dangling. James noticed how pale she was, and how starkly the shadows under her eyes contrasted with this paleness. Not looking at him, she said, 'This expedition to the Southern Ocean, James, how long will it take?'

'Two and a half years. Possibly three .'

She looked up, startled. 'Possibly three ...'

'What is it, Elizabeth?'

'That is so long. And the voyage will be so dangerous.'

'No more dangerous than the Atlantic, or the St Lawrence.'

'To sail to the Pacific means that you will have to double Cape Horn, will you not?'

'The winds mean that that is the usual route taken, yes.' *Why is she not pleased?*

'I have read of those waters. Cape Horn is a perilous passage.'

'It is charted now, and I shall be consulting the charts constantly.'

Ignoring this, eyes glistening, she said, 'I do not want to be a navy widow, James, and I do not want our children to grow up fatherless.'

'Neither do I. That is why I will ensure there will be safe passage.'

Avoiding his stern gaze, she said, 'When you were away in Canada merely for the summer months, I could manage. But for over three years, with four children to care for ...'

He said, coldly now, 'Cousin Frances will be here to assist you.'

'She will not! She is more of a hindrance, lately, with her constant complaints about life here. I intend to dismiss her. She can go back to Cleveland.'

James and Nathaniel, drawings forgotten, were looking from their mother's face to their father's, then back again. Their little faces were grave.

'Elizabeth ... I will be commissioned. I will be a lieutenant. Was that not what you wanted? You have told me you wanted that. Several times.'

'Yes, but I did not want you to be away for over two years. That was why I was secretly pleased when you said that tat other man had been appointed to lead the South Seas expedition.'

'Dalrymple?'

'Yes.'

He permitted a pause, then said pointedly, 'Both the Royal Society and the Admiralty considered I was the better man to command the expedition. Is that not something you can take pride in?'

Shaking her head, Elizabeth picked up the material she was sewing and dabbed her eyes with it. Nathaniel got up, went across and hugged her. Little James was looking down, his expression miserable. His father swallowed hard, several times, willing himself to stay calm, and be reasonable. This was the last thing he would have expected. But there could be no going back now. He said, unable to keep a tone of admonition from his voice:

'Elizabeth, you know how long and hard I have worked for this promotion. For a commission, for a proper command. And I take great pride in the fact that I have come in through the hawsehole.'

'Speak plain English, James, not the language of the Navy.'

James clenched his right hand. 'I mean, it has taken me thirteen years, thirteen difficult years, to progress from able seaman to lieutenant, from the orlop to the quarterdeck. And be offered the command of an exploring ship. Few naval men can claim such a distinction.' He paused. ' And I am determined to succeed, because ...' holding up his right hand, he opened it, to remind her of his old wound '... my first duty is to my country.'

She looked at him with undisguised reproach, then said adamantly, 'No. Your first duty is to your family.'

'So you would have me decline the Admiralty's offer.'

Her expression was defiant. 'I would, yes.'

'And I will not.' He got up and walked from the room.

Pacing beside the river, for once he did not take in any of its water-borne activities. Instead, his mind seethed. His wife was full of conflictions, like tide against wind, with cross-currents added. Measuring the heavens was a simple exercise, he thought, compared to charting a woman's mind. He tried to order his thoughts, to ameliorate his disappointment, to see things from her point of view. She was a devoted mother. Her children were such an important part of her life. Naturally she would find his absence a worry, not knowing where he was, not hearing from him for months at a time. And she would bear a heavy domestic burden, with three young children already and a fourth due shortly after he set sail. It was true, too, that Frances had been of limited help to the household. She should be sent back to Cleveland.

Beside the Thames a coal barge was being unloaded, and a burly coal-heaver passed him, his face blackened, bent double with the load on his back. 'Good-day squire,' he groaned as he passed, and James nodded curtly by way of reply.

Walking on, he presented to himself the other side of the marital ledger. She knew full well, when she married him, that naval duties would take him away for long periods. That was his duty, and as his wife hers was to abide by it. She would be well provided for in his absence, being entitled to draw on his naval savings. This appointment was probably a once-in-a-lifetime engagement. If he declined it, his career would be over.

At Wapping Stairs he turned and walked away from the river. He would arrange for a live-in maid to replace Frances, to assist with the care of the children. And her mother was not far away, to provide her with company and assist with the children. Feeling the heat now, he unbuttoned his waistcoat. Half an hour later, Mile End Road came into sight, then the house. And by the time he opened the front door, he knew what he would say.

'Where are the boys?'

'I have put them to bed. They were upset. Children hate it when their parents argue.' Her expression became accusatory.

Ignoring this, he asked, 'And Frances?'

'She has gone for a walk with the baby.'

'So we can talk frankly.'

'What else is there to say?'

He sat down on the chair under the window. 'There is much to say, Elizabeth.'

She looked at him doubtfully. Her eyes were pink-rimmed, her hair untidy. In her hands was a handkerchief which she was wringing, hard. James began.

'I am fully aware of the strains my long absence will put upon our household. But I will do everything I can to compensate for this. I will engage the services of a housemaid, to replace Frances, who I know has been a disappointment to you. So the severest burdens of child care will be removed from you. '

She was staring at him, clutching the handkerchief, her eyes dull. Placing one hand over the bulge in her belly, she looked down.

Feeling a surge of pity, he went to her, knelt and put his arms around her.

'Elizabeth, you must know, I cannot decline this assignment. It is my sworn duty, as a naval officer, to serve the country we both love. And it will be my opportunity, during this voyage, not only to carry out vital astronomical observances, but to enlarge the King's possessions in the world. It is *possible* that there is an undiscovered continent in the southern latitudes. And if so, I will claim it for Britain. If I do not, then the French or the Spanish will do so, and that is unthinkable to all Englishmen.'

She looked up. Although tears were spilling down her cheeks, she nodded faintly.

He pressed on. 'And although nearly three years sounds a long time, it will pass quickly. You will have the children's interests to occupy you, and to keep you company. Your mother is still close. And I will ensure that you are able to draw on my naval allowance whenever you need to.'

Looking down, he placed a hand on her stomach. 'I may even still be here for the birth of this one, before *Endeavour* sails.'

Blinking away the tears, she said thickly, 'When will that be?'

'It cannot be later than August.'

'The child is due in the last week of August. As you well know.' Her tone was once again reproachful.

He nodded. Then, keeping his hand on her stomach, he said: 'That I can do nothing about. But I have made a resolution.'

She looked puzzled. 'What kind of a resolution?'

'I will write to you, every day.'

'What do you mean?'

'It will be my duty, as you know, to maintain the ship's log.'

'I know that.'

He drew back a little. 'But I will also keep a journal of my private thoughts and feelings. And it will be for your eyes only.'

'But ... what use will that be, if I cannot read it?'

'I will read it to you. When I return. It will be a record of my love and devotion to you, from the furthermost parts of the globe.' He looked down. 'I am not a writer, Elizabeth, I have no way with words, like Daniel Defoe or Thomas Gray or Dr Johnson. And I am not given to expressing my deepest feelings publicly. But in my personal journal to you, I will try.'

She stared at him, her gaze unwavering. 'Is it not the rule that a naval captain's sea log must be sovereign to the Admiralty? That was the case when you served on *Grenville*.'

Looking up, he met her gaze. 'Yes, it is. And naturally, my captain's log will be submitted to the Lords.' He put his arms about her. 'But the other journal will be for you.'

He held her, gently, and felt the tears on her cheeks pass onto his own. Lifting her chin, he looked directly into her filmy eyes.

'I will return, Elizabeth. That is my promise to you. And when I do, I will tell you my story.'

Twelve

He met Captain Samuel Wallis at Garraway's coffee-house on 2 June, an engagement brokered by Philip Stephens of the Admiralty. The idea of such a meeting, though, was at James's initiative. Having heard the rumours of Wallis's South Seas discovery, he could not wait for the official report of the *Dolphin*'s circumnavigation to be published. His own expedition was already a matter of urgency. There were two great oceans to traverse, and Cape Horn to be doubled, if the deadline of 3 June next year was to be met.

Wallis was wearing his gown naval uniform. A man of medium height, he had a round, almost moonish, face, a broad forehead, currant eyes and a small, well-formed mouth. But there were webs of lines around his eyes, his face was pallid and he had a general air of weariness about him. After shaking hands, the two men took a window seat, facing each other across a refectory table.

After ordering coffee for them both, James said, 'Your circumnavigation was successful, Sir, from the accounts I have heard.'

'On balance, yes. But there were many tribulations.' He took a pinch of snuff from a small silver container and held it to his nostrils. 'Excuse me, but I have yet to recover my full health. I was ill for much of the voyage.' Then he continued. 'Passing through the Straits of Magellan took three months. Then, after the Horn, we became parted from our consort, *Swallow*. It was then too that I fell ill. *Dolphin*'s master's mate, George Robertson, assisted by John Gore, handled the ship after that.' He inclined his head. 'Their work was highly commendable.'

James made a mental note of those names. Then he said, 'There are low islands in the Southern Ocean, many of them, south of the Equator. I read that the Dutchman, Roggeveen, foundered on one of them.'

Wallis closed the lid of his snuff box. 'Indeed there are. The Dangerous Archipelago. At around sixteen degrees south latitude. The islands are enclosed by reefs, and are so close to sea level that by the time you come upon them it is almost too late. A man must be posted to the masthead at all times, day and night, to spot them.'

'How can such islands be seen at night?'

'The ocean waves break heavily upon the reefs and the phosphorescence in the water makes them show bright white, even at night. And as it seldom rains in these latitudes, the sky is usually clear.'

'Ah ...' James made a mental note of this, too. Then he said: 'The high island you discovered. There are stories circulating about its beauty.' He smiled, wryly. 'Both physical and human.'

'The stories are not exaggerated.'

'What is the island's location?'

Wallis gave him a reproving look. 'I am sworn to secrecy as to that particular. On Admiralty's orders.'

Annoyed by this pettiness, James said, coolly, 'I will learn of its location shortly, from your report.'

Wallis nodded, but his expression was grudging. Then, leaning forward, he said:

'I *can* tell you that King George's Island is about two days' sailing south-west of the Dangerous Archipelago. It has towering mountains, their peaks pointed, like the teeth of a saw. And the mountains are covered with dark green forest, reaching to their very summits.' He paused. 'In truth there are two islands, conjoined by a low isthmus, one much smaller than the other but very similar in its configuration. Both have many waterfalls, and river valleys where the soil is greatly fertile. It is truly like the Garden of Eden.' He gave a little laugh. 'Certainly my men considered they were in Heaven. There is also a neighbouring island, a short sail to the north-west of King George's, and very like the principal one. I named it "The Duke of York's Island".'

'And the people of King George's Island?'

'They are copper-skinned and black-haired. Very handsome, clean and most healthy. They live in strongly built houses with roofs of thatched palm fronds. Their diet is mostly fish, chicken and pork, with coconuts, root crops and a tree fruit like a green coconut, which was not ripe during our stay. Their canoes are well built, the larger ones double-hulled.' He took another pinch of snuff. 'They all – men, women and children – swim like fishes.'

'How did they receive you?'

'Initially, with hostility. We were forced to fire upon their attacking canoes with round, grape-shot and musket balls.'

James was startled. 'But what weapons did the natives possess?'

'Stones, which they hurled at us.'

'You returned stone-throwing with cannon fire and grape-shot?'

Wallis looked stony himself, conscious of James's disapprobation. He said defensively, 'There were thousands of warriors surrounding the ship. It was my fear that we would be overwhelmed.'

'How many of them were shot?'

'I am unsure. Many, certainly.' He sniffed, hard. 'A show of force was necessary on our part, to repel them.' He paused. 'They attacked, I believe, because they considered us invaders who would occupy their island. After all, they had never before set eyes upon civilised Europeans.' He waved his right hand, airily. 'But thereafter, relations between us became cordial.'

As James sat staring into Wallis's round, fatigued face, he was wondering, what would I as commander have done in such circumstances? Could such an altercation have been avoided? He also thought: this man has found and claimed undiscovered lands. He has given names to islands and other geographical features which would endure. He has circumnavigated the globe. And, most importantly, he has returned safely. James would ensure that Elizabeth was apprised of this fact, it may reassure her. He had further questions for the explorer.

'Did you form any conclusions regarding the existence of a Great Southern Continent?'

Wallis looked uncomfortable. 'I cannot say for certain.' He hesitated, then continued. 'But a day after we passed through the Dangerous Archipelago, we saw lying right across the southern horizon a series of great peaks, swathed in clouds. This caused an outbreak of high excitement on the ship, as it seemed certain then that we had found *Terra Australis Incognita*.' He looked down and pursed his lips. 'But fog then closed in and sight of the continent was lost to us. We did not see it again, so instead we held our course for the high island.'

James frowned. Not only was he irritated by Wallis's use of the Latin term - was he boasting of his scholarship? - but he was puzzled, too. Had *Dolphin*'s crew seen an apparition? And if so, how could such an apparition occur? Then, changing tack, he said,

'Do you consider King George's Island to be a suitable location for the observation of next year's Transit of Venus?'

'I believe so. The astronomers say that the transit will be best viewed in those latitudes of the Pacific. And the natives of the island told us that they have only two seasons, one wet, one dry. The dry season is in mid-year, the time when we were there. The skies were mostly clear, and such rain as occurred, dispersed quickly. Their wet season comes later, during our winter.'

'How could you know this? Was it all conveyed to you in sign language?'

'Yes. They are and intelligent people, capable of communicating eloquently even without English, and very curious about our way of life. Thieves too, many of them. Not having any metal of their own, they have a particular fondness for nails.'

They talked for another hour. Wallis tendered James more advice, some nautical, some social. The bottom planks of *Dolphin* had been sheathed in copper, and so were not eaten into by teredo navalis, the marine worm. There was a sheltered bay on the north coast of the main island, which he'd named Port Royal, readily accessible through a pass in the reef, with an adjacent expanse of level land. This bay made a fine anchorage. The natives' society was very hierarchical; they even had their own queen, a powerful woman called Oberea. The young women were not only healthful, they were shameless in their carnality, something the *Dolphin*'s men greatly appreciated. Sex to the natives of King George's Island was as natural as breathing, the Englishmen had gratefully concluded. A woman could be procured with a ship's nail, and consequently nails had become a kind of currency.

Outside the coffee-house, the two men shook hands. 'Thank you Sir,' said James. 'Your experiences will prove most useful. Your journal and charts will be available to me in due course, I presume.'

'They will. The Admiralty will see that you get them.' His expression became perturbed. 'There is a rumour in the city that the Frenchies are sending an expedition to the South Seas. Commanded by someone called ....' he looked up, as if searching for the name in the London sky, 'Boogannwheel, or some-such Frenchie name. If so, that is not a development to be welcomed.'

'Certainly not.' But James could not resist adding, 'His name, though, is Louis Antoine de Bougainville. He is a scientist and a mathematician. Moreover, he fought at Quebec.'

Out on the street, with a brisk nod, Wallis wished him 'Safe passage,' but at the same time James detected a hint of disregard in the man's eyes. Did Wallis doubt that he, James, a self-taught mariner and just-commissioned lieutenant, could successfully duplicate his circumnavigation? Again he felt old resentments simmering: being regarded as the boy from the farm biggin, the one with the north country accent, reluctantly permitted to keep company with the silver spoon commanders. Then, walking back along Lombard Street, he suppressed this thought, as he had had to on many other occasions. There was one sure way to cope with such disdain – prove that he was equal to the manifold challenges the Navy set him. He had already proved himself, on several seas. And he would do so again. The Admiralty believed in him, the Royal Society had shown its faith in him. And in the face of his sternest test, he was determined to prove his worth again. As he hailed a sedan chair, certain names kept tumbling through his mind: *Cape Horn, The Dangerous Archipelago, King George's Island, Port Royal.* And the date of that appointment with Venus: *3 June, 1769.*

The weeks sped past. There were meetings, meetings, meetings. With the Lords of the Admiralty, with the Navy Board, with the Royal Society, with victuallers, carpenters and sail-makers.

On July 2, when he again took the ferry down the river to the Deptford dockyard, he took both his boys with him. Both gowned proudly in their miniature naval uniforms, they chatted excitedly as they were rowed down river by the ferryman, little James in the bow, his father and Nathaniel sitting on the after thwart. James, though only five, would be tall, his father guessed, and four-year-old Nathaniel stocky, more like his mother. They asked him questions constantly about the moored vessels they passed, and the ones moving up on the tide: schooners, barges, brigs, cutters and other ferries.

Disembarking from the ferry at the place where the Ravensbourne River flowed into the Thames, they took the short walk along to the yard where the newly-renamed HMB *Endeavour* was tied up and undergoing her refit.

Holding his sons' hands, he stared at the ship. The carpenters were working on her extended bow-sprit and fitting the gudgeons for her new rudder, a dab hand was applying paint to the stern embellishments and the caulkers were busy on the main deck with their pots of hot pitch. James felt a swell of pride and satisfaction at the sight of this constructive activity. There had been strife in the docks a few weeks ago, with the coal-heavers and other workers forming an association and withdrawing their labour because of poor pay. The workers were also resentful of the excessive profits suppliers to the Navy were making. Although sympathetic to the labourers' cause, James also was frustrated by the turmoil the dispute had caused. At sea such disorder would be unthinkable. At sea, order was all. Thankfully the dockside disputes had now been settled, and the refitting and provisioning of the Navy's ships had resumed.

He and the boys walked the length of the ship, admiring her in awed silence. This was it, James thought, this was what he had waited so long and worked so hard for. She wasn't a glamorous ship, like the two-decker alongside her, with its busty figurehead and rows of cannon ports. With her blunt, pugnacious bow and narrow stern, *Endeavour* resembled a female bulldog. She didn't even have a figurehead. But style and beauty wouldn't be needed for the voyage. Strength and durability were all. Her flat bottom would be an advantage when she was warped in and out of estuaries, and she was capacious, as she would need to be, with the conglomeration of men, animals and equipment she would be taking aboard next month. There was a satisfying symmetry too in the knowledge that *Endeavour* had been built at Whitby, at the Fishburn yard, one which he remembered well from his apprentice days.

Earlier, while *Endeavour* was in dry dock, the last vestiges of coal dust had been sluiced away from her holds, and she had had her bottom planks sheathed, whereby another 'skin' of thinner boards had been added to her planks, over a lining of tarred felt. The sheathing had been filled with large, flat-headed nails, as added protection against Teredo navalis. Work now was concentrating on the caulking and the fitting out of the Great Cabin. The crane which had stepped the three replacement, square-rigged masts was now being used to swing timber from dockside onto the fo'c'sle, where the carpenters were working. *Endeavour*'s two bower anchors, James noted, were already lashed firmly in place, one on the larboard and the other on the port bow. He was pleased that she would carry five anchors, three bower including one sheet, a smaller stream anchor and another small one, a kedge, to keep her steady in harbour when the tide was turning.

The boys were staring at the ship and the carpenters at work, captivated.

'Which is your cabin, Papa?' asked James.

'There. At the stern. The Great Cabin, it's called.'

'Will it be great enough?'

'Big enough, do you mean?' He laughed. 'I hope so. Big enough for me to stand up in, and for a table and my charts, certainly. A library, too. And see the windows in the stern? They will admit plenty of light, when I'm charting her course. '

'Where are the cannons?' Nathaniel asked.

'They'll be taken aboard later. The decking and the rigging are most important for now.'

'How many cannons?' Nathaniel persisted.

'Ten carriage guns and twelve swivel guns.'

'And lots of muskets?'

'Lots. And pistols. And swords. And daggers.'

'And ... tomahawks?'

'Axes, yes. For any Indians we might meet. But our axes will be presents. We will wish to make friends of the Indians in the Southern Ocean, where they do not know steel.'

The boys nodded, sombrely, but were obviously struggling to comprehend all this.

A stocky man of about thirty with a broad brow and flattened nose, hatless but in naval uniform, came up the after deck companionway and walked down the gang-plank to the wharf. John Gore. He greeted James with a distinctly cool look. The two men had met earlier at the Admiralty. Appreciating that the American-born warrant officer could be as asset to the voyage, in view of the fact that he had circumnavigated the world twice already, James had urged the Lords to appoint Gore to the expedition. He had duly been appointed third lieutenant on *Endeavour*. However Philip Stephens had let James know, in confidence, that Gore had considered himself a much stronger contender for the leadership than James, and that James should be aware of his likely resentment at being passed over.

Determined not to allow this umbrage to affect the expedition's morale, James introduced the officer to his boys.

'James, Nathaniel, this is Lieutenant Gore. He will be sailing with us on *Endeavour*.' He added in a deliberately conciliatory tone, 'He has already sailed around the world. *Twice*.'

Gore nodded at the boys, then said in his unusual accent, 'And will you follow your father to sea?' They nodded, keenly. In fact James had already registered them on the ship's muster book, where they would be listed as 'servants' to the third lieutenant and the carpenter, a common naval practice which afforded the boys notional sea service. That phantom service would give them earlier promotion when they actually went to sea. But he had not yet disclosed this to Elizabeth.

He said to Gore: 'The refit goes well?'

'As well as it can, in the time we have.' His voice was clipped.

'We will need to be at sea by August if we are to close King George's Island by May,' James replied, pointedly.

'We will be,' Gore replied tersely, then strode off down the dock.

That same day, after returning James and Nathaniel to the house, he took a carriage to the Royal Society headquarters. There he was greeted by the Earl of Morton. James had come to like this big, bluff Scotsman. He had shown himself to be an enlightened man, who had been genuinely distressed to learn that Wallis's men had killed many natives during the fracas on King George's Island.

James and the Earl took tea together in the front study of the Society's house, and discussed the scientific aspects of the expedition and the equipment which would be needed for the observation of the Transit. The Society had appointed Charles Green as chief astronomer, with James as his assistant. Green had made a list of the surveying and astronomical apparatus they would need, and James studied it with great interest. Theodolite, plane table, compasses, telescopes with stands, astronomical quadrant, barometer, clocks, dividers, rulers ... The list went on. James looked up, perturbed.

'The cost of all this, my Lord?'

The Earl nodded, ruefully. 'And that is just for the surveying and observation. To which must be added he cost of the botanical apparatus. Nets, trawls, hooks, an amazing underwater telescope, a small boat for collecting specimens at sea. A library of Natural History. In all, it amounts to a cost of ten thousand pounds.'

'Ten *thousand*?'

'Yes. Fortunately, the Society will not have to bear that expense.'

'Who will?'

'The naturalist.'

'Oh.' He had not yet been told who this was to be. 'And who is this person?'

'Someone you will meet shortly.' He withdrew his fob watch and glanced at it. 'He's late.' Putting the watch back he said, 'In the meantime, here is the full list of the equipment he'll be bringing.'

James studied the list of devices which would be used for catching and preserving sea and land creatures and botanical specimens. Where would they all be stowed? he wondered. Then, hearing a carriage draw up outside, he glanced through the window. The Earl looked up.

'Ah ... he's here,' he said, with obvious relief.

He went outside, then returned with the latest visitor. Leading him into the study, the Earl gestured towards James.

'James Cook, meet the Society's naturalist to the expedition - Joseph Banks.'

Thirteen

The tall young man looked much as James remembered from their meeting two years ago in Newfoundland, although his face had filled out. He was wearing a dark brown wig, emerald green brocade jacket, beige waistcoat and breeches. There was a white silk scarf tied loosely around his neck and his shoes had large buckles of polished brass. His eyes were large and dark, his mouth sensuous and there was a playful aspect to his expression.

He shook James's hand vigorously.

'Cook and I have met. St John's, wasn't it? At the Governor's residence?'

'It was. You were meeting to organise a ball.' James put emphasis on the last word.

'Ah, yes.' His eyes twinkled. 'A ball where there were ten males for every female. Not my idea of favourable odds. It was an unmemorable evening. Give me the Hell-Fire Club any day. There the ratio is reversed.'

Banks and the Earl sniggered, James remained usmiling. The Hell-Fire Club was run by John Montagu, the Earl of Sandwich, a well-known aristocratic libertine. Rumours of the club's members' drunken evenings with groups of professional harlots circulated in the City, and were received by most with a mixture of condemnation and envy. James disapproved of debauchery, especially among the high-born.

Banks tugged at his coat sleeves and arranged his face into a serious expression. 'Well, down to business, gentlemen. The expedition's plans are proceeding I trust, Cook?'

James nodded, but he was still disconcerted by the news of the appointment. Banks was a civilian, so would be unused to naval life. He would also not be subject to James's orders or discipline. His background, manner and behaviour marked him as a privileged and somewhat flippant fellow. But, James reminded himself, a naturalist was essential to the expedition. And Banks - what a fitting name, it occurred to him - had invested such a colossal sum of money in it, that surely he would want to ensure that it was well invested. Whether or not James liked it, he would be stuck with Joseph Banks for the duration, land lubber or no.

But as the meeting proceeded, James became more and more disconcerted. With all the nonchalance of a man to whom money was no object, Banks announced to the Earl and James the details of his retinue. Not only would he be bringing his two dogs, he would have with him two Negro servants from the Banks family estate in Revesby ('They're strong, healthy bucks, you'll find them useful') and a boy servant, Nicholas Young. There was also an insouciance about the naturalist's manner, a presumption, James sensed, that he would be the most important person on the expedition. Moreover, Banks also announced that he had chosen as part of his party a botanical illustrator, a young Scotsman called Sydney Parkinson, and another Scotsman as landscape artist, Alexander Buchan ('I am well familiar with their work, it is splendid'). Banks himself would be assisted by a colleague, he informed James, one Dr Daniel Solander, and his friend, Herman Sporing ('Scandinavians, but well qualified ones'). As he announced this extensive retinue, James felt even more uneasy. Was the expedition to be dominated by botanists, illustrators and their pets? What about the astronomy - the principal motive for the expedition? Yet here, in the headquarters of the Royal Society, he could not admit these concerns. He was aware that Solander too was a Fellow of the Society.

James made an arrangement with Banks to meet him at Deptford in three days' time, to inspect the refitted *Endeavour*, then he bid the others farewell and left to take the coach back to Mile End.

As he was driven through the streets of the city, past the Tower of London and down the hill to East Smithfield, his thoughts turned to home and family. Although the plans for the voyage were proceeding apace, in the house at Mile End tensions were growing. Elizabeth continued to show little interest in the expedition, and instead fretted about the children and the unborn child. James had dismissed Frances, as promised, and Elizabeth had hired a girl from Rotherham to replace her, Susan, a slow-moving but mercifully uncomplaining maid who slept in the parlour and attended closely to the interests of little James, Nathaniel and Elizabeth, who liked her immediately. But Susan's presence had made little difference to Elizabeth's feelings about his impending departure.

'How are you, Beth?'

'Weary. My ankles. They are so swollen.'

She was lying on the divan under the front window, face flushed with the summer heat, hair hanging loose, hands clasped across her bulging belly. The window was open, giving some relief from the heat but also admitting the smells of the street, along with the clatter of passing coaches, the clopping of horses' hooves and the shouts of draymen.

'Where are the boys?'

'Susan has taken them to the pond on the common. To catch tadpoles.'

'Ah ... good. And little Elizabeth?'

'She sleeps.'

James went to his wife. Kneeling, he placed his hands over hers.

'How was your meeting?' she asked, without enthusiasm.

'Satisfactory. But there is yet much to consider.'

'You are still leaving in August?'

'We must. The timing is all.' He squeezed her hand, gently. 'And I heard today that your cousin has been added to *Endeavour*'s muster roll.'

'Cousin Isaac?'

'Yes. I requested that he be appointed Master's Mate. He's a good lad. He served me well on *Grenville*. A hydrographer in the making.'

She nodded in an uninterested way, then closed her eyes in a gesture of resignation.

He thought that the news of Isaac's promotion may have cheered her, but it seemed not. Her mind was on the unborn child, he suspected, which was due after he had sailed. This was the way it had been with the others, but this time was different. He would this time be venturing into the largely unknown.

As if reading his thoughts, she murmured, 'I feel ... this child is not the same, somehow. I cannot explain, but there is something ....' She turned away, leaving the statement uncompleted.

Then, seeing that she had begun to doze, he stood up and began to climb the stairs, intending to go to his study. But as he passed the children's bedroom he heard a reedy cry, coming from little Elizabeth's cradle. He went to it, then reached in and picked up the little one. As her large blue eyes stared up at him, he stroked her downy hair. She put her thumb in her mouth and sucked it, without taking her eyes from his face. Dribble leaked from the corners of her tiny mouth. She was getting more teeth, Elizabeth had reported, that was why she only slept fittingly. That and the June heat.

He placed his hand tenderly over her tiny forehead. Now there were two Jameses and two Elizabeths in the house, and this knowledge pleased him. Perhaps the next child would be a Grace. Carefully he placed little Elizabeth back in the cradle, then began to rock it, slowly. His sons he loved deeply, but there was something so special about a daughter. He studied her closed eyes, the long fair lashes which curled upwards and fluttered faintly, her creamy skin. Soon she would be walking. By the time he returned she would be playing, running, skipping, talking. He felt a pang of regret that he would miss these important stages of the little one's life. Then he dismissed this thought. Seeing that the little girl was now fast asleep, he moved away and went up to his study.

On his desk was the large note-book with the marbled covers, which he had bought from a stationer's in Lombard Street. He opened it, picked up a quill and dipped it in the ink-well. At the head of the first blank page he wrote in his long, looping hand: 'Journal for Elizabeth, kept on HMS Bark *Endeavour*, August 1768 ....' He left the ink to dry, then took a sheet of notepaper from a drawer in the desk, the lockable drawer. He thought for a moment, then began to write. When he had finished, he blotted the ink, folded the sheet and placed it in an envelope. After sealing it, he wrote across the front of the envelope: '*For Elizabeth Cook, to be opened in the event of my death*'. Then he placed the envelope in the drawer, locked it and placed the key in the small box on the book-shelf with the others.

Meetings, meetings, meetings. Through the weeks of July, James grew increasingly impatient. Although the principal refit of *Endeavour* was completed on time, the finalising of the crew was at times problematic. There was, for instance, the curious case of the ship's cook. The one appointed by the Naval Board, and who turned up at Deptford on 14 July, looked like a beggar. Haggard and unshaven, with palsied hands and limbs like pea-sticks, James immediately sent him packing. Well aware of the importance of the man who would command the galley, he requested a replacement. Two days later, one arrived. James was again dismayed. John Thompson had only one hand. In place of the other was a steel hook. Again James complained, but the Naval Board official was adamant: Thompson would man *Endeavour*'s galley.

The overly zealous official told James, wryly, 'It's his left hand he lost, and he's right-handed.'

'Can he fillet a fish with one hand? Or peel an onion?' James demanded.

'Be assured that he can,' the official shot back. Then he added, sarcastically, 'And perhaps, given your family name, you could assist him.'

Cursing under his breath, James signed Thompson's papers.

And all the while, at the back of his mind was the concern about the civilian retinue, underwritten and led by Joseph Banks Esq, who would join the ship in Plymouth. How would this lubberly farrago of scientists and artists cope with shipboard life during a voyage around the world?

He made better progress with his insistence that the crew have adequate clothing. Aware from his years in Canada that the high southern latitudes would be bitterly cold, even in the Southern Hemisphere summer, James insisted that thick woollen 'Magellan' jackets, along with 'Fearnought' canvas waterproofs be provided for all his men by the Navy Board. Conscious too of the need for fresh air and personal hygiene below decks, he asked that ventilation scuttles be cut into *Endeavour*'s lower decks. To his surprise, the Naval Board agreed to these requests without demurring.

On 30 July he was summoned to the Admiralty headquarters. There, wearing his new gown uniform with its navy blue full gown coat, cream cuffs and matching buttoned waistcoat, he was greeted by secretary Philip Stephens. He was shown into the Hall, where several of the Lords, including Lord Hawke, awaited him. The Earl of Morton and two other members of the Royal Society, Dr Bevis and the Astronomer Royal, Nevil Maskelyne, were also in attendance. James had seldom been in such esteemed company, and he concentrated on trying to remember the names of the notables as each shook his hand. There was an air of tense expectation in the room, of a suppressed but building momentum.

They all took seats at the long oak table. After James gave them a positive report on the refit of *Endeavour*, coffee and cake were brought in. Stephens left the room and returned with two rectangular, sealed envelopes on a silver tray. He handed them to Lord Hawke.

'Your instructions, Lieutenant Cook,' Hawke announced, gravely. 'The first to be opened now, and to take effect immediately, the second to be opened only after the first instructions have been executed.' He handed them to James, who placed the second envelope on the table, and opened the other.

He read the instructions, which were written in a confident, clear hand. Stephens's, James presumed. They instructed that he should depart Gallions Reach for Plymouth, where *Endeavour*'s complement should assemble and final provisioning of the vessel would be carried out. The crew would receive their clothing and two months' wages in advance. Following embarkation and the reading by the commander of the Navy's Articles of War, the vessel should put to sea. It should proceed to Madeira and there take on fresh victuals and wine, and thence proceed to Rio de Janeiro, and around Cape Horn and on to Port Royal Harbour on King George's Island, to arrive there by May 1769. The party should then prepare for the scientific observation of the Transit of Venus across the face of the sun, on 3 June, 1769. Following the observation, he was to open and follow the Admiralty's second set of instructions.

Although there was nothing in the first instructions which surprised him, James still felt a surge of anticipation as he read them. And the contents of the second envelope intrigued him. Although he made some mental speculations about the nature of the second set, he was sworn to honour their secrecy until next year's astronomical observations had been successfully carried out. Stephens handed him the inked quill, and he signed and dated two copies of the instructions. He handed one copy to the secretary and placed the other in his leather case. Then he stood and bowed towards the assembled Lords, and declared:

'Thank you, my Lords. Be assured, I will do my utmost to serve our King and country to the very best of my ability. I am confident that the expedition I am about to lead will bring honour and distinction to England.'

There were spontaneous murmurs of approbation at this short speech. Lords Townshend and Brett clapped. Then the stooped, craggy figure of the Earl of Morton got to his feet. his cheeks were sunken, his skin sallow. He began to speak, wheezing like a bellows as he did so.

'My Lords, the Royal Society also has instructions for Lieutenant Cook.'

The Lords all looked at him sharply. Clearly, this development had not been expected. Was the Society going to be obstructive in some way? The relationship between the Admiralty and the Royal Society, although necessarily symbiotic for the forthcoming expedition, remained uneasy following the Halley fiasco and the Dalrymple controversy.

Morton extracted a sheet of notepaper from the inside pocket of his top coat, placed wire-rimmed spectacles on his nose, cleared his throat noisily, then began to read, wheezily.

'Instructions offered to the consideration of Lieutenant Cook, Mr Banks, Doctor Solander, and the other Gentlemen who go upon the Expedition on Board the *Endeavour*, prepared by the Earl of Morton, President of the Royal Society.'

Lord Morton's paper reminded the men concerned to, 'Exercise the utmost patience and forbearance with respect to the Natives of the several Lands where the ship was to touch.'

To 'Check the petulance of the sailors, and restrain the wanton use of Firearms. To have it still in the view that shedding the blood of these people is a crime of the highest nature ... as they are the natural, and in the strictest sense of the word, the legal possessors of the several Regions they inhabit ...'

Morton read on, ignoring the fact that the frowns on the forehead of the Lords of the Admiralty were deepening.

'... every effort should be made to avoid violence ...' '... the Natives should be treated with distinguished humanity ...' '... No European nation has a right to occupy any part of their country, or settle among them without their voluntary consent ...'

As James listened to Morton's reading, he thought that these unusual instructions must surely have been precipitated by the *Dolphin* expedition's shooting of the natives on King George's Island last year. As such, he concurred with most of Morton's suggestions. Cannon fire against stones was a shamefully unequal duel, he thought, and it seemed to him that the 'hints' were both enlightened and compassionate. When Morton had finished the reading, he handed the sheet of paper to James.

But around the table there were audible mutterings of discontent and expressions of consternation. Glaring at the Earl, Lord Hawke said, 'Am I to understand that your *instructions* mean, Morton, that the marines and crew of *Endeavour* shall not defend themselves against attack by hostile natives they might encounter?'

Removing his spectacles, Morton returned Hawke's accusatory glare with a hooded look of his own. He brought a big open hand down on the table, emphatically. '*Defence*, most certainly, Hawke. But *attacks* should be avoided. Unlike the natives of the uncivilised world, we are a people blessed with civilisation and humaneness. As an enlightened nation, we must do our utmost to spread and share our advantaged way of life with those who lack our civilised way of life.' Still glowering, he sat down.

At this point James felt the need to intercede. The last thing he needed was ongoing enmity between the Admiralty and the Society.

He stood up. 'My Lords ... both the Admiralty's instructions, and the Society's suggestions, I will follow to the utmost of my ability. The expedition has manifold ambitions and intentions, and will necessarily demand a great many judgements to be made as it progresses. Those judgements will be mine, and mine alone to make.' He glanced down at Morton's paper. 'I can assure the Society, my Lord, that every effort will be made to avoid bloodshed, including the blood of my crew. I can also assure you that the customs and interests of the natives will at all times be considered and respected.' He paused again, his eyes panning the assembly sternly. 'In that, as in all other matters pertaining to the expedition, I give you my word.'

Around the table, there were murmurs of approval. Lord Hawke was nodding; Lord Morton also gave James a short but deferential nod.

Out on the street, Philip Stephens shook his hand. 'Thank you, Cook, for your diplomacy.'

'Thank *you*, Stephens. Captain Palliser has told me how instrumental you were in my appointment. Please accept my gratitude.'

'Your appointment was due entirely to your own abilities.' He gripped James's shoulder. 'It's immensely satisfying to see you in officer's uniform. It has been long overdue. Good luck, and safe passage.'

In the coach back to Mile End Road, the Admiralty and Royal Society instructions secure in his case, James could now only worriedly anticipate his next meeting, and his next farewells.

Removing his hat, he walked into the house. The boys ran to him and wrapped their arms round his legs. 'Papa! Papa!' He tousled their hair, then went into the parlour, where Elizabeth was sitting, knitting.

The boys followed him into the room. Young James picked up a sheet of paper from the floor and thrust it at him. 'Look what I drew, Papa.' It was a pencil drawing of a ship, with sails squarely rigged, flagged with a Union Jack. 'It's your ship, Papa.'

'I know, I can tell,' he said admiringly. 'It's a fine drawing. I will take it with me.'

'And here's my drawing, Papa,' said Nathaniel, handing it to him. It was of a cannon, spouting orange and red fire.

'That looks very real, Nathaniel. I like the colours. I will take that with me too.' He turned to Elizabeth. 'Where is little 'Lizbeth?'

'Upstairs, sleeping. How was your meeting?'

'Satisfactory. I was given my instructions.'

'When do you leave?'

'Tomorrow. *Endeavour* will be taken down river by a pilot. I will take a coach to Deal with Charles Green and join her there, then sail her to Plymouth Sound.'

She got up and walked to him unsteadily, holding her stomach. He enfolded her in his arms.

'Have you decided on a name for the new child?'

'I think ... Mary, if a girl, after my mother. Or Joseph, if a boy. After the Bible story. Joseph and the coat of many colours. My grandmother used to read it to me.'

James nodded. 'Both are fine names.' He hesitated. 'I am so sorry that I will miss the birth, Elizabeth. And by such a short time.'

She looked beseeching. 'There is no chance that your departure will be delayed?'

He shook his head. 'It cannot be. Every week is precious, now.'

She looked away. 'Yes. For both of us.'

He slept fitfully on the last night, aware that Elizabeth too was finding it difficult to sleep. She hugged him tightly from behind, murmuring his name from time to time, and from time to time too he felt the baby move. Its time was very near, that was obvious. It seemed as anxious to arrive as he was to depart. At some time before dawn, he heard muffled sobs, and felt a dampness on the back of his nightgown from Elizabeth's tears. How long would it be, he wondered, before they were together again in this way?

At first light he slipped from the bed, then carried hot water from the kitchen where Susan had lit the fire, shaved and put on his uniform. His packed sea chest was in the hall, by the front door, alongside his polished boots. His other luggage had gone ahead of him, and was already stowed in *Endeavour*. Susan boiled him two eggs which he ate quickly, then she made tea. He poured two cups and carried them upstairs. He went into the room where the children were still sleeping soundly, and placed a kiss on each of their cheeks. Then he went into the larger bedroom. Setting one of the cups down on the bedside table, he placed his hand on Elizabeth's cheek.

'Beth,' he said softly. Rolling onto her back, she opened her eyes.

'Yes?'

'Tea?'

As she hauled herself upright, he placed pillows behind her back, then handed her the cup. She blinked away the vestiges of sleep and pushed her long hair aside. He loved her like this, when she first woke, she seemed so natural, almost childlike in her fresh-faced innocence. She sipped the tea, then asked, 'When does the coach come?'

'At seven.'

'What time is it now?'

'A few minutes before.'

'Oh ...'

He held her tenderly, murmuring into her warm neck. 'I will be safe, dearest. I will be back. And I will bring you my story, which I will share with you. And only you.' She made no reply. Instead she clutched him, as if drowning. Then at last she drew back, wiping away tears with her hand, unable to speak. He placed his hand on the unborn child and held it there for a few moments. Then he kissed her, once, on her right cheek, and left the house.

Fourteen

He was taken down the Thames to Deptford, then took a coach and four with Green the astronomer along the North Downs, with warm rain driving in from the south. When they called at a Maidstone inn for a meal, Green surprised James by consuming an entire bottle of Bordeaux by himself. Already he was revealing himself to be, as others had forewarned, overly fond of the grape.

The coach then crossed the river Stour and took them down to Deal. The sky had cleared and there she was, *Endeavour* at anchor, standing off, half a mile from shore, all sails furled. The wind had dropped and the Red Ensign fluttered at her stern. James felt a rush of pride and exhilaration at the sight. Beside him, Green belched, and James caught a gust of vin rouge. He'd better be sober when he observes the southern heavens, James thought. 'She looks so *small*,' said the astronomer, 'for a circumnavigation.'

James gave him a disapproving look. 'Drake's vessel was a good deal smaller, Green. *Golden Hind* was but 300 tons.' As they stood watching, they saw *Endeavour*'s pinnace being hoisted from the deck, then lowered to the water. Putting on his tricorn hat, James said, 'Time we were piped aboard. Plymouth calls.'

The dockside days were hectic. More provisioning, stowing of gear and scientific instruments, loading of fodder for the four-legged animals and feed for the poultry, the clattering, cumbersome arrival of the marine contingent, final adjustments to rigging and sails. Hawkers and peddlers were allowed aboard, and separated the men from much of their two months' wages. The gentlemen came aboard, among them the frail-looking, long-nosed young artist Sydney Parkinson and his equally delicate-looking fellow Scot, Alexander Buchan, the short, deeply serious Finn, Herman Sporing, the cheery Swede Dr Solander, and others of the civilian retinue. Everyone seemed purposeful and eager as they and their equipment came aboard, everyone sensed an impetus building.

But as James observed the busy proceedings from *Endeavour*'s forecastle, he grew increasingly impatient about the one crucial figure who had not yet appeared. *Where was Joseph Banks?* He detested lateness, it was something which he would not tolerate.

When, by the morning of 13 August, he had still not appeared, James wrote him a curt note, instructing that he report to the ship immediately, and dispatched it express from the Plymouth post office to the botanist's London adgown.

Late in the afternoon of the next day two coaches drove up alongside the ship. Banks stepped out of the first coach and onto the dock. James was relieved at the sight of the botanist, but his tardy arrival still irked him. As Banks emerged from the coach he looked up the ship, noticed James standing on the forecastle and waved at him cheerily. A lanky greyhound leapt from the coach, followed by another, both wagging their tails furiously. The first dog went straight to the nearest bollard, lifted his leg and anointed it. The second sniffed his deposit approvingly. James winced at the sight. *Just what was needed on a ship, two pissing dogs*. Cats were useful on a ship, as ratters, but dogs? A pair of tall negro men and a boy emerged from the second coach, then stood staring at the ship. The driver of the second coach and his assistant began to unload chest after chest from the roof and piled them on the dock. As he watched the luggage mountain grow, James thought, good God, we'll need a second vessel.

Banks, gowned in a heavily embroidered waistcoat and green velvet frock-coat, white silk scarf around his neck, strode up the gangplank and onto the main deck. Smiling, he removed his three-cornered hat and held out his hand. 'Cook, how good to see you.' He looked around the ship. 'All is going according to plan?'

'It is, Mr Banks.' He looked the young botanist straight in the eye. 'But you're late. Where have you been?'

Banks drew back, but just a little. He said carefully, 'When your note was delivered I was at Covent Garden. At the opera. '

James blenched. 'The *opera*?'

'Yes. I was there with my fiancée, Harriet Blosset.' He took a handkerchief from inside his cuff and dabbed his brow. 'We left as soon as I read your missive, so missed the final act. I went directly home, and there made preparations to leave immediately.' He sighed in what seemed to James to be a transparently insincere way, then added, 'Harriet was deeply upset.'

Through gritted teeth, James said brusquely, 'We are all leaving loved ones behind, Mr Banks.'

'Yes, yes, I presume so.' His dark eyes oozed false emotion. 'Lovers, mothers, wives.' He tucked the 'kerchief back inside his cuff. 'Harriet is going to embroider more waistcoats for me while I'm away.' He looked around. 'Now, where is my cabin?'

By August 20, they were ready to put to sea. James told the boatswain John Gathray to order the crew and the gentlemen to assemble on the main deck. Then, flanked by lieutenants Zachary Hicks and John Gore on the quarterdeck, he read the Articles of War to the ninety-three men below.

'....All flag officers, and all persons in or belonging to His Majesty's ships or vessels of war, being guilty of profane oaths, cursings, execrations, drunkenness, uncleanness, or other scandalous actions, in derogation of God's honour, and corruption of good manners, shall incur such punishment as a court martial shall think fit to impose, and as the nature and degree of their offence shall deserve ...'

'... No person in or belonging to the fleet shall sleep upon his watch, or negligently perform the duty imposed on him, or forsake his station, upon pain of death, or such other punishment as a court martial shall think to impose, and as the circumstances of the case shall require ...'

It all, it took him half an hour to read the thirty-five Articles. Below him on the deck, there were mixed expressions: boredom and scepticism on the faces of the old hands, aware that many of the clauses would be more honoured in the breech than in the observance. Whenever had serving seamen *not* uttered profane oaths and cursings, or displayed drunkenness and uncleanness? But among the younger crew there was visible apprehension at the mention of certain phrases. '...punished with death ...' 'shall suffer death ...' '...the detestable sin of buggery...' '.,.. sodomy with man or beast ...' '... punished with death ...' 'punishment...' '...punishment...' 'punishment ...' '...death ...' '...death...' '...death ...'

For all assembled, however, hearing the Articles read aloud was a reminder, if one was needed, that after *Endeavour*'s mooring lines had been cast off and she was properly at sea, the commander's powers were absolute. For good or ill, his Word was Law. And although the civilian retinue was not subject to his authority, they would certainly be behoven to his sailorly judgements.

Then, for the first of many occasions, nature intervened. A storm blew in from the south-west, accompanied by driving rain, obliging *Endeavour* to remain in Plymouth Sound. The gale did not abate for three days. Impatient to be under way, the men paced the decks, staring into the storm or stayed below, smoking and cursing the weather. James remained in the Great Cabin, organising and re-organising his equipment, and hearing Banks and the other naturalists next door doing the same. He pinned little James and Nathaniel's drawings to the wall beside his bunk. Elizabeth's journal, as he already thought of it, was locked in a drawer of the cabin's writing desk. There it kept company with the Admiralty's second set of instructions.

He went over *Endeavour*'s manifest and inventory once more.

Ninety-four persons, including: eight officers, a master and two master's mates, forty able seamen, seven midshipmen, the boatswain and his mates, the surgeon and surgeon's mate, twelve marines (including a sergeant, a corporal, a drummer and nine privates). A cook (one-handed), carpenter, carpenter's mate, gunner, sail-maker and armourer. Twelve gentlemen and their servants.

Two dogs, three cats, one veteran nanny goat (delivered to the ship by Samuel Wallis), four pigs, seventeen sheep, twenty-four chickens and ducks.

Eighteen months' supply of provisions: ship's biscuit, flour, salted beef, pickled beef, salted pork, pickled pork, suet, cheese, raisins, peas, oatmeal, onions, wheat, sugar, oil, vinegar, salt, 1,200 gallons of beer, 1,600 gallons of brandy, arrack and rum, 3,032 gallons of wine (to be taken on in Madeira).

Scientific instruments: two reflecting telescopes, two wooden stands for the telescopes, an astronomical quadrant, an astronomical clock and alarm clock, a brass sextant, a barometer, one journeyman clock, two thermometers, a dipping needle, one portable wood and canvas observatory.

The library: the recently published Nautical Almanac, containing tables of the Moon, for calculating longitude by the Lunar Method, a translation of Tasman's voyages, accounts of the voyages of Anson, Dampier, Byron and Wallis, a copy of

Dalrymple's 1767 pamphlet Discoveries made in the South Pacific, Previous to 1764, containing the routes traced by every traverser of the ocean to date, volumes of botanist Linnaeus's illustrated works, classical writings, the works of Shakespeare and Cervantes, the King James Authorised Version of the Bible. Ink pots, goose feather quills and large quantities of writing paper.

Armaments: ten four-pounder carriage guns, twelve swivel guns, muskets, pistols, swords and a good store of ammunition.

Trifles for winning the friendship of natives and carrying on trade with them: nails, mirrors, fish-hooks, hatchets, beads red and blue, scissors, dolls ...

At last, on the afternoon of 26 August, James ordered the gangplank struck, the topsails loosed, the Jack and the Blue Peter raised, and gave the order for *Endeavour* to put to sea. The master, Robert Molyneux, took the wheel, assisted by Master's Mate Richard Pickersgill. The mooring lines were cast off. Watches were posted by the other mate, AB Francis Wilkinson. Men scampered up the shrouds, yards and ratlines; the foresail and fore topsail were unfurled.

A crowd had gathered on Plymouth dock to watch her leave: Admiralty people, Naval Board officials, curious locals and a handful of the town's harlots who had provided relief for the crew in the preceding days.

As her foresails filled and *Endeavour* moved away from the dock the spectators took off their hats and waved them. Slowly the ship moved out into the sound. Her mainsail, maintopsail and main topgallant were fully let go; sheets were secured. As these sails too filled, *Endeavour* began to make steady progress south, driven by a light nor'easter.

From the quarterdeck he watched the shoreline recede and the green fields of Devon fade into the grey haze. This was it, this was the culmination of all he had worked towards during his twelve Royal Navy years: a bark of his own to command, a voyage to the far side of the world to observe the transits of two planets, the chance to claim new lands for King and country, the challenge of charting the coasts of those lands to make it safer for other Englishmen to follow. Feeling the chill of the breeze on his face, he lifted his chin to the wind. This was it, this was the real beginning.

GRAEME LAY

Fifteen

James rose at dawn the next morning. Brought a bowl of hot water by his servant, the short, chipper New Yorker, Joseph Magra, James shaved and gowned. Then, nodding a brisk 'Good-day' to John Trusslove, the marine corporal standing watch at his cabin door, he went up on deck. It was drizzling and the sea was lumpy, but the wind was still a steady eight knots and *Endeavour* was making way on a WNW course. He checked the bearings with Pickersgill, who was still at the helm, now with Charles Clerke, then went back below. In the Great Cabin he stared for some time through the window at the blue-grey waters of the receding Channel. Then he drew the chair up to the escritoire and his writing slope, dipped his quill in the inkwell and began to write.

26 August, 1768

At 2 p.m. got under sail and put to sea having on board 94 persons including officers, seamen, gentlemen and their servants ... near 18 months provisions ... At 6 a.m. the Lizard bore WNW1/2W 5 or 6 leagues distant.

26 August, 1768, 7 Assembly Row, London

It was a hard labour, the hardest she had yet known, beginning in the late afternoon the day before and ending just before daybreak. By lantern light, near exhaustion, she was handed the bundle by Ella Thompson, the midwife, who had washed and wrapped him and burned the afterbirth in the downstairs fireplace.

'Another boy, Mistress Cook,' Ella said. But there was concern rather than joy in her voice.

Teary, Elizabeth took the tiny package, from which emitted a staccato cry. Pushing aside the wimple of cloth, she peered into the tiny face. 'Joseph,' she whispered, 'Joseph.'

Ella, face drawn, brought the lantern closer. 'He seems to have trouble with his breath, Mistress,' she said. As Elizabeth stared, her own breath caught. The tiny face was screwed up, and instead of the healthy red the others had all had, his cheeks and eyelids had a bluish tinge. His eyes remained closed, and bubbles were escaping from the tiny mouth.

'Put him to the breast, Mistress,' urged Ella, 'that will give him strength.' Holding the child with her right hand, Elizabeth hastily drew aside her gown with her left, exposing her engorged, leaking breasts. Carefully she put the tiny, gasping mouth to her left nipple. There was a faint fluttering of the bluish lips, then the little head turned away.

James put away the official journal in the top drawer of the escritoire, unlocked the lower drawer and took out the other. He set it down on the writing slope, then headed the first page:

27 August, 1768

My dearest Beth

After some days' delay, caused by a squally gale, we are at last at sea, on a course for the Bay of Biscay and Madeira. My thoughts have much been of you and little James, Nathaniel and Elizabeth. Doubtless the children are greatly excited by the imminent arrival of a baby brother or sister, a little Mary or a little Joseph.

Endeavour *promises to be a sturdy vessel for the purposes of this expedition. She is not a vessel of great size or beauty, but I already have a sense of her strength and determination. The holds are crammed, the animals penned, the crew set to with a will, the marines carry out their drills amidships (a spectacle which causes the crew great amusement), and the civilian scientists, though unused to extended life at sea, discuss the voyage constantly and pore over the charts and journals of those who have gone before us.*

For myself, I must emphasise that this appointment and expedition is the culmination of all I have striven for, since I first walked out of that haberdashery in Staithes, a disenchanted young man, twenty-two years ago. The responsibility I have now been given is considerable, but I am confident that I have the abilities to bring the venture to fruition. We have a goodly store of Union Jacks aboard, which I intend to have raised above all those lands I shall claim for our King. Another of my ambitions is to arrive home without the loss of a seaman to scurvy. I will be enforcing a strict dietary regimen to ensure that this aim is accomplished.

But the strongest incentive to bring the ship home safely with its manifold aims accomplished, is to once again be united with you and our beloved children. My thoughts are much with you, night and day.

I have in my cabin a copy of the poems of Thomas Gray, whose verse I was first alerted to by my sister Christiana, following the death of our mother. His Elegy Written in a Country Church-Yard *continues to move me deeply. When I consider this couplet from the poem:*

No children run to lisp their sire's return

Or climb his knees the envied kiss to share

I am reminded painfully of the absence of little James and Nathaniel, and their awe over their Papa's sea tales. I will have many more to tell all four of our children, upon my return.

With all my love, James

1 September 1768

Latitude 44° 56' Longitude 9° 9' West of Greenwich

Very hard gales, with some heavy showers of rain, the most part of these 24 hours, which brought us under our two courses, broke one of our main topmast puttock plates, washed overboard a small boat belonging to the Boatswain and drowned between 3 and 4 dozen of our poultry which was worst of all. Towards noon it moderated so that we could bear our main topsail close reefed. At midnight wore and stood to the southward.

Although the pitching had reduced, the ship was still rolling violently in the Biscayan swells. As he put his journal away, he heard the unmistakeable sounds of human retching, coming from the other side of the lobby, in the adjoining cabin. He left his own, crossed the lobby and knocked on Banks's door. There was a groan from within which James thought meant, 'Enter'.

The two greyhounds were soundly asleep, just inside the door. Banks was lying face down in his cot, hanging over the edge. There was a pool of vomit on the floor below. Hair damp with sweat, face greenish, shirt smeared with vomit, he convulsed again. A stream of pink dribble was added to the pool on the floor, a distillation of the claret he had indulged in over dinner. Suppressing a smile, James said: 'You'll not be cured of the sickness by lying in your cabin, Banks. Get up onto the quarterdeck and into fresh airs.'

'I cannot move. I feel as if I am dying.'

'You will, by choking on your own puke, if you stay below. Get up on deck, man!'

Groaning, Banks hauled himself upright and put his bare feet on the floor. As he did so the ship rolled again. He was thrown forward, then hurled against the port wall of the cabin. He picked himself up, moaning like a pole-axed calf. James opened the door which led to the wardroom, Banks stumbled through the doorway, then tacked across the room towards the companionway. More vomiting noises were coming from Dr Solander's cabin, which adjoined his own. James smiled to himself. The sea was no respecter of class, rank or qualification. And what a grand thing that was.

13 September 1768
Island of Madeira
Fresh breeze and clear weather. At 8pm anchored in Funchal road in 22 fathoms water. Found here His Majesty's ship Rose *and several merchant vessels. In the morning new berthed the ship and moored with the stream anchor half a cable on the best bower and a hawser and a half on the stream.*

13 September 1768
Dearest Beth,
I trust things are well with you and the children, especially little Joseph/Mary, who must now have put in his/her appearance. I trust the new child and his/her siblings thrive. It will be little Elizabeth's second birthday next week, and I know that that will be a happy occasion for all. She is the sweetest child, and makes me think that every man should have a daughter. Wish her every happiness from her now-distant but ever-devoted Papa!

We are now at our first port of call, Funchal, the capital of Madeira, a Portuguese possession off the western coast of Africa. The port is located in a great natural amphitheatre. A British man 'o war, Rose, *is also here, a sight which gladdened my heart as we joined it in the roadstead. The island is very steep, with soaring peaks and terraced vineyards covering the lower hills. There are no proper roads or carriages on the island, the land being so precipitous, so the people rely entirely on horses for transport. The island is quite different from anything I have previously seen, unlike even Spanish Tenerife, where I was on* Pembroke, *a decade ago, though equally sweltering.*

Mr Banks, Dr Solander and their retinue have disembarked and are the guests of the oddly named Mr Cheap, the British Consul here. No doubt they will be carrying out their botanising and will return to the ship with a collection of exotic foliage and blooms for Sydney Parkinson to draw. He is an artist of considerable talent, I have already observed, having witnessed his sketching of the Atlantic sea creatures dredged up by Banks in his trawl. Parkinson, a Quaker like my former employer, John Walker, draws at remarkable speed, but renders his subjects faithfully in all their minute detail.

We have lost our first crew member, and, by a strange twist, not at sea but in port. Endeavour's *quartermaster, Alex Weir, a Scotsman, was carried to the bottom of the harbour whilst trying to retrieve the stream anchor. He had become entangled with the anchor's buoy rope. The anchor was retrieved, along with his body. The incident was most regrettable, as Weir was a capable seaman who had served for many years. I will be writing to his family, giving the account of his death and expressing my sorrow for their loss. We have impressed a sailor from an American ship in port, John Thurman, to take Weir's place. He is from the colonial town of New York, but as such is British, so he will be at home among the crew.*

The Portuguese are strong allies of Britain, so we are treated well here. Provisions are supplied on reasonable terms, and Sam Evans has taken over the Quartermaster's duties from the drowned man. As this will be our last port for some time, the crew is busy stowing provisions we have taken aboard here. These include a live bullock (for future fresh meat), fresh beef, onions (20 pounds per man), more poultry and, Madeira being an island of vineyards, over three thousand gallons of wine. There is the usual maintenance to carry out, caulking, varnishing of spars and masts, and repairs to sails and rigging. The scrubbing of the decks, top and below, is continuous, as cleanliness of the ship is paramount. So too is diet. After two men refused to eat the fresh beef issued to them three days ago I did not hesitate to let the cat out of the bag. I was scarcely able to believe that seamen could refuse fresh beef, which to most is a luxury. The miscreants were given twelve lashes each, for disobeying my dietary orders. If it is necessary to flog the proper diet into the crew, so be it. (Although I ordered the entire crew to witness the flogging, Mr Banks went below to his cabin while it was administered, the gentleman evidently having no stomach for the lash).

We weigh anchor in two days' time, bound for Rio de Janeiro, the capital town of Brazil, another Portuguese colony. We cannot be there in less than two months, so much hot hard sailing lies ahead of us, including crossing the line. This letter I will hand tomorrow to the master of HMS Rose, *as she leaves for Portsmouth in a week's time, in the hope that you will receive it by November.*

If only you were able to send me your news, so that I can learn of the newest little one! Be assured, dearest, that my thoughts are constantly with you and our children, as I go about my daily duties, serving our nation and His Majesty.

My love to all,
James

13 September 1768
Assembly Row, Mile End
'Mama. *Mama!'*

Elizabeth stared into the cradle, hands held up in supplication but unable to move, unwilling to reach down to the child.

Baby Joseph's face was the colour of whey, his little eyes open but sightless. Elizabeth's mother, Mary, ran into the bedroom from the parlour. 'What is it? What's wrong?'

Turning away from the cradle, Elizabeth put her face in her hands. 'Little Joseph. I fear ... I fear...'

Mary bent over the cradle. She put out her hand and laid it gently on the tiny white cheek. Although Joseph's skin was soft, it was also deathly cold, and Mary withdrew her hand sharply, as if she had put it into a flame. Giving a little cry, she turned away and went to her daughter. The two women clutched each other, not speaking, sobbing. Tears streaming, Elizabeth said, at last, 'He was not yet three weeks. *Not three weeks ...'*

The two boys stumbled into the room in their night-gowns, Nathaniel holding his piece of flannel to his face. Their eyes were huge with fright.

'What is it, Mama?' whispered James. 'Mama?' He looked from her to the cradle, then back.

Elizabeth went to the boys, knelt, and put her arms around them. Voice catching with anguish, she said, 'Baby Joseph has gone.'

'Gone?' said Nathaniel, frowning at the cradle. 'Where?'

James said sombrely, 'Mama means he has died, Natty. Joseph was sick, and now he's died.'

Little Elizabeth appeared in the doorway, sucking her thumb. She looked around the room, blinking with bewilderment. 'Joseph? Died?' Then her face too collapsed, and she ran, wailing, to her mother and grandmother.

They gathered beside the miniature grave, adults and children gowned in black, the women with dark veils over their faces. The block stone tower of St Dunstan's Church, Stepney, overlooked the sprawling graveyard, whose remains included hundreds of victims of London's Great Plague of 1665.

This autumn morning it was bitingly cold, the sky matching the drabness of the gravestones which jutted crookedly from the ground. Most of the leaves of the oak and elm trees in the grounds had fallen, and lay strewn dark and sodden over the graves and tombstones, staining them with dark brown smears. A mound of yellow earth lay at the head of the little grave.

The burly, bewigged figure of the Reverend George Downing, draped in his cassock, read from a large open Bible as the tiny pinewood casket was lowered into the grave on ropes by two black-coated attendants. Unable to bear the sight, Elizabeth turned away and fell against her mother, who held her. Their faces frozen, unable to comprehend any of what was happening, James, Nathaniel and Elizabeth stood in a row at the foot of the grave, staring into the little pit. The attendants withdrew, the minister completed his rites. Still unable to look, Elizabeth heard but did not see him recite the bitter words.

'We therefore commit his body to the ground; earth to earth, ashes to ashes, dust to dust ...'

Elizabeth looked up into her mother's ashen face. Her voice broken and barely audible, she said, 'James never even knew the child existed.' She stifled a cry. 'And he may never know who he was, or what happened to him ...'

The Reverend Downing bent, picked up a handful of dirt and tossed it into the grave. Elizabeth's stepfather, John Blackburn, black top hat under his arm, came forward and did the same. The minister said to James and Nathaniel, 'Now boys, you do as we have.'

James stared up at the commanding, frocked figure, then down into the grave where the coffin of his baby brother had been splattered. 'Go on,' said the minister, 'throw down some dirt.'

The five-year-old shook his head, defiantly. 'No,' he said, 'I won't. And neither will Natty. We won't throw dirt on our brother.' Taking Nathaniel's hand, he walked away from the grave.

James spent much of the morning of the 29 September at the masthead, taking bearings and studying the currents which showed up against the shiny surface of the sea like stretch marks on skin. Towards the stern of the ship an albatross was skimming the water, its great pinions veering this way, then that, only inches from the surface. *Endeavour* was making sluggish progress in these latitudes, as the four veterans from Wallis's expedition – Gore, Clerke, Pickersgill and Molyneux – had predicted. The ship's sails were slumped, her buntlines slack, the tell-tales barely moving. The Ensign at the sternpole and the Jack at the bow both hung limp. Yet for James the view from the masthead was captivating.

For the last two weeks he had been in new waters and was well aware that they were bound for even newer ones. And what a mighty ocean this Atlantic was! Its vastness became more apparent by the day, its moods ever-changing. The barometer climbed and temperatures increased to the hottest James had ever experienced. A day last week – September 22 – had marked the vernal Equinox. Now too, when the ship's noon bell tolled, the sun was almost directly overhead. Although he and Charles Green were excited about this benchmark, it produced mainly grumbles from others of the Endeavours about the intensity of the heat. Consequently James had ordered John Ravenhill, the ship's elderly sailmaker, to rig a canvas awning made from a spare sail around the mainmast and over the quarterdeck, as a shelter from the increasingly ferocious sun.

Directly below him, on the main deck, six barefoot seamen were on their knees, canvas buckets beside them, scrubbing at the decking. Others were below, scrubbing the orlop deck, in accordance with James's instructions. Turning towards the stern, he saw that Banks and Solander were busy in the yawl, which was tethered to a cleat on the poop deck. The two naturalists, naked from the waist up, backs lobster-red from the sun, were dragging a net from the sea and emptying the contents into buckets. As James watched, Solander hauled on the yawl's painter and began to pull it alongside amidships, taking it out of James's sight. Banks's two greyhounds were prowling the main deck, impatiently awaiting their master's return to the ship.

30 September 1768

Dearest Beth,

How precious this time is, towards the end of the day, when the Great Cabin is mine alone and I can record my personal thoughts and concerns with you. It is autumn now for you and the English winter will be impending. Strange to consider, when for us the days are unendingly hot. I hope that little Elizabeth's second birthday celebration was a happy event for all of you and I trust that our household's delivery of firewood and coal have arrived in good time, as ordered by me from the yard in Wapping before I left. James and Nathaniel are not too young to assist the coal-heavers with the unloading of the fuel and the fire-making, as I instructed them to.

We have now been at sea for over a month, making steady progress south-west. Endeavour *serves us well and the crew goes about its business purposefully. There are the occasional frustrations, the details of which I will not bother you with, as well as the occasional amusements, such as the crossing the line rituals, which all entered into willingly. I forsook my rum ration rather than be ducked from the yardarm, which seemed to me altogether too undignified a procedure for the ship's commander to undergo. Most of the gentlemen did likewise, but those of the crew who were ducked took the matter in good spirits. A great deal of grog was drunk as part of the equatorial ritual, but this did not concern me, as it is part of a long-established maritime tradition.*

Another entertainment for the crew is afforded by the drill practice of our dozen marines, who exercise their 'skills' on the main deck under the command of their Sergeant at Arms, John Edgecombe. Their antics greatly amuse the crew, due to the clumsiness of their weapon handling and their lack of military formation. I can only hope that our marines shoot straighter than they march. Some do not know their right foot from their left. Their unco-ordinated activities remind me of a troupe of soldier clowns

I once witnessed as a boy, in a travelling circus which visited Great Ayton. I believe it will take Sergeant Edgecombe many more sessions to have his rabble resemble anything else but such a circus act.

I have by now formed some opinions of the personalities of those with whom I share the ship, and it occurred to me that you may wish to learn something of the nature of these men, in order that you may better imagine the company I am keeping.

Joseph Banks you have heard me speak of already. Suffice to say he is as opinionated as he is privileged, and his extravagant entourage (much scientific equipment, plus fellow-scientists and canine company) cause me frustration at times. However I am bound to add that his enthusiasm for his work is limitless and transfers to those around him. His curiosity about the natural world over-rides all other considerations. He is inordinately fond of his two greyhounds. The male, Lord, follows his master everywhere, while the female, Lady, is usually content to stay below.

The Swede Daniel Solander is a scientist of high repute, and utterly dedicated to his profession. Although Banks treats him with some condescension, Solander is mild-mannered and does not retaliate, doubtless because he is aware that he owes his inclusion on the expedition to the Englishman. I have an impression that Solander is the superior cataloguer, probably due to the tutelages of his mentor, another Swede, Carl Linnaeus.

Herman Sporing is quietly reflective, modest, but a man of many parts. He was once a watchmaker, so will be useful if anything goes awry with our instruments. I came upon him yesterday on the quarterdeck, sketching the seascape, and his artwork was impressive. His command of English is inferior to that of Solander, his accent very thick.

Sydney Parkinson, our Scots artist, I admire. Slight of build and quiet of manner, the young Quaker has the elongated fingers of the artist and is able to capture and colour his subjects with astonishing speed. His swiftly executed drawings of sea creatures also depict them as objects of great beauty.

Alexander Buchan, a young Scotsman and a close friend of Parkinson's, is very reserved. As his strength is landscape drawing, he has not yet had the opportunity to demonstrate his principal skills. He is very pale and somewhat tremulous, and spends most time below in his bunk. He seems unwell much of the time, but whether this condition is from the sea or his frail physique I cannot tell.

You will undoubtedly be concerned for the well-being of your young cousin, Isaac Smith. Be assured, the boy is fit, attends to his duties diligently and appears to be relishing the voyage so far. He shows a keen interest in cartography, following his learning while he was on Grenville, *and I have admitted him to my cabin on one or two occasions, to share with him the courses I am charting. I was quite touched when he said to me the other evening, 'Sir, I wish you to know that I seek no special treatment from you because your wife and I are cousins. If I transgress, I must be punished like any other member of the crew.' To which I replied, 'No, Isaac, because you are a member of my family, if you transgress, you will receive* double *the usual punishment.' When he looked askance at this comment, I added, 'I jest.'*

I will report on others of the ship's complement as we proceed further south and I am able to form firm opinions of their respective qualities.

Your loving husband,
James

He tied his quadrant to his belt and climbed down the rigging to the platform on the mainmast. As boatswain Gathray tolled the noon hour on the ship's bell, he took another reading, noted the latitude – 17° 32' north, estimated their longitude – 21° 11' west– and returned to the deck. Nodding approvingly at the men scrubbing the foredeck, he glanced up and saw that the sails were billowing, but with light airs. He went to the wheel and checked the course with Pickersgill, then went down the aft hatchway and through the gunroom and the lobby to the Great Cabin door, which was closed. He shoved it open, then stopped and caught his breath.

Banks and Solander, still barefooted, were bent over the long table on which James laid out the charts. The table was covered with a sheet of canvas, on which was a mass of seaweed and sea creatures: crabs, shrimps, jellyfish, anchovies and juvenile eels. All were writhing or jumping across the canvas in an attempt at escape. Banks was pouring fluid from a large jar into a series of smaller, glass-stoppered ones; Solander was parting the seaweed with his hands and separating the sea creatures from it. Seawater was dripping from the table onto the floor of the cabin, which reeked of fish and weed. Several shrimps flicked their way across the canvas and onto the floor, where they continued their hapless bid for freedom. A purple crab scuttled to the edge of the table, dropped and joined them. Standing in the doorway, James set his hands on his hips.

'What in God's name is going on here?'

Banks looked annoyed, Solander merely blinked. Banks said, 'I should have thought, Cook, that it is perfectly obvious. Solander and I are sorting our collected sea creatures. Preparatory to having Sydney draw them.'

'*In the Great Cabin?*'

'Certainly. And why not? It is sufficiently commodious, for both the classifying and the drawing.'

James inhaled sharply, then said, 'I beg to differ. Might I remind you that that is the very room where I chart this ship's course and write up my log. I cannot share my cabin with these ... zoological activities.' He pointed at the floor, where the patch of seawater was growing larger and sliding across the boards. '*Look at the mess.*'

Shrugging, Banks said, 'I will fetch my niggers to clean it, when we have finished.'

'*And when will that be?*'

Banks turned to his colleague. 'What say you, Solander? Two hours?'

The other man shrugged. 'More like three, if Parkinson is to complete his drawings.'

James gritted his teeth. The impertinence of Banks was almost unbelievable; his carrying out such activity here absurd. The name 'Great Cabin' was a misnomer, *Endeavour*'s was smaller than most commanders' accommodation. Folding his arms, James declared:

'Gentlemen, I am obliged to remind you that I am the commander of this ship. The Great Cabin is my domain. It is the place where I plot the ship's course and record its progress. I cannot share my cabin with ...' he waved his hand at the squirming aquarium on the long table '...with a heap of jellyfish and shrimps!'

Banks pouted, set the jar of preserving fluid down on the table, wiped his wet hands on his breeches and said, carefully,

'And *I*, Cook, am obliged to remind *you*, that I am paying for this expedition. Were it not for my zoological and botanical ambitions and interests, and my capital, this vessel would still be conveying coal from the Tyne to Wapping.' James waited grimly for him to add something like, '... *and you would still be floundering around the coast of Newfoundland.*' But instead Banks declared, 'I intend to return to England having classified for science, by the Linnaeus system, every exotic and unrecorded creature and plant I am able to procure.' He scooped up a large jellyfish. 'For example, I am naming this one Cyanea solandri.'

James met his dark gaze without flinching. 'That is your right as a scientist Banks, and I do not question it.' He waved his hand at the messy table. 'But I will not tolerate this *filth* in the Great Cabin.'

Banks tried not to smile as he said, 'Your initials may be JC, Sir, but you are not Jesus Christ.'

'I never claimed to be.'

'Yet you display messianic tendencies, at times.'

'Your imagination gets the better of you, Banks.'

'Better to have an imagination than to be obsessed with latitude and longitude.'

James flushed. This he would not have. 'Were it not for that *obsession*, as you call it, then you would not survive. None of us would.' He allowed a pause. 'I do not question your right to carry out your scientific work, Banks. What I am questioning is your right to do it here.'

Banks threw back his head and roared with laughter.

'Then where do you suggest we carry it out, in the officers' head?'

James shook his head. 'No,' he said, 'I have a better suggestion.'

A compromise was reached. Banks, Solander and Parkinson would have the use of the Great Cabin from the first morning watch until the midday bell. The long table was to be left immaculate afterwards and the scientists' specimens removed. From midday the cabin would be given over to the main meal with the officers and the gentlemen, and thereafter, for the remainder of the day, it would be James's and his alone, for him to make his journal entries and plot the ship's course.

27 October, 1768

My fortieth birthday today, Beth. An auspicious milestone? Perhaps, two score years being more than a good many naval men attain. My mind was less occupied with my birthday than with thoughts of little James, whose fifth birthday it was two weeks ago. How those five years have flown. You will recall how I mentioned to you that his schooling should now begin, and that I had contacted a Mistress Edmondson, of Stepney Green, who runs a children's teaching establishment there. I have paid his fees for the next year, so it would be as well to enrol him soonest. As for birthday presents for James and the other children, they will have to wait until my return, but be assured, their gifts will be exotic.

The ship's officers somehow learned of my birthday – I suspect it was cousin Isaac who put the word in the ear of Zachary Hicks, my second-in-command – and a toast was proposed to me at dinner today in the Great Cabin, Banks having supplied four bottles of Bordeaux wine from his private store for the occasion. A short speech seeming to be in order, I replied that my birthday did not mean a great deal to me, what truly mattered was the satisfactory discharge of my obligations to King and Country. To return to England having executed my instructions would allow me to whole-heartedly celebrate future birthdays. This sentiment was greeted by general approbation from the officers and gentlemen present, then we returned to the business of dinner.

As I am becoming more familiar with others of the ship's company, I will describe the nature of their personalities.

Zachary Hicks is a Londoner, from Stepney. Aged only 29, he has been at sea for sixteen years. He is highly dependable, as one would hope, and a man of few words, which is much preferable to the opposite. He has a constant, hacking cough which keeps his fellow-officers awake at night. Monkhouse the surgeon administers hot concoctions of laudanum and herbs to him, but with little effect. I suspect he may be consumptive.

You have already heard me speak of John Gore, the American who is my third lieutenant. Having already circumnavigated the world twice, he is rather too fond of reminding me of this fact. He already yearns to be back in the South Sea, which he assures me is the greatest ocean on Earth. A keen marksman, when off duty he spends much time in the bow with his musket, shooting at seabirds and dolphins. 'Trigger-happy' I believe is the term to describe this tendency. Two days ago he succeeded in hitting a dolphin and it was hauled aboard. (Banks immediately seized the creature, and he and Solander spent hours dissecting it and examining the contents of its stomach. They then delivered the remains of the corpse to the cook for preparing for dinner. I found the meat somewhat oily, but palatable nevertheless).

The mate, Robert Molyneux, a Liverpudlian, is only 22, but was part of Wallis's crew so also has valuable experience for this voyage. He is an excellent cartographer, and has proudly shown me the charts he has drawn, including some of Tierra del Fuego. I was impressed by his surveying work.

Dick Pickersgill the master's mate is only 19, but has an old head on his young shoulders. He too is an aspiring cartographer but now has little time for drafting activities, being kept busy with his navigating duties, as well as organising the stores and the stowing of the anchors. He also regales the Endeavours with stories of his amorous conquests in 1767 on King George's Island, thus whetting their appetites considerably for similar pursuits.

Others of the company who are vital to the expedition I will report on at a later date.

As it is my intention to take Endeavour *to Rio de Janeiro for her next provisioning, I will dispatch my letters to you via the next ship which leaves that port for England. Thus you may receive them in time for Christmas. Thereafter it will be some time before I am able to send more dispatches to you, being as we will in the vast reaches of the unknown South Sea. But be assured, Beth, my writings to you will not cease, and my thoughts will always be with you and our four little ones, wherever I may be.*

My love to all at Mile End Row,
James

13 November 1768   Latitude 22° 54' south; Longitude 43° 10' west
A gentle sea breeze and clear weather. Standing along shore for Rio de Janeiro, observed that the land on the sea coast is high and mountainous, and the shore forms some small bays or coves

*wherein are sandy beaches. The Sugar Loaf Hill at the west
entrance to Rio de Janeiro NNW distant 4 or 5 leagues. At 9am
sprung up a light breeze at SE at which time we made sail for the
harbour, and set the pinnace with Lieutenant Hicks and Charles
Clerke up to the city of Rio de Janeiro to acquaint the Viceroy with
the reasons that induced us to put in here; which was to procure
water and other refreshments; and to desire the assistance of a
pilot to bring us into proper anchoring ground. At noon, standing
in for the harbour.*

Spyglass to his eye, James first focused on the entrance to
Guanabara Bay and the islands nearby, then *Endeavour*'s pinnace,
moored to the landing stage on Rio de Janeiro's quay. Behind the
town the land swelled steeply to a range of mountains, their
summits concealed by white clouds. He saw the pinnace cast off,
but moments later saw too that it was being rowed not by Hicks
and Clerke but two soldiers in brown uniforms. Another soldier
was coxing the boat. Puzzled, James went to the port side of the
ship as it came alongside. Calling up to him, one of the officers, a
stout young man with a black moustache, informed James in
passable English that the two *Endeavour* officers were in custody
and would be released only when the ship's commander came
ashore.

'On whose authority are they in custody?' James demanded.

'The Viceroy of Brazil, His Excellency Don Antonio Rolim de
Moura. He also requests that his officers come aboard your ship
and inspect its cargo.'

James felt a tugging at his sleeve. It was Gore. He pointed
shoreward. 'Look.' Another boat was being rowed towards the
ship, its five oarsmen gowned in white military uniforms.

Sixteen

Sweat was beading James's brow now, not just from the tropical heat. They had to provision here, there was no alternative. But why this suspicion? Brazil was Portuguese, and therefore an ally of England. All around the decks, the other Endeavours were watching the looming confrontation closely; James could feel tension mounting around the ship. All the crew had been staring at the land, observing its tempting luxuriance, longing to take a turn on leave ashore. He was also aware that this would be the first test of his diplomacy. Leading over the mid-deck rail, he called down to the Portuguese party:

'This is a ship of the Royal Navy of England and I am her commander. Foreign nationals cannot come aboard without my permission.'

One of the officers, a swarthy, narrow-faced captain, called back in passable English, 'And foreign nationals cannot land in Rio de Janeiro without the Viceroy's permission.'

There was a long pause. Turning to his lieutenant, James said, irritably, 'I fear we have no option, Gore. We must allow them their little exercise, if it permits us a speedier landing.' He laughed, drily. 'And apart from the usual, all they'll find are Banks's pickled prawns.'

Gore nodded. He called down to the boat. 'Your party may come aboard.'

The captain was the only one of the five officers who spoke English. Speaking slowly but officiously, he asked James what the object of his expedition was, how many men were aboard, what cargo *Endeavour* carried and what her armaments were. After answering the questions candidly, stressing the scientific nature of the voyage, James ordered Molyneux and Pickersgill to take the officers on a tour below decks.

After they reassembled on the forecastle the captain nodded curtly at James and announced, 'I will now make my report to His Excellency, the Viceroy.'

'And my two officers? When will they be released?' James demanded.

'After the Viceroy has received my report.' He gave a quick bow. 'His Excellency also instructs that you attend a meeting with him tomorrow morning at his palace. At nine bells.'

James and Gore exchanged glances, looks that said, *Who on earth do these people think they are?*

Wearing his gown uniform, James stepped from the launch onto the stone steps which led up to Rio de Janeiro's quay. The waterfront was crowded with carriages, carts and pack-horses all jostling for position. Goods were being loaded and unloaded from and into schooners and barges by barefoot, semi-naked black men. Seeing the shackles around their ankles, and their cowed expressions, James realised with a jolt, *Slaves.*

The Paco Imperial – the Imperial Palace – was a baroque, two-storeyed building with walls of stone and a half-tiled terracotta roof. Set back from the waterfront and separated from the quay by a broad, paved plaza, it had an ornate marble portal and several balconied windows with iron latticework railings on its upper floor.

James was met at the palace door by an older black man with frizzy grey hair, wearing a red frock-coat and matching breeches. The servant showed him into a large, carpeted drawing room, lined on two sides with glass cabinets, one filled with books, the other with bright pottery plates. On the rear wall was a small fireplace and a polished brass fireguard. A portrait of the extravagantly wigged Portuguese King hung above the fireplace, while on a lower level there were several other paintings, of the Lisbon waterfront and merchant ships flying the Portuguese flag. The elderly black man left the room, then returned, stood in the doorway and announced, 'His Excellency Don Antonio Rolim de Moura, Viceroy of Brazil.'

He was about sixty, a short man with a puffed out chest, a mane of white hair, widely-spaced hazel eyes, a grey complexion and lips which were thin and bloodless. He wore a gilt-edged frock coat with outsized gold epaulettes, a white silk scarf, buckled shoes and a frog-buttoned red waistcoat, over which was a broad scarlet sash bearing the coat-of-arms of Portugal. James extended his hand.

'Lieutenant James Cook. Of King George of England's ship, *Endeavour*. His Majesty wishes me to convey to you his best regards to the people of Brazil.'

The Viceroy shook James's hand, nodded peremptorily, then waved him towards a pair of padded armchairs under the bay window. 'Be seated, Lieutenant. I have ordered coffee.'

After the coffee was brought in and poured by the black retainer, Don Antonio explained that he had served time in London with the Embassy of Portugal there, and so understood English well. But his manner was cold and distant. Determined not to waste time on niceties, and to make his intentions plain from the outset, James set his coffee cup down on the table and said:

'My expedition requires provisions, Your Excellency, including the replenishment of our water casks. And my ship will need to be heeled and cleaned while she is in port.'

The Viceroy considered this for a few moments, puckering his thin lips. Then he said, 'Your first request I will agree to. However the goods must be purchased through an agent of my office, and there will be a surcharge of five percent on all provisions, including water.' He paused. 'Your second request is refused. Your vessel cannot be allowed to dock here. And apart from purchasing officials, only you will be permitted to come ashore. When you do so, an officer of my army will accompany you at all times.'

For a few moments James was speechless. The demands of this over-gowned little man, who resembled one of Banks's puffer fish, were outrageous. Then, leaning forward, he uttered a one-word reply.

'Why?'

The Viceroy's eyes narrowed. 'My officers reported seeing many armaments, and many strange instruments on your ship. Ones they had never seen before. Large telescopes, and ...' his English failing him, he waved one hand wildly '... this and that.'

'Those *instruments*, are for astronomical observations, and for the collection of natural specimens. Here and in other parts of the world. And the armaments are for self-defence, as any ship must allow.'

The Viceroy said, slyly, 'Why should I believe you?'

James was tempted to reach over and tear the puffer fish's outsized epaulettes from his shoulders. But instead he said, carefully, 'Need I remind you, Viceroy, that your country and mine are allies.'

'And might I remind *you*, Lieutenant Cook, that it is within my power to have *no one* from your vessel land in this port.' All pretence of affability gone, he almost spat his next words. 'You speak for your King, I speak for Portugal's, and I obey his orders. He knows full well that Brazil has suffered greatly, for years, from British privateers, and from French smugglers and spy ships. Our coastal towns have been looted, our people killed, our precious metals plundered.' Sweeping back his white hair, he added sourly, 'Is it any wonder that your ship is not welcome here?'

'The vessel I command is neither privateer nor French,' said James, severely.

'But it may still have dishonourable intentions.'

James drew a deep breath, then after a considered pause, declared, 'Our intentions are entirely peaceful. All we require are provisions and fresh water. And a little time for our gentlemen scientists to botanise ashore.'

The Viceroy's already sceptical expression hardened. 'You informed one of my officers, did you not, that you provisioned in Funchal but two months ago.'

'That is correct.'

'So why do you need to do so again?'

'We next face a hard passage, doubling Cape Horn. Perhaps months without fresh water, fruit and vegetables.' He paused, then added forcefully, '*As you must well realise.*'

There was silence for some moments, during which mistrust and acrimony hung between the two men like a miasma. Then, leaning back in his chair, the Viceroy said coldly, 'I do not believe that your expedition has scientific motives. It is my belief that your so-called scientists are here to spy on my country.'

Anger welled up inside James and for a moment threatened to erupt. His scar began to throb, and he clenched and unclenched his right hand. Then he too lay back in his chair, willing himself to stay calm. He would not allow himself to be upset by this absurd little man. But neither would he abase himself. He said, carefully,

'Your accusations are unfounded, Viceroy. Our motives are intended purely to further the interests of scientific discovery. So, once again, I request that my vessel be allowed to take aboard the provisions we will need for the next stage of our voyage.'

The Viceroy looked away, then thrummed on the arm of his chair with his right hand for a few moments. When his gaze returned to James he said, dully, 'You may provision here, Lieutenant, but all purchases are to be made through an agent of this palace.' His hands gripped the arms of his chair. 'As for your other requests, they are denied. Apart from yourself and your provisioners, no member of your crew is allowed ashore.'

James stood up. The man was impossible. Placing his tricorn hat firmly on his head, he nodded curtly at the Viceroy, who remained seated. 'Since you do not take my word on the other matters, I will take my leave. Do not expect to see me again.' He went to the door. Then, turning, he said, 'I will be reporting your hostile attitude to both my King's Lords of the Admiralty, and to the Portuguese authorities in London.'

He called the officers and gentlemen to the Great Cabin before the midday meal and apprised them of the acrimonious meeting. Heads were shaken in disbelief at his account. James concluded, 'The provisioning must be done, even at the extortionate terms demanded. But only the Quarter Masters are to go ashore, to supervise the purchases. The rest of you must remain aboard the ship.'

Banks looked aghast. Leaping to his feet, he cried, 'But what about myself and these other gentlemen?' He waved his hand towards Solander, Sporing and Parkinson. 'We have urgent work to do. There must be a great many new specimens here, on this coast, to be observed and collected. We cannot just ... *pass them by*.'

James considered this, well aware that it was true, and aware too that the scientists were officially beyond his command. But the risks were great. Should the scientists be apprehended ashore, he had no doubt that the entire ship could be seized by the Portuguese authorities. He went to the cabin window, and stared across the water at the coastline, and the forested mountains in the distance. Then, turning back to the others he said, matter-of-factly, 'What you and your entourage do over the next days is your business, Banks.' He paused. 'But I urge extreme caution and common sense while you are doing it.' The scientists looked at each other and smiled, well able to read between the lines of the statement.

Although the anger James felt at what had happened subsided, it did not vanish. Instead it smouldered inside him, like a fire in a peat swamp. He spent the next days at his writing desk, drafting, then rewriting reports on the Viceroy's lack of cooperation until they were ready for dispatch home.

Banks at first sent his servants ashore at night, furtively, to collect plant specimens. But after they returned with a large number of exotic plants, his curiosity could not be constrained. The following night he and Parkinson stole ashore after nightfall in the yawl, rowing and being carried along the coast by the flowing tide. Once ashore they collected more plants, observed the brilliant plumage of Brazilian birds and even fraternised with some locals, who showed them, then sold them, vegetables, tropical fruits, flowers, pork and poultry. These goods and the specimens were smuggled back to the ship, where Solander catalogued them and Parkinson drew their likenesses. The scientists were in their element, the secrecy of their forays adding a frisson of excitement to their discoveries. Fully aware of what was happening, conniving at the surreptitious forays, James avoided speaking of them until at supper one evening Banks said to him, 'Do you recall, Cook, how I once purchased scalps from the Canadian Indians?'

James nodded. It was not an easy story to forget.

Banks continued, a mischievous glint in his eye, 'I thought I might return to the ship with the scalp of the Viceroy, to add to my collection.'

Although James was amused by this suggestion, he simmered still over his treatment at the hands of the Viceroy. Why was it, he wondered, that some men, when given authority, misused it so sorely? Umbrage ate away at him through each day they remained anchored off the coast, intensifying his frustration. In order that the time in the harbour be not entirely wasted, he ordered the men to clean the ship thoroughly, inside and out, and all items of their clothing washed thoroughly. Although there were mutterings from the crew at these instructions, and aggravation at seeing a nearby, enticing shore but not being able to land on it, the work was done. But at the same time the level of grog consumption on the orlop deck rose.

On 20 November James received a report from boatswain Gathray that seaman Nicholson had sworn at the officer on watch and that seaman Sutherland had refused to carry out cleaning duties. Without hesitation James called all hands on deck and from the forecastle read out the charges, then sentenced the two miscreants to twelve lashes each.

The gentlemen remained below, the marines lined up across the forecastle and the crew assembled before the mainmast in the mid-morning heat, their expressions sullen. First Sutherland was stripped to the waist and tied to the gratings by the boatswain. Then John Reading, the boatswain's mate, was handed the lash by Gathray.

The mate, barefoot and naked except for his calico trousers, gave Sutherland his first five, pausing between each stroke and bringing his arm over in elliptical orbits. As he did so James, watching from the port side of the deck, realised what was happening. He could tell full well when a man was shirking, when the lash was not being applied whole-heartedly. Reading was directing most of the cat's force at the grating. By the sixth stroke , when still no blood had been drawn and Sutherland's back was merely striped, James stepped forward and seized Reading's arm. 'Hold it there, Reading.' Turning, he called to Gathray. 'Boatswain, this man is withholding the punishment. Take the lash yourself and *lay it on*. And when the others are done, Reading is to receive a dozen.'

Gathray nodded. 'Aye, Sir.'

Sulkily, Reading handed the cat to Gathray, then slunk to one side to await his thrashing.

When James entered the peace of the Great Cabin, Sydney Parkinson was at the table, huddled earnestly over a large sheet of paper. There was a paint brush in the long thin fingers of his right hand, and pencils, more brushes and a paint box beside him. Also on the table was a wilted cutting of a flowering plant. James greeted him, then said, 'How is your work progressing?'

The young man set his brush down. 'Satisfactorily. Banks and I returned last night with several new specimens. I have been working on one of them this morning. A climbing plant.'

'Am I permitted to see it?'

The Scotsman slowly spread his hands, unveiling the drawing. Smiling bashfully, he said, 'It requires a little more work, yet.'

James leaned over his shoulder, his eyes widening at what he saw.

The painting was of a thorned branch which bore dark green leaves and vivid orange flowers. Both leaves and flowers were veined, but the flowers were delicate and bunched in groups of four or five, bursting forth from the end of their very narrow stems. Each leaf, each flower, each vein, had been rendered and coloured with exquisite detail. The stems were a very dark green, and several of the flowers carried protruding pistils of the same colour. Although the specimen he was copying was dying, Sydney's drawing was bursting with life.

James said, 'That is very beautiful. The flowers are superbly detailed.'

'Thank you. But they are actually bracts. Coloured leaves. The flower itself is inside the bract. And the plant is a vine.'

'Are they indigenous to this coast?'

'I believe so. In this climate they appear to proliferate, and the bracts make a grand display of colour. Not just this orange specimen, but there is a purple variety, too. Spectacular is not too strong a word for this plant, Sir.'

'Indeed. Have you named it?'

'Dr Solander has. He calls it Calyxis ternaria.'

Seeing the wonderful result of Parkinson's foray to the shore calmed James's spirit. The young Scotsman's abilities were consummate. James's own hydrographic drawings captured major landmarks – promontories, islands, bluffs, beaches – but Parkinson's skills were capable of capturing and depicting the minutiae of the natural world. For this reason James did not regret conniving at Banks's and Parkinson's forays ashore in this place. An accumulation of botanic paintings of such quality would go a long way towards justifying the expedition.

At last, after nearly a month in limbo off Rio, *Endeavour* was almost ready to resume her voyage. Provisioned – albeit expensively – freshly caulked and cleaned from stem to stern, on the morning of 2 December James ordered her anchors raised and her topsails hoisted, in order to turn down the harbour and test the rigging.

He stood on the poop deck, Pickersgill and Clerke at the wheel below him, as the men scurried up the shrouds. 'Let 'em go!' called Molyneux, and the topsails were released, dropped and filled with the easterly breeze. Out wide on the fore topgallant, three men clung to the rigging as Pickersgill and Clerke swung the helm three spokes to port. As they did so a gust of wind came across the harbour and *Endeavour* lurched a few degrees to larboard. When she did so the man furthest out on the topgallant arm lost his footing, fell back, then plunged like a gunned duck into the harbour.

The cries went up, from half a dozen throats. 'Man overboard!' 'Man overboard!' 'Man overboard!' Lines were thrown over the port side, the yawl was hastily hoisted out.

Half an hour later a sodden body was hauled up on the end of a boathook by Gathray and laid out on the foredeck, the upper body and face as bleached as a sheet.

'Who is it?' James called down to Gathray.

'Flower, Sir. Able Seaman Flower.'

3 December, 1768
Dearest Elizabeth
We sail shortly from Rio, bound for Cape Horn. Rio de Janeiro has proved to be principally a port of frustration for us, because of the lack of cooperation of the Brazilian authorities, and we will not be sorry to quit its shores.

You may recall my mentioning the name of a seaman called Peter Flower, who served me for some years as an AB on Grenville. *It is my sad task to report that Flower fell from the rigging and was drowned before he could be retrieved from the harbour. I cannot understand how he came to lose his footing, as he was an experienced top man and the winds were light at the time. It is possible that he had been drinking, as the men have been hard at the grog during our time in port, due to frustration at seeing the enticing coast of Brazil yet not being able to go ashore. Flower was no stranger to the mug, and I once had occasion on* Grenville *to have him flogged for drunkenness. Yet he bore no grudge towards me and I had no hesitation in signing him on for this voyage. Flower has been replaced with a local Portuguese, Manoel Pereira. He is grateful for the offer, and as such is the only obliging person we have encountered at this port-of-call.*

Others of Endeavour*'s company I am now better acquainted with are:*

Charles Clerke, the second master's mate. He is from Essex, and although only 25, is a veteran of Byron's voyage. He is a great recounter to the crew of sea stories from the earlier voyage, although I suspect many of his tales are embellished. It is a source of great pride to him that his Accounts of Very Tall Men, Seen Near the Straits of Magellan, *was published in the Royal Society's* Philosophical Transactions *last year. In this account he claimed that the men of Patagonia were nine feet tall. But after several handles of grog a few nights ago, he confessed to me, no doubt in the awareness that we would touch Patagonia before the year is out and that his falsehood would then be exposed, that he had perhaps overstated the men's height. 'The Patagonians were,' he said, 'about your height, Lieutenant Cook.' The man may thus have a bright future as a writer of romantic stories.*

Charles Green, our 33-year-old astronomer will be crucial to the success of the expedition when the transits occur. He is certainly a man of considerable experience, and was appointed to the position of astronomer on Endeavour *by the Royal Society. He relishes the work, and is seen regularly on the after deck by day deploying his astrolabe and at night peering at the cosmos through his scope. A rotund figure, he consumes great quantities of food and drink, and as he does so his face quickly turns the colour of a boiled lobster. However he takes his position with suitable seriousness, is of a generous disposition, and spends some time tutoring the officers and other supernumeraries in the art of astronomical observation.*

I cannot forebear to tell you something of John Ravenhill, the sail-maker and oldest man aboard. No one is sure of his age. When I asked him he was evasive, mumbling something about 'in my seventh decade, Cap'n', but others swear he is nearer eighty. It is somewhat strange to have among the crew a man older than my own father. How such an ancient mariner can maintain such an important role I cannot comprehend, particularly as he is either drunk or half-drunk most of the time. But he can mend a torn sail in a flash, with gimlet, needle and thread, as well as maintaining the spares, and so long as he continues to do so with efficiency he can imbide all the grog he is allowed.

Yuletide now approaches for you and the children in London. How strange it is for me to think of you all in the ice and snow, while here we experience nothing but heat and warm rain. I cannot

quite get used to the fact that here, south of the equator, the seasons
are entirely reversed. However when we reach the higher latitudes,
by Christmas if all is plain sailing, then the temperatures will be
more akin to England's.

From now on we will be entering unknown waters, following the
east coast of South America and intending to double Cape Horn by
the New Year. I know how concerned you will be for my safety,
Beth, but be assured I will take the utmost care of my crew, my ship
and myself. The veterans of Wallis's expedition I am sure will be
valuable in assisting me to chart the safest possible passage from
the Horn into the South Sea.

I will conclude now and dispatch this letter, along with my others
to you, to the shore for conveyance on the ship leaving soonest for
London. My deepest love to you, little James, Nathaniel, Elizabeth
and our newest child, along with warmest wishes to your mother
and stepfather. As it will be Nathaniel's birthday on the fourteenth
of this month, please convey to the little lad his Papa's love and
assure him that my thoughts will be with him on his special day.

A merry Christmas and a peaceful New Year to you all!
Your loving husband,
James

Day after day *Endeavour* butted her way through the South
Atlantic. Although the hours of daylight increased as they moved
into the higher latitudes, temperatures fell. He issued the crew their
Magellan jackets and fearnoughts and when the ship ran into gales
he put the crew on 'watch and watch' – four hours on, four hours
off – which meant they seldom slept adequately. But *Endeavour*'s
performance in the long rolling swells of the ocean pleased him,
and his affection for the ship was growing. She was now far from
her North Sea home, yet plucky and tough, she showed no sign of
pining for it.

Led by Banks, the scientists worked ceaselessly, collecting
marine specimens, observing birds, netting a swarm of butterflies
which were blown onto the decks, seeing their first seal.

Although James remained respectful of Banks's energy, the
naturalist continued to test his resolve.

It was after dinner in the Great Cabin that he raised the subject
of another port-of-call. Seated under the stern window, sipping a

177

glass of claret, he said: 'I am certain, Cook, that the Falkland Islands offers fine botanical prospects. It would be greatly to our advantage to call there.'

The ship rolled and the cabin lanterns swung. James closed one eye. *'Our* advantage, Banks?'

'Yes. Solander, Sporing and myself. No scientist has yet collected specimens from those islands.' He set down his glass. 'It would take but a week ashore.'

'And the consequent loss of a week's sailing.' James paused. 'Might I remind you, Banks, that the primary aim of this voyage is to make King George's Island by May.' He took a mouthful of cheese. 'No number of exotic insects could atone for missing the transit.'

Banks looked grumpy. At the table, Solander stared down at his plate. Banks said, 'Perhaps then for just a few days. Three even.'

James shook his head. 'Time is too precious, so do not raise the question again. Besides, it is said that the Spanish now have a hold on the Falklands, so there is a chance that we would not be welcome there.'

'Are you saying that we will not touch land until we make King George's Island?'

'I am saying no such thing. We will certainly need fresh water by the New Year, so we will go ashore at Tierra del Fuego.'

Banks sniffed. 'A barren place, from what I have read.'

'Perhaps. But the long daylight hours we now have must surely produce plant growth, in spite of the low temperatures.' He turned to Solander. 'Would you not say so, Doctor?'

Solander looked thoughtful. 'Long hours of daylight do encourage plant growth, even in low temperatures. That is certainly the case in the high latitudes in Sweden. So Tierra del Fuego may provide good specimens. '

Looking very disagreeable, Banks picked up the claret bottle and helped himself to another drink. He picked up one of the ship's biscuits from the bowl on the table and tapped it, irritably, on his plate. Then, as he stared down at the biscuit, his eyes began to bulge. Dozens of tiny weevils were streaming away from it, swarming in all directions. Cursing, Banks brushed the creatures wildly from the table with his hand.

Unable to help himself, James said, with calculated calmness:

'There we are, Banks. Some wildlife for you to go on with, in the meantime.'

Seventeen

By New Year's Day, 1769, they had made latitude 43° South. Although the temperature had dropped to 48 degrees Fahrenheit and months of hard sailing still lay ahead, both ship and crew were optimistic over the prospects of the new year. After discussing the subject with the other officers, and in particular with Molyneux and Gore, who had passed through the Straits of Magellan before, James decided to take the alternative passage from the Atlantic to the Pacific, through the Strait le Maire. Though longer, it was considered safer.

11 January 1769

Latitude South 54°20', Longitude west from Greenwich 64° 35'

A steady gentle breeze and fair weather. Sounded and had 64 fathoms, gravel and small stones. At 8am saw the land of Tierra del Fuego extending from the west to the SEBS, distance off shore between 3 and 4 leagues. Saw some of the Natives who made smoke in several places, which must have been done as a signal to us as they did not continue it after we passed.

After they succeeded, on the fourth attempt, at passing through Strait le Maire against the prevailing westerlies, James judged that *Endeavour* should drop anchor in an adjoining bay and shore parties be mounted. The place was called the Bay of Good Success, and the date of their landfall was 15 January.

23 January, 1769

My Dear Beth,

It seems somewhat strange to write that new date. '1769'. What will this New Year bring to you and our growing family? Good fortune, I hope. Perhaps you will be able to visit Christiana and my father in Yorkshire in the spring; I know they would love to see you and the children. If you do travel north, then I urge you to also visit the Walkers, in Whitby.

I write from near the bottom of the world, in a bay of the land named by Magellan in 1519 'Tierra del Fuego'. Banks has been anxious to get ashore for weeks, and has tried my patience in this regard. However our principal need is for water and firewood, so while the scientists proceeded with their plant collecting inland, the crew has been attending to more pressing matters.

The scientists had a sorrowful experience while ashore, which they related to us when they returned to the ship. Banks's two negro servants, Richmond and Dorlton, are dead, frozen to death when the weather turned foul and they were caught in the open. Banks and Solander had been inland collecting alpine plants, while the negroes remained on lower land. The scientists were benighted, but lit a fire and survived their night in the open, but the negroes did not survive the ice and snow, even though they had drunk copious quantities of rum (empty bottles were found beside their bodies).

This news greatly saddened me, as Richmond and Dorlton were strong, reliable workers. However Banks did not seem unduly troubled by their demise. Instead he triumphantly showed me the several bags of alpine plants he and Solander had collected, saying, 'The sojourn was a great success, James.' When I reproached him for his lack of compassion over the loss of his two servants, he merely shrugged and said, 'Some losses are to be expected in these latitudes.' I find this attitude perplexing.

Another troubling episode involved young Buchan, the artist. Monkhouse our surgeon, who was also ashore with the party, reported to me that Buchan suffered what he diagnosed as a fit of epilepsy, a disease of the nervous system, probably brought on by the freezing conditions. This is of concern to me, because Buchan is a landscape artist of considerable talent, and before his fit he produced a fine drawing of a Fuegan village. I expect that the coming warmer temperatures will ensure that he will not experience another seizure.

Monkhouse and I spend much time with, discussing the health of the crew. Another older member of the company (he is 37), he does not inspire my confidence, having little knowledge of the importance of diet in combating scurvy, and being short and hunched of shoulder is not himself the embodiment of good health. A withdrawn and unsociable figure, he informed me that he too is keeping a journal of the voyage, and I suspect that this accounts for the hours when he does not appear on deck. His loblolly boy, Nicholas Young, is a great deal more diligent, and Monkhouse's brother Jonathan, one of the midshipmen, is a more appealing fellow as well.

You will remember my anger at the Navy Board's appointment of the one-handed John Thompson as cook. Well, I now must accept that my judgement of the man was premature. He manages the galley with one hand better than many cooks do with two. He has a great fondness for the grog, which accompanies him at all times, but this does not impair his cooking. Meals are such a vital part of shipboard life, and in this regard Thompson is proving an asset to the company. Drunk or sober, Thompson feeds the Endeavours well.

At last we are in the great South Sea, which I refer to now as the Pacific Ocean. A boyhood ambition of mine fulfilled! Temperatures will rise over the coming weeks and the Endeavours should no longer need their Magellans. First though, I will take the ship further south. Then, by February, I hope to be on a more westerly heading, intending to reach King George's Island in another three months or so. There the great prize – the Transit of Venus – will await us.

My love to all, James

1 March 1769

First part fresh breeze, the remainder moderate breezes and clear weather. The result of the observations gives 110° 33' west longitude from Greenwich and exactly agrees with the longitude given by the log, from Cape Horn. This agreement of the two longitudes after a run of 660 leagues is surprising and much more than could be expected; but as it is so, it serves to prove as well as the repeated trials we have made when the weather would permit, that we have had no current that has affected the ship since we came into these seas. This must be a great sign that we have been near no land of any extent, because near land are generally found currents. It is well known that on the east side of the Continent in the North Sea we meet with currents above 100 leagues from the land, and even in the middle of the Atlantic Ocean between Africa and America are always found currents, and I can see no reason why currents should not be found in this sea, supposing a continent or lands lay not far west from us, as some have imagined, and if such land was ever seen we cannot be far from it, as we are now 5,050 leagues west of the coast of Chile.

'Cook.'

'Banks. Good-day.'

'Almost six weeks now, and no sign of land.'

'No sign whatsoever.'

James peered at the open sea, shading his eyes from the sun with his left hand. They remained on their north-west course, beating into the westerly which had prevailed, to a greater or lesser extent, since they had turned away from the icy latitudes. *Endeavour*'s blunt bow, in which the two men stood, was pushing and pitching her way into the ocean which already seemed infinite. Banks followed his gaze, to where the endless, dark blue Pacific swells rolled on towards them. The naturalist's dark hair was tied in a queue with a blue ribbon.

Pointing directly ahead, James said, 'The swells are regular. And my reckonings show that there are no currents in this part of the ocean.'

Banks looked doubtful. 'Is that conclusive disproof of a continent?'

James's gaze swept the misty horizon. 'I believe so. Were there a landmass to the west, there would be currents, and the swells would be refracted. There are no currents, and no refractions.'

Endeavour pitched heavily and Banks gripped the bower anchor fluke with one hand. 'And yet the scholars say there is a continent out there.'

'Scholars? By that do you mean Alexander Dalrymple?'

'Not merely him. From ancient times it has been postulated that such a landmass exists.'

'And you are disappointed that we have not found it. And so nor any new species.'

'Naturally. But we may yet. Although with each day, and each week, and no sign of a continent, my hopes fade.' His attention caught by a movement in the sky, he pointed. 'But there are compensations. Look ...'

To the port side of the ship, a red-tailed tropic bird soared high in the sky. Pure white except for its orange beak and scarlet, bifurcated tail feathers, the beautiful bird wheeled, spotted its prey, then plummeted into the sea. Banks smiled. 'Magnificent. I've named that one "Phaeton erubescens".'

A light mist drifted across the water. Both men ignored it, and in minutes it had passed, replaced by a delicate, gauzy rainbow. From the other end of *Endeavour* they heard the ship's bell toll three times. James studied Banks from the corner of his eye. He could sense, as well as see, the man's disappointment, and for that reason felt sorry for him. His born-to-rule manner could be infuriating, but his fervour for the natural world, and his determination to plunge himself into the unknown, was undeniable. He nodded dismissively at the naturalist.

'I'm going below, I have work to do. Are you coming?'

'No, I'll remain here a while.'

'Looking out for the continent?'

'Looking out for the continent.'

The best place to view the night sky was from the poop deck. Following their supper in the Great Cabin, James and Green would lie on the deck, telescopes to their eyes, staring up at the blazing cosmos. Green, who seemed to be growing fonder of the bottle the further north they sailed, usually brought a supply of port up on the deck with him, alternatively staring at the stars and swigging from the bottle.

As *Endeavour* rolled on in the gentle swell, James lay on his back beside the stout figure of Green, gazing upwards. A little way along the deck, in her pen, the ship's nanny goat bleated twice, then was silent. Staring heavenward, James was struck in particular by the Crux, the Southern Cross, which he had never tired of observing ever since they had entered the southern latitudes. He raised his right hand and pointed.

'There are the pointers, Green, see?'

The astronomer put his scope to his eye. 'Yes. Alpha and beta Centauri. Brilliant.' He set his telescope down, sat up and took another swig of port.

Although the Southern Cross was the sky's smallest constellation, it was also the brightest, blazing from the centre of the Milky Way like a magnesium flare. Its axis was pointing directly downwards, towards the celestial South Pole.

Scope still fixed to his right eye, James said, 'The Coalsack is particularly brilliant tonight.' Focusing on the dark nebula below the Crux, which was surrounded by the countless, blazing stars of the Milky Way, he said, 'I was reading an account of the 1500 voyage of the Portuguese navigator, Cabral. The one who discovered Brazil. Cabral and his men viewed the Southern Cross as a symbol of their religious faith.' He paused. 'I see it more as an astronomical guiding light.' He moved his gaze slightly upwards. 'You can see that the Acrux is actually a close double star. Hence its extreme brightness. See? Green? *Green*?'

When there came no reply, James propped himself up on one elbow and looked over at the astronomer. The telescope had rolled from Green's hand and he was fast asleep.

March 31, 1769

My Dearest Beth,

You are doubtless savouring, or perhaps still anticipating, the arrival of spring. The oaks and elms on Wapping common will be in new leaf and James and Nathaniel will be practising their climbing skills. I hope that the new nursemaid is proving suitable for little Elizabeth and our baby. I also trust that you received the letter sent to you from Rio de Janeiro, in which I outlined my frustrations with the authorities there. Be assured, that episode is far behind us, and we are again in tropical waters, ones which I hope will prove hospitable to us.

We are now passing through the Dangerous Archipelago, islands so low-lying they are close to the level of the ocean itself. The islands are inhabited – we have seen natives on their shores but have had no intercourse with them, preferring to press on towards King George's Island.

After almost eight weeks at sea our supplies of fruit and vegetables are well nigh exhausted. Consequently some of the men are showing the symptoms of scurvy, and I ordered a dietary regime of wort (an infusion of malt) and pickled cabbage for all hands. The men were at first resistant to eating the cabbage, muttering of its strange taste, so I forthwith ordered it served, with some flourish, to the officers and gentlemen in the Great Cabin. The servants having witnessed us eating it with enthusiasm, they reported this to the other decks. As a consequence the crew, having seen or heard of their superiors consuming the cabbage, set to eating theirs with equal enthusiasm. This, combined with the wort, I am confident will keep at bay the scurvy until we close King George's Island. There are diverse ways of getting men to conduct themselves in ways which are in their best interests. Force is but one; example based on the behaviour of their superiors, is another and a far better way.

A deeply distressing incident occurred a few days ago, one which is without precedent in my nautical experience. A marine, William Greenslade, a quiet young man who had hitherto given no offence to anyone, been given custody of a piece of sealskin, taken aboard at Tierra del Fuego. It was the intention of his fellow-marines to slice the skin up and convert the pieces to tobacco pouches. But when they denied Greenslade of a piece for himself, he was evidently offended and took a piece of the skin without authority. After the other marines learned of this action he was chastised by them. To such an extent that at dusk on 25 March the young man went forward and threw himself overboard. When his loss was reported to me I could scarcely believe that such a petty theft could have such a dire consequence. But regrettably, men confined at sea for long periods are capable of irrational behaviour. In this case such behaviour has led to the wholly unnecessary death of a man of just 21 years.

On a less sombre note, the men grow excited at the prospect of raising the island of which they have heard so much from Clerke, Pickersgill and the others who have already experienced its delights. Before we arrive I will need to remind the crew of the principal purpose of our visit, that is, its scientific motives, and I will be strictly enforcing Lord Morton's rules of conduct with the natives.

I will close this now, as Banks will be coming shortly to the Great Cabin to write his journal, and I have no wish to share the table with him while he is doing so. So I shall, as always, lock my writing to you away before he arrives. Although Banks often shares his writing with me, I have no wish to share mine with him. These words are for you and you alone, dearest Beth.

Your loving husband, James

'Land ho! On the larboard bow!'

Joseph Magra's cry from the masthead came at mid-afternoon on the twelfth of April. Some men rushed to the rails, others scampered up the rigging. James stood on the foredeck, spyglass to his eye. Earlier there had been heavy showers, and now mist still hung across the horizon like a curtain. As the ship moved closer to the island, driven by a light nor-westerly breeze, the misty curtain slowly parted, as if in a real theatre, and all hands stared at what lay upon the stage.

The scene before them reduced the crew to awed silence. The island's shadowy, spired mountains seemed to rise straight from the sea. There were gashes in their slopes, as if they had been slashed by a giant's knife, and traces of cloud remained about the peaks. As the ship moved closer to the land, with Pickersgill and Wilkinson at the wheel, the Endeavours saw that the mountains were covered in forests which reached right to their summits. The welcome smells of land, of damp earth, fresh vegetation and wood smoke drifted across the water towards them. They saw too that there was another island not far to the west, also jagged and forested. Training his spyglass on this other island, James thought, that must be the one Wallis named *York Island*.

Putting his scope aside, James and his entire crew stared at King George's Island, which was now coming into focus. In its scale and beauty, James had seen nothing like it. Even the fiords of Norway could not compare. They had grandeur, certainly, but not a beauty such as this. The island's towering peaks, its forests, the azure sea and the reef which surrounded it like a garland – and all overlaid with blinding blueness – it was the most remarkable sight he had ever set eyes on, so beautiful it was almost unearthly.

Staring at the island, he also felt triumph racing through his veins like a flowing tide. He had succeeded in bringing the ship and its crew half way round the world, to this speck of land in the centre of Earth's greatest ocean. Although there was yet much to do, this was the first real prize, and now it was within his grasp. *He had proved he could do it.*

As he continued to stare at the towering mountains, as captivated as the other Endeavours, James was joined at the rail by Parkinson.

'Quite a sight, Sir.'

'Indeed it is.'

'Those mountains, those peaks. They are as uneven a piece of crumpled paper.'

James nodded. 'But far more beautiful. I suppose you cannot wait to paint them.'

'Yes, I am impatient to begin. The verdure ...' He stared shoreward. 'It reaches to the very summits of the mountains. I have seen nothing like it before.'

'Nor I.'

Through the scope James could now see the island's fringing coastal plain, which was covered with stands of palm trees. In places, smoke rose into the sultry air from this coastal forest. Directly ahead of the ship, spindrift was rising from a line of white water. The spray was caused by the encircling reef, James presumed. He swept the long line of white water with his scope, searching it for a break, for the pass that would lead them into Port Royal. Then, observing that there was a cessation in the spray a few points to the west, he trained the scope on it. The water there was as smooth as silk. *The pass.*

The marines were ordered to stand to on deck and the gunners primed the four pounders, just in case. As the ship moved closer to the reef, they heard the staccato sound of drumming coming from the shore and resounding across the water. At the same time, half a dozen canoes with attachments on their gunwales emerged from the pass. Propelled by semi-naked, brown-skinned men, their paddles were dipping and flashing. As they came closer to the ship, cries from the muscular paddlers reached them across the water. 'Taio! Taio!' James called down to where Gore and Molyneux were standing amidships, their gazes fixed on the canoeists. 'What do they say, Molyneux?'

'"Friend". They are offering us friendship.'

But there was puzzlement, too, among the crew, at the male-only welcome. Banks went up to Molyneux, 'There are no women in the canoes,' he said, a touch accusingly. 'Where are they?' The mate smiled. 'Waiting for us on shore, no doubt.'

The gunner, pock-faced Stephen Forwood, raced up to James and Gore. 'How many cannons shall we fire, Sir?' he asked eagerly.

Mindful of Wallis's disastrous introduction to the island, James shook his head. 'There will be no cannon fire, Forwood, the marines will be our only show of force.' At the gunner's disappointed expression he added, 'But keep the cannons primed and the men standing by them.' He turned to Molyneux. 'The pass is a mile to port. Take over the wheel. You and Wilkinson shall bring her in.'

Eighteen

Alongside Port Royal was an expanse of level land, covered with coconut palms and ironwood trees. A river ran down from the mountains above the bay, then across the coastal plain and the promontory before debouching into the lagoon. A long, black sand beach lay adjacent to the bay's western shore. Once she was inside the lagoon it had been a relatively simple procedure to warp *Endeavour* into the bay, loose her anchors, then hoist out the launch to take parties ashore. The anchorage was firm, the weather fair. But after the natives' initial greeting of the ship from their canoes, they remained strangely distant, offering no ceremonial welcome on the land. No Queen was in evidence, or chieftains, just a few young men – who appeared untitled – who emerged hesitantly from the forest, to offer a few plantains and scrawny chickens for the hatchets, cloth and beads the officers offered them. No compliant young women came, to exchange their alluring bodies for nails. The Endeavours were left largely alone. This was baffling, especially for the veterans of Wallis's expedition, who recalled vividly the initial fatal melee and the subsequent reconciliation and delightful licentiousness.

The advantage of this apparent disregard was that the Endeavours were relatively free to establish their encampment. A shuttle was run from ship to shore in the boats, bringing in the equipment, setting up a camp and organising the marines to guard against any theft by the natives. The fortified camp was set up on the flat land beneath the palm trees, immediately named 'Fort Venus', and the marines were posted around it. Molyneux was in charge of breaking out the stores and getting them ashore, Gore took out wooding parties, Wilkinson and Pickersgill supervised the clearing of the ground and the raising of the fort's breastwork. Some of the palms on Point Venus were felled, to create a wide line of sight for the forthcoming observation.

But although a few men continued to trade food for the Endeavours' trinkets, they still seemed wary, apparently content to observe the visitors from a distance. Probably, Molyneux surmised to James, because they remembered the bloodshed from Wallis's visit. But there was also no doubt, the four veterans of the Wallis expedition concurred, that in the two years between their previous visit and this one, something had changed on the island. Again they noted that the people who came to trade seemed of the lower orders. Also, the grand native houses formerly on Point Venus had gone, leaving only rough huts. Of Oberea, the Queen of the island, there was still no sign. There was no abundant quantity of chickens and pigs, nor breadfruit or coconuts, offered for trade. What had caused these changes? As yet, there was no way of knowing. Furthermore, some of the male natives could be seen to suffering from an itching disease, including yellow pustules on their legs. Could Wallis's men have conveyed venereals to the island? This was by no means certain. As surgeon Monkhouse pointed out to the officers, a disease of the tropics, yaws, had very similar symptoms to those of syphilis.

The death came out of the blue.

Seeing a tall young native rushing the encampment and snatching up a sentry's musket, midshipman Jonathan Monkhouse ordered the marines to open fire on the group of which the thief was a part. The culprit was killed, others were wounded and were carried away by the rest. When the skirmish and its consequences were reported to James on the *Endeavour*, he was outraged. Although the theft was most serious, to fire without first attempting to negotiate the musket's return was a folly, he concluded. The Earl of Morton's enlightened instructions and rules of conduct, which he had recently announced to the crew and urged them to follow, had in one fell swoop been violated. Besides which, he well knew, the killing may well impede relations with the Indians. Already, there was fatal damage to repair.

Then, on the evening of the following day, there was a knock on the door of the Great Cabin.

'Sir!' It was Nicholas Young, the loblolly boy.

'What is it?'

'It's Buchan, Sir. He's poorly. Mr Monkhouse wants you to come.'

James strode from the Great Cabin and followed the lad. Buchan's cabin was off the Gunroom, on the larboard side of the ship. Surgeon Monkhouse, was standing beside Buchan's bunk, sleeves rolled up, attempting to hold the artist still by pinning his arms to the bed. He had only succeeded to the extent that Buchan's arms were still. The rest of his body was writhing and his head was moving violently from side to side. His eyes had rolled far back into his head so that only the whites were showing, and his mouth was wide open, the tongue protruding. Behind Monkhouse, James said quietly, 'When did it start?'

'This afternoon. He was on foredeck, drawing the mountains, when he complained of a dizziness. Then, feeling a tightness in his chest, he fell down. Parkinson took him below, and the seizures started. Parkinson sent for me, but I could do nothing for him. Over the last hours the convulsions have become worse.'

At that moment Buchan gave a horrifying cry which subsided to a stricken sob. His face was the colour of candle wax, froth bubbled from the corners of his mouth and his auburn hair was matted. He lunged forward, almost breaking from the surgeon's grip, then uttered another, louder cry and fell back. The others watched helplessly as his moaning became weaker and lower, until at last he was still, his face a white mask, his mouth agape. Monkhouse waited for some moments, then held the artist's right wrist, feeling for a pulse. Turning to James he said thickly, 'He's gone.'

James nodded, unable to take his eyes from the young Scotsman's face. He felt a constriction in his throat at the sight. He was a good man, and a fine artist. He would be sorely missed, and not just by the gentlemen. The crew admired his drawing skills, too. James said to Monkhouse, 'I'll let Parkinson know.'

Parkinson's cabin was opposite Buchan's. When James entered it the artist was lying on his bunk. He turned, his expression imploring. 'How is he, Sir? Has the seizure passed?'

James shook his head. 'It has taken him. It was too strong.'

With a cry, Sydney turned away. 'He was my friend, Sir. My best friend ...'

That evening they gathered in the Great Cabin to discuss where the burial should be. Parkinson suggested they bury him on Point Venus. Banks was agreeable to this, James demurred. 'The Indians may have their own burial rituals,' he suggested. 'And it may be that they conflict with ours.'

Banks frowned. 'But the island has already been claimed for our King. And as the land is ours, surely we can commit Buchan's body to it.'

James shook his head. 'We have already killed one of theirs. Unnecessarily, in my opinion. So we run the risk of further alienating the Indians if we place the body of one of ours in the ground so soon after arriving here.'

'A fair point,' Banks admitted. He turned to the artist. 'What say you, Parkinson? You were closest to him.'

Sydney's eyelids were swollen. Struggling to contain his feelings, he said weakly, 'I believe the Captain is right. We should ... bury him at sea.'

The next morning the body was rowed out well beyond the reef, and committed to the sea. Later, with heavy heart, James added Buchan's name to the Discharged Dead list in his journal. It now read:

Alex Weir, quarter master (drowned), 14 September 1768

Peter Flower, able seaman (drowned), 2 December 1768

Thomas Richmond, negro servant (froze to death), 16 January 1769

George Dorlton, negro servant, (froze to death), 16 January 1769

William Greenslade, marine private, (suicide at sea), 25 March 1769

Alexander Buchan, artist, (died of epilepsy), 17 April 1769

Studying the list, he thought, my sole consolation is that not one died from scurvy.

The following day a canoe came alongside *Endeavour*, occupied by four men and a boy. Noting the men's bearing and fine cloaks, and thus taking them to be chiefs, James beckoned them aboard and called for Gore to join him. Three of the arrivals had square-cut beards, the fourth was clean-shaven; all were tall and powerfully built, with frizzy black hair. All wore cloaks of bark cloth. They stared around at the ship with intense curiosity, then a broad-shouldered man introduced himself as 'Tutaha', and his compatriots as Tupaia, Tairoa and Nunahau. Tutaha, who wore a polished pearl shell pendant around his neck, pointed at himself and said, 'Ari'i rahi, Pare Arue'. James looked quizzically at Gore. 'What does he say?'

'He is the paramount chief of the island. Arue is a district a little way south-west of here.'

As the men were given a tour of the ship, and presented with hatchets, James sensed that reconciliation was in the air. At last, contact had been made with local leaders. These were definitely men of chiefly bearing and importance. And the one called Tupaia, who appeared to be a kind of courtier to Tutaha, could understand and speak some English. He remembered Captain Wallis, and George Robertson, from the *Dolphin*, he told them. Tupaia was tall and graceful of bearing, with flecks of grey in his dark, top-knotted hair. He had prominent cheekbones and shrewd, slightly almondy eyes. James guessed him to be about forty. The boy accompanying the group was about twelve, and Tupaia introduced him as his foster son. Called Taiata and wearing just a loin cloth, he was slim, with bright, darting eyes.

Using gesticulations as well as speech, Tupaia told the Englishmen that after the *Dolphin* left there had been a great war on the island. Queen Oberea's warriors had been defeated and her court destroyed by a rival chief, a man from Tahiti Iti, called Vehiatua. There had been much loss of life. Oberea had taken refuge with a relative in the district of Papara, where a giant marae, Mahaiatea, had been built under Tupaia's instruction. And with the demise of the former queen, Tutaha had assumed the mantle of leader of Tahiti Nui. But throughout the island, Tupaia said with obvious concern, there was still much tension and uncertainty.

Before his party left in their canoe, Tupaia said that Tutaha would like Cook and some of his scientists to visit his court at Pare Arue, an invitation which James was delighted to accept. The shooting of the musket thief, it seemed, had almost been forgiven.

Now that improved relations had been brokered, the produce began to flow to the Point Venus encampment in great quantities. Banks and Solander were deputed to barter for food, principally pigs, chickens, coconuts, plantains and breadfruit. Other things flowed, too. At last, the vahines came: semi-naked young women, their long black hair glossy with palm oil, approached the encampment, seeking nails and beads. Garlanded with fragrant tiare blooms, they expressed their gratitude to the crew freely with their sleek bodies, thus fulfilling the promise that the four Dolphins had assured the others would be awaiting them. The Endeavours began to satiate themselves with the vahines, on the beach and in the forest, delighting in their wantonness and laughter, the scent of their bodies and their brazen quest for baubles. For the men from places like Bristol, Wapping, Portsmouth and Plymouth, used only to the poor, pasty whores of England's docklands, the women of King George's Island appeared divine.

Banks now began to prove himself an effective communicator with the many of the natives, firstly by gesture, then assisted by Gore and Wilkinson, in a mixture of English and their language. Obviously relishing the natural and human history of the island, Banks was the first one to tell James what its original name was.

'It is called "Otaheite", he said. 'Tutaha told me. And the other island ...' He pointed to the jagged profile to the north-west '... is called Ei-may-o. Those are their proper names.'

'Are you suggesting that we cease using the names "King George's" and "York Island"?' asked James, wryly.

'I am,' Banks declared.

'Why?'

'Because 'Otaheite' and 'Eimayo' were their original names, given to them by their first owners, the Indians. Besides, their names have a musicality which I like.' He waved his hands, extravagantly. 'O-Tah-Hi-Ti, Ei-MAY-o. Don't you agree?'

It was a little over a fortnight after their arrival that Queen Oberea made her first appearance, sweeping down onto the point with her entourage, including the priest, Tupaia. Seeing her old acquaintances Molyneux and Gore, the stout, regal figure, resplendent in a white bark cloth gown and garlanded with tiare blooms, was overjoyed. Taken out to the ship, she met Wilkinson, who introduced her to James, calling her "Ooberea".

'I have heard and read much about you, Your Majesty,' James said, kissing her hand. Oberea beamed with delight. He then took her below to the Great Cabin and presented her with a gowned English doll, which delighted her further. She then invited a party to go ashore.

There the Englishmen were surprised when she introduced them to a husband, a younger man called O-Waamoo. By making suggestive gestures towards her ample loins, then pointing at the priest, she indicated that Tupaia had been her lover, but this was no longer so. Nevertheless he was still the high priest of Otaheite, she also told them.

Banks explained to the others the confusion over her name. 'O-Oberea' means "This is Oberea", he said, in his usual knowledgeable manner. 'Just as 'O-Taheite' means "This is

194

Taheite". So the Queen's name is actually 'Oberea', her husband is 'Waamoo' and her island is "Taheite".' He paused. 'I prefer to call it "Otaheite", however, as the natives do.'

Giving Banks a derisive look, Gore said sneeringly, 'So you have been taking language lessons too, Banks.' It was becoming apparent that the American considered himself to be the leading authority on Otaheite and resented any rival to this self-appointed status.

'I have,' Banks shot back. 'From a very learned teacher.' He laughed, and Gore's scowl deepened.

Banks began to spend more and more time ashore, sleeping at first in his bell tent in the fort, then making forays further inland and collecting botanical specimens for Parkinson to draw. Aware that the flamboyant naturalist was proving popular with the local leaders, James was content to leave him to him to his own interests, while he and Green concentrated on setting up their observatory. But when on the afternoon of 24 April James required Banks to return to the ship and join the officers at a dinner for Oberea and three local chiefs, he decided to venture inland and find him.

The track followed the river, then veered to the right and began to rise. Knowing that there were houses located throughout the forest, and having been told that Banks had been using one above the bay as his collecting base, James followed the track. Although the sun was sinking it was still intensely hot, and he was relieved that he had left his jacket and hat at the fort. He made his way along the fern-lined track, marvelling at the lushness of the foliage and swiping at the undergrowth profusion with a stick as he went. A pair of gaudy parrots swooped from the branches of a breadfruit tree, and he paused to admire its elegantly patterned leaves. Parkinson had already depicted them beautifully in his drawings and watercolours.

James entered the clearing where the open-sided hut stood, its roof thatched with palm fronds. Around the hut a ginger hen and her chickens were pecking in the undergrowth and to one side a tethered pig was rooting in the dark brown earth. Steam from what the natives called an umu kai was rising from plantain leaves covering an earth oven.

As he approached the hut, James heard sounds of human exertion coming from its interior, some deep and guttural, some high-pitched. Then, a few yards from the hut, he stopped and stared at what lay within.

A naked young woman was on her knees on the mat of woven pandanus which comprised the flooring of the hut. Her legs were spread wide, her glossy black hair was hanging loose and she was peering around with an expression of ecstasy on her shapely face, so engrossed in looking back that she was oblivious to the newcomer. Equally oblivious was the man kneeling between her open legs. Gowned in only a sweat-stained shirt, he was thrusting into her with deep, urgent strokes. James watched the coupling for some moments, wide-eyed. So this was what Banks called 'botanising'.

Then the girl noticed the visitor. Beginning to giggle, she brought one hand up to her mouth. As she did so Banks withdrew from her and spun around. Flushed and panting, long hair in disarray, he made no effort to cover his tumescent member. 'Cook,' he gasped. Then, placing his hands gently on the girl's buttocks, he said breathlessly, 'This is my taio, Her name is Tia-tia. Tia-tia, meet James Cook.'

'Ia orana, Ames Tute,' the girl said, dreamily.

James nodded towards her, and she giggled again. Then he said, with mock sternness, 'Banks, I note that your business here is unfinished. Carry on, then return to the ship when it is completed. Your presence is required on board.' He turned away, suppressing a smile.

'Thank you ... thank you .... ,' Banks gasped. Then he turned, lifted his shirt, shuffled forward on his knees and plunged ardently into her again.

On his way back to the bay, James reflected on the incident. Already several of the men had formed attachments to local women. That was entirely natural, after so many weeks at sea. The company of a woman was something he had been sorely missing as well, although as commander he could not himself be seen to succumb to carnal temptations. But the sight of the woman's gaping parts had aroused him, there could be no denying it. However he could not yield, he must not, it was an integral part of his duty. He must leave carnality to the others. However the related matter of the venereals concerned him greatly. The men must not transfer any infection to this lovely island, that would be unforgiveable.

He rounded a corner of the track, and there, spread out below him, was Matavai Bay, its waters shimmering in the late afternoon sun. He stopped and stared. Although small waves were rising, then breaking lazily against the reef, the lagoon water was like a pool of quicksilver. High above the ocean, beyond the reef, a gigantic tower of graphite-grey cloud seemed joined the sky to the sea. A rain storm, building, James realised. But although the clouds surrounding the tower were an unruly mixture of streaks, banks and billows, away to the east was a circle of golden light, a brilliant Cyclops eye in the sky. He stood for some time, entranced by the wild patterns of the clouds and the interplay of light and shade. Then, sensing that the rainstorm was about to break, he hurried on down the track to the bay.

Nineteen

29 May, 1769
My Dear Elizabeth,
As mid-summer looms for you in England, here on this island we
also know nothing except heat. But with the heat there is rain,
much of it, in torrents. As a consequence of this constant warmth
and rain, vegetation is rampant. Palms and forest trees grow
swiftly, and there is a profusion of tropical flowers, so that the
island really does resemble the Garden of Eden. But the heat also
brings a profusion of insects which torment us, especially as
nightfall approaches. Cockroaches which fly, drifting hornets,
swarming ants, aggressive flies and whining mosquitoes are the
worst, and the men light fires to deter them. Parkinson (who Banks
persists in referring to, condescendingly, as 'the draftsman') found
that when painting in the open air the flies even devoured the
paints from his palette, so he has taken to conducting his artistic
work under a net of muslin.

I struggle to comprehend the politics of this island, they seem
even more convoluted than those of Westminster. Since the
authority of the putative Queen, Oberea, was diminished by a civil
war in which her forces were vanquished, the leader of this part of
Otaheite is her relative, Tutaha. A large, powerful man, Banks has
nick-named him 'Hercules'. But there is talk of another leader,
called Vehiatua, whose warriors defeated the Queen's at a battle
on the west coast of the island. Thus, he too could be the paramount
chief. But who to believe?

Banks spends much time ashore now, carrying out his scientific
studies. His curiosity is insatiable. He is assisted by an interesting
older native called 'Tupaia', who comes from another island of
this group, called Raiatea. He speaks passable English, learned
from John Gore when Wallis's expedition was here, and shows
great interest in all things civilised, particularly Parkinson's work.
Being of generous disposition, Sydney has allowed Tupaia the use
of paper and paint, and encouraged by our artist, the native
already shows some ability in drawing and painting. The artistic
interests of the Indians being limited to carving and dancing,

Tupaia thus may well be the very first native of this region to wield pencil and brush.

Theft of our property by the Indians is a constant problem. They steal anything they can, including irreplaceable scientific instruments, and are as adept as London pickpockets at this practice. It has been necessary for me to confiscate canoes and hold some of the Indians' leaders hostage until the stolen items are returned. I have had conversations with Tupaia, over this matter. He informed me that in his society it is not a sin to steal, although it is a sin to get caught in the act of doing so. The people here even have a god of thievery, called Hiro. Tupaia also explained that his people have no concept of personal ownership of property, land or goods. Our firm belief in individual ownership of goods is entirely alien to them, so that everything in a district is shared by the tribe who dwells there. My men take great advantage of this with communality with regard to the local women, who treat them with great generosity. But I have also observed that their favours are given principally for what goods they can receive in return, especially nails, cloth and such gee-gaws as beads. These items they covet and are prepared to go to great lengths to obtain.

I hasten to assure you, however, of my continued fidelity to you. I have no intention of ever breaking my vow of marital faithfulness. To you too I can confess, dear wife, that I find the wantonness of the Otaheitian women troubling, for should the venereals be brought to them by European seamen, their licentious behaviour will doubtless spread the disease rapidly throughout this lovely island.

As the date for the Transit approaches, everything is becoming readied. I have dispatched another scientific party, led by Gore, to the neighbouring island of Eimayo, so that the phenomenon can also be observed from there. As I have explained to you already, but will here repeat for your benefit, the Transit of Venus across the face of the Sun will offer an opportunity to measure the distance from the Earth to the Sun. The black dot, as Venus will appear in its transit, will offer us a fixed point on which to focus. Such resulting calculations can then, by trigonometry, be used to establish accurate figures for an important astronomical yardstick, the distance from Earth to Sun. Green refers to this figure as the 'astronomical unit'.

So, everything is almost readied, and now all that is required on the day is a clear sky, and this concerns me, as lately there has been much cloud and rain.

I must close now Beth, as with the primary aim of our expedition imminent, there is still much to do ashore. So I will close this account with a further expression of my deepest love for you and our children.

Your devoted husband, James

They began to count down the days to the transit. The observation site on Point Venus was complete. Inside a large tent was the clock with its gridiron pendulum and outside the tent and facing the clock was the observatory, in which were set up the journeyman clock and astronomical quadrant, the latter set upon the head of a large cask set into the ground and filled with wet sand so that it made no movement. More telescopes were set up atop other casks, for the purpose of the observation.

Now, with all the elaborate preparations in place, everything depended on the weather. What conditions would 3 June bring?

3 June 1769

This day proved as favourable to our purpose as we could wish. Not a cloud was to be seen the whole day and the air was perfectly clear, so that we had every advantage we could desire in observing the whole of the passage of the planet Venus over the sun's disk. We very distinctly saw an atmosphere or dusky shade around the body of the planet which very much disturbed the times of the contacts, particularly the two internal ones. Solander observed, as well as Green and myself, and we differed from one another in observing the times of the contacts much more than could be expected. Green's telescope and mine were of the same magnifying power but that of Dr Solander was greater than ours. It was nearly calm the whole day and the thermometer exposed to the sun about the middle of the day rose to a degree of heat we have not met with before, 119°.

4 June 1769

Dearest Elizabeth,

The Transit has been observed! You can imagine my relief when the movement of the planet was watched, not just from here on Otaheite, but also from two other bases in the area. Although our observations with regard to the contacts of the planet and the sun

200

varied slightly (probably due to Solander's telescope being more powerful than Green's and mine), this discrepancy I do not believe will be significant in determining the solar parallax. And I do believe, Beth, that the observations made here on Otaheite will prove crucial in determining the precise distance from Earth to the Sun. That figure, when coupled with the perfection of the marine chronometer, will be of enormous assistance to the exact calculation of longitude, and hence precise navigation.

To you, Beth, I can confess enormous pride in this achievement. To have sailed around the world, then establish an astronomical observation site and witness the Transit of Venus were ambitions I knew I was capable of executing. Yet there was always the possibility of failure, both at sea and on land. But it is done, and done well, and so the first aim of our expedition has been achieved. A celebration last night in the Great Cabin was called for, and carried out with jubilation. Green became more intoxicated than usual, being scarcely able to stand after supper, but no one begrudged him this over-indulgence – his astronomical observances have at all times been diligent. And as he blurted out to us last evening, before retiring inebriated to his cabin: 'Gentlemen, today we have begun to measure the Heavens!'

I will end here, dearest, as much now remains to be done before the second set of Admiralty Instructions are opened and followed. Also, the encampment and fort must be dismantled, the rest of the island's coast surveyed and provisioning carried out for the next stage of the voyage. All this I will be describing in the entries which will follow. In the meantime, I am,

Your loving husband,
James

Shared dinners in the Great Cabin were now less common, as most of the gentlemen stayed ashore. But two days after the observation of the transit, James sent an order out that he wished the officers and scientists to attend a dinner on board *Endeavour*, to hear an announcement of great importance .

They sat around the table, finishing a dinner of wild duck, roast pork, sweet potatoes and fruit. Banks and Solander were tanned now, Sporing's face was uniformly red from the sun, Parkinson's was blotchy. Following the meal, they discussed what they had learned of Otaheite. Setting down his brandy glass, Banks said,

'My taio, Tupaia, has been explaining to me the way the society of the island is arranged.'

'Do they have an arrangement?' asked Sporing, doubtfully. 'They all seem the same to me.'

'Indeed they have,' replied Banks, shooting him an irritated look. He took another sip of brandy, then said: 'As we know, at the apex of their society is the ari'i rahi.'

'Tutaha, or your Hercules,' put in James.

'Quite so. He is the paramount chief, although his authority can be challenged in war, as Veihiatua has lately done.' He set his glass down. 'Below the ari'i rahi are the lesser chiefs, the nobility, which they call 'ari'i'. Below them are the people they call the 'manahune', who can own tracts of land. And at the very bottom are the 'teuteu', the commoners. They have no land and few possessions.' He made sharp, horizontal strokes with his right hand. 'It is all highly stratified.'

'Not so dissimilar to England then,' James observed, quietly. Then he added, 'And what of your friend Tupaia? He consorts with chiefs, yet appears not to be one.'

'Ah,' replied Banks knowingly. 'Tupaia is an arioi, a kind of priest. They are a separate, exclusive class, chosen people, skilled voyagers and followers of their god of war, Oro. The arioi are not allowed to father children, but they can adopt them. Young Taiata is Tupaia's adopted son. The arioi travel frequently, from island to island, entertaining the people with stories and leading the religious rituals.'

'So Tupaia knows of other islands?' asked James, thoughtfully.

'That is what he has told me, and I believe him.'

'Islands which we may visit and claim?'

'I cannot see why not.'

James nodded. 'Thank you for that information, Banks. Now we must move on to other matters.'

The company fell silent, contemplating their brandies and wondering what was coming next, as James had risen from the table and collected a sheet of notepaper from the writing desk. Still standing, he announced, 'This afternoon I opened the Admiralty's second set of instructions, which until now have remained sealed.'

The others were instantly attentive, leaning forward under the central lamp's candlelight. James began to read.

"Whereas there is reason to imagine that there is a Continent or land of great extent to the southward of the tract lately made by Captain Wallis or the tract of any former navigators in pursuits of the like kind ... you are to proceed to the southward, to forty degrees south latitude, in order to make the discovery of the aforementioned Continent ..."

'Terra Australis Incognita!' Banks cried out, and the others looked at each other in delighted surmise. *The Great Unknown Southern Land.*

James then declared, sombrely: 'In accordance with my instructions, we will leave at the end of this month and sail southwest, in search of the said continent.'

A deep, considered silence fell upon the cabin. Then, perhaps speaking for all of them, Parkinson said quietly, 'Tis an exciting prospect, Sir.' Then, still looking down, he added wistfully, 'But I will miss Otaheite.'

There was a knock on the door of the Great Cabin. 'Come,' James called, not looking up from his journal.

'Tute, good morning.'

James turned, then was surprised. He set his quill aside. Instead of one of the servants it was the imposing, robed figure of Tupaia. Almost as tall as James, his topknot grazed the roof of the cabin. Under his arm was a roll of paper. Withdrawing it, he handed it to James. 'For you, Tute.'

Puzzled, James unrolled the paper and spread it out on the table. On it was a watercolour painting of four native figures, side-on, two seated on stools, the other two standing between them. The seated figures were semi-naked and were playing nose flutes; the other two wore long robes and were beating drums with their hands. Although naively portrayed, the figures were undeniably realistic, especially the flutists. Tupaia beamed. 'Heiva,' he said. Then, groping for an English equivalent, 'Party.'

James nodded, not taking his eyes from the painting. 'Who did this?'

'Tupaia. I painted.'

'With Mr Parkinson's assistance?'

The priest frowned. 'No. His paints, his paper. But Tupaia's painting.'

James nodded, then said respectfully, 'I like it. It's a very good painting.' He paused. 'Will you give it to Oberea?'

Tupaia shook his head. 'No, it is for you, Tute. Taio Tute. Friend.'

They talked. Tupaia seemed quite at ease in the Great Cabin and his English was now impressive, no doubt because he was spending so much time in Banks's company. When James asked him about other islands in the region, he recited the names of many, pointing in the approximate direction in which they lay. *Tetiaroa, Huahine, Maupiti, Bora Bora.* Then, *Raiatea*, 'My island'.

James was intrigued. If time permitted, they could sail to these other, as-yet uncharted islands, and claim them for England. Thanking Tupaia again for the painting, he decided to call another meeting shortly with the officers and gentlemen and put the suggestion to them.

That evening Surgeon Monkhouse drew James aside. Like Banks, he had been spending most of his time ashore in the company of the natives. Very curious about their customs, he had taken to wearing a Tahitian robe. To James's mind he looked something of a scarecrow in the garment, being a thin, slack-shouldered man. Now he gave James a nervous look. 'Several of the men have the venereals,' he announced.

James was startled. 'You have examined them?'

'Yes. They show the symptoms. Sores on the genitalia, pain on passing urine.'

'But when you examined them earlier, only one man was infected, and he was confined to the ship.'

Monkhouse looked away. 'Seven men are now infected. As the Indian women are so co-operative with our men, it seems that they were responsible for the transmission.'

'So it must have been Wallis's men who introduced the venereals to the Indian women.'

Monkhouse shook his head. 'Wallis swore that none of his men were infected when they went ashore. And Gore has verified the fact.'

James considered the implications of this. If his men had brought the venereals, then it could spread throughout the island people, with dreadful results, as there was no known cure, only the mercury treatment. The old saying, "A night with Venus, a lifetime of Mercury", now took on a dreadfully ironic meaning. Could Monkhouse be wrong? he wondered. He wasn't much of a physician, James had decided. And the men muttered that he had a woman of his own on the shore. Perhaps he had the pox himself. But if he was correct, how could the disease have come to the island except from Wallis's men? After dismissing Monkhouse, he went ashore in search of Banks.

The botanist was sitting under a coconut palm beside the river which flowed across Point Venus. Parkinson and Tupaia were with him and Tupaia's boy, Taiata, sat a little distance away, weaving a hat from pandanus leaves. Even under the trees it was searingly hot. In the distance, under Pickersgill's direction, others of the Endeavours were dismantling the fort and packing equipment into crates. The ground here, James noticed, was pocked with crab holes. Taiata brought over an opened coconut and the three men passed it from one to the other, swigging from it. Banks held the nut up to James.

'A drink, Cook. The finest in the world!'

'Thank you.' James took some of the refreshing drink, and handed it back. Then he sat down next to the others and reported grimly what Monkhouse had told him, ending with the statement, 'So there is no doubt, the venereals have come to the island.'

Banks looked thoughtful. Then he said, 'Naturally, it is only the lower order of the Otaheitian women who have transmitted the venereals to our men.' He turned to Tupaia. 'What is your word for such people, taiao?'

'*Teuteu*,' said the priest, with obvious distaste.

'Yes,' said Banks scornfully. 'Those at the bottom of society.'

James bristled at this. He said, coldly, 'It matters not from which level of society the infected people come in society, Banks. What matters is that the venereals are now on this island, they will spread, and it seems that some of our men are responsible.'

Banks shrugged. 'Perhaps, perhaps not.' He turned to Tupaia. 'My taio here told me last night of another European ship which came to Otaheite, after Wallis's.'

'*Another*?' said James. 'From which nation?'

'He cannot tell. Not England, for they spoke a strange language. But they were pale, like us, and came in a ship like ours. They stayed only a short time, at Hitia'a.'

'How long ago?'

'He thinks, about one year ago.'

Tupaia stepped forward. 'Yes, one year, at Hitia'a.' He pointed to the east. 'The men...' He made thrusting movements with his hips. 'Much ... with the women there.' Banks grinned lewdly, Parkinson looked away.

James considered this. The other ship could have come from Spain or France. Spain had its colony on the west coast of South America, from which forays into the rest of the Pacific had been made, by voyagers such as Quiros and Mendana. Also, Wallis had mentioned that there was a rumour that the Frenchman, Bougainville, had planned an expedition to the South Pacific. And if it was the French, and if their men did introduce the venereals at Hitia'a, then that partly absolved the Endeavours. But the news of the coming of the disease still troubled him. It seemed that Europe was already sullying this lovely island, with its guns and diseases. And now that the world was aware of Otaheite, it was a development that could only worsen.

'Do you still intend to leave the island in two weeks, Sir?' asked Parkinson.

'Yes. After the scraping of *Endeavour*'s hull is completed. And provisioning will begin tomorrow. But first I intend to circumnavigate and chart the island. The repairs to the pinnace are completed, so we will take that vessel. Leaving tomorrow, before daybreak.'

'Who will accompany you?' said Parkinson, looking hopeful.

'Mr Banks,' said James, firmly. 'It's high time he got back to work.'

The others chuckled, Banks included.

As they were rowed down the east coast by the pinnace's four oarsmen, their eyes were fixed shoreward. The island's beauty was overwhelming. The precipitous, forested mountains – their slopes broken by shadowy valleys – rose to a line of jagged peaks. From time to time cataracts tumbled down the mountainsides. Mists rose from the falling water, precipitating rainbows. Streams and rivers poured from the valleys and crossed the coastal plain, which was dense with coconut palms, plantains, breadfruit trees, hibiscus and pandanus. Smoke from wood fires rose lazily from the wooded plain. Everywhere there was greenness, but even from the water they could see flashes of white, red and orange – the blooms of the tropical foliage. Where they saw beaches, the sand was as black as coal. Within the reef the lagoons were a turquoise shade, the seabed cobbled with coral heads, among which multi-coloured fishes darted and flashed and pale manta rays sped away like guilty ghosts.

James sat in the bow, sketching and noting as they went, while Banks stood in the stern and the four oarsmen hauled. As they passed the district of Hitia'a, Banks pointed shoreward. 'I have noticed, Cook, that wherever a river enters the lagoon, there is a break in the reef. See.' James followed his pointing finger, to where there was a satiny stillness between the line of breaking waves. 'Could it be that fresh water is fatal to the coral organism?' James looked up from his sketching and grunted. As usual, Banks *could* be right. It was certainly an interesting theory.

They were rowed steadily along the coast. At times they went ashore and trekked along the plain, pausing to greet the local people, who were cordial, and generous with their offers of food and accommodation. But in the absence of Tupaia, communication beyond the basics was not possible.

On the third day the coast drew inwards to a low isthmus whose name, Tupaia had told them, was Taravao. Then, further to the south-east, the land rose steeply again, culminating in peaks James estimated were over three thousand feet high. This was the sister island which the priest had said was called 'Tahiti Iti'. Here too they saw evidence of the recent war: the stone marae which had been built on most promontories were decorated with human skulls or jawbones, all with traces of fresh flesh. When they came ashore on a plain at the mouth of a wide, crystal-clear river, the recently victorious chief of Tahiti Iti, Vehiatua, came out of a meeting house to greet them. To their surprise he was aged and frail. Welcoming them to his domain, he told them the place was called Tautira.

The east coast of Tahiti Iti was exposed, and James ordered the pinnace's sail raised so that they could harness the brisk south-east wind. The sea developed a steep chop, and James watched with amusement as Banks hung his head over the stern, arms extended, and vomited heavily. James noted that the conjoined island, although much smaller, was in other respects almost a mirror-image of the other, with towering peaks slashed by deep valleys. Doubling Tahiti Iti, they saw that the south coast of the island had rugged cliffs and the reef was close in. The chop grew steeper, and it was a relief when the pinnace turned west and into the lee of the island. They were rowed through a pass and into the lagoon, which was broad here, and with the sun low in the sky reached the sheltered southern side of the isthmus. There, as arranged, in a wide, tranquil inlet, Tupaia and Taiata paddled out to meet them in an outrigger canoe. This place, they told the Englishmen, was called Papeari.

That night the party ate well, on wild pork, fish and plantains baked in an earth oven. Banks had brought a bottle of brandy which he shared with James and the oarsmen, and when the men curled up in the hut and fell asleep, James, Banks and Tupaia sat around the dying fire. With the insects from the surrounding forest providing a screeching chorus, they listened to the legends of Tupaia's people and noted what he told them.

Encased in his bark cloth cloak, a crown of woven pandanus flowers on his head, the priest told them of the origin of his world. In the beginning, he declared, there was only one god, the great Ta'aroa, who existed alone except for a rock, called Te Papa. After Ta'aroa coupled with the rock, a daughter was created from the union, and called Aone. Then Ta'aroa created the sea, the moon and the stars, and a number of demi-gods, including the most powerful, Maui. Then, finally, people were created. Aone and her lover, Te Tumu, created the first man. His name was Ti'i, and he lived on an island far to the north, called 'Hawaiiki'. By his mother and his daughters, Ti'i sired several manifestations of the goddess, Hina. She was the mother of the god of war, Oro, and had three sons. From these three men and the females, all people were descended. The fabled Hawaiiki remained his people's spiritual homeland.

As for the land, the responsibility for its creation lay with Maui, who was possessed of enormous strength. Before he was born the Earth was comprised of one huge piece of land, but when Maui picked it up and shook it, the land broke into many pieces. Thus the islands were created. It was Maui too who hauled the clouds, which before had hung over the mountaintops, into their proper place, in the sky.

His back against a palm trunk, James set his quill aside, then said to the priest, 'They are fine legends, Tupaia, but how do you explain the presence of your people here in the middle of the ocean?'

Keenly, and with elaborate gestures, Tupaia again launched into narrative. Waving towards the north-west, he said, 'Out there, many, many islands. Small islands, big islands. My ancestors sailed from one to another, using stars and ocean currents for guidance. Sometimes they stopped, sometimes they continued, spreading to the east, island to island.' He looked up at the stars, seeking a comparison, then said, 'Like what you call 'stepping stones', across a wide river.' He grinned triumphantly. 'All the way to Otaheite.' Then he stood up, bade them goodnight, and strode over to the sleeping hut.

James and Banks lay before the fire under their blankets. Before they dropped off to sleep, Banks said to James, 'Do you believe his stories? About the man who copulated with a rock?'

'Of course not. It's absurd.'

'Yes.' Banks chuckled. 'Almost as ridiculous as Adam and Eve.'

James swiped at a buzzing mosquito. 'But I feel there may be truth in the other story. The movement from the west, from island to island. It's possible. Think of their great double-hulled canoes – they would be capable of crossing open ocean.'

Banks looked doubtful. 'But might they not have come the other way, from South America?'

James frowned. 'I think not. The distances are too great, and the winds adverse. I do believe his people came from the west, sailing from island to island. All the way back to the Spice islands perhaps.' He drew the blanket over his head as protection against the droning mosquitos. 'How else could they have got here?'

The next morning, while the pinnace was rowed along Tahiti Nui's west coast, Tupaia took the two Englishmen along a forest track to a promontory near the mouth of a river. This was the district of Papara, the priest told them. Then with great pride, he ushered them into a clearing on which stood a great temple he had designed for Oberea, the one he had named Mahaiatea.

Standing under ironwood trees at the edge of the clearing, James and Banks stared in astonishment. The edifice was enormous, consisting of a pyramid made from blocks of coral rock. It had eleven steps, each one about four feet high. 'It is called an ahu,' Tupaia told them. Surrounding the pyramid was a paved area edged with a stone wall. When Banks measured the wall with his tape he found that it was 360 feet by 354 feet – almost square. Shaking his head in wonder, he said to James, 'They built all this, without steel hammers and chisels.' Catching his meaning, Tupaia nodded, his pride obvious. 'Here the gods were worshipped, and sacrifices made to them,' he said.

Then, abruptly, his mood changed. But this was also the site, he told them gravely, of the great battle of a few months earlier, between the warriors of Oberea and Vehiatua. After Vehiatua's victory, the marae had been desecrated, its god images destroyed and the surrounding houses pillaged and burnt. Tupaia's mood brightened as he told them that he had later re-consecrated the marae, accompanied by many ceremonies, including human sacrifices. Now, he concluded, the mana of the great marae had been restored and the ahu was again a place of great sacredness.

James and Banks walked out onto the nearby black sand beach, alongside the river mouth. Tupaia sat some distance away, a drawing pad on his knee, sketching the ahu with a pencil. The inland mountains were shadowy in the morning sun and the lagoon had a satiny sheen. The pinnace was standing off, beyond the reef, and James drew his pistol and fired it, signalling the oarsmen to bring the boat in.

He walked down to the edge of the lagoon, then stopped and stared at the sand. Banks did likewise. Bones, hundreds upon hundreds of bones. Ribs, scapulas, vertebrae, jawbones, arm bones, hipbones, shinbones, skulls, half buried, strewn across the sand as randomly as driftwood. James picked up a skull and examined it. It was the size of an orange. Although bleached, it still contained teeth. Tiny milk teeth. And in one side was a jagged hole. He held it out to Banks. 'A child,' he said, his voice just a murmur. Grimacing, Banks looked away. 'This place must have been a slaughter-house,' he said, averting his eyes. James looked back and up across the forest to the steep, shadowy mountains. The contrast between the natural beauty of the island and the hideousness at his feet had rendered him speechless.

Endeavour's bilges were pumped out and the ship scrubbed inside and out. Laboriously the water casks were filled from the river, rolled down to the beach and taken out to the ship in the launch. The scraping and varnishing of *Endeavour*'s hull was complete, the caulking of the decks would be finished in a few days. The sails were brought up and laid out to air; firewood, coconuts, pork and duck meat were taken aboard and stowed. As James stood on the shore and watched *Endeavour* being readied, it was as if the little lady bulldog, as he now preferred to think of her, was being groomed for a prestigious dog show.

After several consultations with quartermaster Sam Evans, he announced that their departing date would be the thirteenth of July.

Three days before the departure, James made a lengthy entry in his journal. It documented the desertion and recapture of two of the marines, Clement Webb and Samuel Gibson, who had fled inland with their Otaheitian lovers. Tupaia had instigated negotiations with the local leaders, which had culminated in the marines' recapture. As James recorded these events, there was a sharp knock on the door of the Great Cabin, then Banks entered, a roll of paper in his right hand.

He was hatless, his hair was tied in a tail, his shirt was wide open and hanging loose and the sleeves were rolled up, revealing the star tattoo which had been etched into the skin of his left breast by a tattooist friend of his lover, Tia-tia. The intricate pattern of the tattoo showed up strikingly against his deeply tanned skin. Seeing the tattoo, James recalled a recent conversation he had had with Banks, about the imprint on his breast.

'I wonder, Banks, what Miss Blosset will make of this ornamentation.'

'Who?'

'Mistress Blosset. Your betrothed.*'*

Banks snorted. 'It matters not a jot. Our betrothal is cancelled.' *He sighed, theatrically. 'There are far too many wonderful women in the world to settle for just one.'*

Now, taking a chair under the stern window, still clutching the rolled paper, Banks said, in a very businesslike tone, 'I have a proposition for you.'

Irritated by the interruption – had Banks forgotten their understanding that James had the Great Cabin to himself in the afternoons? – he said, snappily, 'Can it not wait?'

'No. It is a matter of great importance. And urgency.'

James set down his quill. 'Very well. But please, be brief.'

'I will.' Then, quickly, 'I wish to have Tupaia and his boy join the ship's company.'

It took several moments for this to sink in. Then James said, 'To be taken to his home island?'

'That first. Then with us to England. Or what he calls *Peretane*.'

James sat bolt upright. 'To *England*? Banks, have you lost your senses?'

'No. My proposal is entirely serious. I wish to take the pair of them to England.'

'*Why*?'

'It is my belief that Tupaia will be of inestimable value to the expedition.' He paused. 'As indeed he has been already.'

'On land, perhaps. But not at sea.'

Banks unrolled the sheet of paper. 'I disagree. Look at this.'

It was a chart, hand-drawn, showing of dozens of islands of varying size, arranged in concentric circles. Each island had a name written across it. James studied the chart for some moments, before he said, 'Did the priest draw this?'

'He did. Using Parkinson's materials.'

'But this cannot be accurate. The Indian has no instruments. No sextant, no compass.'

'The chart is drawn from personal voyaging, and from the accounts of other star navigators he has talked to. He has recounted to me a list, of scores of islands his people know. He himself has visited many, and he knows the way to all of them from Otaheite.'

Without taking his eyes from the chart, James said, 'This is probably an invention. Like the stories of his ancestors.'

Banks's face was set, his gaze unwavering. 'The ancestral stories perhaps, the chart not so.' He came closer. 'His value, I believe, will be in aiding our intercourse with other natives we encounter in the next stage of our voyage.' He gave a knowing little laugh.

'It takes an Indian to know an Indian, as you might say. You know how useful Tupaia was in negotiating the return of Webb and Gibson.'

James nodded, slightly.

'And when he returns with us to England, we can exhibit him and the boy as living specimens of Otaheitian manhood.' His eyes shone. 'They will be of enormous interest to the Royal Society's people.'

James considered this for some moments. As always, practical considerations nagged at him. He said, 'And who will provide their keep and lodging in England? The Naval Board?'

Ignoring James's ironic tone, Banks shot back, '*I will.* I have both the means and the inclination to do so.' He paused. 'Tupaia will be my most valuable specimen.'

James walked to the cabin window, which he had opened to admit the sea breeze. Placing his hands behind his back, he looked out over the lagoon and said, 'And where on the ship would he be accommodated?'

'Buchan's berth is yet unfilled. He can have that.'

James spun about. 'An Indian? In the gentlemen's quarters? Those on the lower deck will not take kindly to such an arrangement.'

'At first, perhaps not. But when they realise his value to us, I believe they will come to appreciate him. He will be our navigator and envoy in these islands.' He waved his right hand. 'As for the boy, he can sleep with the other servants.'

James plucked his handkerchief from his sleeve and ran it over his face. Banks' suggestion had profound implications. Tucking the handkerchief into his sleeve, he said, 'I am unconvinced of the value of this proposition, Banks.' He added, with deliberate slowness, 'Have you put it to the man himself?'

'I have. And he displayed great enthusiasm for the proposal. He wishes to show us other islands to the north of here. And he feels that since the war, his prospects on Otaheite are greatly reduced. He is an exile here, remember.' Banks placed his opened hands on the table, hard, and leaning forward, said firmly, 'Be assured, Cook, I will take complete responsibility for both Otaheitians.'

'Mmm.'

'What does that *mmm* mean, exactly?'

'It means, Banks, that Tupaia and the boy may come with us, but the responsibility for them, now and later, will be entirely yours.' His eyes bored into Banks's. '*Is that understood?*'

The naturalist nodded. 'It is. And I will let Tupaia know, immediately.' He started for the cabin door, then paused and said thoughtfully. 'He may even be able to direct us to the Great Southern Continent.' Then he waved his hand at the sheet of paper laid out on the table. 'The chart is yours, he wishes you to have it.'

After bidding tearful farewells to James and the others, the Otaheitian notables – Oberea, Amo, Nunahau and Tutaha – had climbed reluctantly down from the ship and into their canoes. The windlass was worked by four of the crew and *Endeavour*'s bower anchor came up, her flukes clogged with black sand. Others of the crew sluiced the sand away with buckets of water, and the anchor was manoeuvred into place and made fast. Then, with Gore and Molyneux at the wheel and her foresails filling, *Endeavour* began to move out towards the pass. There was a light wind from the east and the morning mist was dissolving under the rising sun, revealing a radiant blue sky and a glittering sea. Away to the west, Eimayo Island seemed to still be slumbering.

As the remainder of her sails were raised, the flotilla of canoes which had put out from Point Venus surrounded the departing ship. Those of the Endeavours who had not gone aloft were lined along the starboard rail, most glum-faced, waving to their favourites in the canoes. The remaining marines were in formation on the foredeck, muskets at the slope, the drummer Thomas Rossiter beating a tattoo. Tupaia's boy, Taiata, had already teamed up with 12-year-old Nicholas Young, and the lads were climbing happily out onto the bowsprit rigging. Only the would-be deserters, Webb and Gibson, were confined below, awaiting their flogging.

Standing on the quarterdeck in his full gown uniform, heavily garlanded with tiare flowers which a tearful Oberea had placed around his neck, James waved to those of the canoes' occupants he recognised, in particular the Queen herself, her former husband, Amo, and her son, Te Ri'i Rere. Another friend, the chief Potatau, was calling out, 'Parahi, parahi.' ('Farewell, farewell'). Surgeon Monkhouse's lover, a woman as plain as himself, was in another canoe with what looked like her brother, while alone in a small outrigger, Banks's lover Tia-tia was tearing at her forehead with a shard of pearl shell and weeping piteously.

Hearing shouts from above, James looked up.

Banks and Tupaia were clutching the rigging near the top of the main mast. Both men were shirtless and barefooted, and Banks had evidently given Tupaia a pair of his breeches, as he was wearing seaman's trousers. The pair were deeply tanned, their skin so dark that as James stared up at the two men, he found it difficult to tell which was the Englishman and which was the native.

Twenty

27 July, 1769
My dearest Beth,
As we depart the waters of these islands, it seems fitting for me to report on what we can be said to have achieved during our several weeks in Tahiti. I can be frank with you, as I cannot be in my other account.

While our three month stay on Otaheite can in most part be considered a success, it was not entirely so.

Towards the end of our stay there was an outbreak of theft and consequent hostage taking which threatened the peace which we had been so much at pains to establish. The natives' propensity for thievery is almost beyond belief, and the cause of most of the troubles between us and them. Then two of the ship's marines deserted to the island's interior with their women, occasioning the taking of more hostages by us, which caused further resentment. The pair were eventually apprehended, and, after we put to sea, given two dozen lashes each. After these last weeks spent partly ashore, many of the men have become ill-disciplined and resentful of authority. That is over now. Any further breeches of discipline will be severely punished. Enforcements will be simpler now that we are at sea again.

The Otaheitian way of life, though superficially carefree, is on closer consideration not so. Those of our men who are so besotted with the island should pause, I believe, to consider its darker side, as it has been revealed to me. Tribal warfare, accompanied by much killing of innocents, the barbaric custom of human sacrifice – related to me by the priest Tupaia – and the people's incureable thievery and promiscuity, are all alien to our English way of life. Be assured, Beth, I have no desire to romanticise the Otaheitians or envy the way they live, however much some members of my crew have been tempted to do so. My heart remains forever with you and our children, in our beloved England.

Despite the aforementioned troubles, upon our departure most of the natives seemed unhappy that we were leaving and there were many lamentations as the ship drew away from shore. They utter a heartfelt cry at such a time, calling 'Ow-ay! Ow-ay!' Many of the crew, and certain of the gentlemen, had developed relationships with the local women, and so they too were loathe to depart the island.

My circumnavigation of Otaheite and island connected to it, I consider an unqualified success. Their coasts have been charted and soundings taken along their shores. The resulting charts, when published, I believe will prove of great worth to those who follow us.

Most regrettably, and as I feared after learning of the widespread promiscuity of the Otaheitian women, the venereals have become widespread. Surgeon Monkhouse considers that half the men are now infected. This I consider a major failure. Although I am certain that the Spanish or the French first introduced the disease, our role in disseminating it cannot be gainsaid.

The sad loss of our landscape artist, Alex Buchan, has been compensated for by the work of young Sydney Parkinson. As well as his botanical paintings and drawings, which are exquisite, he has produced some superb landscape portraits of the island. I cannot speak too highly of this young man, and his work will surely be acclaimed upon his return to England.

After leaving Otaheite we sailed north, under the direction of a Tahitian man who Banks persuaded me to take with us. His name is Tupaia, he is about my age and height, and is deeply knowledgeable about his people's gods and religious rituals. Banks has taught him some English and he has taught Banks some of his language, so they now converse with ease with each other. Most useful though, Tupaia has navigational knowledge of these islands, having sailed to many of them in the course of conducting religious rites.

The first island we passed was low, with a central lagoon, and its islets were entirely clothed in coconut palms. As Tupaia reported that it was uninhabited, we did not call there. Instead he guided us north-west, to a higher island, called Huahine. (When I asked the priest what this name translated to, he laughed. Then, by gestures, he told me that it was something so coarse that it would offend your delicate sensibilities to hear it, so I will refrain from doing so).

In spite of its vulgar title, Huahine proved to be a surpassingly pretty island, with forested mountains and fertile plains on which

grew a profusion of fruits and vegetables, including sweet
potatoes, yams and bananas, which we made great store of. A pass
through the reef admitted Endeavour *to the harbour alongside a*
village called Fare. Tupaia here proved his worth by conversing
freely with the local chief, a very tall man called Ori, and thereafter
we were made welcome at his long-house near the sheltered shore.
Gifts were exchanged and our visit to this island was entirely
amicable. Whilst in Fare harbour, I was keenly aware of another
island on the horizon, which I estimated to be only a day's sail
away. Its profile was high but irregular, and its peaks were
swathed in cloud. Tupaia too became excited at this prospect, for
it was his home island, called Raiatea, and he was naturally eager
that we spend time there. It was the most sacred island, he said ...

Tupaia and James stood on the foredeck, watching the island
loom from the purple sea. It was wide, high and serrated, and as
they came closer the priest became animated. He pointed to its
three highest peaks, identifying them as 'Oropiro, Toomaru,
Tapioi.' Spyglass to his eye, James focused on the three summits.
Away to the east, a separate, smaller lump of land rose. 'What
island is that?' James asked.

'Tahaa.'

His attention returned to Raiatea. He pointed towards the island's
southern extremity and said, 'Faaroa, where pahi are made.'

'Pahi?'

'Canoes which sail the ocean.' He pointed again. 'Opoa, where
canoes leave from.' He lowered his voice, respectfully, 'And there,
marae Taputapuatea.'

James frowned. 'Tapu ...tapu ...'

'Tapu ... tapu ... *atea*. Most sacred marae.' James saw through
the telescope a level promontory, covered in coconut palms.
Tupaia's finger then swung to the right, to the eastern end of the
Raiatea. 'Tupaia born there. Hamamino.'

'Where is the pass to the lagoon?'

He pointed westward. 'Pass, there. Te Ava Moa.'

'Is it wide and deep enough for *Endeavour*?'

'Oh yes. Plenty wide.'

James called down to where Molyneux and Clerke were at the
helm. 'The pass is four points westward, but dispatch a man to the
chains for soundings, to make certain.'

With *Endeavour* approaching the pass, Tupaia explained that beyond Raiatea was another island, a day's sail away, called Bora Bora. Some years ago warriors from there had invaded his island. The men of Bora Bora were rogues and criminals of the worst kind, he said, led by a chief called Puni, who was now living on Tahaa. It was the Boraboran invasion which had caused Tupaia to leave Raiatea and sail to Otaheite, eight years ago.

With Raiatea drawing closer and its peaks and valleys becoming clearer, Tupaia gripped James's arm and said, urgently, 'Tute, you get ship's big guns ready. To kill all men from Bora Bora!'

James was dismayed. Was this the real reason why Tupaia had wanted to come along? The last thing he wanted was for the expedition to become involved in a local civil war. He shook his head, adamantly.

'No. We wish to see, and chart your island, and trade. That is all. There will be no fighting, and no killing.'

The priest's expression darkened. 'You do not wish to help Tupaia's people?'

'We do wish to help. But peaceably. We will trade, but not fight.' He brought his face closer to Tupaia's. '*There will be no fighting by us*. Do you understand?'

Tupaia turned and walked away, muttering something which may have been an imprecation.

They negotiated the pass and anchored within the lagoon, a quarter of a mile from the shoreline. A pair of canoes put out from the land and came alongside. The paddlers were both mature women, bare-breasted and wearing ceremonial headgownes embellished with red feathers. There was a dead pig, in a basket of woven pandanus leaves, in each canoe. Tupaia greeted the women joyfully and welcomed them and the pigs aboard. Although the pair looked about at the staring crew and the ship nervously, when Tupaia presented them with some beads, they relaxed a little. Then the taller of the two women spoke at length to him, pointing inland as she did so.

James came down from the quarterdeck, from where he had been observing the arrival of the women. 'What does she say?' he asked Tupaia.

'The Boraborans are close. At Uturoa.' His tone was bitter.

James considered the implications of this. It was important to see the great marae which he had heard about, and have Parkinson portray it, but they were not going to become embroiled in an inter-island feud. Shoulders braced, he announced,

'We will protect you and your people, Tupaia. You, Banks and myself will go ashore in the pinnace first.' He called down to Edgecombe. 'Call out the marines and have them stand by, sergeant.'

Taputapuatea was a vast complex of coral rock platforms, thatched god houses and carved wooden boards, placed upright. Some of the coral slabs were upright too. These were the backs of seats, Tupaia explained, where royalty sat. The entire area, about a mile square, was overlooked by towering palms whose fronds littered the ground. Sacrificed pigs, black with blowflies, slumped atop several of the platforms.

Tupaia led James and Joseph to a platform of stones and boards at the shoreline – a kind of marae within a marae – which he told them was the place where sacrifices were made before voyagers set sail.

Adorned in his cloak and headgown, Tupaia recited prayers at the shoreline temple, then led them to the main marae, stopping every few moments to produce lengthy incantations, but glancing inland with obvious apprehension all the while. A light rain was falling, and the place seemed gloomy and full of foreboding. 'What's wrong?' James whispered in Banks's ear. Banks murmured, 'He fears that the Boraborans are watching us, and that they will attack and kill him.'

At last the prayers were over, concluded by Tupaia taking a chunk of volcanic rock from under his cloak and placing it reverentially on one of the stone platforms. He had brought it from the Mahaiatea ahu as a tribute, he explained to them. Obviously bored by all this ritual, Banks wandered over to the nearest god-house. He peered inside it. Then he bent down, pushed his hands into the little hut and brought out a long bundle, wrapped in woven pandanus. Holding it upright with his left hand, he began to tug with his right hand at the sinnet strings that held the wrapping in place.

With a cry, Tupaia ran forward, waving his hands frantically. 'Aita! No! To'o is tapu!'

Ignoring his cries, Banks kept tugging at the bundle's ties, but they were too tight. With a dismissive grunt he shoved the god image – the to'o – back into its shelter and walked away.

With cries of '*Ow-ay*!', Tupaia wrung his hands in despair. The damage had been done, the god-house's sanctity had been violated. He stood before it, his hands over his face, reciting more prayers. James too was furious with Banks. Had he not been instructed to respect local customs? Did he not appreciate the sanctity of this place? Tupaia had explained that Taputapuatea was the most sacred marae in all the islands, and the spiritual font of his people. Here royalty was crowned and vital ceremonies carried out. The place had to be respected, by everyone, natives or Europeans. Back on Otaheite, Monkhouse had been attacked by a man after he merely picked a frangipani flower from a tree which grew on a burial ground. That act had been widely discussed, constituting a violation of what the Indians called 'tapu', and thus was something now well known to the Endeavours.

What Banks had just done – rifling one of the most sacred marae's god-houses – was much worse. James thought: if an Indian had strolled into York Minster and snatched a chalice from its altar, Banks would be outraged. So why had he acted so thoughtlessly in a place so sacred to his friend? He cursed to himself. Sometimes Banks's crassness knew no bounds.

He put a comforting hand on the priest's shoulder. 'Tupaia, I am sorry,' he said. 'I will ensure that that will not happen again.' Still glowering, the priest turned and pointed towards the seaward fringe of the marae, to where three other men in ceremonial robes stood under the palms, clubs in their hands, watching them silently. 'Tute,' he said quietly, 'If I was not here with you, you and all your men would be attacked and killed for what he did.' He pointed at another nearby god-house, in the form of a small upright canoe. Dangling from it were several human jawbones, gobbets of flesh attached to them. Tupaia was tearful as he muttered, 'Much killing here, Tute, much killing.'

By suppertime that evening, Tupaia had recovered. He told them more about his island. The inlet of Faaroa was the place where the pahi were launched. The inlet was deep and sheltered, and at its headwaters rainforest trees were felled and shaped. They were then rolled into the sound and floated down to Opoa for the addition of their prow and stern posts, cabins, thwarts and rigging. After priestly blessings, from there the pahi sailed, under the command of star-navigators like himself, to distant islands of the Pacific.

'So,' mused Banks, 'Opoa is the Plymouth of these islands.'

'And Faaroa the Deptford,' added James. To Tupaia he said, 'Could I see the place where the canoes are made?'

Tupaia nodded. 'Yes. I will take you there.' He went to the open cabin window and looked towards the mountains, which were bathed in a lemony light from an almost-full moon. Turning back to the others, he said, 'And Banks, you will wish to collect plants from Raiatea.'

'Certainly. Are the ones here different from Otaheite's?'

'Yes.' He pointed upwards. 'And there, on the top of Mount Temehani, where god Oro was born, a special flower grows.'

Solander as well as Banks were instantly alert. 'Why special?' asked Solander.

'It grows nowhere else. On no other island.' He held up one hand with the fingers splayed. 'The flower has five petals, one for each finger of a beautiful girl, called Apetahi. She fled to the mountaintop in sorrow when she learned that her husband had taken another lover. Wanting to kill herself, she dug a hole on the mountaintop, cut off her hand and buried it there. She then died from the bleeding.' Tupaia held up both his own hands, dramatically. 'Later, when her friends found her body, they saw that a strange plant, with a flower having five petals, was growing where Apetahi's hand had been buried.' He looked down. 'Very sad story, uh?'

Banks looked sceptical. 'Are you sure the flower grows nowhere else?'

'Yes. My people have tried to grow it on the other mountains. It will not grow anywhere else.'

'A unique soil type, perhaps,' mused Solander.

'We must get a specimen,' said Banks, crisply.

Tupaia said, 'But you must climb the mountain. And is very high.'

Banks looked at him defiantly. 'We'll do it. At first light tomorrow.'

With James and Tupaia seated in the stern, the pinnace was rowed deep into the Faaroa sound. Anticipating the extreme heat,

James had left his jacket on the ship, but he still wore his cocked hat. The sound was sheltered by the sheer slopes of Mt Toomaru, and the water was glassy, the shores overlooked by rank upon rank of coconut palms, their crowns inclined elegantly towards the water. High above the sound, groups of fairy terns wheeled and pirouetted like ballerinas.

The inlet narrowed, then at its head they came to the place where a river entered the sound. Tupaia directed the oarsmen to draw up to its bank, where two outrigger canoes were tied to a mangrove root.

Above the bank a clearing had been made in the forest. It was surrounded by huge trees, their boughs draped with luxuriant epiphytes, their buttress roots like giant scapulas. It had rained heavily in the night, and the foliage was dank and dripping. Unseen insects screeched from the trees and vines as James and Tupaia walked up into the clearing.

In the centre were two side-by-side logs, several feet in diameter, lying across a row of palm tree trunks. Six muscular young men wearing bark loin cloths were chipping away at the logs with basalt adzes, which were lashed to their carved handles with sinnet. The men's hair was long and glossy, their upper arms heavily tattooed. Wood chips littered the ground surrounding the twin trunks.

James and Tupaia approached the men, who looked at them in a curious but not unfriendly way. The presence of the *Endeavour* was by now common knowledge on the island. Tupaia spoke formally to the men, gesturing at James, who caught the words, 'Ari'i rahi'. Then the priest explained the first stage of the canoe-building process, waving his hand at the surrounding forest. 'Tamanu trees. Very strong. From them, pahi are made.' He placed a hand on one of the trunks. 'What is your name for the main part of your canoe?'

'The hull.'

'Yes. Hull.' He smiled, mischievously. 'Your canoe has only one hull, Raiatean canoe has two.'

James examined the work, astonished at what was being accomplished with just stone tools. The giant trunks were twenty yards long. Already shaped into a prow at one end, the workers were now concentrating on hollowing out their centres. Having been forewarned by Tupaia of what to expect here, James took from his pack two axes. But before he presented them to the workers he went up to one of the logs and holding one of the axes in both hands, plunged it deep into the hollow. The craftsmen gasped, then nodded eagerly as he handed the axes over. They passed the tools from hand to hand, testing their edges, and grinning when they felt their sharpness and hardness. Tupaia held up his hand and recited a blessing, then they farewelled the workers and returned to the pinnace.

On the way back the priest told James that to complete one pahi took from two to three years, but if they were blessed properly and looked after well, they would last for many voyages. Standing up, he held up his left hand and waved it towards all points of the compass. 'Sail to many, many islands, far, far away, but always return to Raiatea.'

They reached the place where the sound met the lagoon, then turned north, in the direction of *Endeavour*, the four oarsmen pulling steadily. The sun had dropped below the mountains, and their slopes were in shadow. One hundred yards further on they heard shouts from the shore. James saw a small headland at the edge of the lagoon, and upon it two strange figures, beckoning frantically. They were caked with dark brown mud, their long hair was matted, their garments torn and filthy. Local shamen, perhaps? James wondered. He directed the coxswain to turn in to the shore, and only when they were a few yards away did he see that the figures had canvas packs on their backs. He then recognised them. It was Banks and Solander.

As the pinnace touched the shore, James called to them. 'Well gentlemen, did you collect your flower?'

Banks wiped his face, and gave him a furious look. '*No*. We couldn't get to the top of the accursed mountain.' He wiped his mucky thighs. 'There was no track, only mud, just like ordure. Everywhere. No footing. And very, very hot. We scrambled halfway up, hand over hand, then gave up and slid most of the way down.' Solander just nodded, gloomily, seeming incapable of speech.

James tried to suppress a smile, but was unable to do so. Then he said, sternly, 'Get into the water and cleanse yourselves. I do not wish my ship to become as filthy as you are.'

As the pair washed and rinsed themselves in the lagoon, scrubbing at their naked limbs and soiled breeches with handfuls of coral sand, Tupaia said quietly to James, 'Tiare apetahi is sacred flower. So mebbee better *not* to take it from Mt Temehani.'

That evening, after supper, James and Tupaia walked up onto the afterdeck. Tupaia had requested after supper that they speak in private, and James had agreed. The profile of the island's great volcanic tumescences stood out darkly against the moonlit sky. From the other end of the ship came the plaintive sound of a sailor's fiddle. As the ship's bell rang nine times, the pair leaned on the taffrail and stared towards the island. Holding his hands up high as if in a benediction, he said quietly to James, 'Soon we leave my island, Tute.'

'Yes, once the victualling is complete.'

There was a pause, then Tupaia said, firmly, 'We must sail that way.' He made gestures with his left hand, pointing westward.

James made a pointing gesture of his own, ninety degrees away from Tupaia's. 'No. We will sail south.'

The priest turned, and brought his face close to James's. He repeated his gesture. 'That way, many islands. Many *large* islands, for King George.'

'No.'

James explained that when Samuel Wallis went westward he had found only two small, barren islands, naming them Boscawen and Kepple.

Tupaia's lip curled. 'Wallis did not know what Tupaia knows. His course must have been wrong.' He pointed again, this time more to the north-west. 'Too far that way, mebbee.' He presented his strong facial profile to James. 'I show you the way to the big islands, that way. *West.*'

James felt highly annoyed. This was what he had feared, that the Indian would attempt to usurp his authority. He said, carefully, 'My King has ordered that the ship go *south*, Tupaia. To look for a great land there. So we must go south, to find it.'

With a derisive grunt, Tupaia waved his hand dismissively. 'No great land that way. Only small islands.'

'How can you be certain?'

'Tupaia has been to the small islands. Others have gone south. Many, many years ago. They found no great land. Only other islands, so cold that crops would not grow there.'

James considered this. Could he mean the land Tasman had stumbled upon, in 1642? New Zealand? That was at longitude 172° west, Tasman had estimated. That left a huge void which had not been explored, between here at 152° west, and there. But curious about Tupaia's disclosure, he said, 'Did your people return to the cold land?'

'Yes, from Raiatea. After a war, many generations ago. After that, they did not come back.' He paused. 'But that way ...' he again pointed due west '... are many big islands. Like Otaheite, but very bigger.' He chuckled, cunningly. 'King George would like to have those big islands, I think.'

Turning away, James said, 'King George would also like a *very* big land. What we call a "continent". Your taio, Banks, believes this land is to the south. And I need to find out, for the English King.' He concluded, brusquely. 'So when we leave here, we will sail southward.'

With a disagreeable grunt, Tupaia turned away, muttering. As he watched the priest walk off, James wondered again – was the decision to bring this stubborn, opinionated Indian along the right one?

14 August 1769

Dearest Elizabeth,

We spent several more days on Tupaia's island, and although the winds were in the main adverse, being onshore, we were able to call at neighbouring Tahaa and sail to Bora Bora. This island, the home of people Tupaia calls - employing another English word he has learned - 'pirates', has a block mountain core of spectacular size and only one pass. There was no conflict with the Boraborans, thank the Lord. (During our months in these islands, only one native has died at our hands – the thief shot by one of the marines. Compared to Wallis's visit, when many natives were killed, our stay has been in the main cordial, I am pleased to relate).

We witnessed something of the society of Raiatea when we called at Tupaia's family marae, at a pleasing bay called Hamamino. There members of the priestly class, the people they call arioi, performed dances and plays for us, accompanied by much drumming and singing, gowned in elegant costumes of bark cloth, feathers and head-gownes. The Indians call this a 'heiva'. There was feasting, and gift exchanges, although Tupaia remains resentful that his family's lands are now occupied by the Boraboran usurpers.

Banks and Solander have been heavily engaged in botanising and Parkinson in his illustrating, on the islands of Raiatea and its near-neighbour, Tahaa. The former the Indians consider their most sacred island. Parkinson's depiction of the marae of taputapuatea captures much of the dark presence of that melancholy place where so many rituals and sacrifices have been carried out.

After leaving Bora Bora we sailed west to a small but high island which Tupaia told us was called Maupiti, but there being only narrow passes through its reef, we did not tarry there. Instead we sailed south and after three days sighted an island called Rurutu. Banks was anxious to go ashore, but not only were we greeted with some hostility when we approached, but this island seemed a sterile, rocky shore in comparison with those we had lately visited.

So, Otaheite, Eimayo, Huahine, Raiatea, Tahaa, Bora Bora and Maupiti have been charted. Most are islands of surpassing beauty, as well as luxuriant and fertile. I do believe that there are few other places on Earth to rival their splendour and loveliness. And their inhabitants are on the whole of a generous and amicable disposition, not discounting their predilection for thieving and inter-tribal warfare. It has been my privilege to claim all these islands for King George III.

It has also been my prerogative to name the islands, collectively. As they are in such close proximity – most being within sight of one another – I am calling them the 'Society Islands', as they are a group whose geography and inhabitants have much in common. I have further divided them into the 'Windward' and the 'Leeward' Islands. The former – Otaheite, Eimayo, and Tetiaroa - lie directly in the path of the trade winds and thus are wetter; the latter – Huahine, Raiatea, Tahaa, Bora Bora and Maupiti – lie to some extent in the shadow of the wet winds, and hence are drier. But the whole comprises a uniquely beautiful archipelago. (The members of the Royal Society may well assume that the Society Islands are

227

named after their institution. If they do, that assumption is a harmless one and I will not disabuse them of it).

We are now resolved to stand to the southward, in search of the Great Unknown South Land, the second ambition of our expedition. We are truly heading into the unknown, for apart from Tasman's discovery of a scrap of coastline he named New Zealand, no Europeans have been here before us.

Although I am so far from you, you may take some comfort from the fact that your birthday, and each of our children's birthdays, is marked by a private, heartfelt toast, here in the Great Cabin of Endeavour.

So, as we depart for the unknown and the unfathomable, it is the known and the loved who are uppermost in my thoughts.

Your loving husband, James

Twenty-one

James stood on the afterdeck, one hand on the taffrail. His gaze moved constantly from the sun to the horizon, from the horizon to the sun. By his and Green's observations, yesterday they had crossed the Tropic of Capricorn. Although the temperature was still a mild 68° Fahrenheit, in the Great Cabin last night there had been murmurings of unease about the inevitability of the deteriorating conditions which would face them from now on. Any day now the fearnoughts would have to be brought out of the lockers for the crew. Banks had already issued Tupaia with Buchan's Magellan jacket. The naturalist remained optimistic, anticipating the discovery of the great continent, but Tupaia had said little, evidently still resenting their southward course.

Foam flew from the crests of the swells which rolled towards them from the south-east. Although the sky overhead was clear, dark, billowing clouds extended across the horizon. Storm clouds. The tropic birds had gone, but the albatross which had followed them for days still soared above their wake, watching them like a sentinel. Much smaller pintado birds skimmed the swells.

Endeavour plunged on, heeling to larboard, with Molyneux and Pickersgill at the helm. Squinting at the dark horizon, aware that they were bound where no ship such as theirs had gone before, James wondered: What is out there? Land, or merely ocean and more ocean? And how far must we go before we will know? But as he stared at the vast, empty ocean and felt the spray on his face, he also felt exhilarated. Where they had lately been, others – Magellan, Drake, Roggeveen, Byron, Wallis – had been before them. But no other Englishmen had ever taken the course they were now on, and this knowledge stirred him. He felt no fear, that was an emotion he could not afford, but he did feel apprehension as he peered ahead through the bowsprit stays, watching the swells which came towards them like rolling mountains, because he knew it would require all his knowledge and experience to bring this next stage of the voyage to its fruition.

'Cook?'

Turning, he saw it was Banks. His tan was fading, and for the first time in weeks he wore a jacket. Gripping a foresail sheet, he asked, 'Any signs?'

'No. Nothing but ocean.'

'This morning I studied the Ortelius map, of this ocean. Do you know it?'

'Of course. *Maris Pacifici.*'

'That's it.' Banks lurched as *Endeavour* breasted a swell, then regained his footing. 'The more I studied it, the more I was convinced that a continent lies out here. Between South America and Africa there cannot be merely nothing.'

'There is not "nothing", Banks. There is New Holland.'

'New Holland is in the lower latitudes. And its extent is uncertain. I refer to where we are heading.' He paused, then continued, raising his voice above the wind. 'When I study the disposition of the Earth's northern land masses, and the Ortelius map, it seems certain to me that a similar landmass *must* exist here in the south.'

James nodded, indulgently. 'Perhaps. That is our undertaking, to prove or disprove of its existence.'

Banks closed one eye, slyly. 'Can I make a wager with you? Twenty guineas says such a continent is there.'

'I never wager, Banks. It is against my beliefs to do so.'

The naturalist flicked his eyebrows. 'Have it your way.' He turned to walk away, then stopped and said, with a chuckle, 'But when we encounter the continent, I will have pleasure in presenting you with twenty guineas anyway.'

24 August, 1769

Winds variable. Course SSE. Latitude 32° 44'; Longitude 147° 10' west of Greenwich.

The first part light airs and calm, the middle moderate breezes and cloudy, the latter part very squally with rain.

At noon took in the topsails and got down the topgallant yards. Saw a water spout in the NW, it was about the breadth of a rainbow, of a dark colour, the upper end of the cloud from where it came about 8° above the horizon.

26 August, 1769

Dearest Beth,

I write on the birthday of little Elizabeth. My thoughts have been much with our daughter, and with you and the others. Did you bake our little Beth a special cake? Perhaps you sewed her a new gown with matching bonnet. I think of you all going to the autumn fair on Stepney Heath, as part of the little one's celebrations. No doubt the other children joined in, along with their devoted grandparents.

I write from the high south latitudes, in conditions which are inclement. Temperatures are low, averaging fifty degrees, and are made worse by persistent squalls and gale force winds. The men are grateful for their jackets and dreadnoughts.

The poultry and hogs we took aboard in Tahiti died after refusing to eat their rotted fodder, and the crew's fresh provisions are depleted. In order to keep scurvy at bay I have instructed the men to take their daily ration of wort and pickled cabbage. They grumble at this, as always, but do obey, none wishing to be flogged for disobedience.

The ship rolls constantly in the endless swells, making every activity, from employing the sextant on deck, to writing and drawing in the cabin, most onerous. Parkinson was tossed from his bunk last night, and suffered a bruised shoulder. Banks is ill again and our Indian, Tupaia, spends most of his day staring at the ocean and shivering miserably. He appears to still be sulking because I did not follow his preferred course. Surgeon Monkhouse, who is compiling a lexicon of Tahitian words, says that Tupaia told him he is suffering from not only the cold, but what what he calls 'heama'. This, Monkhouse informs me, is an internal condition similar to an Oriental's loss of 'face'. In the Otaheitian's case, it is a mixture of anger, embarrassment and sullenness, causing intense shame. Used to being treated as nobility in his islands, he is now feeling that a lack of respect is being accorded him by those on the ship, including his friend, Banks. It seems that the botanist, having secured the largest specimen in his exotic collection, is now content to lock him away with his other creatures – birds, fish and plants – then largely ignore him, something which I suspected may happen. Banks lives in constant expectation of sighting the Great Continent, and more than once has mistaken mere clouds for land.

Yesterday in the Great Cabin we celebrated the second anniversary of our departure from England. A cask in which a chunk of best Cheshire cheese had been preserved was opened, and one containing port wine was tapped. Consuming both with gusto, we were able to pretend for a short time that we were in an English country inn, albeit one whose floor rolled constantly. Our Otahetian, Tupaia, liked the cheese, but not the wine, screwing up his face in distaste when he sampled it.

There has been another death, this one self-inflicted. John Reading, an Irishman and the boatswain's mate, died after consuming three half pints of rum, foolishly supplied to him by the boatswain, Thomas Hardman. I severely admonished Hardman for this action, because Reading was known to be overly fond of the grog. I am not averse to the crew consuming their allotted ration of grog, but three half pints in a short time is excessive, as Reading's death proved. We can ill-afford the loss of a hand when we are in no position to impress a replacement seaman.

I will set aside my quill now, dearest Beth. My deepest love to you, to the four little ones, and to all our family and friends.

James

Shortly after dawn he went up onto the stern deck with Green. Both were carrying their sextants. It was the first day of September. Banks was already on deck, Tupaia alongside him at the middeck rail. Banks had his telescope to his eye. The weather was still foul, the seas heavy, with squalls coming at them relentlessly from the south. *Endeavour* was rolling violently. The sea was slate gray, the only colour in sight the scraps of blue sky that briefly followed the squalls. Pickersgill, heavily jacketed, was at the helm, Molyneux on one side of him, boatswain Hardman on the other. Between squalls, Molyneux ordered the fore topgallant and the maintopsail reefed, and a squad of jacketed crewmen let loose the sheets, while others hurried aloft to the yards to take in the sails.

James and Green stood on the larboard side of the stern deck. When the next squall had passed and the sun appeared, James told the astronomer, 'Take your observation now, and I'll take mine.' Both men braced themselves against the taff rail, then brought the sextants' telescopes to their eyes, taking sights on the eastern horizon. A few minutes later, with the ship still rolling heavily and yet another squall coming in across the white-capped water, James looked at Green expectantly.

'Well?'

Green read off his instrument's arc and micrometer. 'Forty degrees, seven minutes, south.' He looked at James. 'And yours?'

'Forty degrees, eight minutes. A minimal difference.'

James folded the sextant and placed it back in its case. Then he called down to the boatswain. 'Order all hands on deck!'

The crew, wrapped in their jackets, many visibly shivering, assembled amidships. They and the scientists were looking up at him expectantly, anticipating something significant. James adgowned them from the quarterdeck, speaking loudly because of the howling wind.

'Men, gentlemen ... this morning we passed through the line of forty degrees south latitude, and an estimated longitude of 146 degrees west of Greenwich.' Feeling his cocked hat beginning to lift in the wind, he pushed it down harder on his head. 'We have thus taken *Endeavour* as far to the southward as I was ordered to. We will now immediately go about and take a nor nor west course, intending to discover the east coast of the land Abel Tasman touched upon in 1642, to determine whether or not that land – New Zealand – may be the Great Unknown Southern Continent.' He paused. 'As that land's east coast is 172° west of Greenwich, we face several weeks more sailing before making landfall.' He called down to the master and his mate. 'Molyneux, Pickersgill, order the men to ready the ship about!'

When he returned to the Great Cabin, Banks was sitting at the long table. In front of him was a crystal goblet, half filled with brandy. His eyes were bloodshot and he hadn't shaved. Looking up as James entered, he said reproachfully, 'You gave up too soon.'

James took the seat opposite him. He said, evenly, 'Do you suggest that I should have sailed the ship right to the polar circle?'

'If necessary. If that is where the Great Continent lies.'

James snapped. 'For God's sake, man! Further south the glass will fall below zero, and there will likely be ice mountains in the sea. The constant squalls and heavy seas have already put great strain on our masts and rigging.' He brought his left fist down upon the table, like a gavel. 'Would you prefer it, *Sir*, that I should put my ship and crew at risk in half-frozen seas, just for you to pursue your ... *fantasy* of a continent?'

Banks took another sip of brandy, then looked up. 'It is no fantasy. And you were over-hasty in turning back.'

James said, frostily, 'I followed my instructions, to the letter, as I am obliged to do.' He stood up, went to his desk, took out the sheet of paper and began to recite the Admiralty's words. ' "You are to proceed to the southward in order to make discovery of the Continent abovementioned until you arrive in the latitude of forty degrees unless you sooner fall in with it. But not having discovered it or any evident signs of it in that run, you are to proceed in search of it to the westward between the latitude before mentioned and the latitude of 35 degrees until you discover it, or fall in with the eastern side of the land discovered by Tasman and now called New Zealand".' He stared across the table at the naturalist. 'That instruction is perfectly clear to me.'

'And which seer decreed that *forty degrees* marked the limit of our exploration?'

'No *seer*, Banks, but the Lords of the Admiralty.'

Banks looked scornful. 'Who have never themselves sailed south of the line.' He gave James another accusing look. 'Suppose the Great Continent lies at forty-*two*, or forty-*three* degrees south. That means we will have missed it.'

'There has not been a single portent of land, Banks. No currents, no driftwood, no land birds, no seaweed. Just great swells, coming up from an empty ocean.' He placed the sheet of notepaper carefully back in the desk. 'Even your Indian, Tupaia, has no belief in such a land.' He sat down again and, seeking some sort of conciliation, said quietly, 'It may be that New Zealand is a large land mass. It could even be a continent. In which case you will have your discovery, and many new specimens, human and animal.'

At that moment the ship rolled heavily. The cabin tilted and the brandy goblet slid down the table. Banks snatched at it, but was not quick enough. Goblet and contents flew from the table and crashed to the floor, the glass shattered and the brandy slopped across the boards. Joseph put his head in his hands and James put a hand on his shoulder. 'Get up on deck, man. You need to witness our new course.'

Twenty-two

29 September, 1769
Latitude 38° South; Longitude 170° West
Strong gales and squally the first part, the remainder fresh
breezes and settled weather. At 1pm was obliged to take in the
topsails, but set them again at 4. At 11am saw a bird something
like a snipe only it had a short bill. It had the appearance of a land
bird. At 4pm saw a seal asleep upon the water, and some sea weed.
Several albatrosses, pintado birds and shearwaters about the ship,
and a number of doves ...

'*Land*! Land! Off the larboard bow!'

The triumphant cry came from the masthead, from Nicholas
Young. It was two o'clock on the afternoon of 6 October. Young
Nick pointed westward. Crew and officers rushed to the rail, but
not being as elevated, could see nothing but sea. And as the breeze
was soft, they could get the ship no closer to the shore.

James ordered the ship kept on close tacks all night, to stay near
the land but without running her aground. Earlier in the evening,
in the Great Cabin, they had celebrated the landfall with a double
issue of rum, and James had presented a grinning Nick with a
gallon of grog, telling him wryly, 'Take care that Monkhouse does
not purloin it all, lad.'

Then, early the next day, the first land they had seen for seven
weeks revealed itself, fully lit by the rising sun at their backs. They
saw a panorama of white cliffs, undulating, forested hills and
further inland, a series of mountainous ridges. Crew, officers and
gentlemen all stared, entranced. *A new land!*

After *Endeavour* was worked in closer to the shore, they saw that
a long, white sand beach curved north from the promontory James
had declared last evening would be called 'Young Nick's Head'.
They could also now see, on the foreshore, canoes and houses.
James approached Parkinson on the after deck, where he was
already seated at his easel, sketching the coastline. The artist
pointed at the northern end of the bay, to a conical hill whose slopes
were surrounded by rows of palings.

'What do you make of that feature, Sir?'

Training his spy glass on the hill, James said, 'It seems to be a settlement of some sort.'

'Or a deer park, perhaps,' suggested Sydney. 'And the white cliffs put me in mind of Beachy Head.'

They were joined at the rail by Banks, telescope in hand. Already booted and gowned for shore, he was beaming. 'A continent, if ever I saw one, gentlemen,' he declared jubilantly.

Quietly satisfied that he had successfully brought the ship across the Pacific Ocean to this coast, James could not ignore the possibility that Banks's glee was justified. Yet doubt still nagged at him, prompted by the navigator's holy writ – facts. The facts of this position were that the longitudinal measurements taken by Tasman and himself – one hundred and seventy-two degrees and one hundred and seventy-eight degrees respectively west of Greenwich – indicated that this land was probably an elongated island. Unless Tasman had been wrong. James was confident that his own longitudinal observations were correct; however he could not be so certain that the Dutchman's were. He said to Banks,

'Much more charting is necessary, before we can be sure.'

Banks continued to stare at the land. 'Let us proceed then, to prove it. Who will go ashore first?'

'Myself, you, Solander and Green will go in the yawl, with four of the men. The marines will go in the pinnace.' He put his scope to his eye again. 'There is a river mouth at the foot of the hill. For ease of landing we will put both boats in there.' Still peering at the river, he added, 'And we will all bear arms for defence. Tasman found the New Zealanders a hostile people.'

The estuary was wide, with sandy banks. The yawl ferried James and his party across to the west bank of the river, then it was left with the men. The pinnace with its uniformed marines was rowed upriver. The sky was clear, the air still and crisp. A little way inland, James and the others came across what appeared to be a recently abandoned village. There were a number of sturdy houses, thatched with broom-like material. Banks and Solander eyed the surrounding foliage eagerly. There were tall, glossy-leaved trees, trailing ropey epiphytes, and plants with long, spiky leaves and orange flowers. 'Marvellous, marvellous,' exclaimed Solander, snipping off one of the flowers. As he did so a throaty but melodious song came from a nearby tree. Looking up, they saw a pair of fowl the size of blackbirds perched side-by-side on a bough. They had iridescent black plumage and cravat-like tufts of white feathers grew from their throats. Joseph snatched up his fowling piece and was about to shoot the birds when from the direction of the river mouth they heard the crackle of musket fire.

That evening the atmosphere in the Great Cabin could not have been more different to that of the night before. Although the lanterns were alight, gloom seeped through the cabin like a London fog, and James could feel the depression in the air. There had been nothing like it since the day the Otaheitian had been shot, way back in April.

Now, one New Zealand native was dead, shot through the heart by the pinnace's coxswain after a party of warriors had advanced on the boat, left unattended when the men went to explore a nearby beach. The warrior's body had been abandoned on the riverbank by his comrades. Coming upon the grim scene, all James and his party could do was place some beads and nails upon the corpse and return to the ship.

He had called this meeting to discuss what they should do from now on. As supplies were very low, he told them, it was essential to take on water and firewood, so they must go ashore again. But how could they do so and at the same time avoid confrontation with the natives?

Banks had remained deep in thought during James's statement of their dilemma. Now, thumbs tucked into his waistcoat, he said, 'I suggest we take Tupaia with us tomorrow.'

Frowning, James asked, 'For what reason?' He was reluctant for the Otaheitian to be elevated to membership of a landing party. Tupaia was haughty enough as it was.

Banks met James's exasperated stare, and said, 'Being a native himself, he may aid our intercourse with those of this land.'

There was silence as the others considered this. Then Monkhouse said, swirling his claret, 'The Indian knows how to handle a gun now. Shoots as straight as any Englishman.'

'I mean *peaceable* communication with the natives, Monkhouse,' Banks replied, coldly.

Parkinson raised his hand, in his usual diffident way. 'I agree with Mr Banks's suggestion. The natives may well react favourably to someone of a similar hue to themselves.'

Solander said quietly, 'We will have nothing to lose by having him accompany us.'

James nodded. It would be worth an attempt. 'Very well, when we next go ashore, he will come with us.' He ran his left forefinger along his hand scar. 'But mind you remain by his side at all times, Banks.'

They faced each other across the river, the Endeavours on the east side, the Maori war party on the western bank. Behind the Englishmen, the bunched, stiffened body of the slain warrior remained where he had fallen, his feather cloak matted with dried blood. The warriors across the river wore skirts of long narrow leaves, feathered cloaks, and their hair was tied in top-knots. Most had spiral tattoos on their faces; all held long, sharpened staves. As the Englishmen lined up alongside James, the warriors began an unmistakeably aggressive dance, chanting, thrusting their arms in the air, pushing out their tongues and stomping their feet in unison. Although brown-skinned like the Tahitians, they were sturdier and more muscular.

James turned to the marine sergeant, Edgecombe. 'We must respond to this. Fire a shot.'

The scarlet-jacketed marine stepped forward and brought his musket up to his shoulder. 'At the natives?' he said, keenly.

'*No*. Into the air!'

When the musket fired with a loud report, the war dance stopped instantly. The warriors looked at one another in confusion. Then Tupaia stepped forward.

'I will speak to them,' he said, and before James could respond he walked boldly to the edge of the river, took off his cocked hat, raised an arm in greeting and called across the water.

'Ia orana ana! Ia orana ana! Maeva! To'u i'oa 'o Tupaia!'

The warriors froze. Mouths agape, they stared at the strange figure who looked like them, was dressed like the other aliens who had entered their domain, but spoke a language which they partly understood. A very tall warrior with a broad, rounded forehead came to the front and called back to Tupaia, who nodded and replied loudly, 'Ay, ay, ay ...'

A further halting conversation ensued. James stood behind the Otaheitian, requesting a translation. Tupaia told him, 'He says this place is called by them Turanga-nui. Their leader is called Te

Rakau. He wishes to know why we are here. He calls us ...' He groped for the right English word ... '*goblins*. They also wish to know why you killed their comrade with the stick that explodes.'

James spoke up, loudly. It was essential to emphasise that he, and not Tupaia, was the commander. He said, 'Tell them that we very much regret the death of their comrade. That was caused by a misunderstanding. Tell them that we come in peace, and that we wish to trade with them. Our need is for food, firewood and water.'

Tupaia related all this, slowly, hesitantly, repetitively, observing the New Zealanders' consternation as they struggled to fully understand him. He continued.'Ua tipae mai nei matou i to outou na fenua. E mea fano mai matou mai te fenua ra o Peretane e Otaheite. Te haere mai nei matou na roto i te hau. Te haere mai nei matou na roto it e hau. Te haere mai nei matou e an ii te pape, te maa e te raau, no to matou pahi. E nau toa rii rau ta matau no outou ei tapihooraa no te pape, te maa e te rau. Ua tia anei ia autou i te tauturu ma i ta matou nei mau anirraa?'

Te Rakau entered the water and waded out to a large rock in the middle of the river. Assuming that a reciprocal gesture was required, without hesitation James handed his musket to Jonathan Monkhouse, then also waded out to the rock. In thigh-deep water the two men met. James held out his hand, but instead of taking it, the native thrust his face into James's and to his dismay brought his nose against his. Then the native turned and waded back to the others. James did the same, wondering at the same time, did this nose-touching mean a breakthrough had been made?

The leader and the other warriors now came across the river. As they did so James ordered a box of nails brought forward. He held out a fistful of the nails to the leader, but the native waved them away dismissively. Instead he pointed first to the short sword at Green's side, then at Edgecombe's musket, and handed James a carved, flat club of jade. The gesture was obvious – he wanted an exchange of weapons. Tupaia stepped forward and spoke firmly to the chief. Turning, he said to James, 'I tell him, we only give them nails, not swords or exploding sticks.'

In response the leader lunged for Green's sword, attempting to draw it from its scabbard. Green reeled back and as he did so Banks raised his fowling piece and fired at the native's legs. Crying out, he clutched his shins. Monkhouse immediately raised his musket and fired at the warrior, at close range. The ball entered his chest and he fell to the ground. Two other warriors ran forward and attempted to wrest the musket from Monkhouse, and while they were doing so Tupaia raised his firearm and blasted their legs with small shot. A short, thickset warrior rushed forward, deftly snatched the jade club from James's hand and grimacing, waved it aloft wildly. Seeing that the club had been retrieved, the other warriors all turned quickly, waded into the river and returned to the other bank.

Blood was gushing from a gaping hole in the chest of the dead man. James led the others a little distance away and when they had grouped around him, said, 'A most regrettable development, gentlemen. It was my belief that a truce was in the offing.' Monkhouse stared at the ground and said nothing. James turned to Edgecombe. 'Leave the body for his comrades.' Glancing back at the river and observing that the warriors had disappeared, he said to Edgecombe, 'Cut a staff and we'll run the Jack up it.'

When this had been done and the pole was planted, they stood around the flagstaff at attention while James declared, 'I hereby claim this land and all it holds for our king, George III of England.' The marines raised their muskets and fired a volley. It echoed from the nearby hillside, then there was a deathly silence.

As they trudged silently back to the boats, James thought, so much for the Earl of Morton's instructions. An English peer in London could hardly have envisaged the circumstances James's party now found themselves in. And other thoughts racked him. The natives obviously would now view them as belligerent intruders, and ones who could kill from a distance. So just how were they to establish relations with these people, in order to obtain their much-needed supplies?

Water was a paramount need. The river had proved brackish, so James ordered the boats to row along parallel to the shore in search of another stream. However a strong swell was now running, and as the waves were breaking heavily, he ordered the boats to return to *Endeavour*. The oarsmen had just begun to row out into the bay when Tupaia pointed and cried out, 'Canoes!'

There were two, each holding seven paddlers. As one approached the pinnace, James told Tupaia, 'Tell them we wish to be friends.' Standing in the bow, the priest called out to them in the language they now knew the New Zealanders understood, at the same time gesticulating dramatically.

The canoeists' response was immediate. One stood up and hurled his paddle at Tupaia like a javelin. It missed him by inches. Another threw a wooden spear, which landed a few feet from the pinnace. Then all the fishermen began to throw objects at the Englishmen: more spears, an anchor stone, and a number of fish, one of which hit Banks in the face. Furious at this unprovoked aggression, picking up his own primed musket, James called to Banks and Solander, 'Fire at them!'

Three shots rang out. Two of the fishermen clutched their chests and dropped to the bottom of their canoe; two others, grievously wounded, slid over the side into the water and sank from sight. The remaining three scrambled overboard and began to swim shoreward. 'Apprehend them!' James commanded the oarsmen. The pinnace pursued the trio, reached them, and they were hauled aboard.

They were mere boys. As they were taken up on *Endeavour*'s deck, grass skirts dripping, they looked around the ship with terrified eyes. Two of them were very young, with thin arms and knobbly knees, the third was much taller and physically more developed. He mumbled something to Tupaia, at the same time putting his hand over his face.

'What does he ask?' said James.

'He wants to know how we are going to kill them,' replied Tupaia. 'With clubs or with the exploding sticks?'

James said, 'Tell them we are their friends. And ...' he turned to a crewman '...bring some biscuits and meat up from below.'

As Tupaia offered them the biscuits and pieces of salt pork, the rest of the crew looked on curiously. One of the midshipmen, Isaac Manley, came forward and handed the oldest boy a red jacket. He stared at it in wonderment. Then, as Isaac showed him how to put it on, his face broke into a grin. The three boys began to nibble the pork and biscuits. Then they became more animated, chatting away to Tupaia as if nothing untoward had happened. Tupaia translated for James, pointing first to the tallest lad. 'This one called Te Haurangi. This one Ikirangi, this one Marukauiti.'

'Can they remain on board?' Banks asked James, his expression wretched. Aware that the naturalist had never shot and killed a man before, James felt sympathetic. He remembered the first time he had killed, while serving against the French on *Eagle* in 1757. Although he had been fighting for his own life, he had never forgotten running a Frenchman through the gut with his small sword, and the memory which had afterwards haunted him. He said to Banks:

'For the time being, yes. They may be able to assist us when we next go ashore.' To Tupaia he said, 'What else do they tell you?'

'That the people north of here kill and eat people.'

The boys kept close to James, Banks and Tupaia after they disembarked on the river bank. Te Haurangi was still wearing Hanley's red jacket. 'This part of the land belongs to their enemies,' Tupaia explained to James. 'Their tribe usually lives further south, across the river.'

The two bodies still lay where they had fallen. 'They are chiefs, so they are tapu,' Tupaia said.' He pointed across the river. 'Look!'

It was another war party, led by an older, portly man. Instead of performing a war dance, the leader called at length across the river to Tupaia, who translated for the others. 'They wish to know, why had the fishermen been killed?'

Suddenly, Te Haurangi came forward and called across the river. Tupaia translated for James. 'He says they have been well treated by the goblins, and given strange foods.' The lad then took off the red jacket and placed it reverently over the bunched body of Te Rakau. At this, the mood of the warriors visibly changed. They looked subdued and thoughtful, murmuring among themselves. Then a stooped, elderly man wearing a feather cloak came across the river, bearing a leafed branch. 'A sign of peace,' Tupaia said to James. 'Same as in my islands.' Emerging from the river, the old man came forward and embraced the youngest boy, Marukauiti, who smiled warmly and clutched him. 'Father and son,' Tupaia announced.

The pair moved over to the body and the old man closed his eyes and began to chant, waving the leafy branch over the dead warrior. James and Joseph stood back respectfully, sensing that a kind of reconciliation was occurring. Tupaia said, 'He is what they call a tohunga, a priest. Like me. And he is praying to their gods, to remove the tapu. Until it is lifted, the body cannot be buried.'

The ceremony over, the old man called across the river to the others. Solemnly they crossed the river and clustered around the corpse. Then two warriors picked up the body of their dead relative and carried it back to the other bank. 'Where will he be buried?' asked Banks of Tupaia. 'In the sand,' the priest replied. 'Above the beach.'

James felt a surge of relief. The killings had been a matter of great regret, but were unavoidable, as he would make clear in his report to the Admiralty. And the decision to bring Tupaia along had, he had to admit, been propitious. As an intermediary he was proving most useful. He said to the others, 'There is nothing to detain us here, we will return to the ship.' Feeling a tugging at his jacket, he looked down. It was the boy, Ikirangi. Neither he nor the other two had crossed the river. He said something to James in his language. James looked quizzically at Tupaia, who grinned. 'The boys wish to come with us on the giant canoe.'

'They may do so,' said James. 'But only to say goodbye. They cannot sail with us.'

They dined below decks, again on salt pork and biscuit, with some baked silver-green fish the crew had seined from the bay. The boys sang harmonious songs for the men, and danced languidly and happily with Tupaia, swaying and moving their hands gracefully. From time to time they stopped and laughed, uproariously. James watched, gratified that a rapprochement had been achieved. Then he ordered the trio taken ashore. When they were put into the yawl they began to weep. And uttering cries of 'Ow-ay! Ow-ay! Haere ra, haere ra!', they were rowed ashore.

At dawn the next morning, James ordered the anchors weighed and a southward course set. Men hastened aloft, the sails were unfurled and filled with a south-westerly breeze. As *Endeavour* began to move out of the bay, they saw the three boys standing on the shore. They first lowered their bodies, then together threw their arms up and outward, three times. Standing on the after deck, James doffed his hat towards them.

Later that day, in the Great Cabin, he wrote:

'11 October, 1769. I first considered naming this place "Endeavour Bay", but instead I have named it "Poverty Bay", as it afforded us no one thing we wanted.'

Their first contact with the New Zealanders had been largely a failure. And James detested failure.

13 October 1769

Dearest Beth,

> *At last I have the Great Cabin to myself again, and so am able to once more communicate with you. I am in blissful solitude this morning, as Banks and Solander are trawling for marine specimens in the yawl and Parkinson is busy sketching coastal features from the after deck. Their absence thus affords me the time and space to write.*

> *Little James is six years of age today! How often he has been in my thoughts these past hours. His schooling is progressing, I am sure, as from his earliest years he showed an aptitude for reading, writing and drawing. Since I have marked him (and Nathaniel) for a naval career, it will not be many more years until he goes to sea himself, and he will do so with my blessing. What stories I will have to tell them upon my return!*

> *As we make our way south, along the coast of this new land, it is my privilege to name the geographical features which appear before us. I am aware that I must be judicious in this matter, balancing the gratitude I feel towards those still in England who have supported me in the past, and those on board whose assistance I value in the present. It is also my duty as an Englishman to commemorate certain features of my home country which resemble those which we encounter. Also, I feel the need to mark signal events which occur during the voyage. Accordingly, I have named a promontory in this country 'Young Nick's Head' after the boy who first saw the new land from Endeavour's masthead, I have called a small island here 'Portland' after Wessex's Portland Bill, a large sheltered bay, 'Hawke Bay' after Sir Edward Hawke, our heroic First Lord of the Admiralty, a cape 'Kidnappers' to mark the abduction by local savages of the Otaheitian's boy (who was, to the great relief of us all, but foremostly Taiata himself) later rescued.*

> *The responsibility for this naming weighs heavily upon me. I am deeply aware that such nomenclatures will not only be enduring, but will be like fiery lightships for those seamen who follow in our wake, and who employ the very charts which it is my constant occupation to construct during this voyage.*

He held his quill above the page for a moment, wondering how much he should write of the killings that had lately occurred. Then, deciding that they would best be confined to his official log, he was about to resume writing when the door of the cabin burst open.

'Cook! Look at this!'

Banks was bare-footed and bedraggled, his trousers saturated. With a red scarf wrapped around his head, he looked more like a pirate than a scientist. In his hand he held the body of a large, goose-like bird. Its plumage was white, with a yellow neck, and its breast was mashed and bloody. Joseph raised it triumphantly and its legs and yellow feet dangled. 'Solander and I were watching them diving for fish, plummeting from a great height, and when this one surfaced I shot it. It is a local species of gannet, I believe, related to the Atlantic genus.' He pulled out one of its wings. 'It has a span of over six feet.'

Getting to his feet swiftly and with quill still in hand, James attempted to cover Elizabeth's journal with the other. Noticing his furtive reaction, Banks said, 'What is that you are writing?'

'My log, naturally.'

Banks gave a half-smile. 'Is that so? From what I glimpsed, the entry seemed more protracted than your usual ones.'

James breathed in deeply, through his nose, then said coolly, 'There is much to record. The kidnapping, the encounters with the natives. As well as the usual observations.'

'Yes, yes ...' But the naturalist's expression remained sceptical.

Then, scowling at Banks, James added, 'Moreover, it is my understanding that the Great Cabin is to be mine at this time of day. Did we not agree on that arrangement?'

'But I wish to dissect this creature,' Banks protested. 'Solander is coming with the scalpels.' He brandished his trophy again, and blood from its shattered breast dripped onto the table.

James paused, aggrieved at both the disturbance to his writing and the discovery of his alternative journal. Then he said, coldly, 'Very well, carry out your dissection. But not on this table when I am writing.' He added, bluntly, 'I suggest the foredeck.'

Although Banks glowered, he turned away. At the door he paused and said over his shoulder, 'After the dissection, I will take the body to the galley and give it to Thompson. We'll dine on the bird tomorrow.'

Still resentful of the thoughtless interruption, James carefully wiped the gouts of blood from the table with a cloth, then dipped his quill in the ink pot and resumed his writing.

We have made numerous attempts at intercourse with the natives here, our need for fresh water and other provisions now being pressing, but have found no suitable landing place. There is also mutual suspicion when the natives appear in their canoes. Several times it has been necessary to fire warning salvoes to curb their natural tendencies to theft and violence. Gifts have been exchanged, however, and the New Zealanders continue to show great curiosity towards Tupaia, our native, who regales them with his personal history and the beliefs of his people. These are so broadly similar to those of the New Zealanders that it is clear from whence they originally came – his island of Raiatea, which they also refer to as 'Hawaiiki'. They call themselves 'Maori'; Tupaia calls his people 'Maohi', generations of time having modified the word but slightly.

It is my earnest hope that we will soon be able to establish amicable relations with these people. Unless we do, there will be little hope of charting the country in the thorough manner with which I hope to do so. We will sail south to forty degrees latitude, then will put about and go northward, following the east coast of this land in search of a suitable provisioning place and natives who are not inimical to our intentions.

I will conclude now. I trust the autumn is proving its usual benign self in England and that the oaks and elms on the common are displaying their golden beauty. Autumn was always my favourite season. Mostly, though, I hope that you and the children – especially little James on this auspicious day – are well and contented. Be assured, Beth, that my fondest thoughts are with you all, wherever I may be.

Your loving husband, James
19 October 1769
Latitude observed, 38° 44' south

The first part had gentle breezes at east and ENE. In the night fresh gales between the south and SW, dark cloudy weather, with lightning and rain. At half past 5pm tacked, and stood to the SE. Soon after a canoe came off from the shore wherein were five people. They came on board without showing the least sign of fear and insisted upon staying with us the whole night for indeed there was no getting them away without turning them out of the ship by force and that I did not care to do. But to prevent them playing us any tricks I hoisted their canoe up alongside. Two appeared to be chiefs and the other three their servants. One of the chiefs seemed to be of a free, open and gentle disposition. They both took great notice of everything they saw and were very thankful for what was given them. The two chiefs would neither drink nor eat with us, but the other three ate whatever was offered them.

After talking at length to the chiefs who had come aboard, Tupaia reported that the news of the great canoe had already spread. Everywhere along the coast, he told them, the natives were talking about the strange newcomers and their giant canoe, exploding sticks and peculiar garments.

'It seems that we are already famous in this land,' Banks remarked delightedly to James, after hearing Tupaia's report. James made no reply; fame was a frivolity which could be left to others, he had more important matters to attend to. Buoyed by the cordiality of these chiefs, and the sighting that afternoon of two sheltered bays, he ordered the bower anchors lowered in the more northern of the two and declared that parties would go ashore the next day. They discussed a proposed programme over supper in the Officers Mess. James decided that he and Green would take observations from a suitable high point, while Banks and Solander botanised and Parkinson drew. Gore and the marines would collect much-needed firewood and freshwater.

There was now an atmosphere of keen anticipation in the Great Cabin, a feeling that after the tragedies of Poverty Bay, this place offered a new and more positive beginning. From the ship they had espied streams and sheltered beaches backed by lowlands. Forested hills rose to the north and south of both bays.

'Very suitable for taking observations, Green,' James remarked to the astronomer. 'Indeed,' he replied. 'There look to be some wonderful promontories, too,' added Parkinson. 'Which I must draw.' Tupaia's eyes were bright. 'I too wish to make some paintings. Can I use your brushes, taio?' The artist nodded. 'Most certainly.' Banks, swirling the brandy in his glass, said, 'I wonder if their women will be as luscious as those of Otaheite.'

James gave him his sternest look. 'Exercise discretion in that regard, Banks. We do not wish to introduce the venereals here. Since the Spanish or French have not been here before us, this time we cannot apportion blame to them.' To surgeon Monkhouse he said, 'Check all the men tomorrow. No infected ones will be permitted ashore.'

Canoes came out from the shore to greet the *Endeavour* after she had anchored. The leading vessel contained two grey-haired men – chiefs, obviously – who Tupaia called down to and invited aboard. One was short and rotund, the other tall but stooped. The faces of both were covered in dark blue tattoos, human molars dangled from their earlobes and they wore cloaks made of animal skin, the taller one's adorned with brown feathers. Jade clubs hung from their belts.

They went directly to Tupaia and offered him their noses. In turn, he pressed his to theirs. They then turned to James, standing behind him. 'You, Tute. Hongi,' ordered Tupaia. James came forward, knowing now what was required, and pressed noses with the pair. Tupaia indicated the taller chief. 'His name, Whakata te Aoterangi. Ariki. Paramount chief. This one ...' he pointed to the stocky figure '... Whakarua te Uawa.' Hearing their names pronounced, the two men nodded, uttering grunts of 'Ay... ay ...' They told Tupaia that the northernward bay was called Anaura, the one further to the south was Uawa.

James gave the men a spike nail each, and a length of English linen. The nails they handed back, the cloth they accepted, nodding with pleasure. Then they all retired to the Great Cabin, whose sash windows had been lowered to admit the sea breeze. The chiefs were offered salt pork and ship's biscuit, which they waved away. Tupaia then told them what the visitors needed: food, water, firewood, and that they would pay with Tahitian bark cloth, beads and axes.

Both chiefs nodded thoughtfully, but at that moment there came a shout from the stern. They all turned and looked through the windows. A warrior in a canoe was yelling at them, rolling his eyes wildly and brandishing a lance. The five other occupants of the canoe were waving their paddles and calling out what were, unmistakeably, hostilities towards the Englishmen.

The taller chief ran immediately to the window, put his head out and unleashed a torrent of what was, with equal unmistakeability, bitter invective. He concluded his tirade with an upraised fist and a cry of 'Ha!' The man in the canoe sank down and turned away, clearly shamed. The others too looked down, then began to paddle the canoe away. The chief put his hand on Tupaia's shoulder and said something to him. James asked, 'What does he say?'

'His tribe will welcome you to his rohe. His tribal land.'

The next day there was a strong swell rolling into Anaura Bay, making a landing there and the transfer of water casks impossible, so James ordered the anchors weighed. After several tacks to the south, *Endeavour* entered the bay called Uawa.

It was deeply indented into an almost perfect U-shape, with a sandy beach and foreshore. Two rivers flowed down from forested hills, meandered, then came together in the centre of a broad lowland before debouching into the bay. There was a rocky island off a headland at the southern end of the bay, joined to the mainland by a natural arch, on the top of which was a pallisaded settlement. Plots of cultivated land showed up as green patches on the hillsides.

On a terrace above the confluence of the rivers were a number of houses, their thatched eaves extending almost to the ground from central ridges. There were porches at the front of the houses, and through their spyglasses James and the others could see adults and children moving about around the houses and maintaining fires in front of them. One larger house which stood apart from the rest had ornately carved barge boards.

The sky was overcast but the temperature mild as the two ship's boats came ashore near the river mouth. A large number of people were waiting there and five canoes with decorated prows were drawn up on the sand. As the Endeavours had fervently hoped, they were greeted peaceably. And although James pressed noses with several of the Maori men, it was immediately apparent that it was Tupaia who was the object of greatest interest to the New Zealanders. James observed their curious expressions as they followed the Otaheitian up onto the plain. Children ran alongside him, touched his coat-tails daringly, then ran away, big-eyed, as if they had stroked a spirit.

They came to the village. Around the houses, fishing nets with gourd floats attached hung on poles to dry, and what seemed to be storehouses – small replicas of the houses – stood atop posts. Fish traps – conical baskets woven from some sort of vine – were heaped below the storehouses. A few small dogs slunk about the village, beyond which were tidily laid out garden plots.

The party followed the people up to the area in front of the large house. There men, women and children gathered about Tupaia, smiling and touching his clothes. Whakata placed a dogskin and feather cloak reverently about the Otaheitian's shoulders, at the same time chanting what sounded like a blessing.

Tupaia responded with a long speech, speaking loudly and with authority, like a King's emissary in a foreign court. Which, James realised, in a way he was. James himself was largely ignored, and even Banks, he noticed with some satisfaction, was having to hover in the background. The other Endeavours could only look on as in front of his now-seated audience, Tupaia spoke with great feeling, turning and gesticulating every now and then towards the east. James heard the names 'Raiatea', 'Hamamino','Taputapuatea' and 'Hawaiiki' mentioned over and over again. His audience – men, women and children – was in thrall.At times they looked perplexed, as they heard some Otaheitian word, expression or inflection which was strange to them, but not once did they interrupt the outlandish, handsome visitor. As he watched, James's feelings were mixed. The man was proving to be a valuable envoy, but how would this adulation affect his already-conceited nature?

The other Endeavours dispersed, leaving Tupaia still soaring on the updrafts of his oratory and genealogy: *'Oro', Ta'aroa', 'Tane', 'Hiro'... 'Matavai', 'Tahiti Nui', 'Vehiatua', 'Hawaiiki','Raiatea' 'Tahaa'...'*

Gore and the marines, accompanied by a lesser chief deputed by Whakata, went inland to gather provisions, while James and Green left to climb the hill at the southern end of the bay. Solander, Sporing and Parkinson went off towards the northern end to botanise and draw, but Banks stayed at the back of the crowd, sitting on the ground like the others.

There was a defile at the end of the bay. James and Green entered it, then pushed up through the undergrowth towards the crest of a ridge. Mature evergreen trees, some with glossy green leaves and orange berries, and a species of palm with a stout green trunk and a bulging crown shaft, grew in the hollows of the hill. Other, taller trees had scaly, branchless trunks with a profusion of leaves sprouting from their crowns. Plump, blue-grey pigeons flew clumsily from branch to branch, and the iridescent blackbirds with tufts of white feathers at their throats croaked and warbled in the foliage. Ferns of all sizes grew amid the forest.

As the two men climbed higher the vegetation became scrubbier, mainly shrubs with narrow twisted trunks, roughened bark and delicate white flowers.

They emerged from the scrub and stood atop the ridge. The bay, plain and rivers were laid out below them. *Endeavour*, reduced to Lilliputian size by distance, had her bow turned into the south-westerly breeze. The sun had broken through the cloud and was rising over the bay, creating diamonds of light on the water. Below, notched into the headland, was a sheltered cove and a beach where three small canoes had been drawn up. Panting, his shirt front open and damp, Green stared out over the bay. 'Tis a fine sight, Cook. And what a contrast with our former impoverished landing.'

'Aye. It could not be better. Water, wood, greens...' They had already noted the wild celery and scurvy grass which grew on the plain. '... agreeable natives'.

James took the sextant box from his haversack. He opened it, took out the instrument, aimed its telescope carefully at the horizon then studied its arc. Looking at him expectantly, Green said, 'Yes?' James smiled, and handed him the sextant. 'Your turn.' Green peered into the telescope, then took his reading.

'Well?' said James.

'One hundred and eighty degrees, forty-seven minutes west.'

James nodded. 'Forty-eight minutes. Good.'

After descending the hill and coming out onto the plain, they came upon Solander, Sporing and Parkinson. The botanists had their collecting bags on their backs, Parkinson was lugging his easel and paint box. Solander was at his most effusive. 'I have never seen such a profusion of new specimens,' he told the others. 'This place is almost as luxuriant as Otaheite.' He removed the bag from his back. 'Yet very different.' He took a stalk and a broad leaf from the bag and held it out. The stalk was dark brown, with curved pods on the end of half a dozen off-shoots. The leaf was grey-green, broad and creased down the centre. Solander said, 'The fibre of this leaf, I believe, could be used to make fine cordage. It grows in damp ground, and the natives make great use of it for weaving baskets. They call it "harakeke", a woman told me when I saw her preparing it.' He raised his wig, wiped his pate with his hand, then reset the hairpiece.

'We climbed the hill,' James reported. 'It affords a fine view.'

Sydney's eyes were shining with anticipation. 'I am sure. I cannot wait to begin my drawing.'

Sporing nodded. 'I too wish to draw this place.'

'Where is Banks?' asked James.

Solander arched his eyebrows. 'He is bartering with the Indians.'

'What for?'

Solander gave a harsh laugh. 'A woman.'

James and Charles approached the cluster of thatched dwellings. In front of the largest house, Tupaia was still holding forth to an audience of several dozen people. Whakata te Aoterangi, a carved stave in his hand, stood beside him, intervening from time to time to ask a question. They heard the words 'marae' and 'paepae' mentioned several times, and again such Otaheitian words as 'Oro','pahi' and 'arioi'.

Two bare-breasted young women with long, coal-black hair and red ochre smeared across their cheeks, were sitting at Tupaia's feet, gazing up at him, spellbound. Both wore jade pendants on woven cord around their necks, miniatures of the clubs the Maori called 'mere'. Standing to one side and watching the scene, James blinked several times, then realised that he was not seeing double. Both startlingly beautiful, the young women were identical twins.

By late afternoon all except Tupaia were back on the ship. James, Hicks, Gore and the gentlemen gathered in the Officers' Mess to discuss plans for the remaining time in Uawa. When James asked after Tupaia, Banks replied sourly, 'He has been invited by the chief to stay ashore while we are here.' He sniffed. 'An invitation which he accepted with alacrity.'

'He has a natural affinity with these people, I have observed,' said Solander.

'He certainly has.'

'Do I detect a note of envy in your voice, Banks?' James asked.

Banks grunted dismissively, then said, 'When I walked inland a little way, I came upon some young women bathing in the river. All they wore was a small cloth over their private parts.' He paused. 'In this respect they are strikingly similar to their Otaheitian counterparts.'

'And ...?' said Monkhouse, leeringly.

'In other respects, not. When they saw me approach they covered their breasts, as modestly as any English debutante.'

The others smiled. Hicks said, 'But not for our Otaheitian friend.'

Banks made a face. 'No. He informed me, gleefully, that the chief has presented him with his daughters for the duration of his stay.'

'The twins?' asked James.

'Yes. And a spacious cave on the hillside, where the three of them can stay. Food and drink will be brought to them there.' Banks ground his teeth. 'The man is treated like royalty here.'

Monkhouse winked at James. 'So you have been unable to barter for a body this time, Banks?'

The botanist pouted. 'Not so. I bartered a piece of Otaheitian bark cloth for a very fine body this afternoon.'

The others looked intrigued. 'Who was it?' asked Gore.

Banks laughed. 'A large lobster. Thompson is preparing it for our supper.'

Hundreds gathered on the shore to farewell the Endeavours. The ship was now fully provisioned with sweet potatoes, yams, live lobsters, wild celery and scurvy grass. James presented both chiefs with more lengths of English cloth, and an axe each. There were speeches, and noses were pressed and re-pressed. But when James looked about, there was no sign of Tupaia. He spoke, slowly, to Whakata. 'Tupaia ... where is taio Tupaia?'

The chief smiled and pointed down the beach. 'Tupaia, Hine, Moana ...'

When they followed his gesture they saw the trio approaching. Tupaia, striding imperiously, still wearing the dogskin cloak over his English garments, cocked hat askew, a bare-breasted twin clutching each of his arms. When they came closer the others saw that the girls were red-eyed from weeping. The crowd stood back while Tupaia released the girls and bade his farewells to the chiefs, embracing them both. As there had been in Otaheite, there were cries of 'Ow-ay! Ow-ay!' from the women in the crowd, and melodious chanting from the men.

Edgecombe, the marine sergeant, approached James.

'Shall we fire a salute, Sir?'

'There is no need. Save your powder.'

James doffed his hat once more towards the crowd, then ordered the men into the boats. Hine and Moana cast themselves down onto the sand, weeping inconsolably as the boats pulled away. James stood in the stern, filled with gratitude for the kindnesses these people had shown them. Would this be what it would be like from now on? If so, there was much to look forward to.

On the ship, he announced that they would weigh anchor at first light on the morrow. In the Great Cabin, mementoes of Uawa were laid out on the table. It resembled a museum display. New plants and flowers by the score (Solander and Sporing), a small flightless bird with a long beak, two dead pigeons and three parson birds (Banks) several sketches of the coast, including one of the pallisaded village atop the rock arch (Parkinson) and another impression of the same feature (Sporing).

With a smile of triumph, Tupaia placed his gifts upon the table. They included the dogskin and feather cloak, jade carvings of what Maori called a 'tiki' – a human embryo representation – a stave they called a 'taiaha' and a flat, sharp-edged jade club. Lastly, Tupaia picked up a delicately carved panel depicting a human figure with a protruding tongue. 'This called poupou,' he declared proudly. He traced the outline of the figure's body. 'This is tupuna. Ancestor.' He had been taken to a special house, he told them, called Te Rawheoro, where young men were trained in the art of carving by skilled older craftsmen. He held up the panel, with its exquisite whorls and spirals, shell eyes and protruding tongue, for them to admire.

Looking covetously at the carving, Banks said, 'What will you do with these things, taio?'

Tupaia grinned. 'Take them with me to England. To give to King George.' Then he picked up a rolled sheet of paper and handed it to James. 'This one for you, Tute. Tupaia painted.'

James unrolled it.

It portrayed in colour two side-on figures. One was a heavily cloaked Maori man, his hair drawn up into a topknot, his splayed feet bare. He was holding out to a frock-coated Englishman a large, many-legged, bright red lobster. But it was on a piece of string, so that it could be withdrawn at any moment. The Englishman was proffering a piece of white Tahitian bark cloth in exchange for the crustacean, but both human figures were clearly wary of each other's intentions.

After studying the painting, James nodded appreciatively. 'Thank you. It is a very fine painting.' Then, glancing at Joseph, he said, 'Could the figure on the right be Mr Banks, by any chance?'

Tupaia laughed, uproariously. 'Yes, yes!' Then, still laughing, he added, 'No vahine here for Banks. Only lobster.'

Everyone except Banks laughed. His face was stony.

As they moved out of the bay, Tupaia stared landward. He said to James, quietly, 'I like these people, Tute. Yes, after I have been to Peretane, and met your King and Queen, I will come back to Uawa.'

Twenty-three

On they sailed north, shadowing the coastline in variable spring weather, passing bays, capes and headlands. Fully provisioned, they had no need to go ashore. Seated on the poop deck, James charted assiduously, relishing the work. From time to time Sporing joined him there, sketch pad on his knee. James had come to admire the Scandinavian's drawing skills. He was particularly adept at rendering coastal features, leading James to name the small island at the southern end of Uawa 'Sporing's Island'. At this news, Herman blushed with pleasure. 'Me, a clock-maker from Turku, haff a whole island named for him. Marvellous.'

More names came. When they doubled what James was certain was this land's eastern extremity, he noted on the chart he was constructing, 'East Cape'. Then, bearing due west and passing a pretty, sheltered cove, and mindful that poor Zachary's cough was worse, he named it 'Hick's Bay'. Following a skirmish during which some hostile canoeists had a warning shot fired upon them and subsequently retreated, James carefully inscribed the nearest landmark 'Cape Runaway'. A cone protruding from a coastal plain he marked as 'Mt Edgcombe' after the Lord Admiral who had farewelled them at Plymouth. And there were more islands, some large, many small. He named one near the eastern end of a long, broad bay, 'White Island' for its pale plume of volcanic steam, and one at the other end, 'Mayor Island', for its authoritative solitude.

The wide bay's coastal plain was obviously productive, with many cultivated fields and fortified villages visible, so that James unhesitatingly named it the 'Bay of Plenty'. A cluster of small, rugged islands a day's sailing north of Mayor Island moved him to extend his metaphor and call them 'The Aldermens'. Then, as they sailed to the west of these and James noted two small islands closer to the shore, he called the first 'Slipper' and the second 'Shoe'. This was work he savoured. He was leaving his mark on the world, as he had long wished to.

As *Endeavour* plodded along New Zealand's eastern coast, more and more canoes came out to greet them. A pattern was established. The occupants of the canoes first challenged them by hurling stones and spears at the ship, then after being warned with a firing of grape shot or cannon balls, either beat a retreat or traded fish and vegetables for the exotic goods the ship carried. Tahitian bark cloth continued to be the New Zealanders' most desired item. At each encounter, Tupaia would call down in their language to the men in the canoes, explaining the visitors' needs, but usually the challengers would shout him down. No further fatalities occurred, however, and the Endeavours now realised that such confrontations carried more ritual than menace.

On the morning of 4 November James and Green met on the quarterdeck. The wind was a steady sou'wester and *Endeavour* was averaging four knots as she continued north. In the distance, to larboard, was a long line of pinkish, fissured cliffs, capped by forest, and spiky islets and promontories. Inland was a continuous wall of rugged, forested mountains.

James peered at the broken coast. 'Only another five days, Green, and Mercury's transit will occur.'

Green looked worried. 'Five days. There will be no time to set up a Fort Mercury, as on Otaheite.' He mopped his brow.

James looked at the sugary cliffs. 'Very little time. But we will still need, along with a clear sky, a suitable shore camp.' Then, trying to keep anxiety from his voice, he added, 'Let us hope that we come upon a sheltered bay within the next two days.'

They did.

On the afternoon of 4 November *Endeavour* rounded a headland, then several steep-sided islands. From the masthead Molyneux reported that there was a sheltered bay due west, and James ordered the ship to put into it. Coming closer, they saw steep, white-cliffed headlands to the north and south of the bay, a long sandy beach between them and a river estuary at the eastern end. The beach was backed by a broad plain. James ordered soundings taken. *Eight fathoms, with a sandy bottom.* A reef-free bay. Perfect.

'Could not be more suitable,' Green mused, in a rare utterance of enthusiasm. On the foredeck, Pickersgill was supervising the lowering of *Endeavour*'s bow anchors. James held his spyglass to his eye. 'Indeed. But first we must negotiate with the local natives.'

Several canoes had put out from the shore and were paddling furiously towards the ship. There were the now-familiar challenges – stone-throwing and a war dance – and Tupaia again called down from the deck and explained what it was they wanted. The ritual continued: James ordered the marines to fire a volley of warning shots into the air, and one of the cannons to be fired. At the sight and sound of these discharges, the canoeists paddled hastily back to a small cove. Satisfied that a kind of truce had been established, James ordered the launch hoisted out. Then he, Green, Banks, Tupaia, Solander and Sporing, accompanied by six armed marines, were rowed to the river mouth and disembarked on the adjacent beach, leaving Gore in charge of the ship.

On the beach a hefty, dogskin-skirted warrior who had been in one of the canoes, greeted them all by pressing noses. He had a large bone pendant around his neck and a piece of jade dangling from each earlobe. Brandishing a carved stick, he launched into a speech.

'Haere mai, haere mai, manuhere. Nau mai, *haere mai.*' He tapped himself on the chest, said, 'Eruera,' then waved his stick at the bay where *Endeavour* was at anchor. 'Te Whanganui-O-Hei,' he declared.

Tupaia translated. 'This is the great bay of Hei,' he said. 'Hei was his tupuna. A famous ancestor.' The man nodded, muttering 'Ay ... ay ...' Then, pointing to the river, he said, 'Awa ... Purangi,' then into the distance, 'Whiti ... anga.'

The introduction over, he waved the others away and beckoned to Tupaia to come inland with him, pointing to a path which ran alongside the river. 'He wishes *me* to see his kainga, his village,' the Otaheitian told James with a triumphant smile. He set off eagerly with the Maori, matching him stride for stride.

Watching the pair, Banks observed, disagreeably, 'Doubtless our Otaheitian is hoping to duplicate his amorous activities with the women here.'

The others walked up onto the foreshore. Looking about, they agreed that the place could not have been better suited for an astronomical observation post. On one side of the river mouth was a headland which overlooked the estuary, the water of which was translucent. Trees with contorted boughs grew on the cliff edge, their roots clutching the crumbling rock like talons. The plain was covered in tussock grass, with flax bushes sprouting from the lower-lying land. Although the wind was fresh the sky was clear, with just a few feathers of cirrus cloud showing up against the pale blue.

Packs on their backs, Banks, Solander and Sporing set off inland to botanize, while Green instructed the marines to erect the tent on a patch of level land a little way along from the river mouth. James walked down to the beach. In the distance, seeming to float on the sea, was a cluster of islands. Already he had a name for them. *The Mercury Islands*. Then, squinting into the morning sun, he saw a canoe come from around a headland and paddle towards *Endeavour*. Seeking to trade with us, James assumed. Considering it best to return to the ship to oversee the barter, he ordered two of the marines to stay with Green and the other four to row him back.

They were half-way to the ship when they saw a puff of smoke come from midships, then a second later, heard the crack of a musket. The canoe began to paddle away, frantically. As it did there was an explosion of cannon fire. A ball struck the water a little way from the canoe. James stood up in the launch. What had happened to precipitate this? Then, as they drew closer to the canoe, he was appalled at what he saw.

The body of a young man, naked from the waist up, was sprawled face down across the gunwale of the canoe. There was a huge wound in his back and blood was gushing from it. Although his right hand clutched a piece of cloth, it was obvious that the wound was mortal. Two other men in the canoe were paddling desperately shoreward. As they passed the launch they shot frightened glances at James and the others.

Gore was standing at the rail, resting his musket across it. Others of the crew were standing about, looking anxious. James stepped quickly from the launch and climbed the ship's steps to the deck.

'You shot the native?' he demanded of Gore.

The Virginian, colouring visibly, evaded James's glare. 'Yes.' He laid his musket on the deck. 'We were trading. The Indian took the bark cloth, which I lowered to him on a rope, but refused to present me with his cloak in return.' His expression was truculent. 'So I shot him.'

'You killed a man ... for a cloak of dogskin?'

'Yes. And the other natives were brandishing their paddles.'

Furious now, James said in a mocking tone, 'What damage could the natives cause you, high above them, with *wooden paddles*?' Struggling to contain his anger, he said, 'Such a killing cannot be justified, Gore. You were not being seriously threatened. It is unconscionable.'

The officer's gaze was now downcast. But for James this was not enough. Thrusting his bunched hands into his jacket pockets, he spoke loudly, so that the crew could hear. 'As civilised men, we cannot condone such a killing. We are not *backwoodsmen*.' At this word, the American looked up sharply and his lip twisted. Ignoring this, James continued. 'We have been in this land long enough for you to know the Indians' ways. Their thievery is to be anticipated. You should have demanded to receive the cloak first.' He added through clenched teeth, 'Your action could well imperil our relations with the people here, on the eve of the Transit of Mercury.' He paused, meaningfully. 'It will be my disagreeable duty to write a full report on this incident. For the Admiralty.'

With a crow-like caw of rage, Gore snatched up his spent musket, turned, ran along the deck and down the companionway. Watching him retreat, James hoped he would stay below. Too often the man was high-handed, too often he reached for his musket. He may have sailed around the globe twice already, but he lacked sound judgement. And to think that some in authority thought Gore should have led this expedition. James strode towards the foredeck. Gore was no leader.

The other crew members resumed their duties, muttering to one another about the killing and the upbraiding they had just witnessed. Still livid, gripping the rail, James looked shoreward. Two other canoes were coming out from the coast and were being paddled in their direction. He waited until they came closer, and to his relief saw that they carried flax baskets filled with sweet potatoes, fish and rock oysters. It seemed that the killing may not, after all, affect their trade with the natives. These people were from a different clan, perhaps.

On 9 November, from noon onwards, Green successfully observed and timed Mercury's transit of the sun. And using the lunar method, James recorded the site's longitude as 175° 40' east. That evening on his chart he wrote 'Mercury Bay' across the cove and 'Mercury Islands' over the group a few miles off-shore. At Parkinson's suggestion he named the towering headland at the northern end of the bay 'Shakespeare Cliffs', and the secluded cove at the foot of the cliffs 'Lonely Bay'.

Gore was now conspicuously absent from the gatherings in the Great Cabin. In a fit of self-pity he had taken to his bunk, instructing the servants to bring his food and drink to him there. While *Endeavour* continued to lie at anchor, he was little missed.

On their last day in Mercury Bay James, Banks, Tupaia and his newest taio, Eruera, were rowed around the Shakespeare Cliffs and into another, wider estuary, the one Eruera said was called 'Whitianga'. The name meant 'a crossing', Tupaia explained. They disembarked a little way up the river, on the south bank. There was an extensive, scrub-covered plain on the other side, and a forested hill on the other, joined to the rest of the land by a narrow neck of land. 'His people come here when their enemies attack,' Tupaia explained. James nodded. The hill would be a natural fortress. Eruera led them across the isthmus, along a track through the forest and across the top of the hill to a place where the land fell away steeply to the river.

James was struck by the beauty of the vista before them: the crystal-clear river, the white sand beach at its mouth and the forested mountain range in the distance. 'So lovely a prospect,' he murmured. 'Uncommonly so,' agreed Banks. 'The mountains put me in mind of Otaheite.' Eruera said something in Maori to Tupaia, then pointed across the river.

Tupaia gave a little cry of astonishment. His jaw dropped. He looked as if he had been struck by lightning. Then he raised his hands and recited a long, impassioned incantation, all the while with his eyes to the north. After his prayer died away, he burst into tears. Turning, he embraced Eruera, who also began to cry.

James and Joseph looked on in astonishment. Two grown men crying. What was this all about?

Wiping his eyes, Tupaia explained. Across that plain, he said, flowing down from the hills, is another river which flows into the Bay of Hei. Tupaia paused, the tears now coursing down his cheeks. 'And this river is called ....' he gave another cry of wonder '... *Taputapuatea*!' He placed his hands on Eruera's shoulders. 'His tupuna, Hei the navigator, sailed here from Raiatea, and named the river in the new land after my island's greatest marae. *Taputapuatea*!' He gave a roar of delight. 'So Eruera is my family, my *feti'i*, and I am his!' And he fell forward, into the arms of his new-found relative.

November 25, 1769
My dearest Beth,
As winter begins to draw in for you, with darkening afternoons,
here in the Antipodes we are now experiencing true spring. As the
holly berries at home herald the approach of Yuletide, there is in
this south land a coastal tree which is now blooming with flowers
of a similar crimson to holly. The natives call this flowering tree
'po-hoo-too-kaa-wah', and it is much in evidence above the bays
and beaches here. And as December approaches, the daylight
hours are longer and much warmer, the winds in general
favourable for our purposes. We are now proceeding due north,
along the eastern coast of New Zealand, in order to determine its
extent and whether or not it is Banks's much anticipated continent.
I am kept greatly occupied, charting, recording soundings and co-
ordinates, and naming landmarks we discover and observe. Some
of the features are thus named: Cape Colvill (after my close friend
and loyal supporter, Lord Colvill), the Firth of Thames and a river,
the Thames (up which Banks and I were rowed some distance
inland), two islands which we sailed past but made no landing
upon, Great Barrier and Little Barrier (so-named because they
formed an impediment to entering a sheltered gulf), the Hen and
Chickens (a farmyard likeness suggested to me by Sporing), and a
cove in which there were islands so innumerable that it declared
its own nomenclature – the Bay of Islands. Tupaia has informed
me that the New Zealand natives have their own names for these
islands, bays and rivers, ones given to them by their ancestors (for
whom they have the highest regard). However the native names are
so troublesome for we Englishmen to pronounce that it is
necessary to supplant them by the ones I have supplied. The natives
continue to challenge us when we approach their domains, and
when on board attempt to steal anything which is not bolted to the
decks. Mediation from Tupaia, the offering of gifts (Otaheitian
bark cloth they greatly prize) and bartering for fresh vegetables
and fish usually results in amicable relations, although it is
necessary from time to time to fire warning shots to demonstrate
to them the force of which our weapons are capable. The Maoris,
I have deduced, are a warlike people, and their many tribes are in
constant conflict with one another. But in other respects the New
Zealanders are a very proud people, capable of great generosity

and gifted in respect of the arts of carving, craft-making, singing and dancing. And their leaders show an aptitude for oratory which would not be out of place in our Houses of Parliament.

I will close now, dearest wife, with the assurance that my thoughts are forever with you and our children.

Your loving husband,

James

Twenty-four

With favourable winds they progressed further and further due north, sailing as close to the land as they safely could, in order to chart the coastal landforms. Near a group of small islands at latitude 35° south, three canoes manned by Maori men came out to greet them. Gathering under the stern, the natives showed no hostility. Their canoes contained flax baskets filled with golden-skinned fish which they called 'tamure' and which they offered to trade. James joined Tupaia and Banks at the open stern window. He said to the Otaheitian:

'Before we barter, ask them how much further north this land extends.'

Tupaia did so, and one of the paddlers, a burly young man with thick lips and a full facial tattoo, replied.

'He says,' Tupaia told James, 'that the land north from here is called "Muriwhenua". Then, three days' paddling after that, the land turns south.'

'Ah ...' said James, grateful for the information. So the end was, if not in sight, then impending.

Banks leaned forward, eagerly. 'Now ask them if there is more land beyond that.'

Tupaia asked the question, and this time the reply was lengthy. The young man stood up, and made emphatic pointing movements to the north-west. Then, accompanied by gesticulations, he launched into some sort of story.

'What does he say?' asked Banks.

Tupaia laughed, derisively. 'He said that many years ago a waka of theirs sailed to the north of Muriwhenua, across the ocean. Only a few people returned here, and when they did they told of a large land they had found. The people there killed and ate booah.'

'Booah?'

'Pigs,' said Tupaia. 'Same word as in Otaheite.'

Banks frowned. 'But these people have no pigs. We have not seen a one in New Zealand.'

Tupaia leaned out the window, spoke again, and waved his left hand dismissively. At this the men in the canoes all began to laugh, falling about helplessly as they did so. Their laughter was high-pitched. *Heh-heh-heh-heh-heh* ...

Banks said, 'That must have been a very funny joke, Tupaia. Tell us what it was.'

'I told them that booah makes very fine food, so their ancestors must have been very stupid people, not to bring some pigs back here from the land that they found.'

Still chortling, obviously un-offended by Tupaia's remark, the men in the canoes held up their baskets of fish. James looked at Joseph. 'That was not a very funny joke, I think. So, why are they all laughing?'

Banks shrugged. 'The Indians, I think, have a different sense of humour to us.' His face lit up. 'But the land their forebears found, to the north ... it must be, *the great continent*.'

James sensed, before he actually saw, the foul weather conditions that lay ahead. There was a brooding stillness in the air, accompanied by intense heat. Two days later dark clouds began to build and the sea appeared to be streaming *away* from the land, making sailing north difficult. Ordering Molyneux to bear away to the east, James climbed to near the top of the foremast and stood, feet braced, on the yard. From there he could see that the swells were not only increasing, they were now cross-hatched with conflicting currents. One arm around the mast, he put his scope to his eye. What land he could see was wide and low, thus providing no barrier to the strong westerly winds. That the sea was in such conflict with itself, James reasoned, could mean but one thing – that two oceans were coming together. That confirmed they were approaching the farthest point of this land, and so soon they must reach whatever landform lay at that extremity.

As James hugged the mast with his left arm, a swell much larger than the rest reared in front of the ship. She plunged into the swell, rose, plunged again. Spray erupted upwards, almost reaching him where he stood. In the distance he could see that the sea was in turmoil, the swells rising, then crashing against one another chaotically. Looking down, he turned. The experienced hands Molyneux and Pickersgill were wrestling with the wheel, and *Endeavour* was making heavy weather of it.

Earlier that day, poring over a copy of Abel Tasman's foreshortened chart of this land, James had seen that before long they would have to double the cape the Dutchman had named 'Maria Van Dieman', after the wife of the Governor of Batavia. Again he noted another name the Dutchman had bestowed: *The Three Kings*, the islands that lay, he had observed, at 34 degrees, 12 minutes south. James slipped his scope back into its holder. The sky darkened further, the squall struck, and rain began to drive in across the decks. Below, the two helmsmen fought with the wheel. James began to climb back down the shrouds, his face and hair dripping. All the sails would have to be close-reefed. Already some splits had appeared in the foresails. They had been taken in and sail-maker Ravehhill was working urgently below decks to repair them.

James stepped down onto the deck, then made his way along to the wheel. 'Order her about,' he ordered Molyneux and Pickersgill. We need to stand off at least eleven leagues!' There was a pause, the ship plunged again into a trough, then the cry went up from Molyneux, 'All hands! All hands! Ready about! Move there, *move* ...!'

There followed three days of constant tacking, amid some of the wildest and most mountainous seas they had ever seen, and against winds that on 15 December reached gale force. Heavy rain drove in on them constantly and the pumps were manned around the clock. Their zig-zag course meant that their progress northwards was minimal, while the land to the west was hidden by the clouds and the incessant rain. More torn sails were taken in and replaced. James constantly scanned the horizon to the west, aware that the land must still be there, and aware of the menace its unforeseen presence presented. Lashing himself to the larboard railing on the stern deck, he took regular sightings whenever there were breaks in the cloud, and made sketches of the intermittently visible coast. Sextant to his eye, legs hard against the rail, he told himself, *Nature will not prevent me from doing what must be done. I will carry out my duty. No part of this land must go uncharted.*

It was mid-morning on 16 December and he was in the Great Cabin, again studying the copy of Tasman's chart, when the door burst open without a prior knocking. 'Cook! Sir!' James looked up, irritated at the interruption. It was Sporing, drenched to the bone and wild-eyed. Tearing his sodden hat from his head, his cape dripping, he said in his strong accent, 'I haff seen another ship! Off our larboard side!'

James sprang to his feet. *'What? When?'*

'Minutes ago. I was on the stern deck, taking air. I had been ill. A squall was approaching, and as I looked to landward I saw another ship. A three-master, but with only one sail raised.' He hesitated. 'She was, I think, about two leagues distant.'

James stared at the scientist. Could he be serious? He said, quietly, 'In which direction was she sailing?'

'South. Before the wind. On a course counter to ours.'

'What flag was she flying?'

'French.'

The word struck James like a blow. *French.* He cursed inwardly. Then, lowering his voice, he said, 'Did anyone else see this ship?'

'I think not. The crew were busy working the sheets, the mates were hard at the helm. No one was at the masthead, in these winds.'

'So ... did you alert the officer on watch?'

'I tried to. Gathray was on watch, and I ran to tell him.' His face crumpled. 'Then the squall struck, and I could see nothing but rain. When it passed the other vessel was gone.' Hat in his hands, Herman's expression became one of pleading. 'I *did* see another ship, one flying the French flag. It was no illusion.'

'And on a southerly course, you said.'

'Yes.'

James nodded. Sporing was a man incapable of fabricating such a story. If he said he had seen another ship, then he had seen one. But the very thought of the French also being in these waters was an abomination to him. He said, 'I believe you, Sporing. But I would ask that you make no mention of this to the others.'

'No?'

'No. It must remain our secret.'

Sporing looked confused, as if he now doubted his very own memory. 'Very well,' he murmured, then turned away and trudged from the cabin. As James closed the cabin door after him he thought, no one must know of this, the incident will go unrecorded. This land had already been claimed for King George. The land and its waters must always be English, and I will ensure it is so. If the French make claim to it, such an assertion will be invalid.

The day before Christmas the wind at last abated. They had been blown several miles north of the land and were yet to double Cape Maria Van Dieman, but the welcome light airs allowed the ship to stand to while Banks and Solander went out in the yawl and shot four gannets as the birds emerged from their dives. Taken down to the galley, they were gowned and roasted by Thompson, then delivered to the Great Cabin for Christmas dinner in the form of a pie, along with baked sweet potatoes, wild celery and sauerkraut.

Endeavour's bow was turned into the breeze and she was rolling gently, the most peaceful she had been for days. The air was warm and there was a light haze upon the sea. The four stern windows were wide open. James had ordered a double ration of rum for the lower mess deck, where the crew were already tucking into their Yuletide dinner, and Green had broached a jeroboam of claret.

Banks filled their glasses, then raised his to the others. 'Gentlemen, the King!'

'The King ...' 'The King ...' 'The King ...'

All except Tupaia drank, then began their meal. The gannet was a fair substitute for goose, James thought. A little stringy, but tasty. And the New Zealand sweet potatoes were excellent.

'I must say,' ventured Parkinson, setting down his knife and fork, 'that I could never get used to having a hot Christmas. Back in Edinburgh this time always brought snow.'

'And in Stockholm,' said Solander.

The others all murmured agreement, remembering their various homes, Christmases past, and absent loved ones. James wondered if Elizabeth and the children would already be at her parents' house, and whether his father was staying with Christiana or Margaret. This last he felt with his usual pangs of guilt. Perhaps his father was no longer alive. He tried to banish this thought, only too aware that he had not been a dutiful son.

Banks swallowed his claret, then said, 'have you ever before experienced such gales as we have had these past days, Cook?'

'Not often, I confess. Even Cape Horn was but mild compared with North Cape.'

The others looked blank. 'North Cape?' asked Green. 'Where is that?'

'The cape we doubled two days ago. This country's northernmost point. I have named it North Cape.' James spoke matter-of-factly.

Banks refilled his glass. Then, tilting his head to one side, he said reflectively, 'East Cape, the Bay of Islands, North Cape. Not very original names.'

James took a sip of wine, then replied, calmly, 'It's my belief, Banks, that a place should be named after an event, for its geographical significance, or after a person who merits the honour.'

Bank's face was becoming flushed. He swallowed another mouthful of claret, then said, challengingly, 'And which of the gentlemen at this table ... "merits the honour"?'

Aware that the botanist was trying to provoke him, James said thoughtfully, 'Well, Herman has his island, at Uawa. Sporing's Island. Zachary has his bay, Hicks Bay.' He smiled, then said with deliberate mischievousness, 'Your turn may come, Banks. Would you prefer to be commemorated by a bay, a cape or an island?' He paused. 'Or some sand banks, perhaps ...'

The others dissolved into good-natured laughter. Then the botanist rose to the challenge. 'I think ... nothing less than a *mountain* would do justice to my notable self.' He looked up and closed his eyes. 'Yes. Mount Banks ... that will do very nicely.'

Green, who had said little until now, concentrating instead on quaffing the claret, said quietly, 'Mount Banks ... That is just a syllable away from a *mountebank*. You may need to think again, Banks.'

All except Tupaia laughed. Puzzled, he said to Green, 'What is this word,

mount-a, mount-a ... what does it mean?'

Banks leaned forward, to adgown the Otaheitian. 'A *mountebank*, my taio, is a fraud.' At Tupaia's still-confused expression, he added, 'A cheat, a dishonest person.'

Tupaia nodded, understanding. Then he shook his head and said, 'That is not you, taio.'

Banks leapt to his feet. 'Thank you, my good fellow.' Turning to James, he declared, 'I have a far better suggestion.' Swaying slightly, holding up his glass, he said, 'Terra Australis Incognita, when we at last come upon it, shall from that day forth be known as ... 'Terra Australis Banksia!'"

Sailing south down the western coast of New Zealand, they kept *Endeavour* well off from the lee shore. The westerly winds persisted, the skies were mostly overcast, and what they could see of the land appeared inhospitable. Powerful swells beat relentlessly against the coast. And with the advent of the New Year, James's concerns grew. The ship had taken a battering these past weeks, repairs to her hull and sails were badly needed, and provisions were running low. Murderers Bay, where Tasman had attempted a landing in 1642, appeared physically suitable, but the Dutchmen's fatal altercation with the Maori there did not bode well. Still, James told himself, they had the Otaheitian with them, to act as a go-between. That gave him reassurance.

On January 13 they were still making their way south. At first light they saw that the coastline was now bearing away to the east. Two hours later the clouds lifted, and at latitude 38° 41', the Endeavours saw a sight which captivated them. To the south, seeming to rise directly from the sea, was a conic mountain. Symmetrical, but with gullied, purplish slopes, its peak glowed with mid-summer snow. Towering over the surrounding land like a gigantic pyramid, it brought all the crew to the port railings.

'What a beautiful sight,' Solander remarked to James. 'What height do you estimate it to be?'

'Somewhat lower than the Pike of Tenerife, I would say,' said James, scope still to his eye. 'And it is surrounded by a plain, which accentuates its elevation. Perhaps ... 9,000 feet.'

Tupaia and his boy joined them on the after deck. 'What is that whiteness at the top of the mountain?' Tupaia asked, obviously baffled. 'Bird shit?'

'No,' said James, chuckling. 'It's snow.' Then, realising that the Otaheitians would never have seen such a thing, he added, 'Frozen water. Caused by the mountain's height.'

Tupaia looked on in wonderment. 'Snow ... snow ...'

Later that day, moving to within four leagues of the shore, they saw a densely forested plain, and just off the coast, several tall, sheer-sided islands. As he sketched them, Sydney remarked to James, 'They resemble loaves of sugar, Sir.' James nodded. 'They do indeed.' Then he resumed his charting.

The next day, on a draft of his chart, James considered a name for the dominating mountain. He hadn't honoured anyone in the Admiralty since Lord Hawke, months earlier. Out of consideration for his own future prospects, it was time he did so again. On the draft he wrote carefully, 'Mount Egmont', to honour Sir John Percival, Earl of Egmont, a recent First Lord of the Admiralty and another of those who had farewelled *Endeavour* at Plymouth. Then, admiring Parkinson's allusion, across the tall islands he wrote 'Sugar Loaves'.

The following day, still on a southerly course, they doubled a rocky cape, the extremity of the

bulge in the coastline. After noting its latitude and longitude, James declared this to be "Cape Egmont". And as made note of the coordinates, he wondered, could this landmark the westernmost point of New Zealand? As the coastline was now trending more to the south-west than the south-east, he ordered an eight-point turn to larboard. With the snowy peak of Mt Egmont still visible aft, they sighted more high land on the horizon ahead, this time a mountain range, and bore south towards it.

As soon as he saw the sound, he knew it would provide them with what they sought. Guarded at its entrance by several islands, it nevertheless offered a broad channel which *Endeavour* passed through, on 15 January, 1770. The airs were light, the sky clear, and just past one of the islands James eyed a cove on the sound's north-western shore, overlooked by forested, undulating hills. He ordered the stream anchor lowered just off the cove. It had barely settled on the bottom when four canoes came out from one of the neighbouring islands.

The usual pantomime occurred. The occupants threw stones at the ship, then Tupaia explained what they required and invited the unarmed natives aboard. These men were darker and looked less well-nourished than the other Maoris they had dealt with, James observed. They told the Endeavours that the sound was called Totaranui, after the large totara trees which grew in the area, the cove was called Meretoto and the island off the cove where their pa was located was called Motuara.

The men then roamed the decks briefly, looking about incuriously, then got back into their canoes and paddled back to the island.

'These ones will cause us no trouble,' Tupaia said to James as they watched them go. 'They are teuteu. Lower class people.' James felt irritated by this precipitate judgement. The Otaheitian could be such a swankpot. He turned to Banks. 'We will go ashore.'

21 January 1770

My Dear Beth,

The first month of not just a New Year but a new decade. What an age it has been since I last saw you and the children. At times I wonder if the boys remember their father at all! Although it is my sworn duty to carry out the Admiralty's instructions, I am aware too that I have other, more personal obligations, to my dear family. Be assured that the most abiding memories I carry with me here on the far side of the world, are not of England and its Navy but of you and our children.

Here, at a place I have called Ship Cove, we have found a safe haven, as fine a bay as one could wish for. It lies on the north-western shore of a long sound which I intend honouring with the name of our sovereign's Consort, Queen Charlotte. The sound is bounded on both sides by high hills covered in dense forest. At our cove there are abundant wild greens and fresh water from two streams to replenish our butts (and a nearby waterfall makes this task more straightforward). There are tall, sturdy trees which the carpenters make good use of to repair the ship's timbers, and by trawling our seine net, we obtain more fish than we can eat. Mussels and rock oysters, too. During the day the air chimes melodiously with beautiful birdsong, although at dusk tiny biting insects swarm and plague us.

Banks, Solander and Sporing botanise doggedly. Yesterday I climbed with them up a steep native trail through the forest to a saddle high above the cove. Along the trail were many large tree ferns, entanglements of tough vines and towering trees whose trunks are covered with a black fungal growth. Beneath this dark coating is a sweet, sticky substance which Banks speculates is secreted by some sort of insect. I was far more interested in the commanding outlook from the saddle, a view of our cove on one side and another equally tranquil bay on the other. Both offer fine anchorages.

Endeavour *has been careened on the cove's shingly beach and her hull scraped, tarred and oiled in preparation for the next stage of our exploration. Her sails are having much-needed repairs, too. The ship, now refloated, is once more in prime condition.*

The natives in this region are poorer than others we have encountered. Their canoes and houses are unadorned with carving and the people themselves not as handsome as those in the north. However although they are at war with other tribes not far away, they pose little threat to us. I did fire at one man who was attempting to steal some of our equipment, but merely with pellets, and only wounding him slightly in the leg. One old chief has become our particular friend. Called Topaa, he has been obliging and has formed a good friendship with our Otaheitian. They discuss their ancestors and their common traditions and deities for hours on end.

I anticipate that we will be ready to leave this agreeable place within the next fortnight, for further charting of the New Zealand coast. Thereafter, who knows? But it is of some encouragement that during this year we will assuredly be turning north on the first stage of our voyage home. That prospect is one which will delight us all, including myself, as it will mean that I will be one ocean closer to you, my beloved wife, and our children.

Your loving husband,

James

At first they thought it was a dead porpoise. Then, as the pinnace drew nearer, they realised it was the half-submerged corpse of a human. Rowing closer, they saw it was a young woman, gowned in a cloak and with long hair trailing. The face was bloated and pale, and there were holes where the gulls had pecked out her eyes. Averting their gaze from the hideous sight, they rowed on and entered the bay which lay a little to the north of where *Endeavour* had been refloated.

This cove too was overlooked by forested hills. Just above the shoreline, a group of men, women and children were attending an earth oven. When they saw the boat and the three men in it, they sprang up and fled into the forest. After beaching the pinnace, James, Joseph and Tupaia saw that beside the opened oven were flax baskets containing the remains of cooked meat. Banks poked at one of the baskets with a stick. 'Dog bones,' he pronounced. 'A rib cage and leg bones. Freshly consumed.' James peered into another basket. It held much larger bones, with scraps of cooked flesh still clinging to them. He picked one up and examined it, curiously. 'That must have been a very large dog,' he said to the others. 'A Great Dane, perhaps.' He frowned. 'Yet we have seen no large dogs here.'

At that moment the family emerged from the nearby trees and approached the visitors cautiously. There was a skinny, dark-skinned man in a grass skirt, with a large whale bone pendant around his neck, a short plump woman wearing a cloak and two small, naked boys. The adults looked at the newcomers in a nervous but not unfriendly way. The boys clung to their mother's legs, regarding the visitors with looks of incredulity.

'Ia Orana,' said Tupaia. The man looked confused for a moment, then replied 'Kia Ora.' He and Tupaia hongi-ed, James and Banks did likewise, while the woman and the boys hung back. James then picked up one of the large bones from the basket and said to Tupaia, 'Ask him what kind of animal this was.'

In response, the man guffawedand the woman giggled. T hen the man took the woman's left arm, held it to his mouth and pretended to eat it, making greedy, gnawing motions. Tupaia's mouth fell open. He asked him another question, and the man answered at length, frowning and pointing out to sea. Screwing up his face, Tupaia turned away.

'What did he say?' demanded Joseph. Tupaia put one hand to his face in disgust, and half-choking, said: 'The bones are the remains of their enemies. A war party tried to invade this bay a few days ago. This family's warriors killed seven of them, and shared the body parts among the victors. His family were awarded the arms. They cooked them overnight and ate them this morning.' Turning away, he closed his eyes. 'Aaaaah ... to eat another person. These people ... they are themselves like dogs!'

James said, 'What about the body of the woman in the water?'

That was not one of the enemy, the man said, but a family member who had died of illness. The body had been buried at sea, weighted down with a stone, but had evidently come adrift. He reported this without a flicker of emotion.

The incident sparked a lively discussion that evening in the Great Cabin. Banks had already christened the bay Cannibal Cove, and had related their find in gruesome detail, down to every last sinew on the bones. Sydney had put his hands over his ears. Minutes earlier he had been showing the others his paintings of two local plants, a honeysuckle and one that Solander had named Veronica floribunda, and a pen and wash drawing of a group of Maoris gowned in feather hats, fishing from canoes. All had agreed Sydney's renderings were exquisite. But now that the conversation had turned to cannibalism, the young artist looked ill. Tupaia was merely disgusted. He said that although his people sacrificed humans to their gods, they never ate people. On some distant islands – he named these as 'Te Hunua Enata' – cannibalism was practised, but never on Otaheite, Eimayo, Huahine or Raiatea. James listened to the others' views, which were unanimously ones of revulsion, then said:

'So, Tupaia, the New Zealanders eat only the bodies of their slain enemies.'

'Yes. They believe that by eating them, they absorb their spirit, and thus they become stronger.'

'So their motive for cannibalism is not appetite.'

'No. The man told me that they only eat their defeated enemies.'

'That then is not a necessity but a custom. An unpleasant one, to us, but one that is part of their culture.'

The others at the table looked perturbed. Frowning, Banks said, 'Do you mean to say you approve of this tradition, Cook?'

'I make no judgement either way. It is merely a fact of their lives. You defeat your enemy, so you are entitled to eat him. As your foes would eat you, if they were the victors.'

Leaning back in his chair, Monkhouse said, austerely, 'It is surely a characteristic of the very lowest order of humanity, that they should eat their fellow human beings. It is barbarism.'

'To us, yes,' James said. 'Even to Tupaia. 'But to them, no. It is an accepted custom.'

Banks considered this for a moment, then said, slowly, 'So, Cook ... if you were to defeat the French in battle – as I know you have done – you would find it acceptable to bake and eat one of the casualties afterwards.'

James looked at him irritably. 'You twist my argument, Banks. I did not say that *I* would do so, I merely said that that is the accepted ritual in this land.' He turned away. 'Besides, the taste of Frenchman would be far too disagreeable.'

The others laughed. 'All that garlic,' muttered Green, chortling into his port.

'Mind you,' said Banks, serious once more, 'I have tasted a French*woman*, and that was far from unpleasant.'

'But presumably,' put in Monkhouse, 'she was alive.'

'Very much so,' mused the naturalist. 'A very lively young Parisienne.'

Tupaia leaned forward. 'The people here collect human heads, Topaa told me.'

There was another silence, then Banks said: 'Of their enemies?'

'Not only enemies. Family, too. They never eat the heads, they preserve them. "Mokomokai", they are called.' He hesitated, then continued. 'The head to these Maohi is the most sacred part of the body. Tapu. So the heads are kept. Those of family, to be loved; those of enemies, to be hated.'

Banks brightened at this news. 'Can we see some of these heads?' he asked Tupaia.

The Otaheitian looked doubtful. 'Perhaps. I will ask Topaa.'

James watched from the quarterdeck as the old man was paddled out to the ship and carried a flax basket up the hull steps and onto the deck. He opened the basket and set four heads down at the base of the mainmast. These were from the enemies, killed recently, and dried over a fire, Topaa said with obvious pride. The crew clustered around the objects, simultaneously repelled and fascinated by the heads' yellowing, shrunken skin, the lank black hair, the blank eyes, the grimacing teeth. Two had tattoos, one had no bottom front teeth, the fourth was a little smaller than the rest and had a wispy moustache.

Banks nudged Tupaia. 'Tell the old man I will buy the heads from him. They will add greatly to my collection.'

Tupaia spoke to Topaa, who glanced at Joseph, then replied, briefly. 'He will only let you have the smaller one,' Tupaia said. 'It was from a young lad.' Then he looked at Banks challengingly. 'What will you give him in exchange for the mokomokai?'

'I will get him something suitable,' the naturalist replied, and he turned and went down the companionway to his cabin. Seconds later he returned, carrying a pair of baggy, stained drawers, which were holed in several places. He held them up to Topaa, while opening the four fingers of his left hand. 'He can have this fine gentleman's garment, for all four heads.'

Tupaia reported this. The chief glowered. Obviously offended, he picked up the head of the lad, and muttered something. Tupaia said, 'He cannot sell the others, even for an exploding stick, they are too valuable to his people. You can only have this one.'

Undeterred, Joseph waved the drawers in Topaa's face, cheerfully, like an auctioneer in London city. 'Four heads, for this valuable garment.'

Topaa's tattooed brow puckered. He said something else to Tupaia. The Tahitian said, 'No. You can have the boy's head only.'

Banks heaved a sigh. 'Very well.' He handed the drawers to Topaa, who then passed the head to Joseph. The botanist held it up by the hair, admiringly. The crew looked on in horrified fascination. On the neck were vestiges of undried cartilage and solidified blood. 'This fellow will cause a sensation at the Royal Society headquarters,' Banks said.

James had watched the transaction from the quarter deck. He found it both macabre and troubling. Within living memory, he was aware, the English had placed the heads of executed traitors on display on London Bridge, as a warning to others. But this was different. In Banks's eyes the head of a recently killed human being had become a commodity, something to be traded. Who knew what might happen if a trade of this nature was encouraged. Might not the natives see a profit in the business, and so increase the killing for it? In this manner they might even obtain their own muskets, and thus compound tribal conflicts, with a consequent mounting death toll. He turned away. He would order that the trophy head be kept well below decks.

During their last week in Ship Cove, seeking to discover what lay to the east of the long sound, James, Banks and Solander were rowed some distance east across the water, to a very long, embayed island whose spine rose high above the sea. Topaa had told them the island was called Arapawa.

The trio made their way up a steep slope, through dense forest and ferns, and emerged from the trees, breathless, onto clear land near the island's crest.

It was a fine summer morning, with almost no wind and skeins of cloud streaking the sky. They had discarded their jackets because of the intense heat. Rolling up his shirt sleeves, James absorbed the panorama before them and was elated by it. He loved ascending hills such as this, had done so since he was a boy climbing Roseberry Topping. Standing on a hilltop was like seeing a map or a chart spring to life.

What lay to the east of where they stood was a vast body of water, calm near the island but flecked with whitecaps further out. It was, James felt certain, connected to the passage which had provided them with egress to the sound. He put his scope to his eye, then panned across the water. In the distance was rugged, shadowy land, quite separate from that on which they stood. Conscious of Banks's silence, sensing his frustration, James said quietly, 'What lies before us is a strait, Banks. And what we have lately circumnavigated is an island.' He allowed a pause, then added, 'Not a continent.'

Solander was nodding, but Banks was not. He made an impatient clicking sound, then said, 'To the north may well be an island, but what of the land on which we now stand?'

'Another island, I deduce.'

Banks regarded James coldly. 'Why not a continent? One that extends far to the south of here.'

James sighed. The man was obsessed. He said, 'Time will tell. We will sail south-east from here and continue our charting.'

'Good. I am still confident that this land will prove to be what we seek.' His attention returned to what lay before them. 'Cook, this expanse of water, this strait ...'

'Yes?'

'In view of your discovery of it ... I propose it be named after you.'

'And I endorse that suggestion,' Solander put in, earnestly.

James considered this. The suggestion surprised him. After all, he had named no feature after Banks. Abashed, he gave a little laugh, then said, 'It seems vainglorious to name such a feature after myself.'

'But it is I who is naming it,' insisted Banks, 'not you.' He held up his right hand, as if taking an oath, and intoned solemnly, 'I hereby name this water, "Cook's Strait".'

Twenty-five

By the last day of January, *Endeavour* was fully repaired, provisioned and ready for sea, with ample wood, water, dried fish and scurvy grass stowed in her holds. There remained just one more duty for James to execute.

He, Surgeon Monkhouse and Tupaia rowed the yawl across to Motuara Island. In the boat was a marker post which James had instructed one of the carpenters to cut, and rout into it the date and ship's name. As they drew into the beach on the island's western shore, they saw old Topaa waiting for them. He was wearing Banks's drawers as a shirt, fastened at the shoulders with strips of flax, and a jade pendant around his neck. He greeted them affably, hongi-ing each in turn with his flat, triangular nose. Then James said to Tupaia, 'Tell him we wish to erect this post on the top of the island.' Tupaia did so, then James handed the old chief some spike nails and a threepenny coin. He accepted the gifts gratefully, then led them up a zig-zag path to clear land at the top of the island. There they set the post in the ground, beside a cairn which they and others of the crew had built a few days earlier. James had buried several coins, musket balls and beads within the cairn, to prove that the natives could not have built it.

A stiff, warm wind was blowing across the sound as the Jack was hoisted upon the post. To the little gathering, the view from the summit of the island could not have been more agreeable: the broad expanse of the sound, in the distance the dark, undulating profile of Arapawa Island, and on the horizon, the outline of the coast of New Zealand's northern island. The flag in place and waving confidently in the wind, James declared gravely: 'I hereby name this inlet "Queen Charlotte's Sound" and take possession of it and the adjacent lands in the name and for the use of His Majesty King George III of England.'

Mindful of the fact that their departure was imminent, James told Tupaia to ask the chief what he knew of his people's land. Topaa launched into a voluble speech, accompanied by many hand movements. Tupaia translated. 'The island across the strait is called "Te Ika-A- Maui", so-named because it was a great fish hauled out of the sea by the Maori god, Maui. The land on which they stood is "Te Wai Pounamu", after the precious green stone found there in some areas. Topaa held up his carved pendant to demonstrate. 'Pounamu.' And the great strait was called "Raukawa Moana", he told them.

'How long does it take to sail around Te Wai Pounanu?' James asked.

'He says it takes four days,' Tupaia replied.

'*Four days*?' said James. That seemed impossible. Tupaia also looked dubious. He said to the others, 'I think his people do not know the rest of their whenua – their own land – well. He knows only these local islands, and the strait.' James nodded. He had already decided that Topaa was the local equivalent of an English provincial person.

Official matters over, Monkhouse took a bottle of burgundy from his pack and uncorked it. He and James filled their pewter mugs from the bottle, then offered one to Tupaia and Topaa, who both declined. William and James raised their mugs to the flag. 'To the King,' James intoned, then drank. As he did so he felt as satisfied as at any other occasion since the voyage began. *I have brought these islands into England's possession*, he thought, *and what an asset to my country they will be*. Monkhouse finished the wine, then handed the bottle to Topaa. The old chief grinned, nodded eagerly, and waved it in the air like a weapon. 'Hah ... hah ... kapai ... kapai ...'

After sailing out of the strait's eastern entrance, James took *Endeavour* north as far as Cape Turnagain. There, with some satisfaction he confirmed to the doubters that the northern island had indeed been circumnavigated. He then ordered the ship to turn south again.

On 12 February they moved past the northern island's southernmost point, which James named Cape Palliser, after his naval captain friend and supporter. Continuing her southern coasting, *Endeavour* was beset by gales which drove her away from the coast, making James's running survey greatly difficult. But on 15 February he charted a high volcanic island at 43° 19' South, and in a gesture of sympathy for Banks, named it after the botanist. Further south the weather grew cold and the fearnoughts were again brought out. As February slid into March the gales did not abate. Great swells rolled up from the southern ocean towards them, and as James lay in his bunk at night, listening to his doughty little ship's timbers creaking, he knew she was taking another fearful beating.

At last, and still in ghastly weather, they doubled a peninsula at the southern island's extremity, which James thankfully named "South Cape". *Endeavour* then began to bear south-west.

Banks was now not only ill, he was melancholic. Discovering the farthest point of the southern island brought a concurrent conclusion – that they had not discovered the Great Southern Continent. This knowledge threw the botanist into a fit of brooding such as he had not previously suffered, and for the rest of the day he remained in his cabin.

It was now James's task to bring *Endeavour* up the western coast of Te Wai Pounamu, to complete its circumnavigation. Most of the crew were now relieved, knowing that when the charting of the two islands was complete, they could begin to consider the return voyage. But below decks there was also conjecture: which return course would they be taking – east to Cape Horn or west to the Cape of Good Hope?

Banks stood on the poop deck, scope to his eye, studying the coastline to larboard. Sydney, legs braced against the tiller, was beside him, sketching. James joined them. It was a rare fine day and the coastline was clear. It was majestic, a line of perpendicular cliffs, soaring above *Endeavour* and plunging directly into the sea. Swells drove in against the base of the cliffs and were dashed into spray. Atop the mountainous wall were dense dark forest and patches of snow, but no signs of habitation. No fires, no huts.

Still with his spyglass to his eye, Banks exclaimed, 'There is a break in the coast. And a wooded island within it. See?'

James had his own scope to his eye. 'Yes. I have already observed it. It is a fiord. Very like those along the west coast of Norway.'

Bank lowered his scope and faced James, his expression eager. 'We can put in there, then.'

'Why?'

'*Why*? To go ashore. And botanise.'

'I think not.'

'Why not?'

'The westerlies have prevailed for weeks, and show no sign of abating.' Pointing towards the island, James continued. 'It would be a simple matter for us to enter the sound, a prodigiously difficult one to exit it.'

'We could warp her out, surely.'

'Not against this wind.' He shook his head. 'We could be embayed for weeks.'

Compressing his lips, Banks said bitterly: 'We have made no landfall since February. Since Queen Charlotte's Sound. We have passed hundreds of miles of coastline without once going ashore.' His voice became a hiss. 'How many new plant and animal species have I missed?'

'Many, probably.' He met Banks's accusatory stare. 'But the safety of my crew and ship are paramount. I will not put them at risk for ... a bagful of plants.' He paused. 'Besides, I have sailed into fjords, in Norway. The walls of such features are sheer rock. That precludes getting ashore readily.'

Banks's face, which had been pale for days, reddened. 'But at the head of the fiord,' he persisted, 'there will surely be a landing, where we could set up camp.'

'*Surely*? How can you be so sure of a place which you have never seen?'

'Along Queen Charlotte's Sound there were many landing places. Why should this one not be the same?'

'The two sounds cannot be compared.' James pointed landward. 'The walls of that one are sheer. And the wind, as I have already pointed out, is unfavourable. The risk is too great, so we will not enter the sound.' Turning away, he called down to the helmsmen, Molyneux and Pickersgill. 'Steady as she goes. Nor nor west.'

'Steady as she goes,' came the reply.

With a grunt of frustration, Banks spun on his heel and strode off towards the companionway. Parkinson, who had overhead the altercation, looked at James nervously. 'I am drawing the coast, Sir, including the sound.'

In the Great Cabin that night, on his latest chart, James wrote carefully across the breach in the coast: *"Latitude 45° 12' South", and to mark his decision, "Doubtful Sound".*

They sailed on north, then at 40° South latitude he ordered *Endeavour* brought east to again enter the great strait which now bore his name. A cove he immediately named "Admiralty Bay" lay on its southern shore, several leagues west of Ship Cove. Broad but sheltered, it looked ideal for the provisioning and repairs which they so badly needed after the gruelling orbit of the southern island. It had taken them almost two months to circumnavigate, and James now knew that having done so, and finding no new land, it was time to give consideration to the return voyage. It was already March, and the Southern Hemisphere winter would soon be looming.

The following morning he called a meeting with Hicks and Gore in the Officers' Mess. Banks, Solander and Sporing had vanished into the coastal undergrowth almost before the anchor was lowered, so anxious were they to make up for lost botanising time. Tupaia and his boy had gone fishing, and the rest of the crew were busy ashore, wooding and watering. The rain, which had been continuous since their arrival in the bay, drummed down on the deck above as James outlined their options to the other two officers.

'To return, we can sail east, in the higher latitudes to pick up following winds, then double the Horn. Or ...' he spread out the copy of Tasman's chart on the table '... we can set a course north-west from here.' He moved his forefinger across the chart. 'That will take us to Van Dieman's Land, and the east coast of New Holland.' He looked at the other two 'Your opinions, gentlemen, before I give you my own.'

Gore, whose attitude had been largely contrite since the fatal incident at Mercury Bay, said:

'The Horn, then the Atlantic, would be the more direct route, would it not?'

Hicks nodded. 'And the Le Maire Strait is reliably charted, whereas the other route is not.' He coughed, cleared his throat, then spat into his handkerchief.

Although James nodded, the gesture was insincere. He had no intention of returning via the Horn. There were no discoveries to be made that way. 'A fair point,' he replied. 'But let us remember that by the time we closed the Horn it would be mid-winter in the south. Short daylight hours, frigid conditions, and contrary winds.'

The other two looked chastened. Rounding the Horn in such conditions was not an appealing prospect. James again put his finger on Tasman's chart, tracing a line across the blank space from Van Dieman's Land to distant Torres Strait. 'We should bear in mind that ours is still a voyage of discovery, and that to this time we have discovered very little. It is for that reason that I propose that our course follows the east coast of New Holland, that we chart that unknown coastline, then negotiate the Torres Strait and proceed thereafter to Batavia and Cape Town.'

Gore looked doubtful. 'The Torres is a formidable passage,' he said. 'Dalrymple makes that plain, in his account of Quiros's navigation of it. With Byron, we bore well north, to avoid it.'

'You doubt my ability to navigate that passage?' said James. It still vexed him, the way Gore reminded him at every opportunity that he had already circumnavigated the world. As for Dalrymple, what did that mere dabbler in voyaging really know?

Avoiding James's confrontational look, the Virginian replied hurriedly. 'Not at all, not at all. With care I'm sure it can be negotiated.'

'Good.' James rolled up the chart. 'Then I shall assemble the ship's company at eight bells tomorrow, and inform them that we will weigh anchor the day after tomorrow, and set sail for New Holland.'

On the last day of March 1770, James stood in the stern of *Endeavour* and watched New Zealand begin to fade from sight. Over the last seventeen months, despite their many tribulations, he had come to love this land – its bays and anchorages, its islands great and small, its estuaries and forests. The people, too, he had come to greatly respect. It was a marvellous land, as yet untamed. But he felt sure that Englishmen would pacify it, in time, and shape it according to their ambitions. Watching the long line of land become less distinct, he wondered, would he ever see it again? He hoped so, fervently.

The wind was favourable for the north-west by west course he had set for *Endeavour*'s master. Although the morning air was hazy, he could still see ocean rollers breaking against the shore of the cape they had lately doubled, the southern island's northernmost landform. Staring at the long, lonely sandspit, he had no difficulty deciding on its name. *Cape Farewell.*

Twenty-six

5 April, 1770
My dearest Elizabeth,
Springtime in England, what thoughts of home that brings!
Walks on the common, the oaks and elms bursting into new leaf,
flowers in the parks, bluebells in the woods, how we welcomed
those arrivals in Ayton when I was a boy. Spring was my mother's
favourite season. The hedgerow primroses, she was especially fond
of gathering. And now, after the hardships of the London winter,
how you and the children must be relishing the season of renewal.
In New Zealand there are no marked differences in the seasons,
and no deciduous trees – all are evergreens – so in autumn the
forests do not assume the shades of gold and russet which they do
at home. The evergreens have a beauty of their own –particularly
the giant trees called the koorri – but they lack the varying hues of
our English forests.

The islands of New Zealand, large and small, have been claimed
for our King, and charted to my satisfaction. It is a fair land with
many resources: sheltered harbours, stands of straight-grained
timber, and, once cleared of forest, fertile land which I believe will
be well suited to agriculture. Although the winds were often
unfavourable to us, Endeavour *proved her fitness for the testing*
voyage and showed again the sterling quality of English ship-
building. The native people of New Zealand, although by custom
warlike towards each other, are also intelligent, open and un-
treacherous, receptive to English influences and customs, and
thus, I believe, capable of attaining a civilised standard of living.
Our own adopted native, Tupaia, who is related to the New
Zealanders, is an example of the degree of civilisation his people
is capable of achieving. His role as mediator between us and the
New Zealand natives has also proved beneficial throughout our
visits to their shores, and it is my earnest belief that he will also
greatly assist our communication with the natives we will
encounter in New Holland.

It is my hope that we will make landfall in New Holland sometime
before this month is out. The crew is already cheered by the
knowledge that we are now bearing in the direction of the equator

*and are thus proceeding towards the Northern Hemisphere. As
your cousin Isaac Smith remarked to me yesterday, 'It is my belief
that the greatest hardships are now behind us.'*

*Every day's progress northwards brings us closer to our beloved
England and those whose affections we hold dearest to us.*

My love, as always, to you and our little ones,

James

'*Land!* Off the port bow...'

The cry came from Zachary Hicks, dangling in the mainmast
rigging like a gibbon. It was two and a half weeks since they had
departed from New Zealand, and the portents had been there for
some days – porpoises cavorting around *Endeavour*'s bow, and a
small land bird, fluttering into, and gratefully clutching, the mizzen
mast's rigging. But the actual sight of land was gratifying, and
brought all the crew on deck. Hicks climbed down.

James shook his hand, vigorously. 'Well done, Hicks. The
landform shall be named after you.'

Abashed, the officer looked down. 'First a bay, then a point. At
this rate I shall grow vain.'

James smiled. 'You, vain? Never, Hicks.'

That evening in his authorised journal, he wrote:

19 April, 1770

*In the PM had fresh gales at SSW and cloudy squally weather
with a large southerly sea. At 6pm took in the topsails and at 1am
brought to and sounded but had no ground with 130 fathoms of
line. At 5am set the topsails close reefed and at 6am saw land
extending from NE to West at the distance of 5 or 6 leagues, having
80 fathoms of water and a fine sandy bottom. We continued
standing to the westward with the wind at SSW until 8 o'clock at
which time we got the topgallant yards across, made all sail, and
bore away for the easternmost land we had in sight. I judged this
lay in the latitude of 38° 58' south and longitude of 211° 07' west
of Greenwich. I have named it 'Point Hicks'.*

They continued on their northward course for day after day since
first raising land, but could find no safe landing or bay to enter. As
the end of April approached and still no landing had been possible,
James's concerns grew. Quartermaster Evans had reported that
stocks of water and food were running low. They saw smoke rising

from the land in several places, but no challenging canoes came out to investigate the ship or offer to trade, while a combination of high surf and rocky cliffs made a landing out of the question. In the meantime, they stared at the coast, sketched its features, watched the smoke, and speculated upon the nature of the people who had lit the fires.

After the noon dinner, and with the ship still making her way north, Banks opened one of the books from the Great Cabin's library and began to read from it to the others.

' *"They are the miserablest people in the world. Setting aside their human shape, they differ but little from brutes. The colour of their skins, both of their faces and the rest of their body, is coal-black. They all of them have the most unpleasant looks and the worst features of any people I ever saw, though I have seen a great variety of savages".'*

'Who penned that description?' asked Green.

'William Dampier,' Banks said. 'The book is his *New Voyage Round the World.*'

'He is describing his meeting with New Holland's natives, in 1688,' said James, who had read it several times.

Solander spoke up. 'But Dampier was a great distance from this coast, I believe.'

'Quite so,' said James. 'He was writing of the natives of the *north-west* of New Holland. Thousands of leagues distant from here.' He gave Banks a meaningful look. 'So the "savages" he describes as being so disagreeable may not be the same as the inhabitants of this coast.'

'Perhaps,' said Banks, his expression doubtful. 'From that description they certainly do not seem in any way related to the Otaheitans, or the natives of New Zealand.' He looked again at the text. 'The colour of Tupaia's people, and the Maoris' skins was never "coal-black". They are chestnut brown.'

'It may be the climate that causes the difference,' suggested Solander. 'Where Dampier came ashore was in the low southern latitudes. The climate there would be constantly hot, almost equatorial.' He shrugged. 'Hence exposure to the high sun, and the consequent blackness of the savages' skin.'

'But not their "unpleasant looks",' said Green, making a face that was itself far from pleasant.

Banks closed Dampier's book and placed it back on the shelf. Peering out the port window of the cabin at the rocky, swell-beaten coast, he said, 'I wonder how much longer it will be before we encounter the natives of New Holland.'

Three more days, it was, the afternoon of 28 April, when James ordered the ship brought through the entrance of a bay they had sighted the day before. The pinnace had been hoisted, and soundings taken by Molyneux from it confirmed that the bay was deep enough for *Endeavour* to anchor in. It was broad, surrounded by white sand beaches and low-lying, scrub-covered land. The afternoon was intensely hot and shimmers of heat were rising from the land as the ship was brought to, opposite the southern shore of the bay, and her bow anchors lowered. From the ship they could see groups of men, women and children, all completely naked. 'And they are indeed black,' Parkinson murmured to James as they stood in the stern watching, spy glasses to their eyes. 'As black as my hat.' 'The women's breasts are pendulous,' observed Banks keenly, 'and their pudenda are uncovered and prominent.' He kept his telescope to his eye.

The women were gathering shellfish, while a little distance away, four men were fishing with spears from small canoes. Tupaia immediately took up a pencil and pad and began to draw the men. Although the fishermen looked up at the sound of *Endeavour*'s anchor chains rattling, their expressions were of total indifference to the vessel. Huge and alien though it must have been to them, it was as if the ship and those aboard were invisible. The natives returned to their spearing, and Tupaia continued his drawing.

That afternoon James, Banks, Solander, Green, Sporing, Tupaia, Parkinson and Isaac Smith got into the pinnace and prepared to go ashore, rowed by four of the marines. James had given Smith special permission to join the landing party, as he had been so diligent with his hydrographical work. Elizabeth would also be pleased with this gesture, when she learned of it, James also reasoned. He carried his musket and a fowling piece; the scientists had their specimen bags, Parkinson his drawing materials.

As the pinnace moved into the shallows, the native women and children stared. Then, obviously alarmed, the women gathered up the children and ran into the undergrowth, leaving only two men on the beach. They were tall and bony, with white stripes painted down their arms and legs and across their chests. Their noses were flat, almost crumpled, their faces deeply pleated. One, clearly much older than the other, had greying hair. Both held long spears and a flat, paddle-like instrument. James nudged Tupaia, 'Tell them we mean them no harm, and that we require fresh water.'

Tupaia joined James in the bow of the boat, then called, loudly, in Otaheitian, to the naked men. It was his now-standard greeting, recounting his ancestry, his people's gods, the islands where they lived, and what the visitors required. The speech went on for some minutes, accompanied by the usual gesticulations and exhortations. But the brows of the men at whom it was directed grew more and more furrowed, the whites of their eyes standing out in their charcoal black faces. Then the older man moved a little way down the beach, shook his lance, then uttered a guttural cry which sounded like 'Warra warra wai!'

Tupaia, shocked that his greeting had not been understood, turned and shook his head. 'These people do not understand my language!' he cried. 'And I cannot understand theirs!'

Sensing the mutual incomprehension that was developing, James reached into his jacket pocket, withdrew some beads and nails and tossed them onto the beach. The men bent down, picked up the trifles and examined them curiously. As they did so James said, 'We can now go ashore.' He turned to Elizabeth's cousin. 'You may have the privilege of first landing, Smith.'

The prow slid onto the sand and the midshipman stepped out, followed by the others. But after they had done so the two natives rushed down the beach towards them, spears raised. James quickly brought his musket to his shoulder and fired a shot, deliberately aiming between the pair. Startled by the report, they both stopped, and turned away. Then the younger man picked up a rock, spun about and hurled it at James. It missed. James snatched up his fowling piece and fired it, aiming it at the men's legs. The older man yelped as shot struck his shin, then ran towards the nearest hut, went inside and came out with a shield which he held up in front of him. The other man hurled his spear at the newcomers, just missing Parkinson. Banks immediately fired his musket in retaliation, also aiming low. The pellets struck the spear-thrower's legs, and he leapt in the air. The women and children emerged from the huts, crying out in terror, and both men limped up the beach and vanished into the undergrowth. The women followed, leaving the few infants and toddlers alone, huddling together in fear. Some began to whimper.

'Not an honourable people,' said Banks as they wandered about the encampment. 'Abandoning their little ones like that.'

He began to collect up some of the spears and paddles that were scattered over the ground. 'Yes, unmanly conduct,' said James. He had tried to pacify the children by giving them beads, but the offering had been ignored. 'Their canoes are primitive,' he observed, kicking at the bark hull of one. 'Held together by sticks. Scarcely seaworthy.' Parkinson looked anxiously at the petrified infants. 'I think we should leave this place,' he said to the others. 'So the parents of these little ones can return to them.'

James nodded. 'Yes. We'll cross to the other side of the bay, and look for water there.' As they returned to the beached pinnace, he felt disconsolate. If Tupaia could not be understood by the natives of this land, and he could not understand them, what hope could there be of productive intercourse with the New Hollanders?

But in the days that followed, the bay itself proved bountiful. Most of the Endeavours spent the daylight hours ashore. Although the aboriginals had not returned, there were fish and oysters galore in the bay, and ample fresh water from holes dug on shore. Stingrays could be skewered with swords in the shallows. And unlike New Zealand, this land had indigenous animal and reptile life. They spotted but could not catch small feral dogs, and saw large lizards, some with frilly necks, which scampered away at their approach. They recoiled from banded brown and yellow snakes which slithered through the undergrowth. Brilliantly plumed parakeets swooped through the trees, and made easy targets when they alighted. There were dozens of species of new plants, many with flower spikes and fruiting cones. Banks, Solander and Sporing botanised blissfully; Parkinson was kept busy all day and half the night, drawing the new specimens, while James sounded and thoroughly charted the bay. There was sorrow, though, when able seaman Forby Sutherland, a consumptive, succumbed to the disease on the last day of April. He was buried ashore, near the place from which the Endeavours drew water. Although Tupaia wandered off in search of natives he could mediate with, when he approached them they either ignored him or repeated the phrase, "Warra warra wai!' Accompanied by shoo-ing movements with their hands, it was now clear what they were saying. *Leave us alone!* Angry that they had rejected his overtures and understood nothing of what he said, Tupaia became openly contemptuous of the aboriginals. 'They are worthless people,' he told James. 'They have nothing that is useful.' He put on his haughtiest expression. 'And they are *ugly*. The women especially.'

'To us, certainly,' James replied. 'But to each other – which is the most important consideration – probably not.'

Tupaia scowled. 'They are bad people. Stupid people.'

'We still must endeavour to communicate with them,' James replied, curtly. He realised that the real source of Tupaia's disdain was not only his snobbishness, deriving from his elevated status in his homeland and in New Zealand, but the fact that the natives here did not appreciate or comprehend him. Hence his value to the expedition as a go-between had gone, and his personal *mana* – to employ his own word – with the gentlemen on the ship, had gone with it.

Hoping perhaps to regain some of his former status, that evening Tupaia presented James with his newest watercolour.

It depicted three of the New Holland natives, in two bark canoes. Two boys in the leading canoe were paddling, towing the second canoe, in which a crouching man held a spear, ready to plunge it into a fish beneath his canoe. The eyes of the two boys were wide and watchful, the spear fisherman was bending forward, staring down at the water. His penis was clearly visible.

James studied the painting, struck by the uncanny way the Otaheitian had captured the personalities of the trio, as well as physical characteristics of the men and their craft. He would never be the artist that Sydney was, of course, but how quickly he had learned the skills of drawing and colouring. There were some, James knew, who denied that natives could acquire the civilised talents of Europeans, but he was not such a denier. The lithic maraes of the Tahitians, the wood and jade carvings of the Maori, were these not artistic achievements of distinction? And this man was also producing images of real worth. Handing the painting back to Tupaia, he said: 'It is a fine work, every bit as good as your Otaheitian paintings.'

Tupaia blushed slightly. 'Thank you, taio. I very much like to draw and paint.' He paused. 'When I am in England, I will paint King George and his Queen.'

The latest collection of new plants was laid out on the table in the officers' mess, ready for cataloguing. Earlier they had dined on fried stingray, which Gore had speared. Also on the mess table was one of the spears which Banks had seized from the encampment. He held it up to the others. 'The savages' principal weapon, I should say. The shaft is hardened wood, strong but flexible. And this ...' He thumbed the point of the spear gingerly '... is sharp enough to penetrate a man's chest.'

Wincing, Parkinson said, 'Is it carved from some sort of animal bone?'

'No. It is the tail of a stingray.'

Intrigued, the others came closer. Banks explained. 'It is lashed to the shaft with a type of fibre. The ray's tail is composed of a bony substance, and is severely barbed.' He ran his hand along its edge. 'The serrations add to its lethal nature.' He laid it on the table. 'A very effective weapon, for a primitive people.'

Tupaia, who had been watching intently, came forward. He said, with enthusiasm, 'My people too, know this weapon.' He drew up his shirt, exposing his chest. Just below his sternum was a shiny scar, about three inches long. 'During a battle on Raiatea an enemy, from Bora Bora, threw a spear which struck me.' He fingered it. 'This was where the stingray barb was pulled out.' Turning about, he displayed his back. 'And this was where the spear went in.' Below his left shoulder blade was a shiny indentation, the size of a florin, which stood out against the surrounding brown skin. The others stared in horrid fascination. James said, 'How did you survive such a drastic wound?'

Tupaia let his shirt drop. 'The spear was cut off at the back, then the point was pulled through from the front.' He smiled. 'There was much pain. But I was young, and strong, so I became well again. A priest treated the two wounds with special plants, and they healed.' He paused, then said, with obvious pride, 'Most men die from such wounds.'

James picked up the spear. 'It makes a very useful weapon, doubtless. And as there are so many of the great fish in the waters of this place, I propose to call it "Stingray Bay".'

Banks smiled. 'You may call it that, Cook. But Solander, Sporing and I have already named the bay.' James frowned. The impertinence of the man. 'And what name is that?' he replied, coolly.

'In view of the fact that we have found dozens of new plants on its shores, we have decided to call it ... "Botany Bay".'

Later that day, upon reflection, James conceded that the name was indeed suitable. Banks and Solander had done sterling botanising here. So upon the chart of the bay he had drawn, on the northern and southern mandibles at its entrance, he wrote 'Cape Banks' and 'Point Solander', respectively. He also labelled a promontory on the south coast of the bay 'Point Sutherland', after his recently deceased seaman.

They weighed anchor on 6 May, and set sail north once again, in favourable weather. The following day they passed a narrow gap in the coast, between rocky, layered cliffs. Through the gap James spied a deep, capacious harbour. Although they had no need of it then, he marked it on his chart as 'Port Jackson', after Sir George Jackson, second secretary of the Admiralty. This gave James particular satisfaction, as Sir George was the brother of Mrs Skottowe, the wife of his family's landlord, from long ago in Great Ayton.

Two weeks later, just south of the Tropic of Capricorn, another inviting bay was spied from the main mast by Nicholas Young. Aware that the water casks needed replenishment, James ordered *Endeavour* to be brought into the bay. When she was at anchor he ordered most of the crew stood down while he and a landing party went ashore. Although Banks and Solander collected several new plants, and Gore shot a plump bustard, the soil James found to be sandy and infertile, and the vegetation mainly mangroves. They saw smoke in the distance but encountered no natives, and after nightfall the party returned to the ship.

As they descended to the after deck, from the lower deck came the sounds of shouting, laughter and fiddle playing. 'The men are making the most of their leisure hours,' Banks observed, wryly. James smiled. 'They will need to. There is much hard sailing ahead.' He would name this place 'Bustard Bay', he decided, as they dined on the bird that evening and found it delicious.

There was hammering on the door of his cabin. James sat up in his cot. What was happening? From behind the door came an anguished cry, and more hammering. It was just after dawn. He pulled on his trousers and shirt in the dim light, then hauled the cabin door open.

'My God, Orton ...'

James's clerk was leaning against the wall, his hands held to the sides of his head. He was barefooted and his shirt was shredded. But what shocked James was the sight of Orton's head.

His forehead and hair were covered in blood. His cheeks were drained of colour, his eyes screwed up with pain. James grabbed his arm. 'What happened, man? Did you fall?'

Eyes tightly closed, Orton shook his head. Then his hands dropped to his sides. James inhaled sharply. The tops of both the clerk's ears had been cut away, and blood was oozing from the lacerations. James led him, stumbling, to the cabin's chair and sat him down. As he did so he caught the thickly sweet smell of stale rum on the young man's breath. He knelt in front of him.

'Who did this?' he demanded.

Eyes still firmly closed, Orton shook his head. 'Don't know.'

'Where were you last night?'

'Below. In the crew's mess.'

'Who were you with?'

Orton thought for a few moments, then began to recite, painfully. 'Johnson, Ravenhill, Magra, Saunders, Wolfe, Moody, Collett, Cox.'

'Were you all on the grog?'

'Yes.' He groaned. 'After my third tankard ... I passed out and ... knew nothing more. Then a few minutes ago I awoke, in great pain ...' He couldn't continue.

James stood up. 'Wait here. I'll get Monkhouse to attend to you.' Rage beginning to build inside him, he added, 'And I'll go below and discover who committed this ... atrocity.'

On James's instructions, bo'sun Gathray had ordered the eight seamen Orton had named to report to the lower deck mess. They sat on the benches there, unshaven, heads bowed, all obviously much the worse for the night's heavy drinking. Assailed by the reek of farts and rum which permeated the mess, James stood, hands behind his back, glowering.

'Last night, while he slept, and the worse for drink, Dick Orton was deliberately and callously mutilated by a member of this crew. His ears were cropped, his clothes slashed.' His eyes roamed over the assembled men. 'You were all drinking with him, so suspicion falls on all of you.' He glared at the cowed group. 'Whoever is guilty of the assault, own up, *now.*'

A heavy silence descended on the mess. The men looked down at the tables, avoiding each other's eyes, as well as James's. Feeling the silence seeping through the mess like a toxin, the anger that James felt intensified. How dare they form a conspiracy of silence! He strode up and down, eyes flashing furiously from one man to the next. Openly incensed, he stopped and demanded, 'Whose hammock hangs next to Orton's?'

Moody raised his hand. 'Mine does, Sir.'

'Did you see, or hear, anything last night?'

'No, Sir.' He looked perplexed, as well as frightened. 'I were on the grog something bad mesself, Sir. I can't remember even slinging my hammock.'

'Collett?'

'It were not me, Sir. I were grogged to the gills, as well.'

James then remembered something, an incident which had been reported to him after they left Otaheite. It had involved Magra, but considering it unimportant at the time, James had taken no action. His gaze fell upon the boyishly good-looking New Yorker.

'Magra...?'

'Sir?'

'I believe you had previously quarrelled with Orton, is that correct?'

Magra shuffled uneasily on his bench. Avoiding James's intense gaze, he said in a low voice, 'I did, Sir, months ago. But I am innocent of this offence.' He looked up, his expression pleading. 'I swear it, Sir.'

'Is it true that you tore Orton's shirt on the other occasion?'

'Yes, I did. We were both under the influence of the grog. We were wrestling, on the floor here, playfully, and I ripped his shirt off.' He appeared contrite. 'There was no malice involved, Sir.'

Although James scowled at the midshipman, he thought he was telling the truth. But he still deserved a punishment. 'You are dismissed from the quarterdeck until further notice, Magra,' he announced coldly. He took a step backwards before adgowning the group once more. Eyes narrowing, he said carefully, 'It is my determination to get to the bottom of this sorry business. Once more, I ask you, *who was responsible for the attack on Orton?*'

When the sullen silence persisted, and their eyes stayed downcast, James spun about and strode from the cabin, cursing under his breath. He was as angry as he had been at any other time on the voyage. A valuable crew member had been callously attacked, by one of his own ship-mates, and he, James, was unable to discover who, or why. It was intolerable. He went straight to the surgeon's cabin. There Monkhouse reported that he had washed and bound Orton's wounds, and relieved him of his duties for three days. 'The lacerations,' he informed James, 'I believe may have been inflicted with the sailmaker's shears.'

It was the next day that James noticed a small piece of folded paper under his cabin door. He picked it up and unfolded it. On it had been written a single word.

Buggaree

As he stared at the word, the rage that had been simmering within him boiled up again.

Orton was the victim of the assault, so was he also the object of another man's lust? Or had he come between two others with feelings for each other? And if so, who? Was it he, Orton, who was guilty of the unnatural vice? Or could it be Magra? Screwing up the little piece of paper, James went through to the Great Cabin, which mercifully was unoccupied.

It could be any of them, he thought, if truth be known, so suspicion fell on all eight. He went to the seat under the stern window and stared out, without really seeing. Sodomy happened, everyone knew it, capital offence or no. It was the unspoken crime of any navy. With men confined for long periods without the relief of women, what else could be expected? But it must never be admitted. But this now was his dilemma – someone knew that the unnatural act had been committed below decks, and that someone knew that he, James, now knew as well.

Turning away from the window at last, he knew what he would do. For the time being, nothing. He wanted no distractions from the arduous navigations that lay ahead. Every man on the ship would have to play his part, and willingly. But when they reached civilisation again he would announce a plan to discover the identity of Orton's assailant. He would get to the bottom of it, as it were. In the meantime, the matter would remain a dark secret.

Towards the end of May, and with favourable airs, Green informed James that from his observations they were approaching the Tropic of Capricorn. A double-checking with sextants confirmed this. From the top of the mainmast, James observed several islands to larboard, and reefs to port, and ordered that from this time the boats would go ahead during the daylight hours, taking soundings, and that at night the ship would lie at anchor. From now on, he was well aware, the tropical waters would allow the growth of more and more coral polyps, meaning that there would be an increasing number of shoals and reefs to negotiate. An undetected coral reef was capable of tearing *Endeavour*'s hull apart as if it was wet tissue paper.

In this manner, slowly and cautiously, they made their way further north and into the true tropics. On 9 June, at 16° south, they passed a low, wooded island two leagues off the coast which James named 'Green Island', in recognition of his astronomer's work. Green was delighted at the gesture, so much so that he drank himself into a stupor that evening. But now the water supplies were again running low, and the coastal land – mainly undulating hills covered with scrubby bush, and acres of spreading mangroves – was unpromising. From the mast heads they could see the spreading, dark brown shoals surrounding them like a stain, with patches of deep, jade-green water between them. They were sailing through a labyrinth.

A few forays ashore found no fresh water. Monkhouse reported to James that Tupaia was complaining of swollen gums, and that livid sores had appeared on his legs – the scourge of scurvy had beset him. Others began to be similarly afflicted, and the surgeon prescribed extract of lemon for them. But it was insufficiently fresh, and so had little effect. As May came to an end the need for fresh fruit and water was becoming desperate, but the coral maze that surrounded them was becoming even more labyrinthine.

As there was a full moon on 10 June, James ordered that they would sail through the night, with topsails close-reefed and a leadsman taking constant soundings. Accordingly, at 11pm that night the man in the chains made the call, 'By the mark, seventeen!' In this depth the ship was safe, and as her course was held the leadsman prepared to cast his line again.

He never did so. At that very moment there came the terrible sound of wood against rock, a graunching and tearing, followed by a series of shuddering thumps as *Endeavour*'s hull was impaled on the reef.

Twenty-seven

Jolted from his cot, James pulled on his shirt and breeches and sprinted up to the deck. Although *Endeavour* was still upright, she was immobile. Gore was in the bow, Pickersgill at his side. The full moon was casting a creamy light across the black water, but the reef itself was invisible.

'Order all sails taken in!' he called to Molyneux, who had been at the helm with Hicks. 'And hoist out both boats. We need to take soundings, fore and aft!'

'Lower all sails!' came the cry. 'Look fast there!'

The stricken ship became alive with dark figures, climbing like spiders amid the rigging. Lines were dragged in, sails furled and tied, the boats hoisted, all the deck lamps lit.

In their pens, the goat and the remaining sheep began to bleat with fear, instinctively reacting to the near-panic of the men around them.

As the boats were being let down, Parkinson and Banks joined James and the other officers in the bow. 'I was almost thrown from my bunk,' said Banks, indignantly.

'Is it bad?' asked Parkinson, eyeing the water nervously.

'We'll know soon enough,' James replied, his eyes on the lowering launch.

The tide was high, and depths varied from 18 to 20 feet on the port side to more than 30 on the larboard. *Endeavour*'s bow was lying north-east, so James calculated that she was lodged on the south-western edge of the reef. The only decent depth, the leadsmen reported, was a hundred feet astern of the ship. James ordered an anchor and cable lowered into the launch. Carried out to the larboard quarter, the anchor was dropped, the cable fed back to the ship and attached to the windlass. But even with all hands to the capstan, and the slack brought in and hove taut, the ship remained immoveable.

'Molyneux, order all the pumps manned!' James bellowed down the deck, and the master obeyed, vanishing below.

The only sound now, in the dead of the night, was the sporadic rush of water being pumped into the sea. And with the tide beginning to ebb, the ship began to rock in the draining current.

Every man jack on board could imagine the extra pressure this was putting upon her wounded hull.

Pickersgill appeared at James's side.

'Shall we carry out the other anchor?' he asked.

'No. It would make no difference.' James's eyes darted to the stern. 'We need to lighten her before the tide falls further.' He called down to Hicks. 'Overboard with all weight! Get the men to go below and bring up the ballast, the rotten stores, water casks ...'

'Water casks?' Pickersgill looked askance.

'Yes, dammit, have them brought up and thrown over. And the carriage guns, and the balls ...'

With the sky lightening and the tide still dropping, over the side they went: cannons, cannon balls, full casks, stinking stores, stored staves and hoops. As the jettisoned items fell, the impact threw up another ominous sight – *Endeavour*'s sheathing boards, floating on the surface. Then, to James's further chagrin, her false keel appeared alongside, indicating that the damage must be even worse than they had thought. Under his breath, he once again cursed his decision to sail through the night.

He knew now that the all-important factor was the tide. Next high at 11am, that would be the best time to try to refloat the ship. But more buoyancy was essential. He ordered spare spars and masts brought up from below and lashed together to create rafts. The men worked in grim silence at this task, aware that they were struggling against overwhelming odds. The rafts were then lowered alongside and made fast to the hull at the waterline.

At late morning the tide rose, then ceased. Slack water. The crew heaved at the anchor lines like a tug-of-war team, struggling to free the ship from the reef's grip. But the morning tide did not reach its previous high mark, and she remained stuck hard. Pickersgill rushed up from below. 'She's taking on water. Fast.'

'All hands to the pumps,' James ordered Pickersgill. 'Organise half hour shifts.'

What he remembered most vividly, later, was the way they all worked in unison, sailors and midshipmen, officers and gentlemen, scientists and seamen. Only the one-handed cook, Thompson was spared. He instead keeping his fire hearth stoked, heating beef bone broth for the pumpers. All were aware, though no one said as much, that if they did not succeed in saving the ship, they would be doomed to a ghastly death on this desolate coast. Natives, probably hostile, awaited them on shore, even if they succeeded in landing there. The nearest European outpost was thousands of leagues away, in the Dutch East Indies. There were two low islets visible to the north of the stricken ship, a league or two away, but they would provide no real sanctuary. As the Endeavours worked frantically below, knowing that they had to get as much water out of the hull as they could before the next high tide, they knew they were pumping for their lives.

Deciding to risk all and try to heave her off, at nightfall James ordered as many hands to the capstan and windlass as could be spared from the pumps. Grunting and sweating, they heaved at the capstan. And at twenty past ten o'clock they felt the ship move, faintly. She stopped for a few moments, then shifted again. All on deck held their breath. She moved again, shifting backwards, then fell free. She was afloat! Under the deck lamps, men looked at each and suppressed the urge to cheer. Knowing that the battle was far from won, James ordered the carpenter John Satterly into the hold to measure the depth of the water there.

Ten minutes later, Satterly returned. Obviously exhausted, he was barefoot, and water ran from his trousers onto the deck. 'Three feet nine inches, Sir,' he reported. Hearing this news, the others on the deck now looked at each other in dismay. At that rate, and with the leak overtaking the pumps, they were doomed.

James grimaced. Impossible odds. But that figure needed to be checked. To Benjamin Jordan, who was standing by for the next pump shift, he said, 'You take a reading too, Jordan.'

'Aye Sir.' And he disappeared below. Under the full moon, the ship was rocking gently in the swell, and beginning to list to larboard. At this rate she wouldn't last the night. James wondered, should he order the men into the boats? Shuttle them across to the islands?

Jordan returned, his expression bewildered. 'My reading shows only a fraction over two feet of water, Sir,' he panted.

'*Two* feet? Are you certain?'

'Yes Sir. I double-checked.'

Mutterings broke out among the others. A considerable difference. The pumps might be able to cope at that rate, James thought. Then a tall, willowy figure appeared at his side. It was midshipman Monkhouse.

'Sir, if I might make a suggestion?'

'Yes?' James replied, impatiently. What could this lad possibly do to help?

'What about we fother the breach?'

James frowned. He knew of fothering, but had not himself experienced it. He shot the midshipman a hard look. 'You are familiar with the procedure, Monkhouse?'

'Yes Sir. Three years ago, while I was on the *Lady Pamela*, crossing the Atlantic, her hull sprang a bad leak. After a gale.' He paused, breathless with excitement. 'The captain had her fothered with an old sail. And it worked, Sir. The pressure of the water forced the canvas over the breach, and she ceased taking on water. We were able to complete the voyage.'

James considered this. It would be worth trying. 'Very well,' he said. 'Where is Ravenhill?'

'He's working the pump, Sir,' came a voice from near the grating. To the midshipman, James said, 'Go below and tell him to get out one of the old sails.' To quartermaster Evans, he said, 'We'll need pitch and oakum, too. And Monkhouse ...'

'Sir?'

'You are to oversee the fothering.'

'Aye, Sir ...'

The big canvas bandage was spread out on the deck, then smeared filthily on one side with pitch, oakum and dungy sheep wool. Monkhouse attached lengths of ropes to each of its corners. Then, with men working on both the port and larboard sides, the canvas was slung over the side, near the bow. It was dragged under the hull, and the ropes made fast to the bollards on both sides of the deck, midships. The bandage was in place, but would the bleeding be stanched?

The midshipman, face crimson with strain, reported to James. 'The fothering's done, Sir.'

'Very well. Now go below and tell the men to keep pumping.'

Twenty minutes later, Monkhouse came up from below, breathless, face still flushed. But his eyes were shining. 'It's working, Sir. The pumps have gained on the leak. When we let the pumps stand, she stayed almost dry.'

From all around the deck rose cries of relief. Chest heaving,

Monkhouse looked down at the deck, exhausted but elated. *Endeavour* had been impaled on the reef for one hour short of a day.

Almost speechless with relief, unwilling to betray what he had feared from the near-catastrophe, James held out his hand to the midshipman. 'Well done, lad,' he said, gruffly. Then to Hicks, standing by the helm with Molyneux, he said, 'We'll set sail at first light, in search of a safe haven.'

20 June, 1770

Dearest Beth,

It is a month and a half since I made an entry in this journal – but a great deal has happened, events which demanded my total attention. Lately the ship, and hence our entire expedition, has been imperilled, and it was only through the crew's unity, combined with good fortune, that we survived a foundering upon a coral reef. I have named the reef after Endeavour*'s most reliable master, Dick Pickersgill. He is singled out in this manner, but in truth the entire ship's company worked as one to save the ship, and ourselves. The blame for the foundering lies with me, as I unwisely ordered the ship to maintain sail at night instead of standing to. If we had been in daylight, the reef would have been sighted from the masthead and hence avoided. I am racked with private guilt, that through my imprudent decision the entire expedition came close to disaster. Never before have I made such a grievous misjudgement. I can confess this guilt to no one but yourself, as my report to the Admiralty will be confined to facts, not feelings. But suffice to say that in all my years at sea I have not come so close to losing a ship, an action entirely attributable to my own indiscretion.*

My relief when we were at last released from the reef and able to set sail again was inexpressible. Yet even free from the coral's near-mortal grip, our tribulations continued, for we had to discover and negotiate a passage which ultimately brought us to where we now are. This was a task of great complexity. Do you remember when we took a launch up the river to Hampton Court Palace, with James and Nathaniel? It was a day in June, 1768, and very hot, as I recall. While there we entered the palace's maze and spent some time going back and forth, seeking an exit from the labyrinth of hedges, not knowing which way to turn, or if having turned, not sure whether that course was the correct one. Cul-de-

sacs confronted us constantly. Well my love, what I have lately experienced was of a similar nature, except that coral reefs are a great deal more hazardous than hedges of hornbeam! And our passage was made even more arduous by unrelenting gales.

But we are secure now, encamped beside the estuary of a river which I have named 'Endeavour', after our long-suffering vessel. After we warped her into the river and she was beached, we saw just how grievous her injuries were. The false keel had been stripped away, several sheathing boards were lost and there was a hole in the hull so large that it must have been fatal to her but for a sizeable chunk of coral rock which had broken from the reef and wedged in the breach, thus fortuitously serving to hinder further intake of water. So, we are now labouring here beside the river during this enforced stay upon the shore of New Holland. Sleeping ashore in tents, we are becoming land creatures again. Our hamlet beside the river is an industrious one. The entire company is busily occupied: the carpenters with repairs to the hull, the smiths forging new nails and bolts, Surgeon Monkhouse tending to the sick (the Otaheitian, Tupaia, largely spurns European food, and so was afflicted with scurvy, but he is recovering rapidly after receiving a fresh diet). The quartermasters seek new vegetables, the most useful of which are the hearts of palm cabbage and the leaves of a root crop which grows in a swamp. Others of the crew collect fresh spring water (the river, being tidal, is brackish), seine for fish and capture the turtles which inhabit the coastal waters. Their meat is rich and nutritious, and we will be taking some of the creatures with us when next we sail. The scientists botanise joyfully, Gore the hunter shoots everything that moves and Banks's greyhounds chase game merrily. The strangest of animals in this land is a kind of giant hare which leaps at great pace, upright, on powerful hind legs. The natives call it a "kangaroo". After Gore brought one down with his musket, the cook roasted it and we ate the creature for dinner. It made splendid eating. The omnivorous Banks made a comment over the meal which amused the rest of us. 'I believe,' he said, 'that I have eaten my way into the animal kingdom farther than any other man.'

We have gradually achieved some intercourse with the natives here. Although as at Botany Bay they were initially indifferent to our presence, and unimpressed with the beads and nails we offered them, they are now communicating more freely. Tupaia in particular has made progress with them, as because of his darkened complexion and earnest attempts at speaking (though in truth they know nothing of his language), they accord him respect. He reports that they belong to a tribe which they call the 'Guugu-Yimithirr'. They are primitive beings who walk about totally naked, sleep under crude shelters of bark and have no true agriculture, supplying themselves with food entirely through hunting and collecting. They are slim of build, very black, and paint their bodies with stripes of white and red ochre. We see mainly men – the women seldom appear. When they are surprised by something, they make a strange whistling sound. They are skilled at making lances and deploying them for spearing game, with the assistance of a propelling device they call a 'woomera'. They are, I believe, contented creatures, entirely at one with the land, river and coastal waters. These offer all they require, and they appear to have no ambition whatsoever to develop or acquire the appurtenances of civilised beings.

This morning I climbed a high hill beside the river in order to see if I could discern a passage through the reef which we can follow after we set sail from here. But I could see that shoals and reefs abound to the north, so the course we follow will be testing, and soundings will have to be taken constantly. But there is much work still to be done before the ship will once more be fit for sea.

I will conclude this entry now, in the hope that you and our family are well and contented. My recent brush with mortality sheeted home to me the knowledge that you and the children are my most cherished possession. In the depths of my secret fear that we would be cast forever on this desolate shore, my deepest dread was that I would never again see you and our children. Now that fear has abated, I look forward with all my heart to completing the charting of this lonely coast, then turning Endeavour in the direction of home.

My love, as always,

James

By late June the little tent town beside the river had become a second home to the Endeavours. While the carpenters worked on the repairs to the hull, the decks were freshly caulked and the sails repaired and set out to dry. The men washed their belongings in the river, sought fresh vegetables and fruit, hunted, fished and caught turtles. The natives were less unfriendly now, although communications remained hesitant.

June 29 was very hot, with a warm wind blowing off the land, helping to dry the crew's washing and the sails, which hung from lines between two poles just above the beach. A cauldron of caulking pitch was bubbling above a fire near the tents, and the yawl was drawn up on the foreshore on its side, awaiting repairs to its hull. On the mid-deck of *Endeavour*, ten turtles caught the day before on the reef by Gore, Evans and others had been hauled aboard and were now lying on their backs, victuals for the next stage of the voyage.

Endeavour had been refloated and Tupaia and James were standing on the afterdeck, watching about a dozen aboriginal men on the other side of the river, squatting beside their canoes. Since they had begun to treat him respectfully, Tupaia had revised his opinion of the New Hollanders.

'They are not bad people, I now think,' he declared to James. 'They are just ... simple.'

'What do you mean by that?'

'They have no proper houses, no temples, no marae. Not even clothes.'

This judgemental attitude continued to rankle with James. 'But they have no need of such things,' he pointed out. 'The sea and the land provided them with everything. And the constant heat here means that clothing is unnecessary.'

Tupaia shrugged. 'The weather is the same on my islands, yet our people build houses and marae. We have clothes, and we worship our gods.' He shook his head, dismissively. 'These people have no gods.'

Persisting in their defence, James said, 'Banks has told me they relate stories to each other, when they sit around their fires at night. And they dance while telling the stories, imitating birds and other creatures.'

'Yes, I too have watched them doing this,' Tupaia allowed. He looked thoughtful. 'Perhaps their stories are about their gods.'

'That may be the case.' James looked across the river at the group. 'And they are peaceable towards us. That has made our stay here more tolerable.'

307

As they talked, the aboriginal men got into two of their canoes and began to paddle across the river towards the ship.

'They are coming this way,' Tupaia said, frowning. 'Why?'

They climbed from their canoes, leaving their spears on board, and climbed the steps on *Endeavour*'s hull. Tall but slim, with wide flat noses, black curly hair and beards, they ranged in age from their early twenties to their mid-thirties. Standing about on the weather deck, ignoring the crew, they were preoccupied by the upturned, white-throated turtles, whose flippers were waving slowly and helplessly. The tallest of the natives, who had a long bone inserted through his nostrils, pointed at the creatures and said something to Gore. Not comprehending, he looked up at Tupaia quizzically. The Otaheitian came down and put himself between the aboriginals and Gore. Through gesticulations, Tupaia asked the tall man what was wrong. He replied, pointing to the turtles, the other aboriginals, and out to sea. Then he bent down and laid one hand on two of the turtles' bellies.

'What do they want?' James called down from the after deck.

Tupaia looked concerned. 'I think, he says ... that the turtles belong to them, because ... what comes from the sea belongs to his people.'

This claim was absurd, James thought. He said to Tupaia, 'Tell them the turtles are ours because we captured them. And that the sea and what comes from it belongs to everyone, not just them.'

Tupaia tossed his hands in the air. 'I cannot explain that to them, Tute. I have not the words of theirs.' He added, hesitantly, 'Can they not have just two of the turtles? There will be plenty left for us.'

James thought for a moment. Relations with these people had been almost completely peaceful. It would be short-sighted, perhaps, to risk amicable relations for the sake of two turtles.

'Tell them ...' he began.

Before he could finish his statement, the man with the bone through his septum dashed forward, grabbed the nearest turtle and deftly turned it over. Two of his companions ran to it and picked it up by the edge of its shell, one on either side. The other men grabbed a second turtle and lifted it up. Gore and Evans charged at them, pushing the aboriginals aside. Both turtles crashed to the deck.

The aboriginal leader raised his fist defiantly, pointed at himself, then the others, then back at the turtles. Clearly, the message was: *They are ours*. But Gore and the others had interposed themselves between the creatures and the natives. Banks, who had been processing plant specimens on the foredeck, rushed up and faced the aboriginals' leader. 'Get back!' he commanded. Realising that this would only inflame the situation, James called down to him.

'Banks! Stand aside!'

The natives' leader pushed Banks away disdainfully with open hands, and he backed into Tupaia, who clutched his shirt.

'No, taio. Leave them,' he pleaded. 'All they want is two turtles.'

Not comprehending Tupaia's attempt at mediation, the aboriginals suddenly sprinted down the deck, yelling angrily, picking up any loose object in their way and casting it overboard: buckets, scrubbing brushes, a fishing net, boat hooks. Then, before they could be restrained, they clambered down into their canoes and paddled furiously the twenty yards or so to the beach, on the encampment side of the river. The Endeavours rushed to the stern, and from there saw one of the younger aboriginal men snatch up a bunch of long, dry grass. The slender black figure ran to the fire under the pitch pot, lit the grass from it, then ran to the scrub which grew close to the camp. Holding the torch to the foliage, he waited until it caught, then ran along its edge, trailing sparks from his brand. Wherever he touched the tinder-dry vegetation, it burst into flames.

The young man then sprinted back to the river, where the others were waiting by their canoes.

The Endeavours scrambled over the side and into the ship's boats, then rowed the short distance to the shore. Too late. The scrub was ablaze and the flames fanned by the land breeze were swirling skywards, accompanied by spiralling plumes of smoke. In minutes the conflagration had encircled the camp and was sweeping towards the two tents and a pig pen on the foreshore. James, primed musket in hand, leapt from the launch and ran towards the tents, followed by Gore and three others. They dragged the tents down, then hauled them away from the encroaching flames. Two men grabbed lengths of canvas and began beating at the flames; sparks flew into the air. Banks called to James. 'Look! By the water!'

The clothesline had been set up just above a flat rock where the men washed and beat their laundry clean. Tied on the line were items of their washing – shirts, breeches, drawers and cloths – along with several fishing nets. A second arsonist stood under the line, fire brand in his hand, holding it under a pair of breeches. Furious, James ran down the beach, aimed and fired his musket. Small shot struck the man in the lower back. He screamed, dropped the burning brand and ran down to where his companions were waiting. Not bothering to collect up all their spears, the men ran into the nearby trees.

Exhausted, the crewmen stood on the foreshore. The fire had burned itself out but the air was filled with an acrid stench and a swathe of the grass was blackened and smouldering. The collapsed tents were further down the beach, saved from the fire, but the seared corpse of a piglet, which had panicked and run into the flames, lay among the ashes. The other pigs were uninjured.

Banks sank to the ground. 'What a mercy it is that most of our equipment is already aboard. All could have been lost.'

James, musket on the sand beside him, nodded. He was bitterly disappointed that it had come to this, after their previously cordial relations.

'What now?' Gore asked James.

'We cannot leave the place in a state of discord, we must try to make peace again.' He gathered up the spears the men had abandoned. 'We'll follow where they went.'

Emerging from the trees, they came to an expanse of scrubby bushland, from which a number of tall brown ant hills protruded, resembling primitive obelisks. Tupaia, who by now knew the area well, led the way. 'Their camp is down this hill,' he told the others. Minutes later, they saw the men, sitting in a circle beneath a tall eucalyptus tree with a pale trunk, strips of whose bark were peeling away like flayed skin. Some of the men held spears. Tupaia stopped. 'Don't come close. If we sit down, away from them, it will show them we mean no harm.'

They did so, also arranging themselves in a circle. Tupaia collected up the spears they had seized. When he gestured for James's musket, he relinquished it, reluctantly. Tupaia placed the weapons on the ground between the two groups. The two parties stared at each other across the open ground. No one spoke or moved for several minutes. Here, away from the sea, the heat was like a blanket which wrapped itself stiflingly around the Englishmen, and the bush insects screamed at them accusingly. James could see blood on the midriff of the man he had peppered. He began to feel uneasy. Was another attack coming?

With the aboriginals was another man, smaller and much older than the rest, with curly grey hair and beard. After a time, at some unspoken command, the old man stood up and came forward. He walked with a limp, his shoulders were hunched and the skin of his chest and torso was slumped into folds.

Coming closer, he beckoned to Tupaia, who got up and walked towards him. The old man spoke, animatedly, then made a loud clicking noise with his tongue.

James called out. 'What does he say?'

'I'm not sure,' Tupaia said. 'But I think he speaks of friendship.'

The old man beckoned all of them forward, and they obeyed, James collecting up the confiscated spears. Approaching the group, he offered the weapons to them, but kept his musket in his left hand. The man with the nose bone came forward, and accepted the offered spears, nodding and saying, 'Hiee, hiee, hiee...' The other men got up, placed their spears under the tree, then came over to James and the others, lifting their splayed feet in high stepping movements. The aboriginals were all chatting and chuckling, as if nothing untoward had ever happened.

Twenty-eight

4 August 1770
In the PM having pretty moderate weather I ordered the coasting
anchor and cable to be laid without the bar to be ready to warp
out, that we might not lose the least opportunity that might offer
for I am very anxious of getting to sea. Laying in port spends time
to no purpose, consumes our provisions of which we are very short
in many articles, and we have a long passage to make to the East
Indies through an unknown and perhaps dangerous sea.

The wind continued moderate all night and at 5 o'clock in the
morning when it fell calm this gave us an opportunity to warp out.
About 7 we got under sail having a light air from the land which
soon died away and was succeeded by the sea breeze from SEBS
with which we stood off to sea EBN having the pinnace ahead
sounding. The yawl I sent to the turtle bank to take up the net that
was left there but as the wind freshened we got out before her, and
a little after noon anchored in 15 fathoms and a sandy bottom, for
I did not think it safe to run in among the shoals until I had well
viewed them at low water from the masthead, that I might better
judge which way to steer ...

It was not until 20 August that they came to the end of New
Holland. It had taken over two weeks of arduous sailing to reach
the tip of the peninsula James named 'Cape York' after the late
Royal Highness the Duke of York. Over that fortnight they had
made their way laboriously northward, with the pinnace and the
yawl preceding *Endeavour*, taking soundings constantly.

Now they were in a complexity of islands, shoals and sand spits,
but after turning west they entered a channel which promised to
lead them ultimately to the East Indies, the strait charted in 1606
by the navigator, Luis Vaez de Torres, and named after the
Spaniard.

After landing on a nondescript island, one of a cluster, James
took possession of the entire coast they had traversed in the name
of the English King, satisfied that he had achieved something no
other European before him had. A pole was set, the Jack was
hoisted, a volley of small arms fired and echoed by one from
Endeavour. The unprepossessing place was named 'Possession

Island', and James named the eastern coast of the continent, 'New South Wales'. Notwithstanding the fact that a Dutchman, Willem Janszoon, had made landfall on the huge indentation in the north coast of New Holland in 1606, and that another Dutchman had named the giant bay the 'Gulf of Carpentaria', seventeen years later, the whole continent the Endeavours now considered England's. Well aware of the Dutchmen's earlier visits, James also knew that none of them had touched upon the east coast of this continent.

That evening, with *Endeavour* on a steady westerly course, James, Banks and Solander stood in the stern watching the sun sliding down a lavender sky. It was still fiercely hot, and they were all in their shirtsleeves. The sea was making a gentle, gurgling sound against the hull as the ship bore steadily west. Knowing how quickly sunset came in these latitudes, James would shortly order her to stand to for the night.

Putting a hand to his brow, Banks said quietly, 'I am feeling nostalgic.'

James frowned. The botanist did not look unwell. He said, 'Have you seen the surgeon about it?'

'Why?'

'Your illness. Nos... what is it?'

Banks laughed, scornfully. 'Nos... *talgia*. And it is not an illness, Cook, it is an *emotion*.'

James felt a familiar irritation. It always rankled with him when Banks paraded his superior education, then condescended him. They had been exchanging journals recently, and James felt envious when he read Banks's vivid descriptions of the places and peoples they had encountered. When ten days ago *Endeavour* was in the open sea and being carried by currents towards the coral reef where there were huge breaking waves, Banks had later written, *'The vast foaming breakers were too plainly to be seen not a mile from us. At this critical juncture, at this, I must say, terrible moment, when all assistance seemed too little to save even our miserable lives, a small air of wind sprang up from the land, so small that at any other time in a calm we should not have observed it.'* Then, when they discovered, almost miraculously, a narrow passage through the reef, and an in-flowing tide took them through it to safety, Banks had written, *'We were hurried in by a stream like a mill race'.*

James knew only too well that the botanist's fluency and lexis were a reproach to the dull prose of his own official journal. But he tried to suppress this fact, reminding himself that his duty as commander was to record, not embellish. He, James, was not a man of letters, nor had he any ambition to become one. His vocation was of a much more practical nature. And that prompted him to imagine what would have happened if Banks had been in command of the ship. *Endeavour* would never have got out of Plymouth Sound! This knowledge consoled him, along with the knowledge that his private journal to Elizabeth contained a record of his true feelings, candidly expressed. He looked away, towards the setting sun. It was gilding the sea aft of the ship, and the wind was soft and warm.

'This ... *nostalgia* ...' James said to Banks. 'How is it defined?'

'A kind of melancholia, caused by a longing for home. I came upon it in Dr Johnson's dictionary. It's from the Greek, nostos, to return home, and algos, meaning pain.'

As always, Solander looked impressed. 'So ... feeling pain for home.' He nodded. 'It is a useful word, I believe, to describe what people feel when they have been away too long.'

James remained silent. But he committed the word to memory. *Nostalgia*. It well described what he was feeling, too. In England now, autumn would have arrived. Season of mists, mellowness and golden foliage. He imagined Elizabeth and the children, walking on the common, perhaps gathering chestnuts for roasting. Did they think of him as often as he did of them?

It was just after daybreak when Gore rushed into the Great Cabin.

'Cook! Come up on deck!'

'What is it?'

'Come and see ...'

They rubbed their eyes, to remove the hallucination. But although unbelievable, the vision was indelible.

An island, but one quite unlike any they had seen in this hemisphere. Its hills and valleys were covered in pasture on which sheep and cattle were grazing. Men in European clothes were riding on horseback across the hills. Palm trees lined a sandy shore, but there was also a village above a cove, with three-storeyed brick houses and a spired church. The Endeavours stared at the outlandish sight. They had seen nothing like it since Rio de Janeiro, nearly two years earlier. James peered at the island through his scope, but could see no flag flying. Alongside him, Hicks said, 'There is no island marked here on any of the charts I have consulted.'

'Nor I,' said James, baffled by the bizarre sight. 'Perhaps it is a fragment of the Portuguese empire.' A few days earlier they had coasted the sizeable island of Timor, divided between rivals the Dutch in the west and the Portuguese in the east. But mindful of the hostility they had encountered in Portuguese Rio, and mistrustful of the Dutch, James had eschewed a landing there. Batavia would be different, it was known to be a truly international port. He lowered his spyglass. 'This may be a place which the Portuguese wish to remain a secret,' he said, wryly. 'An uncharted outpost of their domain.'

As they were in need of fresh supplies, Gore was ordered to go ashore in the pinnace and make contact with whoever the islanders were. When he returned he reported that he had been met hospitably by people who were dark-skinned but not aboriginals, who told him that the island was called 'Savu' and that it was part of the Dutch empire.

'The *Dutch*?' said James, astonished that a chart of the island had not been published.

'Yes,' said Gore. 'And there is a harbour on the south coast of the island, I was informed, which offers a safe anchorage.' Noticing James's doubtful expression, he added, 'They seemed willing to exchange our goods for fresh provisions.'

'Very well,' he told Gore. 'Go back and tell them we wish to trade.'

When the Virginian returned from his second visit ashore, in the pinnace with him was an enormously fat, bearded native of about 35 years, gowned in European clothing, and a florid-faced European man a little older, in wig and frock coat. They lumbered up onto the deck and Gore introduced them to James and Banks.

'This is Herr Johann Lange, the Hamburg representative of the Dutch East India Company on Savu, and Ma ... Ma ...' As Gore stumbled over the name, the fat man came forward, pressed his palms together, nodded solemnly and pronounced, '*Rajah* Madocho Lomi Djara.'

James shook hands with the two men. Then, wishing to talk terms, and as it was now early afternoon, he said, 'We would be pleased if you would dine with us.' He was also aware that one of the *Endeavour*'s last sheep had been butchered yesterday, and was in the galley being prepared for the table.

It quickly became evident, as the officers, gentlemen and their two unusual guests sat around the dining table, that both the Rajah and the company man had a great fondness for liquor. Banks raided his supply of burgundy and he, the Dutchman and the Rajah drained glass after glass of it, Banks almost tripping over Lord, his male greyhound, whenever he got up to provide refills. The dog was lying on the floor next to the table, gratefully accepting scraps of mutton from the Rajah. And as they ate, drank and talked, with Solander translating for the two guests, their promises to the Endeavours grew extravagant.

'Our friends say,' Solander reported, 'that there are great numbers of cattle, pigs, sheep and poultry on Savu, and that tomorrow we will be able to buy as many animals from them as we wish.'

Lange's head bobbed. 'Ja ... ja ...' Then he pointed to his plate and said something else. When James looked at Solander quizzically, the botanist said, 'And he loves this English mutton, and wishes to buy a sheep from us.'

Assured now that there would be replacement livestock available, James said, 'Herr Lange may exchange our last sheep for three of theirs.' Then, turning to the Rajah, he said, 'And what would you like from us?'

The Rajah burped, took another mouthful of wine, pushed his chair back and pointed at Lord, the greyhound. Banks eyed the Rajah groggily. 'You ... would like to have ... my dog?'

The Rajah bent down and stroked the greyhound's ears. 'Ja!' he said.

Banks raised his glass, which was full again. 'Then, my good man, you shall have him!'

Parkinson froze. Horrified, he said, 'Banks, you cannot give Lord up to a stranger. It is unthinkable.'

Turning a baleful gaze on the artist, Banks said, carefully, 'Don't tell me what I can and cannot do. I will still have Lady. So if my fat brown friend here ...' he placed a hand on the Rajah's shoulder

' ... wants this dog, *he shall have him*.'

Colouring, Parkinson stood up abruptly and left the table. Sympathising with him, but ignoring his exit, James said to Solander, 'Ask them how we can purchase the livestock.'

It was arranged that the Savuans would bring the animals down to the island's southern shore the next day, so that the Endeavours could purchase from them whatever they wanted. Upon hearing this good news, Banks fetched two bottles of claret, opened them, and refilled all the glasses, except James's, who again demurred. Observing the conversation but tiring of this wine-fuelled talk, James thought that the saying 'A drunk's best friend is another drunk', was rarely seen to be truer. And by the time the intoxicated pair of visitors departed the ship, Lord the greyhound was in the launch with them, huddling miserably in the stern.

Next morning the pinnace tied up to the stone jetty in the centre of the bay, which had a white sand beach and a line of coconut palms along its foreshore. At the end of the jetty was a brick warehouse, and a little settlement was clustered behind the palms. They walked up to the town, which had an unpaved square, an administration building above which the Dutch flag flew, and a number of detached brick and thatch cottages, straggling up the hill behind it.

James, Gore, Banks, Solander and Sporing strode into the square, expecting to see it filled with livestock pens. But the only creatures in sight were three native women in colourful, head-to-toe saris, who were drawing water from a well in the centre of the square, and a group of barefooted men, squatting on their haunches in front of the administration building. A solitary horse was tied to a rail beside the open entrance.

Confounded by the almost-empty square, James led the others through the door of the building. Inside was a spacious but sparsely furnished room with bare floorboards, a portrait of William V of Holland on one wall and three oil paintings of tulip fields in full bloom on the other. In the centre of the room was a round table, and sitting at it were Lange and the Rajah. Lange looked up blearily as the others entered; the Rajah kept his head in his hands.

Puzzled, James said to Solander, 'Ask them where the livestock are.'

Mopping his face with a large cloth, Lange replied, dully, and

Solander translated. 'He says he is ill today. And so is the Rajah.'

James looked at the Hamburger sharply. Ill? The worse for the wine, more like. 'What about the livestock?' he demanded.

Solander looked uncomfortable at the next reply. 'He says that he has just received instructions that the Englishmen must negotiate for the livestock with the local natives, not with them.' Lange shrugged; the Rajah avoided their gaze.

James was livid. The pair was nothing more than a couple of ill-disciplined wineskins, full of empty promises. Trying to curb his anger, he said, 'Ask him, from whom did these "instructions" come?'

They were from the Governor of Timor, he was told, in Concordia. *Endeavour* had been observed coasting the colony, and the governor had sent word that were she to call at Savu for provisions, they were to be provided only by the natives, and in the shortest possible time. When James glared at the Dutch officer, he again shrugged and gave him a daft grin. Banks tugged at James's sleeve. 'This "letter" is a fiction, I believe,' he murmured, 'they are merely seeking excuses for themselves.' James nodded. He had already come to the same conclusion.

The Rajah raised his head and spoke, slowly. Solander said, 'He says, as we entertained them to dinner, they will provide a meal for us, here. And by the time the meal is over, the livestock we want will be on the beach. Buffalo, pigs, chickens.' James ground his teeth in frustration. But if they walked out and left the island, which he was inclined to do, they would forgo the chance to obtain any of the needed provisions. 'Tell him,' he said reluctantly, that we will be their guests.'

The meal – rice and boiled pork – was served in woven pandanus baskets as they sat on mats in the square. The food was excellent, the sky a brilliant blue and the sun was high, beaming down fiercely into the little square. Banks sent out to the ship for more liquor, but this time the Rajah declined. Herr Lange resumed his imbibing enthusiastically however, and his face, which had been waxen-white when they arrived, resumed its terra cotta shade.

Towards the end of the meal a native messenger arrived, gowned in a loincloth. He informed Lange that there were three sheep on the beach, ready for the English.

'*Three sheep*?' James was incredulous. After all this, merely three sheep?

Again he adgowned Lange, who replied, casually, 'The natives who own the animals want cash for them, not bits of cloth, or some such trifles.' He rubbed the finger and thumb of his left hand. 'They want money.' He chortled. 'The rest of the animals will be on the beach for you tomorrow.'

They returned to the ship, well fed but otherwise frustrated. On the row back, Banks said to James, tipsily, 'We'll be lucky if we get a leg of lamb from these people. This island is farcical.'

This prediction proved correct. When they returned the next day they were accompanied by crewman John Dozey, who spoke Portuguese. They party was met on the beach by a short tubby native holding an emaciated buffalo on a rope leash. Ask him how much, James asked Dozey. 'Five guineas,' Dozey told him.

'*Five guineas*?' James shook his head in wonder. These people were unbelievable. He dispatched Dozey up to the hall, with an instruction that they would pay no more than three guineas for the scrawny beast. Minutes later, Dozey came back with the Rajah's reply – 'Five guineas, take it or leave it.'

As they stood on the beach digesting this unpalatable message, they saw a group of militiamen coming down the hill, on foot. They were natives in rag-tag uniforms, bare-footed and hatless, but carrying spears and muskets, led by a moustachioed white man in a blue uniform, complete with sword, gold epaulettes and a blue plumed hat. The group assembled shambolically in front of James and the others, then the commander announced, in broken English: 'My name Senor Luis del Gardo. Me is Herr Lange's assistant.'

Unfazed by this rabble, James said calmly, 'And where *is* Herr Lange?'

The commander jerked his thumb in the direction of the village. Standing ramrod-straight, he announced loudly, 'There will be no trading. You are ordered to leave Savu by nightfall.'

James was incensed. This whole landing had been an utter waste of time. 'We will return to the ship,' he announced. 'To hell with this place.' They were turning away when they saw a thin, elderly Savuan man in a white skirt and turban walking up the beach towards them. Earlier in the day the same man had greeted them affably and presented them with some plantains and coconuts. Grateful for the gesture, James had presented him with a magnifying glass, with which he was obviously delighted. Now the old man walked past them, strode up to the Portuguese commander and began to berate him, gesturing fiercely and firing a burst of invective at both him and his raggedy troops.

'What's he saying?' James asked Dozey.

'He says ... these people are our guests ... that they are here in peace, only to trade ... and his people want to trade with them.'

'His people?'

'He is another Rajah. More important than the fat man. And he leads the people who want to trade with us.'

'Ah ...'

James removed the sword from his belt, went up to the old man and handed it over to him. It was a ceremonial weapon only, and could be spared. Chuckling with delight, the elderly Rajah accepted it. Then he went up to the troops and began brandishing the sword at them and rebuking them once more, until, shame-faced, they all turned and trudged back up the hill, trailing their weapons, followed by their commander.

There then appeared over the brow of the hill another group of a dozen natives, driving before them a mixed herd of animals: buffalo, sheep and pigs. Others carried chickens in bamboo cages, baskets of fruit and coconuts, and jars of palm wine.

Banks grinned at the sight. 'Let the trading begin,' he announced.

Once again *Endeavour* became a menagerie, the deck pens filled with some undernourished buffalo, plus pigs, sheep and many chickens. Provisions – fruit, firewood, vegetables and animal fodder – were unloaded from the longboat and taken below. It was not an overly-abundant supply, but it would suffice until they reached Batavia.

With the sea around the ship an indigo shade, the sky flaring red and orange and the humped profile of the island standing out darkly against it, James and Parkinson stood on the quarterdeck, staring back at Savu.

'A strange visit, this has been,' James reflected. 'Outlandish.'

'Aye,' said the artist. 'Almost unreal.' He gave his little, high-pitched laugh. 'Dream-like.'

'But you have drawings to prove Savu's reality, I trust.'

'Aye Sir, I have. Of the land, and some of the natives.'

'Good. And I have charted its coast.' He turned on his heels.

'Now, on to Batavia.'

Twenty-nine

In the Great Cabin following supper, Banks took a volume down from the bookcase. 'I have been reading this with interest.' He showed James the cover. 'Have you read it, Cook?'

'I have. Some years ago,' James replied.

'What is it?' asked Solander.

Banks held the book up to the cabin's lantern light, then recited. '*A Narrative of the Dutch Settlement of the Spice Islands*, by Heinrich Van Ensing, published in an English translation in 1735. 'Listen to what he writes of our next port-of-call.'

' *"Following the heroic subjugation of the native ruler and his troops by Dutch forces in 1619, led by Jan Pieterszoon Coen, Batavia was built on the ruins of an ancient town, known as Jacatra. Renamed 'Batavia', after the Germanic warrior tribe, the Batavians, ancestors of the Dutch people, it was subsequently fortified and became the base and principal port for the Dutch East India Empire, which is administered by the Vereenigde Oost-Indische Compagnie, or the VOC. Batavia was designed and constructed as for a Dutch city, complete with canals, warehouses and churches such as were found in the capital of the Netherlands, Amsterdam. The VOC grew immensely wealthy through the spice trade in the East India archipelago, over which it gained a monopoly, and the company possesses its own large merchant and naval fleet."* '

The others looked displeased at this Low Country boastfulness, but Banks continued.

'*Jan Pieterszoon Coen was determined to eliminate all but Dutch interests in the Banda Islands, where nutmeg trees grew. In 1621 he led 1500 Dutch soldiers and 80 Japanese samurai warriors in a gallant attack on Lonthoir Island, in the Bandas. After the Dutch victory, Governor-General Coen commanded the samurai to behead and dismember 44 Bandanese troops in front of their families, to provide a practical example of Dutch authority. The heads of the natives were mounted on pikes, as a warning to other native rulers who may have been tempted to challenge lawful Dutch authority.*'

Banks put the book down. 'Hardly the actions of a civilised

nation,' he said, scathingly.

James considered this, then said, 'That was one hundred and fifty years ago, Banks. Civilisation has advanced greatly since then.'

'For we English, certainly, but I have never found even the modern Dutch to be a compassionate people.'

'I am confident that England will soon surpass them, in imperial possessions and trade,' James ventured. He paused. 'A progression which began when we defeated the French in North America. That acquisition, combined with our trade bases in India, will enable us to eclipse all remaining Dutch authority. '

'Our own expedition has already significantly enlarged Britain's colonial empire, has it not?' ventured Parkinson. 'Think of New South Wales.' The others nodded, but James was thinking, ruefully, *yet our discoveries have been minimal.*

Banks flipped through the book's pages, then stopped some way further on.

'Some of the personal testimony in this book speaks highly of the *native* people of the East Indies.' He stared at the page. 'This is what one Dutch settler has written about the women of this land':

"They are all most ardently addicted to the sensual pleasures of love; and goaded on by the hottest fires of love, are ingenious in every refinement of amorous enjoyment. Mr Van Pleuren, who had resided here for eight years, and several other credible people, informed me that among these women were many who possessed the secret of being able, by certain herbs and other means, to disqualify their inconstant lovers from repeating the affront to them, insomuch that the offending part shrunk entirely away ..."'

Banks cleared his throat, noisily, then added, 'Not that I am in any need of such a prescription myself.' Glancing at Solander, he said, 'I shall go ashore immediately we are permitted to do so by the authorities, and take lodgings in Batavia. 'Will you join me, Solander?' The botanist nodded, enthusiastically.

1 October 1770

First and latter parts fresh breezes at SE and fair weather, the middle squally with lightning and rain. At 7pm, being then in the latitude of Java Head and not seeing any land assured us that we had got too far to the westward, upon which we hauled up ENE, having before steered NBE. At 12 O'clock saw the land bearing east, tacked and stood to the SW until 4 o'clock then stood again to the eastward, having very unsettled, squally weather which split the main topsail very much and obliged us to bend the other. Many of our sails are now so bad that they will hardly stand the least puff of wind. At 6 o'clock Java Head or the west end of Java bore SEBE distant 5 leagues, soon after this saw Princes Island and at 10 o'clock saw the island of Krakatoa.

As they raised the southwest head of Java, then turned east towards the island's northern coast, an air of intense expectation settled over the ship. The majority of the crew were well and could hardly wait to go ashore in Batavia, the fabled Dutch port which Molyneux and Gore had told them so much about.

Others, however, were ailing. Tupaia was ill again, afflicted with headaches and nausea but refusing to eat the ship's food or be treated with Monkhouse's principal remedy, extract of lemon.

'I believe he has the scurvy,' Banks reported to James in the Great Cabin, as he was making an entry in his journal.

James looked away. This suggestion was anathema to him; he hadn't lost a single man to scurvy, and didn't intend to now. He turned back. 'Is his boy similarly unwell?' he asked.

'No. Taiata is as chirpy as ever.'

'Well, the other one will recover, once we are ashore. The food there will be similar to what he was used to on Otaheite, I believe.'

Banks gave James an edgy look, then said, 'You don't much like the man, do you.' It was a statement rather than a question.

Momentarily taken aback by Banks's bluntness, James said, carefully, 'I have no strong affection for him, it's true. His conceit is misplaced, on this ship.'

'But he led us to Huahine, Raiatea, Tahaa and Rurutu Islands. No Europeans had been there previously. And now they are part of Britain.'

'They were but minor discoveries.'

'Discoveries, nonetheless,' Banks replied. 'And later, in New Zealand, you were most willing to make use of Tupaia's linguistic talents.'

'We all did. But thereafter he was of little use.' James paused, then added, 'And now he is ill and refuses treatment.'

Banks peered through the portside window, at the coast, then said, 'You will recall that I said that Tupaia and his boy would be my responsibility throughout the voyage.'

James nodded. 'That was a condition of them joining the company. A condition which still applies.'

'Indeed. So while we are ashore at Batavia the two Otaheitians will accompany Solander and myself.'

'As you wish.' James stood up. 'Now, is there anything else you wish to report? I have a letter to write, to the Admiralty.'

Banks grimaced. 'Yes. Surgeon Monkhouse tells me that Green and Hicks are also unwell. Green is struck by the flux and Hicks is coughing up blood. Monkhouse himself is also feverish.' Banks harrumphed. 'His condition recalls Shakespeare's entreaty, '*Physician, heal thyself.*' He moved towards the cabin door. 'I must prepare to go ashore.'

James was about to resume his journal entry when he again felt the cramp in his gut. He held his breath as the cramp grew stronger, then when it passed, let out breath slowly. The constipation had been affecting him ever since Savu. However rather than report this to Monkhouse, he had been taking syrup of figs, his mother's age-old remedy. This worked, but only sporadically. As the cramp subsided, he picked up his quill and resumed writing.

After the midday meal the next day, with the coast of Java now clearly in sight, James had the officers, midshipmen and able seamen called together so that he could adgown them from the quarterdeck.

'Tomorrow,' he began, 'we will be anchoring in the roadstead of Batavia, and thereafter going ashore. I anticipate that we will be in the port for some weeks, having repairs made to our ship, which has taken a beating these past weeks.' He moved closer to the rail and his gaze moved over the men below. 'I am aware that many of you, not merely the officers, have kept written accounts of our voyage. These must not be retained by their authors. Instead, to preserve the confidentiality of the voyage and its associated discoveries, all journals are to be handed to me before we go ashore in Batavia. Only the gentlemen scientists are absolved from this command.' There was a muttering from the assembly, and James paused, to allow it to subside. 'In accordance with my instructions, I will be despatching all journals, charts and drawings constructed during this voyage to the Admiralty in a sealed package, on the next ship which sails from Batavia to London.' His gaze again swept the now-silent crew. 'I say again, no written accounts of this voyage by crew members may be retained by the writer, neither are the achievements of our expedition to be disclosed to anyone not of this ship's company. Is that understood?'

Calls of 'Aye,' 'aye,' 'aye,' came from below, although with no great enthusiasm. Most had hitherto considered their journals to be private property, possibly for London publication and profit. Now they were resigned to the fact that this would not occur.

'Those of you who have kept journals are to deliver them to the Great Cabin from this time onward.' He allowed another pause, then said, 'You will all recall the matter of the grievous assault on my clerk, Orton, which remains unresolved.' All heads, including Orton's, looked at the deck; James gripped the quarterdeck rail.

'I am determined to settle the matter, as it has placed a shameful stain on the fabric of this ship. Thus, I am offering a reward of one guinea, and fifteen gallons of arrack, to anyone of this company who will name the culprit.' All heads looked up, sharply. *A guinea, and arrack.* 'I will be available to receive any information pertaining to this regrettable incident, in my cabin.' He concluded, 'I estimate that we will be entering the harbour of Batavia in less than 24 hours. That is all. Resume your duties.'

As he returned to the Great Cabin, James was well aware that in retaining his clandestine diary to Elizabeth, he would be in breach of his own, just-declared decree. He felt a pang of guilt at this deception (and heard a favourite saying of his Ma's, whispering in his ear – *'Do as I say, not as I do'*). It was a transgression which would have bemused her, he thought. But he was obliged to make it, in view of the vow he had made to Elizabeth. No one need know what lay locked in the lower drawer of his writing desk, certainly not the Lords of the Admiralty. That account was a personal record, not a political or nautical one.

There was a knock on the door of the Great Cabin. 'Come,' James called. On the table in front of him was a pile of journals which he was preparing for despatch, along with his own log, and a covering report. Looking up, he saw Midshipman Magra, holding out a solid, foxed, book. 'My journal, Sir, as instructed.' James took it. 'Thank you, Magra, it will be added to the others. You relished keeping it, did you not?'

'I did, Sir. It is my hope that it may be published one day.' James nodded, and was about to dismiss him when the New Yorker said, hesitantly, 'There is something else, Sir.'

'Yes?'

'Saunders, Sir.'

'What about him?'

'He has gone, Sir.'

'*Gone*. Where?'

'No one knows, Sir. It's my belief that he has slipped ashore.'

There was a long silence. Magra's expression was nervy.

'It were nothing to do with me, Sir,' he said. 'And he told no-one anything of his intentions.'

James remembered that Saunders had been present on the night of the attack on Orton. He considered this, then asked, 'Was it you who left a one-word note under my cabin door the day after the attack on Orton?'

Magra looked bewildered. 'I know nothing of a one-word note, Sir.'

James levelled his gaze at the midshipman, searching his eyes for a lie. Finding nothing of the sort there, he looked down, at the young man's journal. 'Very well,' he said quietly. 'That will be all.'

When Magra had gone, James thought, the note must have been left by one of the others, someone who knew of one of the others' unnatural lust. The attack on Orton must have been due to carnal jealousy. Now he was certain of the culprit's identity. *Saunders*, he thought, a would-be sodomite, and now a deserter. He would not order the marines to search for him, the ship was well rid of the sod.

There were sixteen other vessels in the roadstead, most flying the Dutch flag. The pilot boat which rowed out to *Endeavour* after she dropped anchor in the harbour contained a pair of VOC officials. The two Dutchmen were listless and very pale, like plants deprived of sunlight. 'Yet there is ample sunshine here,' said Parkinson, puzzled, as he observed the wan pair. 'Why are they so ashen-faced?'

James was rowed ashore and taken to the residence of the Governor, Petrus van der Parra, Hicks having earlier gone ashore to forewarn the Governor of their arrival. The residence was within the city walls. Like something from central Amsterdam, it was a two-storey building with pale brick walls and a roof of orange tiles with dormer windows set into it. There were tall colonnades around the entrance, and above it a hexagonal bell tower. James was shown into a reception room with a polished wooden floor, filled with carved hardwood furniture, glassed-in bookcases and framed marine charts. Racks of native spears adorned one wall, and a small turbaned Malay man of indeterminate age was working a large fan which was having a minimal effect on the heavily humid air. The Governor entered. In his mid-fifties, he had a plump face, a small chin and a moustache of fine gold hairs. His wig reached to the shoulders of his brown velvet, gold-buttoned jacket.

Not speaking English, Governor van der Parra had engaged an interpreter, a tubby, lugubrious Scotsman who was a merchant in Batavia. James greeted the Governor and introduced himself. Through the interpreter, the Governor opened their meeting by stating, 'It was a great shame, Lieutenant Cook, that you were not here two days ago.'

'Why so, Governor?'

'It was a public holiday. I declared it, as it was my fifty-sixth birthday. There were many celebrations in the town.'

James nodded, but thought, here is yet another official full of his own importance.

The Governor pressed his hands together. 'So, to business, Lieutenant. Where has your expedition come from?'

James smiled, thinly. 'That is not information I am authorised to share with you, Governor.'

The Governor's eyebrows arched. 'Is that so? I ask merely out of courtesy.'

'Thank you. But all I am permitted to tell you is that my ship is King George III of England's naval vessel *Endeavour* and her home port is Plymouth. I wish to apply to you for leave to heave her down and carry out repairs.' He paused. 'And to purchase necessary provisions, fresh beef and greens, water and firewood, for the next stage of our voyage.'

'Which is to?'

Annoyed at this flagrant insistence, James said, 'I repeat, Governor, I have no authority to divulge where we are bound after we leave Batavia.'

When this was translated, the Governor scowled. Getting to his feet and waving his hand in irritation, he said, 'I suggest you careen your vessel on Onrust Island, outside the harbour, which has the necessary facilities. Your crew must remain on a neighbouring island, Kuyper.' Then he left the room, followed quickly by the fan-wielding Malay and the Scotsman.

The carpenter, Satterly, had a bent nose, broken in a waterfront brawl in Wapping, and missing front teeth. But he knew his craft, and his repair work on the ship after the misadventure on the reef of New Holland had been admirable. Now, though, he looked crestfallen. Scratching his head, he reported to James:

'She'll never make it to England in her condition, Sir. Her false keel is gone beyond the midships, from forward and perhaps further. She's leaking six to twelve inches of water an hour, caused by the main keel being wounded in many places. The scarf of her stern is very open and one pump is not working. There's weeks of work ahead, Sir, in my estimation, to get her ship-shape again.' Then he brightened a little. 'But the yards, masts and hull are satisfactory ....'

New planking, replacement keels, repairs to sails. He'd never imagined she was this bad. *Weeks of work*. He mopped his sweating brow with his sleeve. England was still half a world away and there was much hard sailing still to come. Weeks of work? Well, so be it. He instructed Satterly and his assistants to begin the repairs.

He took accommodation in a boarding house near the harbour front, run by a Dutch couple who spoke a little English. It was a tall, slim brick building, side-by-side with dwellings of identical design. James's small room was on the highest level, and although it afforded him a view of the harbour, the atmosphere was sweltering.

Enquiries at a shipping agency nearby informed him that one of the Dutch ships, the *Kronenburg*, was leaving for Europe via Cape Town, in ten days' time. There was a desk and a writing slope in the little room, and James immediately went to work. First he collected all his charts of the South Sea, New Zealand and New Holland, his astronomical observations and his journals, and wrapped the considerable package in canvas cloth. Before sealing it, he penned a covering report to Philip Stephens of the Admiralty.

'*Although the discoveries made in this voyage are not very great, yet I flatter myself that they are such as may merit the attention of their Lordships, and although I have failed in discovering the much talked-of Southern Continent (which perhaps does not exist) and which myself had much at heart, yet I am confident that no part of the failure of such discovery can be laid to my charge. Had we been so fortunate not to have run ashore, much more would have been done in the latter part of the voyage than what was, but as it is I presume this voyage will be found as complete as any before made to the South Seas.'*

He concluded:

'In justice to the officers and the crew, I must say that they have gone through the fatigues and dangers of the whole voyage with that cheerfulness and alertness that will always do honour to British seamen.'

He paused. Should he mention the Otaheitians? He decided not. They were Banks's responsibility and as such were sure to be included in his own gaudy chronicle of the voyage.

As he bundled the precious documents together, adgowned the package to Stephens and sealed it, James experienced pangs of anxiety. Supposing *Kronenburg* should founder en route to Europe, taking his priceless records down forever. This thought was horrifying, and he was unable to dispel it.

He patted the bundle, affectionately. 'Go well,' he murmured. 'God speed to Whitehall.'

It was late afternoon when he picked up the journal which had not been packed with the others. He placed it on the writing slope and once again picked up his quill.

Batavia, Dutch East Indies, 23 October, 1770

My Dearest Elizabeth,

After anticipating that I might possibly be home for Christmas and thus reunited with my loved ones, those hopes have now been dashed. It seems that we will be fortunate to leave *this place by Christmas, owing to the damage* Endeavour *has sustained over these past months. Although aware that this restoration work must be carried out, the crew, as well as myself, became despondent when we learned of the delay. We had all anticipated seeing the shores of England again, much sooner. Instead most of the ship's company, having broken out Endeavour's stores and ballast, are accommodated in tents on Kuyper island, which is low-lying, damp and infested with insect life. An unsatisfactory place in almost every respect.*

However we have received here some news of England, which at least gave the impression that we are nearer, although it was a far from encouraging bulletin. It is reported that there is unrest in our American colonies, which caused us concern, and equally so when we learned that there is a threat to our monarch's authority in the form of street disturbances, led by a troublemaking politician called Wilkes. It is my earnest concern that these troubles have not affected you or our family, Beth, and that they will have by now subsided. As for the possible loss by insurrection of our American colonies, that is a prospect too distressing for words.

I am accommodated on shore in Batavia, in a house owned by a Dutch brother and sister, Herr and Frau Van der Wavern. Their place is clean and the meals satisfactory, but the environs are far from agreeable. Never have I experienced such a pestilential place as Batavia. The Dutch have been here for many years, and in their determination to create another Amsterdam in their Indies, constructed a town laced with canals, 'a grave mistake', in the words of Dr Solander. Amsterdam's climate is cool, here it is constantly tropical, so that the canals have become putrid. Batavia now sprawls beyond the city walls and its streets seethe with people of every nationality and hue: Malay slaves, Chinese merchants, Dutch troopers, Arab traders, Japanese mercenaries and Dutch burghers. But unlike the Dutch capital's canals, these waterways are nothing more than cesspools - slimy, filthy and filled with human and animal ordure. And in the town's constant humidity and rainfall, whining mosquitoes hover over the surface of the canals in a low, swirling cloud. Many of the European people here suffer from pestilential diseases and fevers. And the stench! Even the Londoners among the crew from the industrial parts of our city have smelt nothing like it. The odour is sulphurous, as if – forgive my vulgarity, Beth, the colourful metaphor was coined by Banks – an invisible giant is constantly farting over the city. Dutch architecture and fine carriages cannot compensate for the air's foulness.

Banks and Solander are unable to tolerate the stench, but to my surprise the two Otaheitians are so enamoured of the city that they cannot get enough of the town. They exclaim at the European buildings, the carriages and coaches, the wares on sale and the

exotic costumes of the soldiers and of the other Indians who are
seen on the streets. So much so that Tupaia returned to the ship,
retrieved his Otaheitian bark cloth cloak and head-gown, and after
putting on his traditional garb, parades with Taiata around
Batavia in it, aware in this conceit that they are sole wearers of
such a costume in all the Dutch Indies ...

'Cook! Are you there?'

It was Banks's voice, coming from the street below. James went
to the open window. The naturalist was standing on the cobbles
alone, looking up. His blouse was open and he was bare-headed,
using his hat as a fan against the fetid air.

'What is it?'

'I have made a discovery. Can I come up?'

'Very well.'

James blotted the entry in Elizabeth's journal, closed it and
placed it under the bed. Moments later, Banks burst in, his face
flushed and wet with sweat. James invited him to sit by the
window, then curious, said, 'What sort of discovery?'

Banks waited to fully recover his breath, then began.

'You will recall that while on Otaheite we were told by a native
that another European ship had been there, some months after
Wallis's left.'

'Yes. At Hitia'a.'

'That's it. A Spanish expedition, we surmised.' Banks held his
breath, then added, 'Yet it was not Spanish. It was *French*.'

'*French*? How do you know?'

'Tupaia and I were walking along the Middelburgstrasse this
morning, he in his Otaheitian costume, when a Dutchman
approached us in a state of excitement and asked where Tupaia was
from. When he was told, the man said that nearly two years ago
another Otaheitian had come to Batavia, gowned in such a
costume. He was brought here from the island by a Frenchman,
Louis-Antoine de Bougainville, who called here in 1769, on his
way back to France.'

James considered the timing for a moment. 'Bougainville ... Yes,
that could be correct.'

'It *is* correct. The other Otaheitian's name was called ... Ahutoru.
Tupaia knew of the man, he was some sort of leader in the eastern
part of Otaheite. Bougainville was taking him to France, in much

332

the same way as I am taking Tupaia and Taiata to England.'

Struck by an unwelcome possibility, James asked, 'Did the Frenchman lay claim to Otaheite?'

'The Batavian did not know.' Banks shrugged. 'But if Bougainville did, his claim would not be legitimate. Wallis had already declared the island was Britain's, albeit less than a year before the Frenchies landed there.'

'Yes, yes. So Otaheite is ours, there can be no doubt of that.' He paused, meaningfully. 'So Tupaia and his boy will not be the first Maohi to see Europe, as you had planned, Banks.'

'No. But they will be the first to see *England*,' countered Banks, irrepressibly.

'*... Banks has just left, after dropping in with important news which I am not yet at liberty to divulge. He and Solander are planning to move inland, to a house on higher land where they can botanise and escape the vapours which permeate Batavia. They are taking the two Otaheitians with them, along with a pair of Malay slaves which Banks has purchased for the sojourn. As I expected, Tupaia has now recovered his health, doubtless related to his intake of fresh local plantains, juices and green vegetables, confirming the intimate connection between diet and scurvy. I will thus ensure that* Endeavour *is well provisioned with these victuals before we weigh anchor for the next stage of our prolonged voyage back to England. My charts, astronomical observations and Admiralty journals have been dispatched to London, Beth. Only this one remains in my hands. It is my most fervent wish that before much longer, I can place it in yours.*

Your loving husband, James

The first to die was surgeon Monkhouse.

Crippling headaches and a heightened fever were followed by discharges of blood from his bowels, and he was found dead in his bed in Batavia, on 5 November. Banks and Solander were too ill to attend his burial but James, although feverish himself, managed to. He made a brief speech over the surgeon's grave, after a rotund Dutch minister had given an equally brief Bible reading, in Dutch. The European cemetery was on a hillock at the rear of the town, and during the Monkhouse's interment James was distracted by the sight of fresh graves being dug and of horse-drawn hearses being unloaded of their caskets. Grim-faced men in broad-brimmed black hats and sobbing women in dark veils followed the coffins. Dozens of semi-naked Malay grave-diggers were at work in the sweltering heat, hurling dirt over their shoulders, so that the scene resembled a building site rather than a graveyard. In a way it *was* a building site, he later reported to Banks, as they were actually digging the foundations of a necropolis.

Banks's fever was treated with his personal supply of chinchona bark, given to him by a botanist friend in London, which proved effective. He and Solander, accompanied by Tupaia and Taiata, then sailed across to Kuyper Island. As the monsoon season was imminent the rain was coming more frequently, making the ground around the tents sodden. Many of the tents were filled with sailors too ill to work, and their moaning and coughing were incessant. Tupaia chose a place under some tamarind trees, away from the others, to pitch the tent for himself and Taiata. But days later the young Otaheitian developed a cold which rapidly worsened to a fever. Sweat flowed from his body like a river, but he also complained of waves of coldness. His whole body trembling, he cried out, 'Taio, mate ua!' and the others realised that he was saying. *'Friends, I am dying!'* Tupaia was constantly at his bedside in the tent, wiping his fevered brow and whispering incantations in their language.

'Ow-ay! Ow-ay!'

Tupaia's anguished cries could be heard throughout the tent settlement, and they found him lying across the body of Taiata, which was still at last. Weeping inconsolably, Tupaia had to be pulled forcefully from the body of his adopted son, and when he saw Taiata's corpse being taken away he threw himself on the ground, calling out, 'I should not have come away, I should not have come away. This is Oro's punishment.' The body was rowed across to the nearby island of Edam, where there was a cemetery, overlooked by giant fig trees.

Then, bereft and grief-stricken, Tupaia too fell ill again. Shuddering uncontrollably, refusing food or drink, he lay on his back in the tent, staring sightlessly upward. Three days later, he too was dead.

Parkinson was the only one of the gentlemen well enough to attend the Otaheitian's burial; Banks and Solander were still feverish and James's constipation had given way to bouts of diarrhoea. When Tupaia's grave had been dug, beside Taiata's, and his canvas-shrouded body laid within it, the burial party stood back to allow Parkinson to stand over it. Bowing his head, the artist intoned, 'Parahi, taio. Farewell, my friends.' Then grief overtook him, his eyes filled with tears and he sank to his knees at the head of the grave. He got to his feet, wiped the tears from his face and placed upon the body of Tupaia one of his finest paint brushes.

As the grave was filled, the light warm rain which had been falling grew heavier.

James roused himself from his own sick-bed to write 'DD' beside Monkhouse's name in his journal. Now he could not wait to be gone and to put this malodorous place behind them. And he wondered, constantly, what is the cause of this illness and death? It could not be scurvy, for their fresh-food diet was now far healthier than it had been at sea en route to Batavia, when no one had died. Recalling the cadaverous specimens who had met them in the pilot boat on their arrival, James reasoned that it must be the foulness of the air, which was probably absorbed into its inhabitants' lungs and guts. Batavia's sole saving grace, he concluded, was its shipyard, whose efficient workers had restored *Endeavour* to a condition suitable for setting sail again. He was also able to take on several more crewmen, Englishmen mainly, who also longed to leave the cesspits of Batavia and work their passage home.

By Christmas 1770 the ship was ready for sea, although with forty sick men on board there were only twenty men and officers capable of working her. There were no shipboard Yuletide celebrations this year. On the morning of 27 December, to James's huge relief, *Endeavour*'s anchors were weighed and her sails loosened. He had set a course for the Sunda Strait – entranceway to the Indian Ocean – and Princes Island, where he had been told that fresh provisions and water could be taken aboard.

By 14 January they were fully provisioned with turtles, chickens, fish, venison meat, coconuts, limes and plantains from Princes Island. Firewood had been stowed and the water butts filled from the island's ponds. They weighed anchor, stood out and bore ENE into the Indian Ocean, bound for the Cape of Good Hope.

James stood on the foredeck, watching Sumatra fade against the eastern horizon. Although he still felt unwell, and the crew were far from recovered, his spirits were rising. The foulness and pestilence of Batavia was behind them. At last they were entering open ocean, at last they were surrounded by clean air and bright, pearly light. They had fresh provisions aplenty, the decks had been scrubbed above and below with vinegar, and they were bound for home. Gripping the rail, James lifted his chin and drew in the clean air gratefully. Ahead was the fathomless dark blue of the Indian Ocean, whose swells were already rising and falling with soothing regularity. Charted waters, the known coast of Africa ahead. He breathed in the ocean air as if he was drinking spring water. Plain sailing again, at last.

Thirty

Discharged Dead
John Truslove, marine corporal, 24 January
Herman Sporing, scientist, 24 January
Sydney Parkinson, artist, 26 January
Thomas Dunster, marine, 26 January
John Ravenhill, sail-maker, 27 January
Charles Green, astronomer, 29 January
John Thompson, cook, 31 January
James Nicholson, able seaman, 31 January
Sam Moody, able seaman, 31 January
Archibald Wolfe, able seaman, 31 January
Francis Haite, able seaman, 1 February
John Gathray, boatswain, 4 February
John Bootie, midshipman, 4 February
Jonathan Monkhouse, midshipman, 6 February
John Satterly, carpenter, 12 February
Daniel Preston, marine, 16 February

Endeavour had become a death ship, its men falling like swatted moths. Too weak to make the head, they fouled themselves in their hammocks, so that the stink of shit and puke permeated the ship below decks. Death bloomed and spread like a deadly mould. The progression of the fatal illness was identical: an onset of burning fever, then violent dysentery which first immobilised its victims, then drained the life from them. Day after day they rolled on towards Africa, but a mood of melancholy saturated the decks. The few remaining healthy crew struggled to work the ship. All the living had been close to the dead, so that as the ship stood in towards the coast of Africa the mourning seemed perpetual.

The cause of the plague remained an enigma. But there was speculation.

'Cook?'

'Yes?'

'Can we speak?'

It was Solander, holding a pan of water. James beckoned him into the Great Cabin. He too had barely recovered from the fever. His long face was pale and drawn and his hands trembled as he placed the pan on the table. He looked earnestly at James.

'I have been checking the water casks.'

'Why? Are our supplies short?'

'The quantity will suffice.' The furrows in Solander's brow deepened. 'But the quality ...' He bent over the pan. 'Look.'

James followed his gaze, then saw the object of his attention. Tiny creatures, dozens of them, moving across the surface of the water in short, jerking movements. Frowning, James said,

'What are they?'

'Larvae.'

'Of what insect?'

'The mosquito. Its eggs are laid in still water, then hatch into the buzzing insects which have tormented us in the tropics. And in the water hold there are hundreds of them.' He opened his hand. 'I killed one just minutes ago. Look.'

On Solander's palm was a smear of blood, and the black, squashed corpse of the insect. Staring at it, he said,

'I placed one under my microscope. It has a proboscis which can penetrate human skin. It uses it to draw our blood into its body, which I believe is then nourished by it.'

James rolled up one sleeve of his shirt and held out his arm. It was covered with red blotches. 'I have been kept awake by their interminable droning, and bitten by them, over these last days.' Struck by another thought, he said, 'Could the water we took on from Prince's Island have contained their larvae?'

The naturalist nodded. 'I am sure it did. Moreover, I believe that the fever which has afflicted us is caused by the insect's bite.'

'How so?'

'A toxin is perhaps transmitted from the insect into the human bloodstream, through its feeding.'

James blinked. 'A tiny creature, able to weaken and kill a human being? That seems preposterous.'

Solander's face fell. 'I have no proof, yet. But before Sporing fell into his fever, he had been bitten severely by the insects. He showed me his neck and arms.' Looking away, clearly distressed at the memory, he added, 'The agitation then began, and he was dead three days later.'

'Yet I have been bitten, and I am still alive,' said James, unconvinced by this theory.

Solander rubbed at his chin, thoughtfully. 'The effects of the bites may vary according to the constitution of the person bitten. You are a tall, strong man. Sporing was not. Neither was Parkinson.' He persisted. 'And you were feverish in Batavia, were you not?'

'I was for a time.,' James conceded. 'And I still sweat. At night, especially.'

Solander rubbed his palms together, to wipe away the blood. Walking over to the cabin window, he said, 'I recall that in Otaheite the natives burnt coconut husks to keep the insects at bay. Perhaps smoking out the water hold with rags would help to repel them.'

James rolled down his shirt sleeve. 'It would do no harm to try. I will order that smudge pots be burned there.' He nodded, dismissively. 'Thank you Solander, for bringing this matter to my attention.'

17 February

Dearest Beth,

I write in sorrow, the deepest I have known these past two and a half years. Since leaving the Dutch port of Batavia, where seven of my men died, we have now lost another twenty-three, to the flux and fever. Although replacements were obtained for those lost at Batavia; we cannot replace those whom we have lost since we left, the day after Christmas. For these past six weeks Endeavour *has been a hospital ship. Sea burials have been an almost daily occurrence and we are running short of canvas from which to make the victims' shrouds. For myself, who has been so proud of not losing a man to scurvy, the death toll from other causes has been devastating. As commander and guardian of my crew's well-being, the deaths strike me to my very heart. No voyaging successes can atone for the loss of so many men. A short time ago the crew joked that the oldest man amongst us, sail-maker John Ravenhill, was the only fit man left because of his constant imbibing and consequent state of intoxication. But that hypothesis and jest died the same day Ravenhill did, on 27 January. For me, the most grievous loss was the death of Sydney Parkinson. A young man of exceptional talents and industriousness, his botanical drawings and landscape paintings comprise a priceless record of our voyage. To me he had become almost an adopted son. So when his body was committed to the deep I have to confess it required all my self-control not to shed tears. Others tried, but failed. Banks wept openly (but without noise), while Solander's eyes remained firmly shut during the committal and his face was contorted with grief. We had all lost not just a shipmate, but a close friend and a young man of the finest sensibilities. Then it was Banks' and my sad duty to deal with what Parkinson had left behind.*

'Good grief Cook, look at them all ...'

Parkinson's cot had been folded away, along with his easel, brushes and paints. Banks had opened all the drawers of the cabin's chest. Every one was filled with folios, and every folio was filled with drawings. The larger drawers contained his paintings, of plants, people, birds and landscapes – all rendered in beautiful detail. More paintings were pinned to the wall of the cabin, and these too they paused to admire. The largest was of two naked New Hollander men. One was holding up a spear, the other a shield, and the two figures overlapped, so that their private parts were discreetly concealed. The artist had entitled the depiction, 'Advancing to Combat'.

'Remarkable,' said James. 'It is just as they were in reality.'

Banks pulled the bottom drawer of the chest fully open. Along with more folios was a small round box, carved from pale wood. Banks removed its lid, peered in, then showed it to James. It contained a locket of glossy black hair. Putting it to his face, Banks inhaled, then smiled tightly.

'A keepsake, from his Otaheitian lover. It carries the fragrance of the island's coconut oil.'

Startled, James said, 'He had a lover on the island? I never knew.'

'Only a few of us did, and he swore us to silence about her.' He closed the little box. 'Tehani, she was called, and she was very beautiful. Parkinson promised her he would return to her one day.' His eyes became misty. 'As we all did, to our special taios.'

There was a wide shelf above the chest of drawers, crammed with books. Banks reached up and took down a large, hard-backed volume. He opened it and began to read aloud. '"Journal of A Voyage to the South Seas and Regions Beyond, 1768 – "'

His expression brightened. 'Parkinson's record of our expedition. This will be of great interest to readers in London.' He handed it to James, but considering it disrespectful to look into the account so soon after its author's death, he placed the journal back on the shelf. Then he turned back to Banks.

'Sydney's botanical and animal drawings must go to the Royal Society. But what of the rest? The journal, and his curiosity collection. Who will receive those? His parents were both dead, he once informed me.'

'Yes. But he has an older brother in London. Stanfield Parkinson. I will see that Sydney's curiosities, and his painting equipment, are passed to him.'

'And the journal?'

'I will take it. And ensure that it is published.'

For a few moments, James was speechless. Then, shocked, he said:

'You cannot do that, Banks. The journal was Sydney's personal possession. Therefore it belongs to his estate. Which should now pass to his closest living relative, his brother.'

Banks sighed, impatiently. 'Cook, you should know the law. I commissioned Parkinson to draw what Solander, Sporing and I collected. Therefore all his work belongs to me.'

James eyed him coldly. 'I *do* know the law. And I am aware that you and the Royal Society have the rights to Parkinson's natural history illustrations.' He stared hard at the naturalist. 'But you have no rights to his journal. That is private property. As a supernumerary, Sydney's record of the voyage was retained by him when the crew's accounts were handed in. And now that he is no longer alive to claim ownership of it, the journal must go to his brother.'

Banks's eyes narrowed. 'I cannot agree. Parkinson was in my employ, therefore anything which he produced during the voyage is my property, to make use of in any way I consider fit.' He paused. 'Including his journal.'

Shaking his head, James said quietly, 'There are some things which should *not* be collected and disseminated, Banks. And a personal journal is one of them.'

'That is your view.' Banks held his gaze. 'But it would be interesting to ask a notary for another opinion on the matter.'

A long, icy silence ensued. Then James concluded, 'This is an unseemly dispute to hold, in the very cabin where poor Parkinson worked, slept and died. We will speak of it no more.' Then he added, pointedly, 'For the time being.'

Leaving the cabin, James seethed. Nothing had really changed between Banks and himself, even after nearly three years. The man's vanity still led him to believe that he was beyond all authority. No doubt he would even try to possess the Elizabeth journal, should he be made aware of its existence. Returning to the Great Cabin, James had another thought: if Banks remained as high-handed as this while at sea, what will he be like when we return to London?

15 April, 1771

Dearest Beth,

Cape Town, which we finally reached on 15 March, was salvation to us. Overlooked by a great flat-topped mountain, the town's harbour was filled with Dutch, Danish and French vessels. As we stood out of the bay we received a salute from an East Indiaman, and her cannon fire was like an orchestral symphony to us. And unlike Batavia, Cape Town provided for all our needs. The ill men were taken ashore and nursed back to health (albeit at considerable expense), the air was wholesome, the water clean, fresh food plentiful and the townspeople attendant to our requirements. Replacements for our lost seamen have been obtained. There can be no finer port or facilities for the repair and provisioning of an ocean-voyaging ship and the needs of its crew than this Dutch outpost.

Now it is half-way through April and we are again at sea, at last truly bound for home. Although thoughts of England and our waiting loved ones make us buoyant, I still cannot disregard the calamities of the last few months. The fact that a third of my ship's complement has been lost on the last leg of the voyage distresses me so greatly that I constantly struggle to keep it from the forefront of my consciousness. Moreover the deaths have continued. My trusted young Master, Robert Molyneux, succumbed to the flux shortly after we departed Cape Town. He had been a fine and reliable seaman, as well as an accomplished draughtsman. Molyneux's loss was as if Endeavour *had been partially dismasted. How I now regret my foolish boast of not having lost a single man to scurvy! I realise now that it matters not what is the* cause *of death at sea, what really matters is the* incidence *of fatalities. And this voyage has seen far too many deaths. The huge toll from the fatal fever cannot compensate for the certain knowledge that an anti-scorbutic diet prevents the outbreak of scurvy at sea.*

I apologise if my recent entries have been in so melancholy a vein, but if I cannot express my deepest feelings to you, who then can I relate them to? The truth is, I am weary, as well as disillusioned, at the way the voyage has declined into frustration and fatality. There have been too few discoveries, and too many deaths. I believe, also, that three years is an excessive time for a voyage, even for a circumnavigation, though much of this time was unavoidably expended in undertaking repairs to the ship.

Day after day, all I enter into Endeavour*'s log are the briefest descriptions of weather and sea conditions. But as I write this intimate entry to you, dearest Beth, I am encouraged, as we all are, by thoughts of England and our loved ones. The next few weeks cannot pass too quickly.*

Your loving husband,
James

On 29 April he observed that they had crossed the Greenwich Meridian, confirming that *Endeavour* had circumnavigated the entire globe. There was quiet satisfaction rather than riotous celebration at James's announcement of this achievement that evening in the Great Cabin. Since the Batavia plague and its ghastly consequences, the mood of the ship had changed. A kind of muted resignation had settled upon the decks of *Endeavour*. Although each man continued to go about his duties punctiliously, his thoughts were now principally elsewhere. The primary ambitions of the expedition had been acquitted; home was where the Endeavours now needed to be.

On 1 May they stood off St Helena, but only Banks went ashore, and only briefly. However thirteen ships of the East India fleet were anchored in the island's roadstead, and when they weighed anchor on 4 May, *Endeavour* sailed with them. Her crew appreciated the companionship the compatriot fleet afforded, even though the merchantmen were much larger than their own lumbering vessel.

On 15 May an eclipse of the sun was observed, another event which caused only mild interest. After all, considering everything that the Endeavours had done and witnessed, what did a mere solar eclipse have to offer? Likewise, the sighting of Ascension Island a few days later was not considered a significant event, and there was a similarly subdued reaction three weeks later when they crossed the line and entered the northern latitudes. The crossing itself was a far less celebratory occasion than the knowledge that they were now in the hemisphere of home.

On 19 May a surgeon from one of the East Indiamen was boated across to *Endeavour*, to attend to Zachary Hicks, whose consumptive lungs had been worsened by the foul airs of Batavia. However the surgeon could do nothing for him, and a few days later Hicks died, of asphyxia. He was 32. Although James was aware that his disease had been contracted prior to leaving England, so that in a sense he had been dying throughout the voyage, his death caused further sorrow, and James ordered that his body be committed to the sea with full naval honours. Somewhat reluctantly, he then promoted Gore in Hicks's place, and much less reluctantly, declared master's mate Charles Clerke *Endeavour*'s third lieutenant. James had never quite forgiven Gore for the Mercury Bay killing, but Clerke had proved to be the most conscientious of crewmen.

As May melted into June *Endeavour* continued to battle her way north, in the wake of the merchant fleet. To ensure that the crew remained dutiful, James ordered constant activities: great guns and small arms drill, the repair of split sails and snapped rigging and the scrubbing of decks and clothing. The men went about these duties silently, and largely without complaint. The end of every watch, and every duty, brought them closer to home.

Until the mid-summer solstice they remained within sight of the East Indiamen convoy, but from 23 June *Endeavour* proved unable to keep up and their ship was solitary once more. Staring up at her mainmast, James now thought of her as an arthritic old lady, determined to make it back home, but condemned to a slow, painful pace. Her timbers creaked and groaned and every other day at least one of her sails needed replacing.

Then, on 4 July, there was yet another death.

Banks burst into the Great Cabin at first light. James was shaving, and he was startled by the sight of the naturalist, still clad in his nightshirt, his hair awry, his eyes wild.

'Cook! She is dead!'

'Who?'

'Lady. My faithful bitch. I found her a minute ago, lying on the chair where she always sleeps. Rigor mortis had already set in.' He put his hands over his face. 'She must have died in the night.'

James then remembered. 'I heard her whining, loudly, last night. Then all was quiet, so I paid it no attention. Did you not hear her?'

Banks, his hands still covering his face, shook his head. 'Would that I had. I may have saved her. She was such a companion to me, more devoted than any woman. I cannot believe she is gone. *Gone.*'

James put his hand on Banks's shoulder. 'I am sorry for your loss.' He allowed a pause, before adding, 'You will dispose of her body with your own ceremony, I presume.'

Banks nodded, then turned away and left the cabin, too distraught to speak. James's sympathy for the man only extended so far. He recalled Banks callously giving away his male dog to the degenerate pair from Savu, in the face of Parkinson's protests. Banks was such a paradoxical mixture of sensitivity and crassness, James concluded. This prompted a further thought. Would the other woman in his life, Miss Blosset, be still waiting for him in London?

'Land! Land ho! Off the port bow!'

The eyes of all those on deck lifted to the masthead, where the crewman on watch was the lad, Nicholas Young. It was 10 July, 1771, and a fine mid-summer day. Young was clinging to the rigging with one hand, and pointing north with the other. The others followed his gaze. On the horizon they too saw it, a low, undulating coast of green. Men ran up from below and joined the others at the rail, exclaiming at the sight. Amidships, Banks, Solander and Gore all had their scopes to their eyes. On the quarterdeck, James trained his own spyglass on the horizon. Through it he could discern breaking waves, dark cliffs, farmhouses, patches of forest. 'Land's End,' he murmured. '*I have done it.*'

London, 15 July, 1771

The boys had been given their gifts and had gone outside to play in the street, but the other presents lay unopened in the sea chests on the parlour carpet. James and Elizabeth sat side-by-side on the couch under the bay window, she with her face pale and pinched, he numbed by what she was relating to him.

'Joseph was baptised, but lived for only three weeks more. He was a poor, sickly mite, but his passing still tore me apart.' She paused to blow her nose on the handkerchief she clutched, then continued. 'I blamed myself for his weak constitution, I should have given him better nourishment ...'

When her body began to convulse, James drew her closer to him.

'That cannot be so, Elizabeth. Some infants are born weak. It is no fault of the mother.'

There was a long silence. His arms around her, he could feel her still trembling. At last he asked, fearing that his voice would break, 'And our little daughter?'

Elizabeth tipped her head back and drew a long, deep breath. When she replied her voice was merely a whisper. 'Three months ago, just before Easter, she developed a cough, a sneeze, and a runny nose. I kept her indoors, thinking it were just a cold. But the cough grew worse. She had fits of coughing, terrible fits ...' She turned to him, her eyes huge, haunted by the memory. For some moments could not go on. James said, quietly, 'Did you call for the doctor?'

'Yes. My mother fetched Doctor Bartlett. He prescribed hot compresses for her chest, to ease the coughing, and told me to confine her to bed. I did so, but the fits still came. She struggled for breath, and when she did breathe in it made a terrible noise, a kind of whooping and rasping. For that reason they call it the "whooping cough".' Her expression was now agonised. 'Oh James, it was heart-breaking to see her struggling for breath. Then the coughing worsened, and on Easter Sunday morning ... she breathed her last.'

Now there were no words to express what they both felt. Instead they clutched each other. He felt her tears streaming down his neck and the wracking of her body. The same thought, the same useless thought, kept running through his mind. Their daughter, their beloved only daughter, had died on the 9 April. Not long after he had left Cape Town. Had he arrived home earlier, he may have been able to help save the child. The sweetest child, the most loveable child, her mother in miniature.

At last he said, in a whisper, 'Where are the children buried?'

'St Dunstan's graveyard.'

'We must go there. I must see the little ones' graves.'

'Yes.'

After a long pause, he said gently, 'There will be other children, Beth, to replace Joseph and little Elizabeth. There must be.'

Her eyes became fixed on his. Although there were dark shadows beneath them, the eyes themselves were as clear and penetrating as ever. Forcefully, and with a tinge of reproach, she said:

'Joseph and Elizabeth cannot be replaced. They were unique. So both are irreplaceable.'

He nodded, understanding too well. Only now did he fully realise the sorrow she had gone through these past years. The loneliness, the grieving. And that awareness filled him with remorse. And yet ... and yet ... what could he have done?

'And James ...'

He put his hand softly on the back of her neck, and brought his face closer to hers.

'Yes?'

'It was said ... around the docks, and in the City ... when *Endeavour* hadn't returned by last Christmas ... that your ship must be lost at sea. Some said it had been sunk by the Spanish, near the Falklands.' She hesitated. 'I felt so distressed, and I did not know what to do. So I wrote to Mr Stephens, at the Admiralty, and asked if there was any firm news.'

'He would not have known,' James put in. 'My letter to him from Batavia did not arrive when I hoped it would.' He put his hand under her chin, and held it there. 'But I did write, Elizabeth, to let you know when I hoped I would return.'

She nodded, blinking away the tears, then said:

'I had begun to think you and the ship must surely be lost, and the thought was devastating to me. I said nothing to the boys, but already I had begun to mourn for you.' She swallowed, twice. 'Then yesterday Mistress Norman, from Number 12, came rushing in here, waving a copy of the *London Chronicle*. There was a long story in it, about the *Endeavour* arriving home safely. I have never felt so thankful. I could not sleep all last night, for the relief and excitement I felt.' Then her expression became one of puzzlement. Blinking, she said, 'But the newssheet story was mainly about Mr Joseph Banks. It was all about where he had been, and who he had met and all the plants and creatures he had collected during the voyage.' She shook her head in bewilderment. 'There was scant mention of you, James, just a statement saying that you were *Endeavour*'s commander.'

Through the heaviness of his grief, James felt a slight leavening of validation. What he suspected may happen had already begun. Banks the self-promoter had taken it upon himself to tell their story: Banks as heroic botanist, Banks the conquering adventurer, Banks the great seducer. Well, James thought, let him be what he wants to be. He – James – knew otherwise, and in time the record would be set straight. In the meantime, Elizabeth and their surviving family here was all that really mattered now. She had had to grieve for so long without him, now they needed time to grieve together. He owed that much to her.

'And the newssheet story said something else.' Elizabeth's eyes continued to bore into his. What else, he wondered, could possibly be coming?

'Mr Banks said that he was going to sail around the world again, very soon, to discover the Great Southern Continent they did not find on the *Endeavour* expedition.' Her frown deepened. 'What do you know of this plan?'

Averting his eyes, James shook his head, wearily. 'I know nothing of Banks's latest scheme.' He paused, listening to the sound of his sons, playing outside with their Maori fighting sticks. Then he added, 'Although I venture to say that before long I will.' And he thought, *Yes, there is still unfinished business, and it will not be Banks who will finish it.*

Releasing her, he walked over to the chest which lay open on the parlour floor. From beneath his folded clothing he brought out the journal. Holding it in both hands, he carried it over to her, and said:

'For you, Elizabeth. With all my love.'

ACKNOWLEDGEMENTS

A Man of Endeavour – a novel is by definition a work of fiction, but it is one founded on fact. What might be called James Cook's 'outer world' has been chronicled by scholars and writers ever since his first biography, *The Life of Captain James Cook* by Andrew Kippis, was published in 1788, just ten years after the subject's death. Since then Cook's voyages have been exhaustively documented, so that today the voyager's bibliography is immense.

Instead of reading every Cook biography or article published, which would have been time-consuming as well as repetitious, I drew on a few selected works to familiarise myself with the actualities of the first forty or so years of Cook's life. These books included JC Beaglehole's monumental work, *The Life of Captain James Cook* (1974), and Anne Salmond's gripping accounts of Cook's voyages, *Between worlds: early exchanges between Maori and Europeans* (1997) and *The Trial of the cannibal dog: Captain Cook in the south seas* (2003). For a depiction of the traditional Polynesian world which shaped the life of Tupaia, the Raiatean who sailed with Cook on the *Endeavour* after Tahiti, Joan Druett's book, *Tupaia – Captain Cook's Polynesian Navigator* (2011) was enormously helpful. *The Captain Cook Encyclopaedia* by John Robson (2004) was an invaluable reference for fact-checking, when pure facts were called for. Other biographies I referred to were *Captain James Cook* by Richard Hough (1994) and *Captain Cook: Obsession and Discovery* (2007), by Vanessa Collingridge. I am also grateful to Joan Druett for her expert advice on maritime matters, and to writer and artist Don Donovan for his reminiscences of growing up in England, albeit 200 years after James Cook's boyhood. My gratitude must also be extended to my editor, Stephen Stratford, for his skills and unerring eye for detail. He is the best in the business. The words of Cook himself – short extracts taken directly from the journal he kept on *Endeavour* – appear throughout the text of the novel. They consist of careful observations of weather and sea conditions, the ship's course and bearings taken, with the occasional avian or ocean creature also noted. The official journal illustrates Cook's ability to closely observe and record the physical phenomena which surrounded him. Scrupulous in his day-to-day documentation of *Endeavour*'s progress, his personal feelings never intrude.

The above references provided the foundation upon which I constructed an imagined version of Cook's 'inner' life, told mainly through a personal journal dedicated to his wife, Elizabeth. Given the paucity of facts about Cook the man, it seemed to me that such an invented account, in which crucial events of his life are viewed through the eyes of Cook himself, could paint a portrait of the explorer which is very different to conventional depictions. Accordingly, I have spliced into the facts of his life, during his formative years and his later maritime career, an interpretation of Cook's principles, motives and deeds, in the hope that these may provide insights into the inner nature of this remarkable man.

The personalities of the other principal characters in the novel, such as Michela, Elizabeth Cook, Joseph Banks, Tupaia and Sydney Parkinson, and their relationships with one another, are the result of the author's imagination.

Hence the story, as told here, is primarily fiction.

The rest, as they say, is history.

My final acknowledgement is to my agent, Linda Cassells. I am deeply grateful to her, not only for planting the seed which ultimately grew into this book, but for her sound editorial and publishing judgements along the way. Without Linda, this book would never have materialised.

Graeme Lay

*

Printed in Great Britain
by Amazon